OBSERVATORY
MANSIONS

EDWARD CAREY

OBSERVATORY MANSIONS

A NOVEL

Crown Publishers
New York

Grateful acknowledgement is made to Marin Sorescu for permission to reprint an excerpt from *The Biggest Egg in the World*, translated by Paul Muldoon with Ioana Russell-Gebbett (Newcastle upon Tyne, England: Bloodaxe Books, 1987).

Published by Crown Publishers, New York, New York.
Member of the Crown Publishing Group.

Random House, Inc. New York, Toronto, London, Sydney, Auckland
www.randomhouse.com

CROWN is a trademark and the Crown colophon is a registered trademark of Random House, Inc.

Originally published in Great Britain by Picador in 2000

Printed in the United States of America

Library of Congress Cataloging-in-Publication Data
Carey, Edward, 1970–
Observatory mansions / Edward Carey. – 1st ed.
1. Eccentrics and eccentricities – Fiction. 2. Collectors and collecting – Fiction. 3. Apartment houses – Fiction. I. Title.
PR6053.A6813 O27   2001
823'.92 – dc21   0-034645

ISBN 0-609-60680-8

10   9   8   7   6   5   4   3   2

First American Edition

For my mother and father

Acknowledgements

Very many thanks are due to Elizabeth Carter, Pascal Morisset, Sonja Müller and Claudia Woolgar for providing me with places in which to write this book, and also to Robert Coover, Isobel Dixon, Ann Patty and Richard Milner for their excellent advice in helping me to finish it.

I gloved and greaved
my hands, my legs, my thoughts,
leaving no part of my person
exposed to touch
or other poisons.

Marin Sorescu

I

THE ARRIVAL

I wore white gloves. I lived with my mother and father. I was not a child. I was thirty-seven years old. My bottom lip was swollen. I wore white gloves though I was not a servant. I did not play in a brass band. I was not a waiter. I was not a magician. I was the attendant of a museum. A museum of significant objects. I wore white gloves so that I would not damage any of the nine hundred and eighty-six objects in the museum. I wore white gloves so that I would not have to touch anything with my bare hands. I wore white gloves so that I would not have to look at my own hands.

I lived in a city, as many people do, a small city, an unspectacular city, a not very famous city. I lived in a large building but had access only to a small part of it. Other people lived around me. I hardly knew them.

The building we lived in was a huge, four-storey cube in the neo-classical design called Observatory Mansions. Observatory Mansions was dirty. Black stains like large unhealing scabs fouled the exterior, and sprayed on its grey walls in red and yellow car paint were various messages delivered at night by some anonymous vandal. The most immediately noticeable being: *And even you can find love.* The building's only notable features, save for its plainness and size, were the four simple columns that supported the entrance portico. The columns were badly scratched and dented, one in particular was inclined to slouch. The building's only other irregularity was the dome on the slate roof, directly above the entrance hall. In this dome, once upon a time, was an observatory. An observatory now lacking telescopes, now an unproclaimed

3

sanctuary for pigeons, their shit, their young, their dying and dead.

Observatory Mansions once sat in the countryside, surrounded by outhouses and stable buildings, parkland and fields. In time the city crept up to it, covering with each new year more fields, until it reached the parkland, which it smothered in asphalt, and the outhouses, which it knocked down. Only the house itself, that large grey cube, remained. They built a circular wall, ten foot high, around the house, a barricade, a statement that this was as far as the city would get. But the city carried on, way beyond our home, building yet more roads and houses. And as the city continued, the roads that neighboured Observatory Mansions became ever wider and more frequented, a river growing in confidence, until an ox-bow lake was formed and Observatory Mansions became an island. A roundabout, a traffic island, forgotten by the city but surrounded by its quickly flowing business.

I often thought of our home as a solid, hairless and ancient man. This man, sitting with his flabby arms hugging his round knees, stares hopelessly down at the traffic, at the smaller, modern, neighbouring buildings, at the countless people rushing by. He sighs heavily; he's not sure why he's still here. The old man is not well, the old man is dying. He suffers from countless ailments, his skin is discoloured, his internal organs are haemorrhaging.

This was our home and we were even tolerably happy living there, until a new resident came.

Our first rumour of the new resident came to us in the form of a little note pinned on to the noticeboard in the entrance hall. It said:

Flat 18 –
To be occupied.
One week.

A simple note that filled us with fear. The Porter placed the note there. He knew what we wanted to know: we wanted to know who it was that wanted to occupy flat eighteen. He placed the note there because he knew it would upset us. He could merely have kept quiet and a week later we would be stunned to hear someone busy about the living business in flat eighteen, unannounced. But he warned us, knowing how it would upset us. His only motive was to upset us. He knew that we would all separately be spending the week worrying over the mysterious person who was to occupy flat eighteen, and that he alone would keep the secret because no one ever spoke to him.

The Porter would not open his mouth, except to hiss. The Porter hissed at us if we came too near to him. That hiss meant – *Go away*. And we did. It was not pleasant to come too close to the Porter's hiss. It was not pleasant to come too close to the Porter. So even if we were to have enquired about the new resident the reply would have been a hiss. *Go away*. We had to wait. And more than anything else we hated waiting. Suspense was bad for our unfit hearts. We were left to imagine the future occupant of flat eighteen – for a whole week.

And for a whole week we were terrified. We slept short nights. We would find each other examining flat eighteen, as if by simply being in that specific section of the building which filled us with disquiet we would immediately understand what sort of person it was that was soon to occupy it. When we saw each other there we backed away, ashamed. If we entered the flat while the Porter was cleaning it, he would hiss us out of the place. We would run back to our own homes, shaking.

Flat eighteen, which had been a large dressing room and bedroom when Observatory Mansions was a country residence, was now similar to the other flats on the third floor; we found no clues inside it. We wanted to take floorboards out, damage the plumbing, cut the electricity lines. Anything to make the new resident know that he was unwelcome. We wanted to, but we did nothing. We sat thinking, paralysed by panic, with sweat on our foreheads, on the privacy of our lavatory seats, behind locked doors. We ate less. If the week had been any longer than a week we should all have been noticeably thinner.

Before the new resident arrived there was perfect stagnation. Years had sat on years and we had not been able to distinguish any difference between them. We were growing older, true, but since we saw each other every day, we had all (as if in conspiracy) not noticed, or pretended not to notice, the particulars of ageing. Our home was a different matter. It is probable that many of us were keenly aware of our home's slow but gradual disintegration – on every floor large strips of the ubiquitous blue and white wallpaper had peeled itself from the walls, the carpets were faded and full of holes, the banisters on the top floor, where the cheaper, smaller flats were, had already collapsed. The plumbing was somewhat erratic. The electricity frequently failed.

We who lived in Observatory Mansions were a small and peculiar group of people. Group is perhaps the wrong word since it was only because we lived in the same building that we could in any way be thought of as belonging to one another. Or perhaps we had become alike after spending so much time in solitude, the more time people spend alone the more difficult they become. How strange the people are who, past a certain age, find themselves blocked in every direction, these people who are convinced they will no longer be employed, these people who live alone. And of course they spend their time working out how to get by or thinking about their pasts, but they have only themselves to reminisce with. And how dull that is, how painful it is when it is only, day after day, their own reflection that appears in the mirror. How they long to get away from themselves, not just to get out of their own skins but to get out of their pasts and presents and futures; to leave, in short, everything that has anything to do with them behind for ever.

But I liked to think of these people as pure people, as concentrated people, or, to put it another way, as how everyday people would be if they were subtracted from work, friends, family and all the motions of life which we are told we should take part in. These people are obsessive; sometimes it is easy to spot them, sometimes not. Sometimes when you see them about the city their eccentricities make you laugh, but more often they make you feel miserable. They are a rare group of individuals, bizarre creatures, who seem to have walked out of strange, dark fairy tales, but they are real enough, they are about, they are to be found amongst cities' Coca-Cola signs, evening paper stands, waiting for the traffic lights to change with the rest of us. We seven from Observatory Mansions were a little like that.

We seven.

For years we had been used to residents leaving. Residents either packed up and left, or died in their flats and were taken away. After their departure the flats remained empty and with each vacation our home seemed larger and larger. It was well known to us that the value of our individual flats, though once good, had been steadily decreasing and that if we decided to sell we would be unlikely to find a buyer.

Observatory Mansions was designed to house twenty-four different families but, just before the new resident came, only seven individuals lived there. It was supposed that that number would be likely to gradually decrease but most unlikely ever to increase. All we were worried about was being the last person remaining. Living in our vast home, walking around all those empty flats, perpetually alone, was not something to look forward to. Though we were not happy together, and though we were only intermittently friendly towards each other, though many of us lived in virtual solitude, there was some solace to be drawn from the fact that our misery was not borne alone. It was shared, between seven. There was a certain pleasure, or fraternity, to be gathered from living with people whose lives had ended as unspectacularly as each other's. We had little to look forward to. Little changed. The only change was the occasional arrival of demolition experts who appeared, uninvited, and never stayed very long. On their first visit, some twelve years ago, we were naturally worried. The demolition experts arrived with representatives of the property company that owned Observatory Mansions, the company that paid the Porter. We waited for something to happen. Nothing happened. The fear, though, we had been able to share, between seven. For a while we communicated with each other, dividing our anxiety. When a suitable amount of time had expired, and it appeared to us that nothing, in fact, was going to happen, we each returned to our solitude. We shut up our doors, ended communication until the next visit by the demolition experts. Each time the visits caused us less worry. We had convinced each other that nothing was actually going to happen, so much so that on the last visit, before the new resident came, we paid no attention to our uninvited demolition experts and did not even consider opening our doors to each other.

We continued, waiting patiently for the moment when one of us would be the last person left in our home, for the time when there would be no one left to ignore. Solitude is only good when surrounded by other people. I, being the youngest resident, had the most to fear. I was thirty-seven at the time the new resident arrived. It may be presumed then that I would be glad to have another resident in our home, but that was not the case. It was not the case with any of us, and this is the great contradiction with the lonely. Though we longed not to be lonely, we also feared the pain it would take us to be brought out of our lonely states. And after that fear, could we be guaranteed that we would never be returned to a state of loneliness again? We could not.

Though we did not necessarily enjoy our condition of loneliness, we were at least used to it. It was dependable, almost a friend. We wanted nothing to change. Though we longed not to be the last resident, we also longed for our anodyne days to remain the same. We wanted no noises. We wanted no sudden movements.

On the day before the new resident came we were all united in an all-consuming anxiety. We had not yet opened our doors to each other, but the option was there. We could feel the door handles twitching. We were restless. We entertained the possibility that the new resident might be a person, like us, who deplored sociability. We entertained the possibility that the new resident would be old or dying, and could perhaps even die during his first night here. We entertained the possibility that the new resident might take one look at our home and decide to leave. If that were the case we would be offended for a few minutes and afterwards relieved for eternity.

There was nothing we could do but wait and make his stay with us, which we were sure would be short, unpleasant. But no one was more worried than I, being the youngest resident in our home and subsequently the one, if the new resident proved neither to be old nor to be dying, most likely to suffer his company for the longest time.

The day came.

It was a bright morning. It should not have been, it should have been overcast. It was a pleasant late spring day. It should not have been, it should have been shrouded in miserable winter pessimism.

I was up early, I had fed my mother, my father and myself. I suppose that many people would, if they woke up at the age of thirty-seven to find themselves living with their parents, be filled with dread. To them, spending every day with their parents would be suffocating; those people would feel cramped, they would say that the air they breathed was somehow contaminated. Perhaps they would even kneel by their beds at night, as good children do, and pray that their parents be dead by morning, as bad children do. That was not the case with me, I was not unhappy living with my parents.

On the morning of the day that the new resident came to us, I crouched by the door waiting for noises. Silence. At half past eight I had to leave home to go to work. I climbed the stairs to flat eighteen, the door was open, the flat bare. He had still not come. The only life from the third floor was the friendliness pouring out of Miss Higg's pet television set in flat sixteen.

I had to go to work.

The journey to work.

I usually travelled to work by using the public bus service. Any person who could produce the correct amount of money on request was entitled to sit in its confines and endure the rather dubious comfort of its dirty and ripped seats. The dirt was, of course, perilous to my white gloves, and whilst on board I had to be careful not to touch anything. The bus was old, but it moved. It moved but slowly. Its driver was a young man who had surely failed all his school examinations and was thus forced to endure for the term of his working life the daily ignominy of driving this dinosaur of locomotion. This man had also to suffer the screams, giggles, dirt, loves and hates of the schoolchildren: the bus was the school bus too. It trundled all the local children to their hours of misery every day during school time. When school was on holiday it was possible to see who the bus's other users were. There were various diagnosed imbeciles. Among the imbeciles was

Michael, a giant of a man, more sensitive, I believed, than the others. Michael was always observing, he examined each of his fellow passengers, considering them through his delicate blue eyes. The imbeciles went to school too, a different type of school. This school did not teach them history or languages, mathematics or science. This school taught them to be happy, to smile, to read their digital watches and, most of all, not to worry. The other passengers were mainly old men and old women, sometimes couples, mostly not. The old were off for a trip in the city centre where they would sit in cafés, underneath flashing electric signs, listening bemused to the vapid music, sipping tea and coffee, sighing and drooping. Two other passengers I found worthy of attention. The first was a small boy with bright fair hair, who was always accompanied by his dark-haired mother (though she barely deserves a mention and is easily forgotten). The boy wore glasses and one of the lenses was gummed over so that it could not be looked out of. This was because the boy had a squint. By using only his squinty eye, that eye was supposed to slowly repair itself. I do not think it ever did. The other passenger was a man in his forties, stunted by timidity. This man was a poet, he wrote beautiful odes to trees, flowers and country animals which he had not seen since he was a child. He was reminded of them by photographs he found in the city library. And it was the city library where the bus would drop him. And myself too.

The day of the arrival of the new resident was during school time and the sad bus was full of children. Some of the children were inevitably female. And some of those female children were inevitably pubescent. These girls would usually sit by the bus driver and stare at his hairy arms and talk to him, lift their skirts, make him laugh, encourage him to pinch them.

We passed the shops, the burger restaurants, still quite new to our city, with their clean plastic signs. We passed the large supermarket, one of three we have here, each of which employs an army of pathetically thin, pale girls with peroxided blonde hair. What exotic delights there are to be found there: ostrich steaks, pulped papaya, a drink called Sex on the Beach. En route to my work that day I saw a curious sight, something new. A vehicle moving slower than our bus was blocking the traffic in the opposite direction. This vehicle was cleaning the streets. It is a fact that our city is dirty and repugnant. It is a fact that dust covers every object moving and stationary. This vehicle was in its slow but methodical way attempting to remedy the dirt of our city. I had never seen a vehicle designed to shampoo streets before and neither, judging by their reactions, had the other inhabitants of our city. The vehicle was new, it glistened. People stared in wonder at the machine and carefully stepped over the clean path it left behind.

After the school exodus and peace came the library. The poet and I descended. There is no darkness but ignorance, said a stone above the library's portal. And by this threat bent people's backs and kept the opticians in business. I walked to the door in the library labelled GENTLEMEN, for such a type am I, and behind the locked door of a cubicle, readied myself for work.

The work.

There is, in our city, in the centre of our city, that part of our city most populated by people with a little excess money, that part of our city where people who are not from the city are most likely to visit, a plinth. A statue plinth. A statue plinth lacking a statue. A statue plinth which once had letters on it naming the statue that once stood upon it. The statue had gone, the letters on the plinth had been erased.

It was on that statue plinth, in the centre of the city, that I worked. The words erased on the plinth could perhaps have said my name, for no one else used it but me. Had it said my name, it would have said: FRANCIS ORME. What was the work that I was employed in whilst standing on that statue plinth? I was a statue, I pretended to be a statue. For this occupation I earned enough money to feed myself, to feed Mother, to feed Father and even occasionally, when I felt the need, to feed a man named Peter Bugg.

I wore white. White cotton gloves, as has already been admitted, these I always wore, but, when busy at my employment, I wore whiteness everywhere, not just on my hands. White linen shrouding my body, a white curled wig to conceal my not-white hair, white trousers, white shirt, white waistcoat, white tie, white face. I painted my face white every day before work commenced. I blotted out all those little moles, freckles and the swollen bottom lip that signified Francis Orme. I stood without identity, a statue of whiteness.

I stood two feet from the ground, elevated by my plinth. Beneath me was a tin box in which coins were placed as the day's work progressed. One other thing is necessary to mention: in my right hand I held a white enamel pot. In that pot was a small stick of white plastic with a wire hoop at its end. In that pot was a soap mixture. I stood still, holding the pot, with my eyes closed. When I heard a coin drop I would open my eyes, take the plastic stick with the wire hoop at its end from the enamel pot and blow out soap bubbles to the person who had dropped me the coin. The soap bubbles were an annoyance that I had to put up with. If people part with money they demand some compensation. Soap bubbles were the cheapest compensation I could think of. After I had blown out a soap bubble I would close my eyes, resume my pose and remain absolutely still until I heard another coin drop. Then I would open my eyes, move and blow out another soap bubble.

When I opened my eyes I saw in front of me many people. People who had never before seen a person keep so still.

People who were confused, wondering whether I was made of flesh or of plaster. Until I opened my eyes. The white of my body was so precise in its whiteness that the whites of my eyes looked dirty by comparison. Dirty, but alive. When I closed my eyes I resumed my perfect stillness, and the people around me, who only a moment ago had seen my living eyes, began to wonder all over again whether I was of flesh or of plaster. That was how perfect my stillness was. How had I learnt to achieve such inanimacy?

The art of stillness.

As a child I often played a game with my toys. I would place them all in a circle, leaving a space for myself. We would sit together. I would look at them all, each in turn, for exactly the same amount of time. I would consider what it could be like to be an object. These objects – a teddy bear, a tin soldier, a clockwork robot, a stuffed fox and a plastic frog – had all at times been given voices by me, I had temporarily made them live in the games of my childhood. I considered it only fair that since I had made them feel what it might possibly be like to be living that I should in turn try to discover for myself – but with help from them – what it was like to be an object. I kept still. I felt my heart slow down. I closed my eyes.

When I grew up I was given employment by the wax-work museum in the city. This was a popular job, the waxworks was a popular place. For my interview I was informed that I had to stand still amongst wax dummies. Five of us interviewed for one job. The job was stillness. The art of keeping still. We were informed that if none of us were still enough no one would be employed and the job would remain vacant for another year. It was a popular part of the museum that housed wax models that pretended to be people to also employ people who pretended to be wax models. When the public perused the objects they liked to guess which ones were wax, which ones were flesh. Often they made mistakes; this was because the army of flesh dummies were such experts, masters of stillness. When a dummy that was presumed to be made of wax moved, the public was astonished. They gasped and then they laughed. This was considered entertainment. In the interview we had to prove that we were capable of holding a pose for a very long time. Five of us were interviewed with five wax dummies. We all wore different costumes from different ages. I was given a white shirt with frilly cuffs, breeches, a gabardine, white stockings, black buckled shoes and a curled white wig with a purple ribbon at its back. I remember this costume extremely well, not only would I wear it for my interview at the waxworks but I would also wear it for my subsequent employment there. In fact, after my employment was terminated, I kept the costume and used the shirt and the wig (with the ribbon removed) whilst standing still on my plinth. Once costumed, we five interviewees were shown our places between the five wax dummies. We selected our poses. The interview began. A fat man walked in wearing a cream three-piece suit, who I later discovered had come all the way from the largest of all the wax museums, in the capital city of our country, to take the interview. He walked up and down the line of wax and flesh dummies, pausing for a long time in front of each. He sat down and watched us from a distance. He took out his fob watch and waited. In half an hour three flesh dummies had made themselves known. They had moved. They were dismissed. We were now seven. Three quarters of an hour later a fourth flesh dummy fainted. We were now six. After an hour the fat man in the cream three-piece suit took a plastic box from one of his pockets. It was full of flies. He opened the box, the flies flew around us, landed on our faces, walked around our noses. But we did not move.

After an hour and a half someone else made himself

known. But it was not me. One of the waxworks had really been made of flesh.

The fat man said (to the wax dummy who had revealed himself as a flesh dummy), I'm afraid we must dismiss you, thank you for all your work. The flesh dummy said, But I have been working here for three years, how will I feed my family? The fat man said, *Get a movement job.*

We were now five.

After nearly two hours the man in the cream suit clapped his hands, he said, Very good, that will do, please step forward. But I did not move. Another trick. After two hours and a half an employee of the waxworks entered the room carrying a food tray. Roast pheasant, roast potatoes, broccoli, claret, lemon tart, stilton, port. The employee left. The man in the cream suit gradually consumed his lunch. Pausing between courses, eating everything, watching us as he ate and drank. After three hours and a quarter, the fat man fell asleep, or pretended to be asleep, to this day I am not sure whether it was another trick or not.

It was not until I had been standing there for nearly four hours that the fat man shook himself from his sleep, or pretended to shake himself from his sleep, and left the room, closing the door behind him. Shortly after, another man came in, he said the interview was now officially over and that Francis Orme would be employed by the waxwork museum. But I did not move. Then the man said, Thank you everyone, and all of the waxworks moved forward and walked out of the room. Unassisted. There had been no wax figures. The man came up to me. He said, Thank you Francis, that will do, don't boast.

I was by far the youngest flesh dummy ever to be employed by the waxworks.

The job was more complicated than it may sound to the uninitiated, and we who were employed in our jobs of stillness were a very proud group of soldiers. We believed ourselves half flesh and half object. To achieve that standard of professionalism it was important to gain not only outer stillness but also inner stillness. Inner stillness was an art I learnt from my father.

My father and his (inner) stillness.

Father is not a famous figure of today, will not be one of tomorrow, and his yesterdays were as eventless as an unfilled diary. Father will never be a famous figure.

Father considered himself a parenthesis in his own existence. Convinced that he was the essence of insignificance, he determined to live his days out of the light, in shades of darkness that might discourage people from confusing him for a piece of life. He felt comforted making friends with all that never answered back, with all that never moved, with all that others disregarded or simply never noticed.

Father kept his young body still to observe all about him. Keeping his body still helped him to see what was around him with patience and with consideration. Father was the friend of gradually changing levels of light, of a snail's odyssey, of dust's snowfall. One day, though, Father was caught in the light. One day mother drew open the curtains and marched Father to church. One day Father looked terrified and fragile. He was forced into the outdoors. Father caught a suntan (caught in the way that other people catch a disease). In time his wife stopped playing with her new toy and he was discarded. His short term of significance was over and he calmly sought the shadows again. The suntan ran away.

Then Father was alive and not alive, Father was dead and not dead, he lived and died still. Still. He kept his old body still. He kept time still. Time is movement, and Father and movement treated each other with caution. When Father, in his more active days, decided to move, the decision would only be acted out after great tangles of exhaustive internal considerations. Later when Father moved he was either being moved by someone else, or his body was involuntarily moving him. Don't be fooled, that was not Father moving, that was Father's body. The pair, though they had known each other all each other's lives, were not one. Father's body twitched without warning Father. It was an old creased rebel. Father, inside Father's body, watched his body moving with surprise, admiration and a quiet terror.

For larger sorties into the world of activity, we operated his limbs. Father was our own, grown-up, ugly dolly. We pulled his strings. Our mannequin made of flesh. Years ago, Father made a decision. Father's decision was to keep his old body more motionless than his youthful body. Thereafter he lived in a chair, a large red armchair made of leather. If I had not introduced him as my father, then he might have been called a man in a chair – or a chair with a man on it, since the chair was at first sight more significant than its occupant. In this way, seated in his chair, death forgot Father. Death paused for a moment in front of stationary Father and then moved on thinking his business had already been accomplished. Father's decision was not made out of a fear of death. Father's decision was made out of convenience. It was convenient for a man who loved stillness, who sat in a permanent state of torpidity in a comfortable chair, to remain motionless. Father's decision was made out of a love of stillness. Father was a genius of the stationary. Father was an enigma.

However.

However, on the day that the new resident arrived I was unable to perform my perfect stillness. I was able to achieve outer stillness, but not inner stillness. I was unable to concentrate because I knew by then that surely the new resident had taken possession of flat eighteen. My stillness was not perfect and it being imperfect made me feel wretched. Without perfect outer and inner stillness I was no better than any of the other city buskers. What made it worse was that once, when coins fell into my tin, I opened my eyes to blow out the bubbles and saw Ivan, one of my former colleagues from the waxworks, one of the proud group of half-wax-half-human dummies, and I could see how ashamed he was of my performance. When I opened my eyes the next time a coin was dropped, he was gone.

We half-wax-half-human dummies that were still left were by that time no longer employed by the waxworks. Our roles had been taken over by electronic dummies, deemed in the long run cheaper than us and also, the shame of it, more impressive to the public. The art of stillness had become a forgotten art. It was then still possible to see some of us half-wax-half-human dummies about the streets, walking dolefully through the city, pausing to look with envy at some statue or pillar. And it must have seemed to Ivan, my former colleague, as if I had forgotten my art, as if I was betraying it, as if I was a has-been still pathetically trying to earn money from a half-remembered trade.

I left work early that day.

Peter Bugg.

For my first visual pictures of the new resident I had to rely on the reportage of Mr Peter Bugg. Mr Bugg lived in flat ten, which, when our building was still in the countryside, was part of the nursery rooms, its bedroom and classroom. Peter Bugg, retired schoolmaster, retired personal tutor, retired person, lived, if it could be called living, off a small pension rewarded him by the father of one of his former pupils. Peter Bugg bald as an egg. Peter Bugg dressed in his two-piece black suit with its flared trouser bottoms. Only the second suit he ever possessed and certainly the last. This suit a gift from former pupils. But not out of gratitude. Out of obligation. The pupils had ruined the first suit he owned. They had painted the white seat of his classroom chair. White. Peter Bugg's first suit, which had also been black, had sat with Peter Bugg inside it on the classroom chair and had become, in and around the region of his skinny bottom, white. A white and black suit. The pupils bought him a new one, under obligation. They wasted all their pocket money on Peter Bugg's skinny bottom, an action which further reduced his popularity. But he did not care, not then, for then the ever-changing tides of pupils seemed to stretch out before him, an horizon filled with educational possibilities. He was a cruel teacher. But he was, in his way, fair. He handed out his cruelty to the brainy and the brain-dead. He allowed himself no favourites. He was feared and he smelt that fear, breathed in that fear through a sommelier's nose. Then Peter Bugg found a favourite and something went wrong. Something went unspeakably wrong. Peter Bugg decided to leave his precious school and become a private tutor. For twenty-two years.

One day this stern man noticed that he was crying. For no discernible reason. He surmised he was suffering from conjunctivitis. But no matter what medicine he poured into his eyes, Peter Bugg continued to cry. The doctors could not explain the crying. Peter Bugg cried on. Some people, he was known to say, cry. They cry, he was known to say, for no apparent reason. They are not sad, he said, they just cry all the time, without the tears letting up. It happens to some people, he said, it just happens and there's nothing they can do about it. A year or two later Peter Bugg noticed that he was sweating. Almost continuously. All over his body, whether he was moving or stationary. He called that sweating hyperhydrosis. But no matter what medication he took, whether taken internally or externally, Peter Bugg continued to sweat. The doctors could not explain the sweating. Peter Bugg sweated on. Some people, he was known to say, sweat. They sweat, he was known to say, for no apparent reason. They are not unfit or overweight, he said, they just sweat all the time without the sweat letting up. It just happens to some people, he said, it just happens and there's nothing they can do about it. Peter Bugg stocked up on anti-perspirants, foot deodorizers, body rubs, aftershave lotions. He smelt of a hundred different smells. Peter Bugg noticed that he was sweating most on or near to those regions of his body where hair grew. So he shaved himself. He shaved off the hair on top of his head. He shaved off his eyebrows. He shaved off the hair in his armpits. He shaved his legs, his chest. He shaved between his legs. He did not let any of the hair grow back.

Peter Bugg knew what was happening but he was a private man. A man who found it difficult to speak about himself. A man who found it difficult to speak to anyone. A man who was made nervous by verbal contact and hysterical by physical contact. A man who kept himself to himself, with a few exceptions, of which I was one. He knew what was happening to himself and it terrified him.

His whole body was weeping.

His whole body was sobbing.

He knew that. What he wanted to know was:

Why?

A bespectacled blur.

When I returned from work, I climbed the stairs past flat six, where I lived with my parents, up to the third floor. The door of flat eighteen was closed. The new occupant had occupied. The door was shut and I did not knock to introduce myself. I put my ear to the door. I heard nothing. All that I could hear on the third floor was the friendliness pouring out of Miss Higg's television set.

I returned home.

I had a visitor.

The visitor, who also kept a key to our flat, had let himself in. He was sitting in our largest room, a room that was a kitchen, a dining room and a sitting room. He was sitting on an upright pine chair facing a large red leather armchair. He was holding the hand of Father sitting in his armchair. The visitor was crying and sweating and smelling of a hundred different smells: Peter Bugg. Beads of sweat, islands, a-top his white shining skull.

Peter Bugg proceeded to tell me about the person who had occupied flat eighteen. I knew this was the reason for his visit. He did not usually come to me on that day. He arrived, punctually, twice a week to help me change Father. And he looked in on Father when I was at work (Mother, who lived in the largest bedroom of our flat, mercifully changed herself). Peter Bugg's visit was an exception then. Peter Bugg spoke.

The new resident in flat eighteen, he explained, was not:

1. Old.
2. Dying.
3. Male.

The first two I had, I suppose, been expecting. It was unlikely that we would be so fortunate. The third was a shock. I had always considered that my imaginings of the new resident might be wildly inaccurate. I had tried to allow for that. But I had never considered, even for a moment, that the new resident would be a female. As to whether she was pretty, ugly, obese, skeletal, slim, freckled, fair-skinned or dark, Peter Bugg was unable to inform me. Nor could he remember her age.

I can see her. I just can't see what it is that I should see, what it is that I should describe.

What do you see?

I see ... I see ... a vague mass. Blurred. The mass was smoking a cigarette. There was smoke in my eyes. I was crying. Wait! There were two slight reflections around the region of the head. Yes! She was wearing spectacles.

Anything more? There must be more.

The poor weeping bundle had never, he elucidated, never been able to focus his eyes around the female form. It was a complete mystery to him. Even his mother? His mother, yes, he could remember better. She was the one married to his father, wasn't she? Yes, he supposed, that was her. A vague, well-meaning fog.

It transpired that Peter Bugg had met the new resident on the stairs and even spoken to her. He saw immediately, though not precisely, that she was not the sort of resident we could ever be happy with and told her so. He had twisted his face into a mask of bitterness and hate, a particular expression that had always horrified his pupils, and pointed words decisively and unpleasantly around the place where he believed a head might normally be expected to be placed on the female anatomy. These words:

Go back to your home. Go away.

And Peter Bugg believed that his intentions had been perfectly met in those two sentences. He was quite satisfied. But he had not expected a reply:

This is my home now.

It was her home now, she announced, and apparently she considered it to be. She continued up the stairs. Peter Bugg, appalled by her response, found himself a virtual waterfall of sweat and tears and nervously scrambled back into his home, flat ten.

Frustrated by the selective nature of Bugg's remembrances, I decided the first night that the new resident of flat eighteen spent with us to call on someone else in Observatory Mansions to try to discover more. We would visit Miss Higg of flat sixteen. But not immediately since it was then the time when Miss Higg would be sat in front of her television watching one of her favourite transmissions and we would certainly not be granted admission. We would politely wait until the transmission had finished. We ate. Why, I wondered aloud, and I had never considered this before, why was it that Peter Bugg could so effortlessly spend time with Miss Higg? She was, after all, female. He winced, sighed and then explained:

I have never considered there to be anything remotely feminine about Claire Higg.

Claire Higg existed rarely in the present, rarely in the past and certainly never in the future. She had created for herself an alternative time frame called fiction. Miss Higg lived for fiction and she had been so completely living for fiction for such a long time that fiction had become, for her, reality. Despite the colours that poured out of Miss Higg's television set there was something black and white about her, something almost moth-like in her pale, dry, youthless skin and in her dark, dusty clothes; she was a woman without moisture. And Claire Higg had contrived to completely forget what Claire Higg looked like. There were no mirrors in flat sixteen where she lived.

Her flat consisted of six rooms, but she occupied only four of them, the other rooms growing ever-thicker rugs of dust in her absence. If she were to have walked into those other rooms she would not have been able to recognize them, she would be sure that she was somewhere else, that she had got lost. The other rooms were not fenced off from the rest of her flat, not at all, but there was a certain point in her flat that she had not crossed for quite some time. Nothing stopped her from crossing to the other side, she just didn't. There was nothing for her there. All that she needed she had in her four rooms: kitchen, sitting room, bathroom, bedroom. She spent the majority of her days sitting in the warm comfort of her favourite armchair, facing and enjoying the friendliness that poured out of her television set. Her days were happy there. They were spent among friends. Among characters from soap operas. She loved them all, even the villains. Inside that magical television box were such beautiful colours, such beautiful people, such beautiful lives. Outside there was only little Miss Higg. But that did not matter to her. Since most of the day was spent amongst beautiful characters the remainder of the day could be spent thinking about those beautiful characters. Her brain would replay the day's events, and she would giggle, tut-tut, cry and sigh with her loved ones once more. It was a full life. The days were so busy, in each one she had to cram funerals, weddings, births, scandals, love affairs, parties by the pool, important meetings in enormous offices, walks on the beach, rides on horses, surfing on the waves, tantrums, tears, kisses, the occasional prelude to sex and much else besides. When she went to sleep, she went smilingly to ready herself for another full day.

Miss Higg's magnolia-painted walls were once – before they were hers, when their windows looked out on to parkland filled with nonchalant cattle – decorated with a series of hunting prints. Now they were spotted with photographs carefully scissored out of magazines, pinioned there by blue tack, drawing pins and sewing needles. One man occurred particularly frequently: moustached, with a toothy grin and bronzed flesh. This man was also to be found on her mantelpiece, clamped between the glass and wood of a picture frame. This portrait included the hand of another alien person that rested on his right shoulder. The photograph had been cut so that the other person, certainly female, was lost. In her small kitchen, with its diminutive gas stove and baby refrigerator, Miss Higg exhibited a cork pin board on which were displayed more cut-outs of her television heroes.

There was a rectangular mark on one of her magnolia walls where a photograph had once lived. This photograph was from Miss Higg's very own, and once very real, life. A passport photograph of a sickly looking man: Alec Magnitt, former resident of flat nineteen. Deceased. On the back of the photograph was an epigraph which read – *Claire, Claire, I love you so*. And signed: *A. Magnitt, flat nineteen, Observatory Mansions*. But the photograph was no longer there (lot 770).

On that particular evening, Miss Higg's transmission having ended and the news broadcast just beginning, an inconvenience she never watched or listened to, Miss Higg turned down the volume of her television set and heard a knocking on her door.

An unscheduled programme replacing the nine o'clock news.

Who? She wondered.

It's Peter, came the response. Peter and Francis Orme.

She sighed, her mind on other creatures – other beautiful, sun-gold creatures who spoke of love and dollars. We were not part of her beautiful life. I had a swollen bottom lip, Peter Bugg was bald, was crying, was sweating. Our skins were pale. We had little money. At best we could have been extras, padding for the crowd scenes, kept in the back. But that evening we had come forward and were threatening to place ourselves in front of the viewer's eyes. And Miss Higg's eyes had adjusted themselves to beauty only. Coming out of that state of mind required a little concentration. She would have to convince herself that we were characters from the television and that the characters from the television were the real people. She would have to convince herself that she had switched the channels over and was caught on some documentary, probably, or some small-budget black and white film that was concerned solely with non-beautiful people without suntans and without money. She would have to convince herself that the actress who was about to perform the role of Miss Claire Higg had absolutely nothing to do with her. The name was just a coincidence. The real Miss Claire Higg was on a beach oceans away. How much convincing would that take?

I'm busy.

It's nine o'clock. The news is on.

I'm watching the news.

.

You never watch the news.

I've got company.

Yes, but at the moment on the wrong side of your door.

You can't stay long.

We shan't stay long.

No longer than half an hour.

We know the news is only half an hour long.

Come in. Sit down. Let me fetch you a martini.

Miss Higg's martini tasted more like tea. She sat in her favourite armchair and as we talked she placed sun cream on to her face and arms. She was still in her nightdress, she rarely wore anything else, she had no reason to venture outside, there was nothing for her there. Peter Bugg did her shopping. In her list of bare essentials there would often be a more idiosyncratic item: sun block, a bikini, a champagne glass, a red rose. These requirements were hidden between tea bags, mulligatawny soup, tuna chunks, tooth glue. Occasionally, though, even she went outside, but only when there were power cuts. When the electricity failed Peter Bugg and I would always go straight to her flat. There we would find her in a state of panic. We would put her in her coat and, each taking one arm, escort her downstairs. Time for your walk, we would say on those occasions. Everyone's died, she would say. They haven't died, we'd say, they'll be back soon, time for a little fresh air. Then she would smile. You're my beaux, don't go taking advantage of me, she would say. We would say: We won't. Peter Bugg and I, more lifting Miss Higg than escorting her, would walk her around the walled enclosure of Observatory Mansions. If, during the walk, the lights came back on inside the building she would begin to panic, and we would immediately cease our stroll and return her to her flat. Those were the only times Miss Higg left it.

She had not always been like this. There were other Higg

times too. She loved and was loved once, weren't you Claire? I was, wasn't I? Wasn't I? But that is another story.

Miss Higg had her reasons for not wanting a new resident. Particularly one living on her own floor. She wanted nothing to interrupt her viewing hours. She wanted no more company, considered it dangerous. A new companion might become attached to her television set, might have affairs with her beautiful friends. Worse though, a new companion might encourage her to see less television, might encourage her to visit the outdoors.

She had, she told us, heard the new resident moving into flat eighteen. She had heard voices. Plural. Who was she conversing with? we enquired. With the Porter, she said. Impossible. Talking and hissing, we suggested. Talking and talking, she insisted. We ignored that comment, put it down to Miss Higg's lack of concentration. Called the voices noises from her television. Later during the day someone had knocked on her door. The knock, she said, was a new knock. Was neither the knock of Peter nor the knock of Francis Orme.

And?
The knock had a voice with it.
And what did it say?
It said, Hello.
And?
It said, I know you're in there I can hear your television.
And what did you say?
Nothing.
Good.
And then the knocking came back, and the voice with it.
And what did the voice say?
The voice said, I'm your new neighbour.
And what did you say?
Nothing.

Good.

And then the voice said, I hope we can be friends.

And what did you say?

Nothing.

Good.

And then the voice said, I'll call back later, shall I?

And what did you say?

I said, No. Never.

Very good.

Then, explained Miss Higg, the voice and the knocking went away and never came back. We praised Miss Higg for her dialogue. We said, it's all for the good of Observatory Mansions. Oh? she said. We said, it's for the good of her privacy. Yes, she said, it was well done then.

I asked her if there was anything about the voice that might describe its owner. Miss Higg thought it the voice of a woman, a young woman, probably in her twenties or thirties.

We decided that through whatever means possible, the new resident must be out of Observatory Mansions within the week. I stroked my gloves – that white, that cotton – thinking hard. Claire Higg offered noise intrusions as a possibility. She proposed to keep her television set at all times (except during news broadcasts, documentaries, financial bulletins, weather reports, black and white films, wildlife programmes and police appeals) at its highest volume. Bugg and I thought this a good beginning. I suggested that, for my part, I follow the new resident wherever she went to try to discover what it was that made her want to live in this part of the city and what, if anything, might make her leave Observatory Mansions. Higg and Bugg thought this an excellent suggestion. But when it came to Bugg's turn, he could think of nothing he could do to help.

And so, after stroking my gloves for a few minutes, I came up with a task for him. Peter Bugg was, by use of the Porter's ladder kept in the basement, to climb up to the window of flat eighteen. Whilst the new resident was out he was to enter her flat, make a note of all her possessions and move those possessions about, shift their places. Place everything in a different order. This was sure to intimidate the new resident enormously. It would cause her great concern, not only for the safety of her possessions, which we were to move into different places, but also for the safety of her person, which we were not to touch. A person's objects make up their identity, they are placed inside a person's home according to their specific tastes. When a person's objects are moved by an unseen force, it feels to that person as if their soul is being played with, as if someone were messing with their insides.

If all the windows of flat eighteen were shut Peter Bugg was instructed to try to wedge one open, but if that was not possible then he should carefully smash a pane of glass. But he, poor Bugg, nervously sweating and crying, wondered if perhaps he wasn't the man for the job and if he could possibly do something else. What would happen if the police became involved, he added, he would surely have left his finger prints everywhere. I told him to wear gloves. Poor Bugg didn't have any so I leant him a pair of pink rubber ones. These I wore over my white gloves when I washed dishes.

It's nearly half past nine.
Good night, Miss Higg.
Good night, Francis Orme.
Good night, Claire.
Good night, Peter.

And a little later . . .

Good night, Francis.
Good night, sir.

Glove diary.

I felt comforted to be back in my bedroom. Everything, I thought, now that we had decided to take action, would soon be sorted out. The threat would be moved on, we would become a calm people once more. No one was going to take away the peace in Observatory Mansions, no one was going to change our lives, no one was going to infiltrate flat six. I looked around my bedroom, soothed by what I saw.

Lined up by the foot of my bed were three wooden boxes. The boxes were the same size. They were made by a carpenter to my specifications. Eight inches by thirteen inches, thirty inches in height. In all three boxes there were two vertical slats of half an inch thickness which divided the interiors perfectly in three. Two of these boxes had already been filled. They contained my gloves. My old, obsolete gloves. The two full boxes each held a total of six hundred pairs of gloves, two hundred in each compartment. I was still using the third compartment of the third box. The third box would be full in twenty-three pairs time. Between each pair of gloves I laid a piece of tracing paper and wrote on a small piece of watercolour paper, two inches by two inches, the date that I began wearing the gloves and the date that I finished. This was my glove diary. From the dates written on each piece of watercolour paper it was possible, by referring to the relevant school exercise books (numerically stacked in rows underneath the bed), to discover what had caused me to cease wearing them. I never allowed myself to wear gloves that had become remotely dirty, my hands were always to be an immaculate white.

The new resident would be encouraged to leave the next day. Everything would be as it was.

No one was going to touch my glove diary.

Looking at Mother.

Mother's bedroom had always been a bedroom, it was a
bedroom when Observatory Mansions was a country residence, it displayed old-fashioned crimson flock wallpaper
which had been decorating the walls undisturbed for over
sixty years. My mother's bedroom contained a mother, a
bed, books, paintings, photographs, hats, shoes, mirrors,
knickers, bras, magazines, gramophone discs, empty bottles,
umbrellas, pressed flowers, teacups, sherry glasses, a man's
wristwatch, a walking stick, an abacus and many other things
besides. The curtains in Mother's bedroom were closed; they
were always closed, day or night. On a small teak table stood
a porcelain night lamp designed for infant children. The
night lamp, which was never turned off, was in the shape
of a mushroom and had a hollowed-out centre where a
small porcelain rabbit resided. The porcelain rabbit held
up a porcelain lantern which contained a tiny twenty-watt
bulb. This lamp was mine, it was given to me when I was a
child.

The objects about Mother's room were her aids to memory. Each object opened up for her a passage of time. When
Mother could not remember her happier days naturally, she
opened her eyes and looked around at the objects in her
room. Her looks stroked them, she closed her eyes and
retaining the image of a particular object took it with her,
back into her past. Mother never opened her eyes to a person,
only to objects, those certain objects collected in her room. I

had not seen my mother's eyes, which were blue in colour, for some years.

So when, the next morning, I went in to tell Mother of the new resident and to ask her for advice, she did not even acknowledge me. I would often go into her bedroom to speak to her, to tell her all my fears and, though Mother never spoke back, I felt comforted, that she was – by simply being there, quietly breathing, never interrupting – calming me. But that morning, with such news, I hoped she might say something to me, I hoped she might at least move to indicate her alarm, I hoped she might somehow show that I had her sympathy. But she didn't take hold of a gloved hand and squeeze it tightly, she kept her eyes closed, kept her long grey hair still on the pillow, kept her breathing regular.

Motion.

The new resident didn't leave her flat all morning. I listened out for her footsteps for an hour, and even twice went up to the third floor, listening at her door to make sure she was still in.

But she couldn't keep me indoors all day, waiting for her to make a move. I wouldn't be trapped like that, I would leave Observatory Mansions, I could follow her later. That day of the week I customarily took off work, and on all my days off I went to the park.

I walked out, I stood by the entrance of Observatory Mansions, there was once a gate here, now there was just a gap in the brick wall. I stood on the perimeter of our traffic-island home and watched the cars rush around. I thought: everything goes around but nothing comes in. I waited for a break in the traffic. This is a procedure that must always be enacted when leaving a traffic-island home. Sometimes it takes minutes before a break occurs, sometimes only seconds, and when it comes you must run for your life. Yes, traffic must never be underestimated when leaving a traffic-island home, the little girl from flat seventeen learnt that. Too late. She was in too much of a hurry, she went over one car and under the next.

Finding the required pause, I dashed across to the street on the other side. Into an any people place, into the stupidity of the city. A girl chewed gum – I could smell her coming. An adolescent with a skin that betrayed his diet listened and hummed to thumping rhythms as he moved, his gait attempting to acknowledge the music. Young, beautiful horses of girls clopped their high-heel hooves. Men in suits walked alone, contriving to be serious. An old woman paused every six or seven steps for breath. Her mouth worked quicker than her legs – she sucked a boiled sweet. Children ran; they're the noisiest. They barged into me. I did not complain. I would have liked to complain, but I lacked the guts. I found nothing more terrifying than youth.

Weighing the world.

I reached the entrance of the park. The park was not an exceptional park. It was a very ordinary, a very uninteresting park, called Tearsham Park Gardens. I stopped outside. There stood the man who worked in front of Tearsham Park Gardens. There stood a man sacred to his duty, providing the public with his everyday service. Bank holidays inclusive. He was never late, he put in long hours, he was loyal to his work. What was his work, what were the tools of his trade? There was only one implement necessary to earn him his meagre living. He stood behind it with great pride. He was, I believe, the only man in the city who worked in this way. He was an original. His object was a set of bathroom scales. For two coins you could afford yourself the pleasure of obtaining your weight in stones and pounds. I stepped on the scales, I stepped off the scales. I gave the man two coins, as I did once a week, always on this day. The man, I never knew his name, began his employment many years ago. It was an extraordinary enterprise to give up days for, it was extraordinary to put your bathroom scales at people's disposal. At first he had few customers. This is perhaps not surprising. Bathroom scales are not uncommon objects. But he stuck to his post. His presence was noted. He was viewed with some fondness as an amiable imbecile, his list of clients grew. They were mainly old women, sometimes young men, never alone, who considered the action of weighing themselves amusing. His clients were never young women. I had never heard him speak, the procedure did not require words, I appreciated that.

The man noted down the weight of each customer in a little notebook. I do not know why. I never asked him why. He recorded the weights of the people of the world, it was his business. Perhaps he had noticed trends in corpulence or slenderness. Perhaps he worked out the average weight of a certain height. Or of age. Or of sex. Perhaps he just wanted to be near people. (Once he misplaced his weight notebook. Confused for two weeks, he left his post vacant. Eventually though, he bought himself a new notebook and returned to work. Lot 644.)

My weight was recorded, as it was every week in the same way. It was our routine. He noticed me as I came out of Observatory Mansions. I smiled at him, he smiled back from behind his scales. Then I rushed across the road and walked over to him.

I never asked him about his scales, about his notebook. He never asked me about my gloves. We communicated through smiles. Once a week.

Since it was my day off, I went and sat in the park.

Love and hate in Tearsham Park Gardens.

1. LOVE. I loved Tearsham Park Gardens for its beautiful white, sad trees that had been stripped of their bark by pollution and autographed by young vandals with their sweaty-handled magnifying glasses. Someone loves someone, someone loves a football team, someone burns letters of abuse, another scratches with a knife.

I loved this park for the couple that passed me that day: an old man with his grandson riding a tricycle in front of him. The old man walked slowly, slowly (there's time, there's always time these days) from one end of the park to the other. The grandson was supposed to keep to his grandfather's pace, but he was always at least two metres ahead. The boy stopped to observe a pair of lovers kissing on a bench. The grandfather stopped, he watched too. Eventually they set off again, but not at the same time and not at the same pace.

There was a concrete square in the middle of the park. Its paving stones were uneven. In its centre was a rusty fountain. I do not recall the fountain ever working. It had always been dry, save when the rain came, when the rain came it flooded. I called it a fountain out of optimism perhaps, but also out of regret. By the unworking, rusting fountain, which lacked water and appreciation, sat a beautiful girl. Whenever I saw a beautiful girl I thought of my own best interests.

Late teens. Ripped trousers. Jeans. Chequered coat. Dyed ginger hair. Brown freckles. Moon face. Beautiful. She worked chalks on to the paving stones, she worked many colours into the uniform grey. She smudged them, blended them. The subject that day was an angel. The angel was by some Renaissance master, she copied it down from a postcard, the likeness was not good. A handkerchief with stones in each of its four corners had a message above it. THANK YOU. She was thanked with coins. Generously. Not because of her angel, but because she had large brown eyes. We had known each other for two years.

I had never spoken to her.

People, all people, old, young, ill and well, spoke to her. I would have liked to have collected her chalk drawings but they faded quickly. People walked across them as soon as she had gone. The rain diluted them and then scrubbed their faces blank. Once, in a fit of stupidity, after she had left, I rubbed my gloved hands across her art. My gloves showed dirty, ugly, smudged colours. I had to replace them. I was ill for days. She looked at me once, smiled at me. I did not smile back. I was frightened. She stopped smiling and went back to her colours.

Whenever I saw a beautiful girl I thought of my own best interests, for a short term.

It was late spring; with the blossom in the park there was a hint of hope.

2. HATE.   This park was detestable because of its memory. It was sad, like so many people, because of its memory. It enjoyed, like so many people, passing its sadness on to others. This sadness, though not a dangerous disease, was infectious. It had a habit of getting through the pores of a person's skin. People sat in the park perfectly happy but before they stood up again sad thoughts would have stroked their lungs. The park remembered what it once was. It remembered other trees. It remembered grass, acres of grassland. It remembered the feet of cows and of calves. It remembered. Penned in by wrought-iron fencing was all that remained of a once wide and plentiful park. The parkland was churned up, houses were planted on its soil. The cows were moved on, people were herded in. And here I must admit that I walked on the streets surrounding this park when I was a child. I was there, the streets were not. It was all my home once.

The Ormes had lived on this land for centuries. They lived

in a house not far from this park: when I was young the building called Observatory Mansions had a different name, it was called Tearsham Park. Tearsham Park was a large eighteenth-century building. There had been an older Tearsham Park, a sixteenth-century manor house, but this had been destroyed by fire. Many objects had been rescued from inside it, but the building itself had been lost for ever – its beams and oak floorboards had ignited so easily. The new Tearsham Park, built on exactly the same spot as its predecessor, was a large grey cube with a central courtyard and, unusually, an observatory built into a domed roof directly above the entrance hall.

When Tearsham Park became Observatory Mansions, the centre of what was once the courtyard became a lift shaft. In the remaining space of the courtyard, square passageways were constructed on each floor with stairs connecting them, all the way to the top. The original grand mahogany staircase and the back servants' stairwell were both pulled out. Where windows had once looked into the courtyard were now doors around landings. The building was divided into twenty-four flats. The observatory, in shape though not in purpose, remained. I recalled large spacious rooms: the library, morning room, drawing room, smoking room, dining room. They had all been divided up, segmented by plasterboard. But I had remembered how it all was once. The park remembered. Father remembered too.

It was in this park, the reduced version, that my father had a stroke. People brought him home. His skin was lime-coloured. Ever after, one of his eyes drooped, the lower lid showed its pink inside. On that day Father was sitting on a bench observing the small part of park that he was once master of. He saw people, heard noise. He had a stroke and tipped off the side of his bench on to the ground.

Dogs and the Dog Woman.

In the park worked the Dog Woman. The Dog Woman smelt of dogs, a smell like ammonia with a little vomit and urine and shit added in. The Dog Woman wore a dog's collar around her neck and clothes (old, greasy) and was clothed with the hairs of dogs. She had many friends, all canine. Her clothes were ripped, as was the skin of her hands and thighs and ankles and breasts, by the clawing of dogs: memories of other times. Some were fresh, still blood-coloured, others were old, almost skin-coloured. Happy times, heavenly moments.

In the city there are many dogs. They have worked themselves into a social order, into different castes: those with collars and those without. The Dog Woman, greasy, matted hair like an old mongrel, breath smelling of a dustbin diet, loved all dogs without collars. Pissy knickers. Dribbly mouthed. Dog lover. She fed the dogs in Tearsham Park Gardens. In return they whined at her, scratched her, licked her, bit her. She fed them with disowned morsels; she, in an understanding with them, shared the same diet. She barked too, and growled, and rolled on the ground and sniffed under dogs' tails.

She was the Dog Woman of Tearsham Park, loyal to her brood, huge and breasty like some great whelping bitch. That day I sat in the park, she wound her large-hipped, hairy way across the nearly beautiful angel of the beautiful girl that I had known for two years. The girl said nothing, immediately repaired her angel's smudged and swollen-looking face, made her thin again.

The Dog Woman had another name – she was also called Twenty. Two names never to be written in a passport. She was also called Twenty because she lived in flat twenty of Observatory Mansions. A convenient kennel, so close to the park. It might be considered that Twenty would surely have preferred to sleep outside with the dogs. But she chose not to, since she didn't want to wake with one of her dog-friends pulling her insides out, since she needed somewhere to lick her wounds clean, to hide her bones.

We called her Twenty because she had declined to give her real name. She was, before the new resident of flat eighteen arrived, the Mansions' most recent resident. She arrived during a storm, a rare day when all the dust in the city was peeled off the walls, off the streets, off the few trees, off the people too, and rushed, in chalky, ashy colours into the darkness of drains.

During that particular storm Twenty, the Dog Woman, climbed through an open window of one of the unoccupied flats on the ground floor of Observatory Mansions with her ailing dog, a pathetically thin Great Dane, its ribcage piercing through its scarred pelt. In the night, after many hours of sobs and groans, with one final spasm of its back legs, it died. It was a great, black, ugly corpse. It must have been a titan of a dog. A dog, Twenty's companion, equal to her in size. The pair of them had got caught up in a fight, a dog fight, and running away from that fight the Great Dane had bounded into the roundabout traffic. And was hit. It was thrown from the corner of a car into the brick wall of Observatory Mansions, its hips smashed. And Twenty, more careful of the traffic, rushed over to stroke it during its final breaths and to carry it to our home.

Twenty buried her husband outside Observatory Mansions the next morning, under the hard, dusty earth where flower beds used to be. She pushed down her knickers and pissed over the grave. Twenty sniffed around the flats and chose flat twenty. Flat twenty, top floor, outside the lift that didn't work, outside the lift that once worked and once worked so swiftly that it killed Mr Alec Magnitt and shattered Mr Alec Magnitt's calculator (lot 737). But Twenty knew none of this. Twenty used the stairs. Out of choice even though there was no other.

Twenty, Dog Woman, did not pay rent.

She had no reason to welcome a new resident either. Since the residents of Observatory Mansions were of the human kind, she detested them all. She loved only . . . dogs.

And for us Twenty was the perfect resident. She did not pay rent but that was no concern of ours. She kept herself to herself. Spent her days (and most of her nights) in the park.

That day in the park, I watched her lie down, belly sagging, on the patchy grass of Tearsham Park Gardens. She yawned, she placed her chin on the ground, wagged her bottom, closed her eyes.

A child's toy.

That day in the park I saw a child. I saw a mother carrying the child, way above the ground, way above child level, somewhere high up – mummy level. I saw the child's hand gripped around a child's toy. A lock of love. The object, before unimportant but then, suddenly, most notable, fell to the ground. The child screamed. The mother walked on, told the child to close its mouth, separated child from child's toy for ever. I saw that object, once smothered with attention, now abandoned and lonely, another casualty of love.

So I stood up, approached, stopped, stooped, checked the object for unreasonable dirt, for child's saliva and snot, for white cotton dirtying substances, for gloves' enemies. Found none. Found the object most collectable. Found the object alone, childless, in need of a collector. And so, always friend of the friendless and quick as a magpie, I swiped it.

A child's toy, rescued from the park's floor, found a home in my pocket. A small metal Concorde aeroplane, with teeth marks around its cockpit, flaking off the paint, with one of its plastic wheels missing. Where would it fly to? Where was the hangar? There was a little space, more than enough to land in (never to take off again). A plot. Labelled lot number nine hundred and eighty-six.

I didn't go picking up every abandoned object, that has to be clear. Requirements must be met. The teeth marks around the cockpit, the missing wheel had given the object some history. Showed that it was loved. Marked it out as relevant.

So I rushed across the park, dodged the traffic and returned to the building signed:

OBSERVATORY MANSIONS
Spacious Apartments of Quality Design

Stepping into Observatory Mansions, cramped apartments of inferior design, I met a person.

A *sphincter muscle named Porter.*

The man with many keys. The stoic. The Porter, busy about his cleaning business, busy trying to kill all dust, busy breaking his heart. He saw me but made no greeting. Not even a hiss. As I passed him he turned his back to me, walked out to where I came in and re-entered the building, crawling forward with his dustpan and brush, rubbing out my footsteps. The keys jangled. The teeth of his brush scrubbed the grey, faded carpet that was once blue. The dirt and dust of the city had added its own colour, but first the Porter scrubbed out the blue, cleaned it away, swept it up. In this manner he tidied away all colours. He broke everything down to a ubiquitous grey. He would have preferred white. But white was not possible. White does not last. White, he wondered – probably – are you a myth?

I held the colour white in my hands, my gloves, but the Porter thought: Whiteness has gone from the city. He thought, it packed its bags years ago, leaving behind one, sad, orphaned boy, orphaned by cleanliness, who climbed the stairs every day, Sisyphus like, with his dustpan and brush, leaving a trail of only slightly cleaner carpet behind him, like the antithesis of a snail. *Be not like the slimy snail and leave behind a litter trail* – those were the first words he said to me.

But for a long time I had not heard the Porter speak – the last time he broke out of his word-fast was during his attempt to expel Twenty from twenty. Two years before. She paid no rent. She bit him.

The Porter lived below us. In the centre of the dirt, in the basement. Amidst the dust and dirt was an oasis, amidst the dust and dirt was a three-roomed cage of undiluted tidiness. I saw it once. I came down to inform him that the Mansions had again been burgled. I came to inform him that this time the burglars had not got so very far. As far as the entrance hall, as far as the cupboard in the entrance hall. The cleaning cupboard where the vacuum cleaner was kept. It's gone, I said. Stolen. No one can afford to replace it, I said. With a smile.

The Porter used to help me clean Father once a week. But once, the last time, while we were lifting Father from his red leather chair on to a neighbouring pine chair, a single drop of spittle fell from Father's mouth and found temporary lodging on the Porter's right cheek. The Porter dropped Father. Father fell on the floor. The Porter scrubbed his cheek. *He never cleaned Father again. He never vacuumed again.* I took the vacuum cleaner. No fingerprints were to be found on it. I wore gloves. White cotton gloves.

The vacuum cleaner has gone – I said. Stolen – I said. Translation: Your best friend ... is deceased (lot 802). And then, in that moment of vulnerability, I saw what no one else had ever seen before: the Porter's flat. As the Porter rushed up to the entrance hall, leaving his flat door open, I went inside and found ...

The three-roomed cage of undiluted tidiness that had declared enforced exile on cockroaches, slugs, flies, spiders, moths, silverfish, ants, bats, mice, rats and intimate ephemera. Though, under the bed, away from light and vision, was a trunk. The trunk was secured by four latches and two large padlocks. What was entombed inside it? I made a guess: non-regulation togs, untyped dispatches, extra-curricular manuals and photographic portraits – in short, collections from an average human life. Of the Porter before he became a porter, of a man who once had a name before he became a job. The trunk had a dual purpose: first for suffocating fragments of biography, the second for providing extra firmness to the already hard mattress above.

There was a bathroom. I do not suppose the bath had ever been used. That is not to say that the Porter did not ever wash himself. The clue is in the shower head that leered authoritatively down at the hot and cold taps as if they were filthy children. The bath, I imagine, was considered by the Porter an instrument of sloppiness and relaxation. Washing of a vigorous nature could never be accomplished in such a construction. In a bath one lies in one's own dirt. The shower, on the other hand, positively rips grime off and sends it promptly through the plughole into oblivion.

Directly above the lavatory tank was, curiously, a mirror where the Porter must have watched his face while he urinated, or perhaps porters call the action micturition. Through the mirror the Porter saw his face. And in that face he must have seen a time before porterdom, he must have seen a childhood, perhaps toys. Perhaps even some happiness. On that face were marks. Marks that stepped over each other. Marks all over. Pinpricks of imperfection.

The Porter had ginger freckles.

They obscured his face completely. Untidy groups distorted the precision of his nose, his cheekbones, his eyelids. He had been scrubbing for over fifty years and still they hadn't come off. They made him look childish. It was as if his body insisted on retaining the semblance of a child until he stopped being a porter and became one final, happy day a person. A porterless person. A person person.

Porter was his name: porter, beside being the name given to gatekeepers or doorkeepers or caretakers, is also the title of the pyloric opening in the stomach. The pylorus is terminated by the porter, a strong sphincter muscle, which connects the stomach to the duodenum, safely allowing the journey of food to progress down the alimentary canal. This ring of muscle decides when to allow the passage of food to progress or when to constrict its access completely. A condition known as pyloric stenosis occurs when the muscle tightens and refuses to allow anything to pass. This causes repeated vomiting, sometimes of food eaten twenty-four hours previously, and generates alkalosis – when there is too great a quantity of alkalines in the body. If this muscle refuses to relax surgery, known as a pyloromyotomy, is necessary to unbolt the gate by force.

The Porter, muscle not man, may refuse to open, thereby stopping the breakdown, expulsion and digestion of food, and hold the entire body in check to calamitous outcomes.

The Porter, man not muscle, oversaw the expulsion of dirt that lay in the body of Observatory Mansions. We left our full dustbin bags outside our flat doors every night, the Porter removed them every morning. And the Porter expelled, with the exception of Twenty, any intruders who happened upon Observatory Mansions, particularly the adolescent boys who sometimes crept through the broken windows of the ground-floor flats to smoke cigarettes, drink cans of beer and examine magazines filled with naked women.

If pyloric stenosis occurred, if the Porter ceased to clean, we would drown in dirt and rubbish.

On my single visit to the Porter's flat I gave myself a

souvenir. The Porter's duplicate uniform was hanging tidily, spotlessly in the Porter's wardrobe. I took for myself a single brass button (lot 803). A while after taking this button the Porter confused me. I always saw him immaculately dressed in his uniform *without a button missing*. At first I presumed that he only wore one uniform. Then I presumed that he purchased a replacement button. Finally, I understood. Three buttons down, the thread was always a slightly different colour. I imagined the Porter settling himself down when the time came to change uniforms, with a needle and thread, transferring a single brass button from uniform jacket to uniform jacket.

On that first day the new resident spent with us, the Porter, having finished removing proof of my entrance, went in search of other dirt. I descended to the cellar.

The journey to meaning.

Down below where the carpet stopped, where nothing was on display for the residents and was out-of-bounds for all but the Porter, the dust lay heavily. It had blunted every corner and, resting on foundations built by spiders' webs, it had created phantom ceilings and phantom walls. The cellar was the length and width of the floors above it, it had a vaulted brick ceiling, the same ribbed pattern all over it, with plain columns at every segment, like roots to an enormous tree. These multitudes of columns that supported the house were ideal to hide behind. Ideal, I remembered from my childhood, for tying fishing line around at ankle height and watching servants trip over. And there was also a tunnel which began in the cellar and ran all the way to the nearest church, some half mile away. This tunnel was all that remained of the sixteenth-century manor house that had burnt down.

This is where I went. This is what I was searching for. Past the Porter's flat, past the boiler rooms, past the sheets of plasterboards and rolls of blue and white striped wallpaper (remnants of the conversion of Tearsham Park to Observatory Mansions) was a door. I can see it now and as I see it I become vaguely tearful. A door marked DANGER – ENTRANCE FORBIDDEN. My door. Sealed with a heavy padlock to which I alone kept the key.

Stretching out across the long passageway that led to the church, kept in existence by numerous wooden beams which supported the roof and walls, with just enough space remaining to provide a narrow walkway, were the nine hundred and eighty-five objects of my exhibition.

It was possible to understand my history from this exhibition. Like layers in a rock face, the years and stages of my life were encoded there. The exhibition also revealed the life of the city, changes in taste, in fortune, in its people.

Each exhibit was placed inside a polythene bag and sealed with tape to keep away damage from condensation. At the foot of each exhibit was a small sign written on cardboard in standard biro black: the exhibit's number.

I, the exhibition's owner, archivist, attendant and public, wandered down the fringe enumerating: One, two, three . . . There they all were, all swaddled in polythene, all the dears, many years' work. All my own.

I began the collection, my pride and joy, way back when at fourteen years of age I found a till receipt that had been exhaled by the wind on to the driveway of Observatory Mansions, a time ago when the house was called Tearsham Park. I was outside, ordered under the sky by my mother for the purpose of taking some physical exercise. My white, lace-up footwear, designed for sportsmen (a fraternity that I have never belonged to), was enjoying the pursuit of kicking a pebble up and down, forwards and back. I missed the object, scarred the earth and brought the till receipt accidentally to the surface. Lot number one, by the entrance:

Fine Quality Foods

9	0.79	
3	1.07	
1	0.35	
	2.21	st
	2.21	tl
	2.50	ca
	0.29	cd

Thank you for your custom

This seemingly dull piece of flotsam ensnared my inquisitiveness. I rescued the tear of paper. Who was at the shop? What did the person buy? Where did the person live? Male or female? Married or single? Ugly or pretty? Young or dying? Will I ever know you? All the questions were unanswerable, so I conceived people from my mind to fit the receipt. The receipt was wrapped in cling film and hidden under my bed and bothered daily for many a week and month until it was creased all over and became extremely fragile.

Other articles supplanted the love I felt for the first. New histories were created. At first I collected unimpressive objects: empty boxes, plastic bags, empty bottles and cans, used envelopes, pencil stubs – in short, objects that had been rejected, that had either been spent or disregarded, objects that other people might have termed collectively *rubbish*. Then one day I set out a new rule. I bought a hard-bound notebook, hereafter called the exhibition catalogue, and wrote on its first page: IT IS REQUIRED OF ALL EXHIBITS, FROM NOW ON, THAT THEY ARE TO BE EXHIBITED SOLELY FOR THE REASON THAT THEY ARE LOVED; THAT THEIR FORMER OWNER PRIZED THEM ABOVE HIS OR HER OTHER POSSESSIONS, THAT THEY ARE ORIGINALS, THAT THEY ARE IRREPLACEABLE.

In time the collection grew too abundant to keep in my bedroom and was relocated piece by piece to the cellar, a three-month programme of exodus. At first they were hidden in the wine cellar, which like many parts of the estate was out of bounds for children; this parental warning ensured that these forbidden corners quickly became my favourite hiding places.

Time walked on.

Then Francis Orme, not one day out of many, but not unsuddenly, was child no more. Then Francis Orme, white gloved, was declared past child age.

Time walked on.

Then it was announced that the park was changing its name to Observatory Mansions and building work began. The wine cellar was to be transformed into a basement flat. A three-roomed cage hidden amongst the dust and dirt.

The fat and thin Cavalier.

I had been told ghost stories of the corpulent courtly gentleman (also an Orme, also called Francis – every first-born male Orme was named Francis – though this Francis Orme was called Sir Francis Orme) who was too large to escape down the cellar passageway to the sanctuary of the church, which, by fault of design, narrowed as it progressed. I had been told how the Cavalier became stuck down there in the dark, wedged himself in so perfectly that he could neither advance nor retreat. And in the miserable darkness, his ribs crushed, unable to turn around, bleeding at head and broken at fingers, he died. His skeleton was discovered decades later collapsed on the floor, with his once tidy uniform rotting around him. Only after death had the Cavalier thinned enough to be set free. This legend had been told to my child self with the correct degree of drama and suspense that I swallowed it utterly and vowed never to wander along the church passageway where I would surely be trapped against a circle of wall and be unable to wriggle free. Nobody, I was told, would ever come looking for me if I got chocked up there, for that is where the Cavalier lives, and no one wants to meet the fat and thin Cavalier.

So, armed with burning candle and box of matches, lest I should shiver the flame out, I moved the exhibition once more to that safest of places where my parents wouldn't come searching if I screamed out at eighty decibels. No one must discover you. *Never. Never, ever.* It was such a perfect hiding place, even the Porter did not come to this part of the cellar. Too much dirt. Of course, I had to protect my gloves down there. Small concession. Whenever I went to the cellar I wore my father's brown leather gloves over my white cotton ones. And for nineteen years I kept the exhibition a secret there. Until the new resident came.

The Object.

One object was always moving. This was my most precious possession. It was the inspiration for which the exhibition kept multiplying. It was the most delicate, intricate and clever object that I had ever known, the object above all other objects, which was always moved to the end of the exhibition. It must always seem to be the exhibition's newest item, never supplanted in love by any other exhibit. It was the exhibition's greatest glory and was called simply, with love and awe, *The Object.*

And next to that sacred object I placed so tenderly object number nine hundred and eighty-six. A scratched toy Concorde. I did not need to conceive a history for this object. I had viewed enough by seeing the child's tears as the plane and child parted company.

As I concentrated I licked my bottom lip, as had been my habit for a long time when gripped with exhibition passion. And so, after a while, my lower lip became swollen.

I spent an hour amongst my friends, walking up and down the narrow corridor, seeing that they were all safe, talking to them, sharing with them. Eventually, I returned, with regret, to the world above.

On reaching the top of the stairs that led to the entrance hall, I heard a voice. The voice that belonged to the bespectacled blur I have already mentioned. The blur was now in focus. The voice said:

What's down there?

It said:

What's down there?

II

MEETINGS

Our first conversation.

What's down there?

I was looking into the pale face of the new resident. It was a round face with a tight chin, delicate, well-formed ears and a small nose which pointed slightly upwards. She had two freckles, neither big – both about the size of a pin head – one on the left cheek, the other on the tip of the nose. She had clean black hair, which had permission to grow to just above the nape of the neck, and thick black eyebrows. There was nothing else of immediate significance, save the two objects worn by her face. The first was a cigarette; the second, a pair of round, steel-rimmed spectacles, their powerful lenses magnifying the eyes behind them. The eyes, and this was difficult not to notice, were green and seemed extremely sore, somehow infected. Combining all the features together (though they may perhaps have been separately attractive) resulted in a slightly sickly, unenviable portrait. The new resident was not pretty.

What's down there?

The new resident stood a little over five feet tall, she wore a plain, dark blue dress and flat-soled, black, lace-up shoes. Her hands were thin and bony. The right hand had a mole between the knuckles of its forefinger and thumb. Both hands were ugly, both were callused.

What's down there?
Nothing.

Is it the cellar?

What are you doing here?

Sorry. My name is—

Don't tell me your name. I've no need of it.

Then what's your name?

You've no need of it. I shan't tell you.

Do you live here?

I do. Get out.

Good. Let me explain, I'm new. I live in flat eighteen.

Why?

It's my home, I've bought it.

Why?

I liked it.

What about it?

I wanted to live in this part of the city.

Why?

That's my business.

When are you leaving?

I'm not leaving.

I want you out by the end of the week.

But the new resident, rather than beginning an argument or bursting into tears, simply smiled, as if she had suddenly seen or understood something, and said:

Of course, you're the one who wears gloves.

Don't touch me.

You're Francis, aren't you?

The Porter told you my name!

You'll get used to me, Francis. See you later.

And I stood, mouth wide open like an imbecile, and watched her walk out of Observatory Mansions. I don't think she had listened to me at all, I don't think she had any intention of leaving. I closed my mouth and stepped out after her.

The new resident was the other side of the roundabout being weighed by the man with the bathroom scales. She was talking to him, he talked back. I did not hear the words, I was too far away, held back by the constant traffic. I felt slightly betrayed, the man with the scales and I had known each other for several years. What upset me most was that he seemed to enjoy his communication with the new resident and was smiling after she had left him. As I hurried across I smiled at the scalesman, an enormous smile, a smile larger than any smile I have produced before or since. A smile performed entirely to impress the bathroom scalesman with my friendliness. He did not look up, he was smiling to himself, looking at his notebook.

Strange events in the park.

I could not immediately find the new resident in the park, though I did see a mother consoling her wailing son as the pair looked unsuccessfully, desperately, for a lost toy Concorde. When I did see the new resident, I noted to my dissatisfaction that she was near the broken fountain, looking at a chalk drawing created by the girl that I had known for two years. I was further betrayed that day. The new resident spoke to the girl. *The girl spoke back.*

What followed can only be described by that hideous word, chatting. They chatted as if they were long-lost friends. Words tumbled out of them both. Indeed it looked to me, sitting a safe distance away on a park bench, that they were having problems getting the words out fast enough. I was amazed how freely they conversed. The words moved up their bodies through pipes inside them and gushed out of their mouths. I had heard rumours of these sort of people. These people who could, seemingly without any effort, communicate with every single living person. These people who by their mere presence were able to open up the lid of the most closed person and look inside, without causing any damage to the person whatsoever. In fact the person probably even enjoyed the experience.

I was so taken by the novelty of the uninhibited communication that day that I would have, had I not been Francis Orme, enjoyed the spectacle of it. It would have made me smile. It would have made me feel light and alive. It would have done, but it did not. Taking that joy of speaking and placing it inside Observatory Mansions, I saw dangerous times ahead of us. I saw doors opening, I saw secrets unearthed. It is known that such a type of conversation, as I was then witnessing, was relaxing, and relaxation is a danger. During relaxation we drop our guard. Particularly in conversation. Relaxed conversation leads to openness. And in openness we often reveal what should never be revealed.

Finally, their conversation was over. The new resident went to another part of the park. To my delight, that other part of the park, that corner of patchy grass that she chose, was well known for being occupied by a certain terror of a person. A loather of humanity. A misanthrope on all fours. Twenty. Dog Woman.

A word about Twenty, Dog Woman.

Twenty, we other residents believed, was to be greatly pitied. We had decided that she was the product of some unspeakable domestic unpleasantness. Probably, we thought, she was from the countryside. For in the countryside, isolated and quiet, so many unthinkable crimes can happen. We imagined her chained up as a child. Probably, we thought, in a dog shed. Probably, we thought, with only a dog for companionship. She was fed on scraps, we decided, which she shared with the dog. She had not been taught to speak. She was what is known as a feral child. At some point her parents, her keepers, must have died – or perhaps Twenty had escaped from them.

On this we were not decided, this we argued over. We were, however, collectively convinced that somehow she escaped her terrible predicament and, with her dog companion, had entered the city. The dog, as was well known, died in one of the ground-floor apartments of Observatory Mansions. Afterwards, she had decided to stay with us, in the place that was honoured by the dog's grave.

We had read, admittedly rare, accounts of feral children in our newspapers. These reports encouraged us to decide Twenty's appalling past.

Yes, Twenty was pitiable indeed.

The taming of Twenty, Dog Woman.

Twenty, Dog Woman, did not permit anything to trespass on to her piece of patchy grass. Occasionally dogs wandered casually up to it, generally to sniff at Twenty, but they were soon chased away. Humans found the piece of grass an unpleasant place to stop, and walked on. The piece of grass wasn't the problem, it was what lay on top of it: a woman, dirty, greasy, with a dog's collar around her neck, dressed in ripped clothes and dogs' hairs, smelling of a sewer. She was an offence to the olfactory senses, a point which no doubt pleased her greatly, as anything did that kept human contact at bay. Dogs, however, seemed to find her stench fascinating, and would, when invited, happily nuzzle between her legs; the place, I presumed, where the strongest odours were kept. Twenty lay on her belly on the grass, lightly dozing, just as she had been when I saw her earlier that day. When the new resident approached, she opened her eyes and stood up. On all fours. The new resident sat on the grass – three metres from Twenty. Twenty at first looked surprised, then her backside went up (indicating her rising hackles) and she began to growl. But the resident did not move. The resident smiled. This smile may have worked on other people, may have worked on the chalk artist, may have worked on the man with bathroom scales, may even have worked on the Porter. It did not work on Twenty. Twenty growled, her lips curled up, her eyes stuck out. She was offended. This was her patch after all, what right did this cigarette smoking, bespectacled biped have on it? Truly this woman was amazing. She was the sort of person who walked all over other people's privacy; the sort of person who, when walking along a country path, would come across the inevitable sign saying PRIVATE PROPERTY – KEEP OUT and deliberately enter.

But Twenty was not allowing it. She barked. She bared her teeth. Black and yellow they were. She growled closer, so close that her nose was practically touching the new resident's face. I thought I ought to call out to the new resident, tell her that she was in danger. I thought I ought to perhaps warn her that unless she moved she would surely be bitten. I thought I ought to take her away from that place, instruct her never to go there again. That is Twenty's patch, I ought to have said, and no one goes near Twenty's patch, unless you're a dog and only then if you're invited. All this I ought to have said and done. Instead I did nothing, I sat and watched. I smiled, I stroked my gloves and thought what really I ought not to have thought at all. I thought: *Go on, Twenty, bite her. Bite her! Make it really hurt.*

And Twenty did. Twenty bit her on the hand, and blood trickled out of the new resident's hand and tears sprang up in her eyes, testifying that the bite certainly hurt. There, I thought, now you know. Leave Twenty alone, the pain will go away, the wound will heal up, go home, bandage your hand, dry your tears. But the infuriating new resident did not budge an inch, instead she raised up her hand to Twenty, Dog Woman, inviting her to have another go. It was as if she were saying – Go ahead, Twenty, Dog Woman, take the whole arm off for all I care, I have another. Twenty looked at the hand, considered it, considered what the offering meant. If she had a tail she would surely have stopped wagging it at that instant, for the offering of hand, and arm too if required, meant only one thing: that the new resident was not frightened of Twenty. Twenty was confused. I, a short distance away, was confused also. The new resident looked determined. She pushed her hand towards Twenty's face, and then the first extraordinary thing happened – Twenty backed away.

The new resident stood up, Twenty backed further away. The new resident raised her hand higher than Twenty's jaw level, to head level. She placed her hand on the top of Twenty's head, on Twenty's hair. And then the second extraordinary thing happened – she started stroking Twenty, the Dog Woman. And Twenty, the Dog Woman, let herself be stroked.

Five minutes later the new resident was sitting down on the piece of patchy grass formerly considered Twenty's property, with Twenty's head in her lap, stroking, still, Twenty's hair. Twenty smiled contentedly. (Now, I would not have touched Twenty's hair for the world, I had my gloves to think of. I feared for the new resident's hands.) In this manner, sitting an inconspicuous distance away, I watched the happy coupling for half an hour – the new resident stroking and smoking, Twenty smiling and sighing – until I was unavoidably distracted.

A brief history concerning passport photographs.

My passport photograph collection began when I had ended my habit of going for walks in the city (shortly after Tearsham Park had changed its name to Observatory Mansions). I set off from home and looked about the city for an interesting person to follow. When I had found such a person, I would simply follow him or her, at a discreet distance. Sometimes I would follow a man, sometimes a woman. I made no preferences. The first interesting person that came my way would be followed. Regardless of sex. Or of age. Or of race. I would follow the chosen person for as long as they walked. I would observe them, and as I observed them I imagined for myself the sort of life that that person was living. I did not much care if my imaginings were accurate or not. What mattered was that I felt at the end of the day that I had met someone new. These walks sometimes lasted a long period of time, hours perhaps, sometimes only a mere few minutes. It was not important. What was important was that I felt, however briefly, that I had witnessed a moment in an interesting person's life. It may not have been an interesting moment. I did not care. I had been close to an interesting person, someone, perhaps, whom I might have liked to have made friends with. But I found friends were predominantly absent things. I had only one true friend, but I did not meet him until I had begun my employment at the waxworks. My walks through the city streets were, in a way, a consolation. Through them I came as close to interesting people as I was happy to come. I would not have wished those city perambulations, those city chases, to have terminated in a conversation, less still an exchange of addresses.

My city walks were ended on the day I began my employment at the waxworks museum. Then my days were full. Our working hours were long and we were employed for seven days of the week. I could not, therefore, walk the city streets in pursuit of interesting people any more. I was confined, admittedly happily, to the waxworks museum throughout the day. In the evenings, when my work had ended, I was too tired to spend the time roaming the city in search of interesting people. Though, I remember, I missed them.

A solution came to me one day on the way to work. On a street pavement I found an abandoned passport photograph. I picked it up. I considered the face. I conceived a history for that face. I kept the passport photograph. In time I had enough passport photographs to form a collection. This collection, though admired by me, was never a substitute for my major work: the exhibition of objects to be found in the cellar, in that tunnel that led to the church (an exhibition which itself contains a passport photograph, lot 770). It may be realized that passport photographs are not common objects to be found on city pavements. After I had found the first passport photograph, I always walked to the waxwork museum with my eyes watching the city pavements, in search of passport photographs. After three months I had only found one other passport photograph, one other face to consider. I had to change my tactics. It did not take me long to think up a solution.

Every morning I changed my route to work to include a passport photograph booth. There I preyed on the impatience of man. Passport photographs once taken are not ready for collection for a good three minutes. That is the time it takes for the machine inside the passport photograph booth to develop the passport photographs. This time, a mere three minutes, is considered interminable by a good many people. This is where I took my advantage. By the passport photograph booth that I passed on my way to the wax museum were various shops, shops with window displays, window displays with which to pass away those three minutes while the passport photographs were being developed. Often people waiting for their photographs, and looking through the shop windows to pass away the three minutes, would spend longer than three minutes there. If I saw no one approaching the booth's photograph dispenser when a sheet of photographs plopped out, I would seize the photographs, I would call them mine and (always careful of the still-drying chemicals) I would hurriedly, in case I was seen, continue on my way to the waxworks museum. I was only caught once and made profuse apologies to the man whose passport photographs I had stolen. I told him: I thought they would be mine, I felt

I had been waiting for such a long time. I returned the photographs and he accepted my apology.

In this fashion my passport photograph collection progressed to such an extent that I had at one stage one hundred and twenty-six different passport photographs of people I had never met. For one hundred and twenty-six different faces, one hundred and twenty-six different histories were conceived.

On the afternoon in the park when the new resident had tamed Twenty, Dog Woman, I spied a forsaken passport photograph by the park bin nearest to me. It was of a young man. Thirties. Black hair, in need of a brushing. Square face, in need of a shave. Denim shirt, in need of an ironing. I struggled to imagine his life from his face. Another human being, yet another I had never seen before. What did this one know? Was he happy? Was he cruel? Did he worry? The more I stared at his face, the less I understood him. This is not unusual, the same procedure happens whenever I examine a person either on photograph or in reality: in my first glimpses I always think I can read someone fairly quickly, that the snap judgements I make are surely accurate, but the more I observe the less I understand, the more I realize how difficult the art of judging a person is.

When I looked up again from the passport photograph I saw that Twenty was lying on her patchy piece of grass alone. The new resident had gone.

Outside the church.

I could not see her anywhere in the park. I considered immediately returning to Observatory Mansions to warn Peter Bugg that I had lost her. But if the new resident had returned to Observatory Mansions then it was already too late. If, however, she had not, then she must still be somewhere in the city and Peter Bugg could continue his work in flat eighteen uninterrupted. I had not looked far when I was halted by an idea. The new resident smoked a great deal, she had not yet been seen without a cigarette in her mouth or in her hand. When cigarettes are finished the cigarette stub is generally discarded, thrown casually on to whatever piece of ground the smoker happens to be crossing. I could therefore follow the new resident by means of collecting her cigarette stubs. I approached Twenty, not getting too close, to pick up a cigarette stub which had certainly belonged to her (careful not to let any ash fall on my gloves, using a pair of tweezers which I always carried with me). Printed on the cigarette's paper in black ink, just by the filter, was a circle in which was written the words LUCKY STRIKE. Now I could follow her discarded stubs through the city until I found that place where they ceased being discarded, the place where the new resident would be. I noticed that her cigarette stubs bore her teeth marks. This was useful: it meant that I was unlikely to waste time following some other person who was not the new resident, but who also smoked Lucky Strikes.

I followed the stubs, they came every two hundred metres or thereabouts. When I found a stub I had to pursue all directions until I came across the next one. In this way I eventually found myself outside a church. On the steps of the church was the final cigarette stub, though this was more than a stub: half a cigarette, abandoned. I presumed, therefore, that the new resident was inside the church. There were two exits from the church, the first was past the porch through a large oak door, the other was to be found by shifting the stone lid off a false tomb within a private chapel. Having moved the lid aside you would find yourself descending roughly cut stairs, heading off into the darkness. You would find yourself in a tunnel, a tunnel which widened as it progressed. Along that tunnel you would discover numerous objects, nine hundred and eighty-seven to be accurate. I considered it unlikely that the new resident would take that exit, so few people knew of it. She would surely leave via the porch, so I waited for her in the church graveyard.

I had not been in the graveyard for several years, and seeing it again that day I found a peculiarly moving experience. I knew someone who was buried there, someone who I had once loved. I took some flowers from a fresher grave and placed them at the grave of my old friend. The gravestone was simply marked, it merely said, in large bold capitals, the single word:

EMMA

For there it was that Emma was buried.

A short voyage around the memory of a woman named Emma.

Long before the time when Tearsham Park changed its name to Observatory Mansions, shortly before the time when I began wearing gloves, was the time known as Emma-months.

Emma, already an old woman when I knew her, was the saviour of the village of Tearsham, in which my father's house, Tearsham Park, was by far the largest dwelling. She helped the old bachelors and old spinsters in our village. She taught children to swim. She visited the sick. She prayed for the dead. Among, I suspect, her less-remembered acts was the miracle she once performed in Tearsham Park.

Emma taught me to speak.

I was viewed as being somewhat behind as a child, though I would rather refer to my lack of speaking not as stupidity but as stubbornness. I was in no hurry to speak. I could not imagine what possible advantage words might have for me. Words usually meant company and I was always happiest on my own. Many teachers and therapists had been sent into the Park and they had all left without finding a word in me. My parents had run out of teachers, someone must have suggested Emma as a remedy for my silence, and though sceptical (but without any other options left open to them) Emma arrived the next day.

Emma's exterior.

Emma, never married, was never referred to as Miss something, just Emma, only Emma. That's what I called her, that's what everyone called her. She lived on her own in a small cottage on the edge of the village. Emma wore black. All-dressed-in-black Emma. Always black. Home-made black clothes. Black beret, black shirt, black skirt all the way down to her ankles. Thick black material, even in summer. Itchy. Emma smelt. I spent many days searching for the particular ingredient that might describe the stench. I found it in the kitchen. Emma smelt like boiled carrots. Emma had long grey hairs hanging from her face, as if she had dipped her chin in a cobweb. Emma's skin was the worst thing. When she first came to Tearsham Park I was afraid of her. I was afraid of her beard, her clothes, her smell – but most of all it was Emma's skin that terrified me. I often closed my eyes so I would not have to look upon her skin. Difficult to describe Emma's skin. Ingredients for a description of Emma's skin:

> Take one orange. Peel it.
> Leave it for several days in the summer sun.

The orange in the sun loses colour, turns white and develops thick, deep wrinkles. It diminishes in size. Open the orange out and, taking one of the thick, wilted and creased segments, tear it in half. Inside, at its very centre, is a tiny piece of the orange that used to be – still fleshy, still clutching to a little juice. Were I to have peeled Emma, I think that somewhere deep within her, past all that thick seemingly dead cover, I might have found a little life, a little blood.

I didn't like Emma. Not at first. I wanted her to leave, I made a fuss, I banged things about. Later I'd pray for her to live for ever, but first I'd beg for her to die painfully during the night. And yet, through my child's mind, I thought there was little hope for such an exit, for despite her hoary exterior her eyes betrayed more energy, more life than could be found in my youthful body.

Liquorice hours.

Blacked out and bearded Emma closed and locked the nursery door behind her. She did not smile at me. She regarded me briefly, but without expression. She sat down. She opened her (black) bag, took out a tin of tobacco and a wad of black liquorice rolling papers. She rolled a cigarette. She sat smoking. She took a small (black) plastic ashtray from her bag, put it on the table in front of her, and filled it with ash. When the cigarette was finished (this took some time and she smoked it almost until its dampened end burnt her fingers) she tapped her fingers on the table. She was waiting for something to happen. I sat at the other end of the table waiting for whatever it was that was meant to happen to happen. Silence. Emma took a piece of liquorice from her bag and noisily sucked it. Finally that too was gone. She sat still. I waited. Nothing. She rolled another black cigarette. She smoked on in silence.

My first Emma day was counted out with cigarettes and liquorice. She did not speak. I did not grunt, just watched. Hours of watching with just cigarette and liquorice consumption for diversion.

When the small black tips had filled the ashtray and her bag of liquorice seemed to have been emptied, Emma stood up again, she pushed the chair neatly under the table, walked to the window, opened it, emptied her ashtray, replaced it in its black home, closed the window, unlocked the door, exited and locked the door again. That was my first day with Emma.

The echo.

For days two and three with Emma read day one. Twice more. The fourth day brought a new experience.

69

I was not enjoying my hours with Emma. I was restless. I was waiting for her to do or say something. I fidgeted. I swung my legs up and down under the table. I began stamping my feet. Emma looked up, she nodded. I stamped my feet harder, she began clumping her (black) clogs. We made a terrific din. We banged on. Her wooden shoes made impressive thumps on the floor. When I stopped stamping, she stopped her clumping. Silence again. She lit another cigarette. I stood up, ran to the nursery door and pummelled my fists hard against it. I groaned. I whined. I yelled. Only when I had quietened down a little did I realize that Emma was clapping and smiling even. She held out a piece of liquorice, clearly for me to eat. I took it. I threw it on the floor, I stamped on it, I flattened the damned black thing. She took another piece out, dropped it, squashed it under her clogs. I screamed. Emma screamed, just as loud and just as panicked. I graced her with an infuriating whine. She did her best to respond to it but hers lacked my resonance. I stopped screaming and whining, there was little hope in those gestures. Emma only copied my sounds and showed no fear of noise. In any case, nobody had come running to save me.

Emma spoke:

Frrrrr. Fffffrrrrr.

I looked at her offended. I understood. If I was to leave the nursery it would only be after a performance of the noise: fffrrrrrr.

I learn to talk.

Fffff-rrrrrr, instructed Emma.
Ffffff, attempted Francis.
Rrrrrr.
Errrrr.

Rrrrr.
Rrrrr.
Fffffrrrrrr.
Ffffff.
Rrrrr. Fffrrrr.
Fffffrrr.
Aaaaaa.
Aaaaaah! (I knew this one.)
Fffrrrraaaaarrr.
Ffffaaaarrr.
Ffffrrraaaarrr.
Ffffrrraaaarrr.
Fffffrrraaarrrnnnn. Nnnn.
Nnnn.
Ffffrrrraarrrnnn.
Ffffrrraaaarrrnnn.
Ssssss.
Ssssss.
Frarrrnsss.
Frarrnssss.
Iiiiiii, sssss.
Iiiiissss.
Fraarrnssiiissss.
Ffraaarrrnssiiisss.
Francis.
Frarncissss.
Francis.
Frarncisss.
Francis.
Francis.
(Pause.)
Francis. Francis. Francis. Francis. Francis.
Francis.
Francis!

And Emma pointed at me. I was that sound. I was this – Francis. Said I: Francis. And pointed to myself. Emma held out her wrinkled and cold hand. I flinched. She took my hand and placed it in hers. We shook hands. Francis and Emma shook hands.

Meeting Mother.

Emma unlocked the nursery door. We went to visit Mother in the drawing room. Francis, I said. Mother kissed me all over my face and stroked my hair, she said to me: Mother, Mummy. Say Mummy. Francis, I said.

Skip some months, and many pieces of liquorice.

I could talk. I could deliver sentences. I could speak with anyone and comprehend their responses. I had entered, with regret, the world of communication. But I would not have remained there were it not for one thing . . .

The nursery days' entertainment.

Clump, clump, clump! The confectioner, the tobacconist, the audio-library was on her way. In she came. She shook my hand. We bade each other good morning. She sat. She rolled a cigarette – too slowly, she knew what I was waiting for, she was doing it purposefully. She took out her matches – too slowly, too slowly. The first one blew out before it had achieved its function – she had let it blow out, deliberately, I was sure of it. The second one lit the cigarette. She took a long drag. Smoke left her mouth. Silence.

What shall we do today?

That's it. That's what I was waiting for.

A story, a story, I cried. That's what I wanted always forever.

Emma's stories became more complicated and fascinating the more I learnt to speak. Emma's stories had been passed down from generation to generation – always changing slightly from mother or grandmother to child. Emma had heard many of the stories she told from her grandmother: she learnt them by heart then embroidered them or forgot parts and replaced the missing segments with her own additions. Often I'd demand her to repeat certain tales again and again – sometimes she'd change the ending or leave it open for me to finish. How can I explain Emma's stories? They were alive. They moved. *They lived!* They were a swirling mass of colours and smells that could never be caught. They shifted shape, swallowed themselves whole, contradicted themselves, ends chased beginnings, they leapt off at tangents or into other stories as if switching trains, hurled in strange directions, forgot themselves, remembered themselves, metamorphosed from romances to tragedies and back again by way of comedy. I heard of princes and princesses, of stepmothers, of donkeys that shat gold, of dragons, magic kingdoms, beasts, bluebeards, witches, goblins, ogres, trolls and many other phantasms.

As well as the standard fairy-tale characters, Emma added her own. And of her own tales, a certain group began, not in some imagined kingdom but in Tearsham Park. These tales would often start with – They didn't know it up in the nursery, but down below in the library, something extraordinary had begun to happen to Mr Orme. My father, absent-minded and mysterious, who we saw so often around the house staring into nothingness or crouched with intense curiosity in front of some object or other, became with Emma's help, the most magical of characters. Emma would tell of Father's adventures.

When Father had been ordered out for a walk by my mother, Emma would tell me he had gone on safari into strange, distant lands where people had heads in their stomachs; when we saw him in the parkland fascinated by molehills, Emma would send him deep beneath the earth where odd, hairy people lived; or she would summon gales to fly Father up into the sky to visit the strange weightless people who lived in the clouds. And I almost believed all these stories. Looking at Father they seemed entirely plausible.

The ending of a thousand tales.

On a certain day Emma was late. I went down to tell Mother. She told me to wait in the nursery, Emma would come. But when she didn't come, I went. Emma's front door was shut but unlocked. I let myself in. Emma was sitting in front of her fireplace. The fire had exhausted itself many hours earlier. Emma's eyes were closed. With her eyes closed, her one sector of energy was absented. She looked as if her skin was made of burnt paper and her clothes of cigarette ash. If I blew I was sure her head would sink into her chest and the two parts, connected and unreadable as Emma, would soon float down to what was once Emma's feet, and then all Emma, old Emma, would lie tidy in a little mound waiting to be swept away. The spent fire would look like her twin sister. But I did not blow. Emma did not subside; I'm just thinking my childish thoughts.

I tugged her elbow. Emma did not look up.

The library was closed, the stories were padlocked under her stiff tongue and would come out to play no more. All the creatures from trolls to princesses, all her heroes and adventures had sunk down her throat into the abysses of her stilled organs, amongst blood that had lost the idea of action. Emma was a dead thing. The centre of her lips were burnt, she had been smoking a liquorice-papered cigarette when she had died and it had gone on living after her. It had extinguished itself in the cooling blood of her mouth, it had heated her lips while the rest was going cold. The last warm place on the person who had taught me how to speak and to think, how to use my imagination and how to conceive histories, had been the lips and the tip of her celebrated tongue.

On a table by the fireplace was a tin of tobacco and a wad of black cigarette papers, I took them for my friends, I gave them to my pockets (lots 44 and 45).

But Emma was still to be found in the neglected graveyard of the church. I sat, that day, looking at the tombstone:

EMMA

Our second conversation.

I became aware of the new resident standing in the church porch, smoking a cigarette, looking at me.

You've been following me, haven't you?
No, thank you.
Why have you been following me?
I'm laying flowers at the grave of a friend.
No. Do you want something from me?
You'd better be out by the end of the week.
I've no intention of leaving.
It's been known for people to change their intentions.
I won't.
It's been known that people who promise never to change their intentions actually do change their intentions.
Well, I won't.
We'll see.
Are you trying to threaten me?
You may come across unforeseen obstacles.
You really are an exceedingly malicious little man.
If you have to put it like that, I prefer the word malignant. In any case, I'm taller than you.
I won't be frightened.

We'll see.

The Porter said you were slightly backward, is that true?

I've had enough of this conversation. (I began to leave.)

Is it the truth?

The Porter knows nothing about me. (I began to leave hurriedly.)

My name is—

I've no need for names!

Oh, you'll need this one, Francis Orme. Learn it.

I'm not listening!

My name is Anna Tap.

The findings of Peter Bugg, retired schoolmaster, retired personal tutor, etc.

Peter Bugg was waiting for me when I returned that day, just after my second conversation with the new resident who now, I was forced to understand, went by the name of Anna Tap. Peter Bugg was puzzled. Puzzlement in the guise of drops of sweat and tears trickled out of him. Had he been into Anna Tap's temporary residence? He had. Had he made an inventory of her possessions? He had. He held the sweaty list in his sweaty hands. Had he moved the objects into new positions? He had. He promised. Though, he said, it had been difficult. Heavy objects? No. Too many objects? No. Delicate objects? No.

He showed me the list of his findings:

An inventory of the possessions of Anna Tap,
18 Observatory Mansions.
Temporary resident.

Bed 1
Sheets, pillowcase .... (of each) 4
Pillows 2
Blankets 2
Towels (white, identical) 3
Chairs (identical design – Prussian blue, plastic, metal
    frame) 2
Tables (identical design, Formica top, metal frame) 2
Coat (black) 1
Blue dresses (identical) 8

Black lace-up shoes (flat soles, all identical) .... (pairs) 3
Socks (black, identical) .... (pairs) 8
Undergarments (bras, knickers) .... (pairs) 8
Spectacles case (empty, steel) 1
Toothbrush, toothpaste, soap, shampoo,
   deodorant .... (of each) 1
Bottle of pills (labelled DIHYDROCODEINE TARTRATE) .. 1
Suitcase (black) 1

These were all the objects to be found in flat eighteen. I insisted that there must be more. Some writing implements, some letters? Some photographs, books, periodicals? No. Some paintings, posters, ornaments? None. He had not searched everywhere. He insisted that he had. The only things he neglected to place on his list were, he said, various items of food. He also added that she had no kitchen machines. No refrigerator, no cooker. The food, he said, was either fresh or in tins. All to be eaten cold.

The difficulty poor Peter Bugg had was in arranging Anna Tap's possessions in such a way that would make them look as if they had assumed new positions. His first attempts at moving dresses and shoes (which were distributed, before he arrived, in various different places throughout her flat) had resulted in the flat looking identical. As if Peter Bugg had not been there at all.

I did not touch the undergarments. Though I noticed that the knickers had tiny little white bows on them. The bows made me feel sad, I'm not sure why.

He did not move the bed either. Too heavy. The chairs he did move, but afterwards they did not look as if they had taken up dramatically different positions. They were both identical. In the end Peter Bugg chose not to be subtle about his displacing. He moved the bed linen into the living room. He moved all the dresses and shoes into the dining room. He placed all the washing items (towels, toothpaste, etc.) in the kitchen and all food in the bathroom. The spectacles case (empty) he placed in the spare bedroom. But he did not, he maintained, touch the undergarments.

The procedure had been further complicated for poor Peter Bugg by the pink rubber gloves that I had pressed him to wear. The gloves, he said, had made his hands even more sweaty. What's more he was very nervous about his tasks and sweated and cried a great deal during their enactment. Wiping his forehead or his eyes with rubber gloves proved of little use, the rubber wouldn't soak up the wet.

The lack, and the similarity, of Anna Tap's possessions worried us deeply. The repetition of the items, we eventually decided, was the choice of a tidy, too tidy, mind. They also showed a remarkable lack of vanity or love of objects. We managed to convince ourselves that Anna Tap's somewhat frugal style of living was only temporary. The rest of her belongings were sure to follow on shortly. We would, of course, ensure that Anna Tap had left us before they arrived, more items would only encourage her to reside with us for longer; personal effects give people a sense of security. We were pleased that she had not completed the business of moving in. This meant, happily, that there was less to move out.

We heard Anna Tap returning to her temporary home, and then, a little later, a sudden scream came down to us from the third floor.

Down below, in flat six, Bugg and I smiled.

A death upsets us more than the bereaved.

At the appointed hour, during the evening news, when we went to pay a visit on Miss Higg to inform her of our progress, we heard talking coming from inside her flat. The voices, there were two, did not belong to a television set.

The voices belonged to Miss Claire Higg, television anchorite, and Anna Tap, temporary resident of flat eighteen.

Two hours later, during the next news broadcast, we received an explanation. Claire Higg had suffered a distressing loss. There had been a death. We were surprised, we could not remember her having any friends or relations, we could not imagine anyone whose death might have upset her. The news of the death had caused her to scream. It was Claire Higg who had screamed and not Anna Tap on entering her temporary residence, as we had first believed. She had opened her flat door to scream, hoping that that scream would reach the ears of Peter Bugg or even Francis Orme. She wanted some company. She needed consoling. But the company she had required had not been forthcoming. Instead she had been visited by Anna Tap. Claire Higg was quick to point out that, unlike Peter Bugg and Francis Orme, Miss Tap had immediately come to console her.

The death had come as a great surprise. The deceased had been shot, she said, at point-blank range. Seven shots. He fell to the ground. He didn't have a chance.

Who is dead? Who was shot?

Miss Claire Higg pointed at one of the photographs, scissored from a magazine, of the man with the moustache.

Now it may be thought that such a death, the death of a fictional character, may hardly be a cause for sobbing. Generally such deaths perhaps merit a sigh, no more. Not to Miss Higg. To her that death was a genuine tragedy. To her the moustached man was a real person, her friend. Taken cruelly from her by what she believed were genuine bullets. There was even fake blood to prove it. We could not say – Don't worry, Miss Higg, it's only a story. The actor with the moustache is still alive and well. We could not say that. If we had attempted, Miss Higg would only have looked at us with incredulity and sighed – Poor thing, poor thing. Been in the sun, have we? No, no, we had to continue the absurd charade of consoling Claire Higg because we wanted to find out what it was that had happened between her and Anna Tap.

Anna Tap had been very kind, apparently. She had even offered Claire Higg one of her cigarettes. Smoking was a habit of the deceased. A different brand, but the effect was the same, Higg felt closer to that moustache. Anna Tap had listened, patiently it seemed, to all Miss Higg's remembrances of the dead man. Dead *character*, that is, I forget myself. Miss Tap had even said that she wished she knew what such a loss felt like.

But no, Annie dear, you mustn't mind if I call you Annie dear and not Anna. You must consider yourself lucky never to have suffered such a loss. It's a terrible thing. I shall have to wear black now, probably until I'm dead.

You see, Miss Higg . . .

Call me Claire, all my friends call me Claire.

You see, Claire, I never had anyone to lose.

No one to lose? Nonsense.

You see, I'm an . . . orphan.

On encouraging the new resident to leave.

The next day, I had been out early and purchased from the locksmith's, a ten minute walk from Observatory Mansions, a new door lock, which came with two keys.

Bugg and I heard Anna Tap leaving and, armed with screwdriver, chisel and hammer, we approached flat number eighteen. Outside flat eighteen was an unpleasant welcome. Tufted-haired Twenty, the Dog Woman, crouching, a little cleaner than usual perhaps, but still repellent, standing guard for her new friend. A human watchdog. She growled at Bugg, who began to sweat, and also at me. I put my hands behind my back.

We returned downstairs.

That's it then, there's nothing we can do.

Stupid Bugg, dense old schoolteacher, dense old tutor. A head for books, a head made of books, a head of sheets of paper, the typefaces all tiny. Skin of paper, the paper of his skin burnt with words, words that glistened under sweat. Who has read the book of Peter Bugg? No one. Who wants to read the book of Peter Bugg? No one. It remains on the library shelf. It was placed there shortly after publication, an edition of one, and no one has ever asked for it. It would be dusty, but this type of paper sweats. No one wants to borrow the book of Peter Bugg. The last pages remain blank. For the moment. It's a book covered in black woollen material, which sags outwards at its bottom. It's called *The history of Peter*

Bugg, retired schoolteacher, retired personal tutor, etc. There it sits, one book in many. It's not a love story, it's not a thriller, there's no murder hidden between its jacket covers, no adventure either. There's a few pictures in amongst the pages to break up the tedious reading: one of the subject's father, the others are all school photographs, happy, smiling boys – where are they now? That's all. It's rather an old-fashioned book, to be honest. Not that it was ever in fashion. Nor will it ever be. Peter Bugg was born, Peter Bugg taught, Peter Bugg breathed. Who cares?

So that's it then, there's nothing we can do.

There was, Peter Bugg, there was, sir, everything that could be done. I sent him out. Off you go. Go fetch a dog, one of the city dogs, a wild one, not too wild, try not to let it bite you, bring it back.

He came back crying, sweating and moaning, his nervous body terrified of what it barely managed to carry: a dog, a flea-infested puppy. I placed some raw bacon on the stairs just beneath the third floor and sent the puppy up to fetch it. The puppy fetched. But the puppy came back rushing, yelping down the stairs, sprinting for its life. After it came Twenty, Dog Woman.

There, sir, that's what could be done.

We changed the locks of flat eighteen that day. Bugg kept the old lock. I kept one key to the new lock, Peter Bugg the other.

There.
Now she's sure to leave.

Now I could return to work.

Work.

Of work during that morning, I have little to report. Save that I was back on my usual unusual form. I was able to achieve both outer and inner stillness and my public rewarded me tolerably well for my concentration.

Of work during the afternoon, I have a matter of some unpleasantness to report. I was quite happy until I noticed on one of the occasions when a coin was dropped (when I opened my eyes) that among my crowd of appreciators was Anna Tap. When I closed my eyes I realized that I could no longer acquire my inner stillness. When I opened them again I noticed (by following the sounds) that the coin had been dropped by Anna Tap. I blew bubbles in her direction. I closed my eyes. A coin was dropped. I opened my eyes. Anna Tap had dropped the coin. What I heard though, between coin drops, is the most unpleasant part of this history. The coins that were dropped by Anna Tap were not coins taken from her pocket. They were taken from my box of coins which lay at the bottom of the plinth. Anna Tap was taking a coin from the box and throwing it back into the box. Again and again. Each time one of these coins was dropped I felt myself forced into the action of blowing bubbles at her. I noticed, too, that during Anna Tap's disgraceful abuse of my talents the number of my appreciators decreased. Anna Tap picked up my (hard-earned) coins some ten or twelve times during that afternoon, and during the intervals I noticed that she smiled each time a little more fully. Finally there was a long gap between coin throws and when I opened my eyes again she had left.

Temporary relief.

On my way back from work, walking this time, furious with my lack of inner peace and unable to remove the image of the smiling new resident from my brain, I found relief through an overheard conversation. Two elderly women walked and talked and stopped to look in windows:

Yes, it does look lovely on you.

It's a family heirloom. My grandmother used to wear this sable stole. Sadly, the weather's getting warmer and I'll have to put it away again until winter. I almost chide the summer for being so warm, it means I can't wear my stole. It feels so soft. Feel it.

I'm sure it's lovely.

Feel it.

Yes, so soft.

Take it. Wear it for a while if you like.

Really?

Yes, of course.

So soft. It feels wonderful wearing it.

Look in the window there. Look at those silks!

What colours!

Do you think we dare go in?

Oh, let's!

Darling, where's my sable?

Just here, around my neck – Oh!

Where've you put it?

It was just here.

Where's it gone? My sable stole! My stole!

I don't know.

It's been stolen!

Perhaps on the floor. No. Oh, no.

You bitch, you let it be stolen!

Then I felt happier (lot 987).

Peter Bugg's betrayal.

When I had finished cataloguing my new exhibit, I travelled up to the third floor to see what had happened to Anna Tap, and found an unpleasant progression: the original door of flat eighteen had been changed, the old lock had been replaced, the new lock was nowhere to be seen.

Miss Claire Higg's television set could not be heard, despite it being her usual viewing time. Instead came the distasteful sound of talking; there were not two, but four voices. Higg had company. Two of the voices I immediately recognized. Claire Higg. Anna Tap. Of the other two, one confused me, the other confounded me. The first of these two I could not recognize at all. I had not heard it before. What was more, I could not understand a word it was saying. It was speaking, in a somewhat broken fashion, a foreign tongue. Suddenly this voice, the first voice, laughed. It was like a child's laugh but it wasn't coming from a child. That beautiful laugh, so natural, so disturbing in its beauty, was completely out of place there; Claire Higg's sitting room should not have a laugh like that inside it. The second voice conversed alternately in the foreign language, but more fluently than the other voice, and then in our own language. It belonged, I am ashamed to admit – ashamed, that is, not for myself but on behalf of the owner – to a retired schoolmaster, retired personal tutor and ex-companion of mine who reeked of a hundred different smells. Peter Bugg, without a doubt. I even knocked on his flat door, labelled ten, on my way down the stairs just to make sure. No one replied to my knocking. Peter Bugg was out, call back later. Peter Bugg was out, indeed he was. Out of favour and out of his flat, upstairs with Higg, Tap, a foreigner and himself.

They've all been taken in by Anna Tap, all gone:

The Porter (I wasn't concerned about this one, let him go)
The man with the bathroom scales (his pockets will
    weigh, each week from now, two coins less)

The girl that Francis had known for two years but never spoken to (struck off my list)
Twenty, Dog Woman (I only ever cared for one dog, and she's been dead these many years)
Higg (wait till the next power cut)
Bugg (who cares about Peter Bugg?)

I did. Francis did. I raised my hand in the school classroom of Peter Bugg's mind. Please, sir. Sir! Sir!
Silence.
Wait, I thought, they'll be back. One by one, in reverse order, they'll all come running back. Just wait. And so I waited. For three hours. And then, finally, I heard a quiet knocking on our door. And who did that knock belong to? The man with a hundred smells.

A dog collar.

Peter Bugg was, as was his custom, sweating and crying an extraordinary amount, though these I noticed were excretions of excitement and not of nervousness. He told me that a wonderful thing had happened. *The lock, the lock.* Some other time for that. *Now! Now, Peter Bugg* (not sir, this time), *now!* Listen, something wonderful has happened to the woman who lives in flat twenty. *But the lock!* Later. Listen. Sit down.

The woman who lives in flat twenty has begun to speak. I'm sure you never heard her speak. Well, she started today. At about five o'clock it happened. No sentences yet. But a communication of a kind has gradually begun. Just words. Foreign words. But being a teacher of many subjects, as I am—
As you *were.*
—I have managed to join some of the words together into a kind of meaning. It seems that the woman, whom I have seen about but never paid much attention to, is very attracted

87

to dogs. At first that was the only word she came up with – just dog. In her own tongue of course. Then, with our encouragement, she went a little further. A name. Max. The name, we wondered, was it Max, short for Maximilian? When we said the name in full she yelped with excitement. A yelp that was not unlike a dog's yelp. We tried to find out who this Maximilian was. Her husband? No. Her father? Her boyfriend? Her brother? No. All she kept saying was dog, dog. We presumed that she was stuck upon the word dog. But then she showed us a dog collar. On the dog collar was a name tag, the tag said MAX, in capital letters. Max *was* a dog, you see. That was what she was trying to tell us.

Fascinating. And the lock? Anna Tap's reaction?

It was Miss Tap, the new resident, who discovered that the woman could speak, though she could not understand her, she was sure that she was speaking words, but in a different language. She asked Claire if she understood, if she spoke the language. Claire suggested, and rightly so, that I might be of assistance, explaining that I am a teacher and personal tutor—

Were a teacher. *Were* a personal tutor.

I could understand the woman, you see. I knew the language. And we're trying to find out more about her. It appears she's been in some terrible tragedy. She, as yet, seems unable to remember anything about her life except that she had a dog named Maximilian. Indeed, she clutches the damn collar to her and won't let anyone touch it. It's the sole clue to her life and she's petrified that someone might steal it.

My ears pricked up. Doggy fashion.

And when we make progress the woman from twenty laughs. It's such an extraordinary laugh, Francis, you should hear it. We're endeavouring to find out more. She's very stuck on Anna, won't say a word unless she's by her. She keeps licking her face and hands when she has the opportunity and she whines when Anna's out of the room. I just came down to tell you. I'm going back up there now, they're sure to be ready. Anna and Claire have been washing her; she's in a terrible mess. She smells too, but that can all be remedied.

And the lock?

Ah, yes. The lock. I'm sorry, Francis. Shortly after you left for work, someone knocked on my door. I opened it. There stood the Porter with Miss Tap. The Porter hissed and then spoke: Give me the key to the new lock on the door of flat eighteen.

You denied having it, of course.

No. I gave him the key. Then he said: Give me the old lock to the door of flat eighteen. It seemed a trifle difficult for him to speak. His sentences were, I believe, rehearsed.

You insisted you didn't have the old lock.

No. I gave him the lock. You know how I abhor physical violence. The threat of it was certainly there. I was sweating and crying so.

Sir!

The Porter took the key and lock and left.

Useless!

Miss Tap remained behind and had a few quiet words with me. Did you move my possessions around in my flat? I did. Do you promise never to do such a thing again? I did. Thank you, she said, and began to leave. I tried to say something, stammer a kind of apology. She turned and said, rather kindly I remember – she said – Don't say another word. We'll forget about it. It never happened. Besides, I am entirely convinced that you were put up to it. Goodbye, she said, and left. She came back later, enquiring about my knowledge of foreign tongues. I hope you don't mind, Francis, not now, not now this business with the woman from twenty has cropped up. I was sure you wouldn't mind. All that fussing with locks and keys and things suddenly seems rather petty, don't you think?

It seemed to me now that it was most unlikely that Miss Anna Tap's stay in flat eighteen would be a temporary one. Her arrival had changed time in Observatory Mansions. Like the arrival of Christ which ruptured time and shifted it from BC to AD, Anna Tap's arrival and presence had somehow applied sutures to the broken years of the inhabitants of Observatory Mansions, and by doing so had, unintentionally perhaps, unleashed an inferno. Unlike Christ, Anna Tap, an amateur in controlling time, was not able to stand us on our feet and say – Forget all the yesterdays, let's start from today and go forward. No, she was unable to do that, instead she sent us hurtling back into our pasts.

I went to bed early.

That white.

That cotton.

I slept, while above me memories began to flutter awake.

III

THE FOUR OBJECTS

The Time of Memories.

We now entered the time known as the Time of Memories, a strange time in which we residents of Observatory Mansions were forced to ingest the recollections that were sent out of each of us to knock on each other's doors, to fly around our rooms, to swim up our nostrils while we slept. Memories were everywhere during that time, they lurked soppy-eyed or listless with unspent energy, begging for attention on door handles, on window sills, on bedheads. We could not ignore them, we listened to them, we drank them up, we swallowed them and still they would not go away. In that time filled with our memories it was difficult to find the present. We did not know what the hour was, or the day, some of us even searched for the name of the month. During the Time of Memories we saw our rooms and possessions and ourselves shift through clouds of history. No object was to be trusted, for all the objects of Observatory Mansions gleefully took part in this confusing episode in our lives. If we reached for a chair, we might find that that chair was not actually there: it had been years ago, we had just remembered it, that was all.

The Time of the Four Objects.

A sub-division of that time went under the name of the Time of the Four Objects. The idea of these four, contemptible possessions entered each of our brains and once inside expanded until they were all that we could think of. A leather dog collar (with a name tag inscribed MAX), a pair of round steel-rimmed glasses with thick lenses, a black and white passport photograph of a sickly man (inscribed on its reverse – *Claire, Claire, I love you so* – and signed – *A. Magnitt, flat nineteen, Observatory Mansions*) and a wooden mahogany ruler with markings on its sides to indicate the length of inches.

The air had grown sticky with memories, we had to struggle to breathe and as we breathed we sucked in yet more memories. Everyone was remembering. Childhoods ran up the stairs of Observatory Mansions, deaths lay in our beds. In the dust of our home were minute skin particles which we had shed sometimes years, sometimes only days before. These particles began to connect themselves so that we saw the skins of our former selves take up our shapes, their former shapes, and wander about us, ghosts of skins past. Only Father, agile in his stillness, managed to gracefully step over, managed to dance around all the histories that tugged at his socks. He did it by keeping his thoughts empty, by achieving that perfect inner stillness where there are no thoughts, where memories suffocate.

The prologue to the Time of Memories had begun with the arrival of the new resident, Miss Anna Tap. And it was she who conducted the histories out of us, until, that is, there were too many voices, too many ghosts of objects for her to control. But the Time of Memories proper began with a dog collar belonging to the woman who lived in flat twenty and ended in a death, not in the memory of a death, though memories do sometimes end (or begin) with deaths, but in a real death. In a real body that refused to sink back into a past when we touched it. The body was cold and it was solid.

The residents of Observatory Mansions were trying to populate their present lonely lives with people from their pasts; so that they might feel sociable again. They didn't realize that memories could hurt, but soon they would.

Memories should be locked up inside skulls or in a tunnel that narrowed as it progressed. At first I did my best to ignore the business that went on two floors above me in flat sixteen but only one evening later, after a more successful day at work, I was disturbed again by the knocking of the man with a hundred smells who insisted on introducing me to the memories that had been set free.

Twenty remembered – 1.

The woman we called Twenty had been washed, her face, body, hair were clean. They had put her in one of Claire Higg's dresses; she looked quite different, I was told. She had remembered and laughed some more too.

Twenty remembered the number twenty. It was the number that had pulled her up to live on the top floor of Observatory Mansions. Twenty, the two and the zero, placed together in that order, held an irresistible attraction for her. She remembered that during the days when she lived in a foreign land, in fact her homeland, she lived in a block of flats and the number on her door had been the same. Twenty.

Claire Higg remembered – 1.

The original object of the Time of Memories was to allow Twenty to find herself, to remember as much of herself as she could. But it is only human nature that once one person has started to reminisce, another will immediately feel an irresistible urge to do the same. And so it was that Claire Higg remembered her wooing days, years of them there were, when she set her heart on a man named Alec Magnitt. Not a beautiful man. He grew no moustache, he had no magic smile. But he was loved by Claire Higg. He lived in flat nineteen and she would follow him on his way back from work. Magnitt was an accountant, she remembered, he was never without a calculator. She remembered all this while sitting with Anna Tap, Twenty and Peter Bugg.

Higg was wearing black. She had walked around her room looking at all the photographs of the deceased moustache man while Twenty was busy remembering, and as she looked around her room she noticed a square of magnolia wall less dirty than the rest. There, on that spot, once lived the photograph of Alec Magnitt, she remembered, aloud. Where had it gone to? I loved Alec, she remembered, aloud, to her three visitors. And Alec loved me too, she entreated. Though she did not actually remember him saying it. Indeed, he never did. He wrote it once though, on the back of a passport photograph, he wrote – *Claire, Claire, I love you so.* He had, she insisted, he had written those words so close to Claire-Claire's fat covered heart. He had even signed it, she recalled. Proof, she said. Proof of her memories. But where had that proof gone? Yes, where is that passport photograph? It was there, she told her three visitors, pointing at the wall. And she made them all, each in turn, inspect that sacred piece of wall where once there was proof that Claire Higg had indeed been loved. They believed her, they wanted no proof. But *she* did, oh yes, Claire did. Proof, where are you? Where are you, dear photograph of darling Alec? It was the only photograph she had of him. Then she started panicking, she screamed. Anna Tap gave her a cigarette but it didn't seem to help. What was wrong? they asked.

I can't remember his face any more!

She closed her eyes and all she could see on the magnolia walls of her memory was the face of a man with bronzed flesh and a moustache who smiled a perfect smile at her.

Alec? she had called, though never to his face, that sickly face she was trying so hard to remember. There was a kind of proof of that face's existence on her magnolia-coloured wall. There was even a kind of proof in her head, though she couldn't entirely trust in it. Each time she thought of her past it turned sensational, the off-white dingy rooms of her youth turned into vast golden beaches. She could not trust her brain, so much that it recalled, and she was realizing, remembering, thinking this now, had never actually belonged to her.

She needed proof, not to show those three visitors but to show herself. Where had that passport photograph gone?

Twenty remembered – 2.

After Claire Higg had calmed a little, Anna Tap again tried to encourage Twenty to speak. And Twenty, with time and patience, laughed her sweet laugh again and remembered aloud a little something more. She remembered walking the Great Dane across a great expanse of rocky ground. There were trees, too, and there was blood on her head. She presumed, not remembered, that she had cut her head. And then Anna Tap looked at Twenty's head and said that there was a scar there. So that then they all celebrated Twenty's presumption about cutting her head because now it was certainly a remembrance too.

And wasn't that progress?

Claire Higg remembered – 2.

And after Twenty had remembered that little bit more there was a slight pause. And into that pause jumped Claire Higg, taking full advantage of that most little of silences to fill it with herself. She remembered a time when she lived and worked in the capital city of our country. She worked in a large department store, the largest, she remembered, that there was. She was proud of the place, she had worked there for twenty-three years, and in those twenty-three years she had seen the ever-increasing rise in the popularity and shares of the department store. She worked in the hosiery department.

She sold stockings, garters, tights. She remembered that when she began working in hosiery there had been little range in the products she had to sell. She sold mostly stockings, nylon, wool, silk. Her customers then, she recalled, were mainly women of her own age, buying, as she saw it, sensible garments. Then tastes changed and she had to begin selling other items. She thought these were ugly looking objects, particularly the ones in red satin. Her customers changed too, she recalled. They suddenly seemed less sensible, more frivolous; not necessarily younger, but with fuller bosoms and thicker make-up. It occurred to her in time that she was aiding the sexual adventures of the people of our capital city. This made her sad. It particularly upset her when men came to buy these, as she saw them, ludicrous objects with their buckles, straps and clips. Claire Higg felt more and more degraded as the objects she was forced to sell became more and more erotic, for there was little of the erotic about Claire Higg. In time the shop owners felt that, in fact, Claire Higg was putting off potential customers in hosiery; her shy, rather desperate, looks, her skinny, unconfident body did not increase sales. They let her go, giving her a cheque. And with that money, combined with a portion of her savings, Claire Higg bought herself a home away from the capital city, a place she had found increasingly bewildering, and moved to a smaller, hopefully kinder, city where she prayed, she remembered, she might be more at ease. She bought flat number sixteen in an old building recently converted into flats, called Observatory Mansions.

Twenty remembered – 3.

Claire Higg was very sad after revealing this memory, and the atmosphere up in flat sixteen became tired and melancholy until Twenty, who had not had Miss Higg's story translated for her, suddenly laughed (at which Miss Higg looked deeply offended) and remembered aloud that after she had cut her head she was unable to remember anything. She remembered she had nothing in her pockets to tell her who she was and only a Great Dane, who wore a dog collar with the name tag that said MAX, to reveal even the barest hint of how her life had been before her head was cut.

The Porter remembered.

And elsewhere in Observatory Mansions, the Porter remembered – while considering the new Twenty, whom he had seen earlier that day, now clean and washed – that he had once attempted to remove Twenty, in her unwashed state, from flat number twenty. And he remembered that she bit him. The wound, he remembered, he cleaned and now, due to his hygienic efforts, there was no souvenir of where Twenty's teeth had been on his speckled skin. Seeing, in his remembrances, the old, dirty Twenty enter Observatory Mansions, set off other remembrances of other residents. These other residents, the ones he liked to remember, had all gone now. They had, he remembered, a certain tidiness about them, a certain class. And this made him remember, with sadness, the time when Observatory Mansions had been full, when all twenty-four flats had been occupied. It was a time when Observatory Mansions was seen as a desirable residence, and that time was only shortly after he had changed his name to Porter. He remembered this with nostalgia, for then the carpets were a perfect dust-free blue, the papered walls were a perfect stain-free blue and white. The Porter remembered, feeling his large bunch of keys, a time when those keys could open doors to so many different people's lives. He was a happy porter then. But he had only vague recollections of how a state of happiness felt.

Mother remembered.

Mother, positioned horizontally on her bed, remembered a time when she was perpendicular. She remembered the same time that the Porter had remembered, the time when Observatory Mansions had been seen as a desirable residence. But her memories of that time did not include dust-free blue carpets or stain-free blue and white striped wallpaper. Those she had neglected to remember. She remembered a time when flat eight was occupied by a slim bachelor. She remembered the slim bachelor's double bed that was large enough to hold a bachelor and a woman, be she spinster or widow. She remembered she used to call herself a widow, though even then she remembered that her husband was still alive. Here my mother's remembrances were stopped, momentarily, by the entrance of Father into her memory cinema. And when his face came on to her screen it was as if THE END were written up there, for Father's face stopped her memories, dried them up. When she saw Father's face, she counted to ten, or twenty, or fifty, sometimes a thousand – but usually, she remembered, the numbers blocked him out. She always stopped her memory showings each time Father arrived as a character in them. She did not want to remember Father as part of those times when she had been perpendicular. And horizontal. And then she remembered that bachelor's bed in flat eight again. She had remembered lying naked there and the bachelor lying naked beside her. She had got so excited by her remembrances that she stretched her hand out to touch the bachelor between his legs but he was not there. Ah, yes, she remembered, miserably, he's gone, hasn't he? Left flat eight, left Observatory Mansions, left Alice Orme. But she remembered to call him *bastard* before he left.

Mother remembered through objects, as I have already indicated, and this particular memory was brought to her by a pair of men's Y-fronts that sat, unoccupied, on one of the chairs in Mother's bedroom. In days long since spent, she slipped them off. He slipped them on and his suit trousers over them and, shortly afterwards, he was completely dressed, and then he was going, with all his Y-fronts (save one pair), away. But she remembered to call him *bastard*, for the second time, before she started crying, though she had only really said it once. Repetition. Mother had probably said *bastard* to the bachelor and started crying twelve or thirteen times already that day. The memories in her head went around like a Ferris wheel, she often stopped the wheel when it got to Y-fronts. Mother kept catching herself in a memory circle that began with Y-fronts and ended in *bastard*.

Father remembered.

But Father remembered nothing, Father sat in his red leather armchair, still as the numbers on a clock face, watching but never moving, with the hour and minute and second hands running around him (in an anticlockwise direction). If he remembered anything, which I do not think he did, he remembered not to remember.

Anna Tap remembered – 1.

Claire Higg up in her flat sixteen with her guests, who were now silent and feeling more than a little awkward, was still vaguely thinking of her old job in the hosiery department, and asked Anna Tap how she had been employed. So it was that Anna Tap remembered her work, which had been in the city museum textile conservation department, third floor. She remembered the door to her office. The other side of that door were workbenches, microscopes, magnifying glasses on stands, dyes, waxes, cotton, organic solvents, resins, entomo-logical pins, curved surgical needles, filaments of silk and polyester, and many other objects besides, all connected to her work. And what was that work? Anna Tap was employed in the city museum, until her dismissal, as a textile conservator. She cleaned and consolidated dresses, tapestries, chair covers, kimonos, bedspreads, sheets, embroideries, suits, ties, handkerchiefs, lace veils, flags, puppets' outfits, shirts, blouses, socks, gabardines, doublets, tights, pantaloons, bishops' mitres, trousers, skirts, hats, gloves and many other objects besides. She worked on horsehair, on human hair, on furs, on feathers, on lace, on wool, on cotton, on nylon, on velvet, on felt, on silk, on hessian and many other fabrics besides. She remembered what it was like to touch those different materials, she cleaned them, she conserved them so that they would be remembered for years to come. Though she remembered that as she stooped over her objects that the objects' wearers or owners had died years ago, sometimes centuries ago. The objects had outlived the owners. The objects had won every time. And she painstakingly ensured that they would go on winning for generations to come. She even, she remembered thinking, helped the objects' victories to be complete. Part of her work as textile conservator was cleaning the objects. And as she cleaned them she removed all the various pieces of autobiography that were left on them. She took out all the marks and stains, all that remained of the objects' owners. She removed sweat, lipstick, food, mud, wine, blood, semen and many other memories besides. She removed all the secrets from these objects until all that was left was the object itself, clean, uncreased – the creases too, those folds that showed where humans had been, were lost. She was a virtual washing machine of history.

But these objects, rather than being grateful to the woman that had so generously preserved them and aided them in their victory over man, took revenge on her. Her eyes, they believed, had seen too much, had read all their little secrets before removing them.

Anna Tap, crouched over so many fabrics, focusing her

bespectacled eyes on minute strands, had begun to go blind. She wore, over the years, ever thicker spectacles, until it was that she had to rely more on touch than on sight. And this was not good enough. She might mistakenly snap one of those tiny fibres, she might make stains of her own, she had to go. For the objects' sake, the objects had decreed it. Once her eyes had become too weak, she was dismissed.

Then Anna Tap, out of work, had little to think about except for her eyes, and the last eye surgeon had said that, sadly, there was nothing he could do, that, sadly, she was going to go blind. After the failure of the trabeculectomy, he said, and continued resistance to acetazolamide and pilocarpine, it seems it is impossible to reduce the pressure building up inside your eyes. We are incapable, in short, of reducing the production of aqueous humour. The eye tissues are being stretched, he said, the conjunctiva will grow intensely inflamed and with that the eyeballs will become as hard as two small rocks inside your skull, after which I am afraid, but there can be no doubt in this, the vision will go. The process will cause you some severe irritation which you will relieve by taking these. He handed her a bottle of pills labelled DIHYDROCODEINE TARTRATE – High in codeine, he said, that should dampen the pain. Anna Tap remembered how many eye surgeons she had visited and how they all could not remember a case as bad as hers and that there was nothing they could do for her. Soon afterwards Anna Tap began praying. She prayed for her sight to be saved, and, she remembered, her prayers had not yet been answered, though she was certain that they would be in time. Just in case, she had sold many of her possessions, reduced them to a manageable few and positioned them carefully in her new home so that she would be able to recall their places if she went blind, practice for her all-night years to come. But that was only if her prayers failed, she remembered, which they wouldn't, she insisted. There would be no need for this dihydrocodeine tartrate, even with its high level of codeine. What were pills when compared to the strength of faith?

Claire Higg remembered – 3.

Then Claire Higg, needy for attention once more and having lost it during Anna Tap's reminiscence, remembered placing a full and unopened milk bottle outside her door every morning at seven o'clock. She also remembered opening her door again at half past seven to retrieve the milk bottle. And at precisely picking-up-milk-bottle time a certain Mr Alec Magnitt would be seen leaving his flat for work. They would see each other through the caged walls of the lift shaft. They would exchange smiles usually, sometimes swap a good morning, sometimes comment about the weather. That was all. But that was something. She at least saw him every day. And all because of those milk bottles of hers. Milk bottles of love she used to call them, she remembered. Poor Alec Magnitt never did work out that the milkman did not call at Observatory Mansions.

Peter Bugg remembered – 1.

And after that memory, Anna Tap suggested they all take a break, and took Twenty, who seemed increasingly restless, across to her flat to feed her. Peter Bugg, during the day's lunch break from their memories, in the privacy of his rooms, neat, tidy, smelling of a hundred smells, was not one willing (as yet) to share his past, but he remembered too. In his largest room with its strange and inappropriate wallpaper (left over from the tenant before him) of greatly enlarged photographs of some distant port in some faraway land with bizarre ships and scantily dressed fishermen, Peter Bugg let in his remembrances. He stared at his own photographs, sealed in frames, of schoolboys stacked together for their yearly portrait. These boys had been neatly hung over ships, fishermen and port buildings, but Peter Bugg didn't see the foreign harbour, he saw only the boys from his life. He put names to the faces of each of those smiling boys. Then he saw, quite by accident, for he tried never to look in that corner, the face of his father, a black and white photograph. And he remembered how that face of his father's moved. Then he started sweating and crying a little more than was common for him. And in so doing he remembered a time when he neither cried nor sweated. But once his remembrances had been connected to his father, his father would not let him go. He kept his son in his seat, watched his son sink down that seat, petrified. Remember that fear, Ronnie? – for his father always called him Ronnie, he remembered that, couldn't forget that – oh yes, Ronnie remembered the fear.

It was that same fear, he remembered, that he handed out so easily to his pupils. And especially to one pupil in particular. His name: Alexander Mead. No, put that name away, screamed Peter Bugg (aloud now), for he was suddenly terrified. His heart began to race. Sweat and tears rushed on to his skin. Put that name back, he screamed. Put it back, back, back into the abysses of my brain. Let it stay in the darkness. But the boy, encouraged by his name being remembered, comes out to play. A fair-haired boy: tidy, precise, an exceptionally bright, friendless student. Go away, boy – screamed, aloud, the boy's retired schoolmaster. Go and do your homework. But the boy says he's done his homework, sir. Peter Bugg opened the window of his sitting room but the boy wouldn't go out with the heavy air smelling of one hundred smells. Instead, he sat on Peter Bugg's head and slipped off every now and again when the sweat became too slippery. Into Peter Bugg's eyes.

Yes, Peter Bugg remembered too.

Twenty remembered – 4.

Twenty, when they had all returned to flat sixteen after their lunch break and with some encouragement from Anna Tap, remembered walking for days, perhaps months, maybe even years, she had no way of knowing for sure. The time, she said, was vague in her, as yet, still vague mind. She did remember, though, certain dogs on this long walk of hers. She remembered she took her food from the dustbins kept outside people's houses. Some of those people kept dogs. She remembered dog fights. Ferocious dog fights. She remembered licking the dog Maximilian's wounds after the fights. She remembered the taste of dog blood.

Each time Twenty remembered she grew a little less confident.

Anna Tap remembered – 2.

Then Anna Tap remembered the second time that she visited the museum in which she was employed for so many years, in which her eyes were irreparably damaged. She could not remember her first visit at all. When she first visited the museum she was only a few days old. She had been wrapped in blankets and left in the women's lavatory, in a basin with her head beneath a tap, she explained. She thought it might have been the hot tap. She was found, she did not know by whom, and taken into care. That was all that Anna Tap could recall being told about her first visit to the city museum.

Her second visit, however, she remembered without help. She was sixteen then. She had been told that she had been abandoned in the women's lavatory in the museum and wanted to see it for herself. She saw it, she spent two hours inside it, trying to get closer to Mummy, she remembered. Then, when she had seen enough, she walked around the museum. She called the museum objects her brothers and sisters. The closest, she explained, she was ever likely to get to brothers and sisters. She decided she wanted to work in the city museum, to be in a place where, she believed, her mother had once been, and also to be close to those so-called brothers and sisters.

She had never, she remembered aloud, lost her fondness for women's lavatories.

Francis Orme remembered – 1.

This recollection, when it was presented to me later that day by Peter Bugg, reminded me of one of my own memories. And so it was that even I remembered. Anna Tap's museum story breathed life into my own first visit to a museum. The museums are different. The museum I remembered was a waxworks museum. I was taken by my father to the waxworks museum shortly after the death of Emma. I was taken there, I suppose, to cheer me up. Emma's death had saddened me greatly and I was deeply preoccupied in mourning her. I even insisted on being bought liquorice.

But nothing, save the beginnings of my own exhibition, thrilled me quite so much as that afternoon I spent wandering around and between the men and women of wax who loomed over little me. I considered then that since I had no friends the wax museum would be an admirable place to find them. I could spend, I remembered thinking, my days here surrounded by people and never get lonely. I could talk to them, I could give them voices and I could keep still and close my eyes, as I had practised at home with my toys, and imagine that I was made of wax.

I was impressed that day, so much so that I forgot to mourn Emma. Father, I remembered thinking, was impressed too. I vowed that when I had grown beyond child age to adulthood I would get myself employed at the waxworks museum.

Twenty remembered – 5.

Twenty remembered, earlier that day than my remembrance of the wax museum, that she walked from her homeland all the way to Observatory Mansions. She remembered that when she set off she did not say to the dog Maximilian – We shall carry on until we reach Observatory Mansions. The fact that she arrived at Observatory Mansions was entirely coincidental. On the evening before she took up residence in flat twenty, Twenty and Maximilian had got caught in a dog fight, a particularly bad one, she remembered. That night the dog who fought with them was particularly fearsome. It had scratched Twenty in many regions. But it had, she remembered, chewed poor Maximilian nearly to death. And running from the fight, she remembered in tears, Maximilian had been hit by a car. He howled so when he was hit, she said, and later he whimpered and whined and shivered. She needed, she explained, in her foreign tongue, with Peter Bugg translating, a place of shelter to lick Maximilian's wounds. But Maximilian, sad Great Dane, died during the night. She buried him, she remembered, under some dried earth outside Observatory Mansions. Then, she recalled, she did not know what to do with herself, nor could she remember why she had walked so far, or in what country it was that she had ended up. Looking around Observatory Mansions she saw the number twenty written on a door and that number seemed to mean something to her, so she decided, she remembered, to stay there. In flat twenty.

Twenty was not laughing when she remembered this.

Claire Higg remembered – 4.

One morning Alec Magnitt, remembered Claire Higg without invitation, had come out of his flat to go to work and had as usual smiled at Claire Higg as she came out to pick up her milk bottle of love. But that day Alec Magnitt had said something, he had said – I didn't know that we had milk delivered here. Oh, yes, Higg said, Higg lied, Higg remembered aloud, I can fix it for you if you want. Would you really? said Magnitt. Absolutely, said Higg. And she did. She bought an extra milk bottle every night, one for Higg, one for Magnitt, and placed one outside her door and one outside Magnitt's door every morning at seven o'clock. She remembered that morning very clearly, she said, because it had seemed to her on that occasion that Alec Magnitt was in fact flirting with her. He didn't have to ask me about the milk bottles at all, did he? she asked. And receiving no response she went to her kitchen to pour herself a glass of milk. She said, on returning:

I always love to drink a glass of milk.
Personally, I can't stand it.

Anna Tap remembered – 3.

It was Anna Tap who remembered her detestation of milk. Claire Higg looked offended. Anna Tap offered her a cigarette and went on to remember a time when she was sent to orphanages. We lived in dormitories sometimes of only ten, sometimes of fifty or more, she said. One orphanage dormitory she remembered particularly. This one, she said, was so full that there were two girls in every bed, and girls lying between the beds, and girls along the passageways. If you slept on the floor you slept on a mattress, she said, if you slept on a bed you slept without a mattress, lying on the cold stiff planks with only a sheet between those planks and yourself. The sheets were dirty, almost always. And there was only one pillow to each bed or mattress, so that the weakest child in each pairing always went without. We lay down with our heads at opposite ends – if we were found lying or sleeping together head to head we were beaten. There were windows there, but the windows needed cleaning and were bolted and barred. And during the night the dormitory door was always locked. The beds were wooden and on each bedhead and foot were scratched children's names or words of hatred or of love or simply scrapes and dents, signatures of those children who could not write. The children might remain in that orphanage or be moved on (at least three quarters would be), and so the priests who ran the orphanage took less care over those potentially temporary boarders, since they could be sent away before they had even had a chance to learn their names. It would have been easy for the priests to sit down and listen to each child's story, to pass her a handkerchief and comfort her as she went through it. Each story carried a similar charge and passion, the priests could spend their lives listening to them. If they stopped for one child, then others would insist on attention too, and so all were left alone. Cried alone. Covered the already dirty sheets with their snot and tears. The sheets, such flimsy mothers, too weak to resist, would be stretched, ripped, loved and smudged over and then left without a goodbye for the next girl to mistreat. Sometimes we lay there all day as well as night. During the day the door was always open. From the door a stone passageway could be seen and, every now and then, other children, better dressed than us, Anna Tap remembered, would pass. Adults passed too: priests, cleaning women, doctors. But only the other children looked in and they never stopped to speak, offer comforting words or insults because on a wooden stool in the doorway sat an orderly. The orderly was a well-built man in his twenties. He sat there on those days and in those hours when we were forced to stay in the dormitory. He sat with a paper, reading it through and through, starting with the sports pages and then working backwards. He only looked up if one of us approached the door. Then he would point the child back to her bed or stand up filling the whole door frame.

Everything was temporary; all those little bodies would lie there for no longer than three months. Only the stains, the beds, the orderly were permanent. During the day when the orderly sat at his post with his paper (unless we were allowed to sit outside or in a large classroom) everything was silent, only the rustling of blankets or sheets was heard or the quietest of whispers, for the orderly's presence was a perfect notice – BE QUIET. But at night, after the meal of a glass of milk (she remembered, looking at Claire Higg, for it was the glass of milk that had sparked off her memory), soup, bread and biscuits, after the door was locked and the passageway was silent, the noise gradually began.

At first there were quiet whisperings from here and there, from this bed or that bed, this mattress or that mattress: never progressing beyond the originating bed or mattress where the occupants were whispering to each other. So the first conversations were only between two. Couples whispered, whispers that began timidly, not knowing if the neighbour would react, with – It's dark, or It's cold, or You awake? And then the answers came back – You'll get used to it, or Am I taking too much blanket? or I'm awake, I don't mind talking for a bit. And then they'd ask each other's names, where they came from, did they know where they were going next, how long do we stay here? The talking gradually grew in confidence, the words came quicker, were spontaneous now, she remembered, not carefully thought out. All about the dormitory the numerous private conversations grew in volume, and those other pairs at first too scared to talk gradually let out their own sounds – and so the words fell from bed to bed or leapt across to the row on the other side, darted from head to head: words not coming from one or two places now but from numerous, uncountable origins. Anna Tap said at this point, when everyone was talking excitedly, sitting up in their beds, calling to the new girls many beds away, that those were the sounds she loved most. They meant to her company, pure, necessary company noise. The girls in that dormitory shook hands, imitating adults, feeling for them in the dark, smelt each other's voices, told of their lives so far. And if one child told a life story that was exceptionally sad or frightening or funny or moving, she would be asked to go to another part of the room so that others might hear it. This task – the sifting and swapping of stories – was executed by the senior girls who had been there for weeks or months. They acted as editors, organizers, not brutally controlling the nights but rather helping them along; encouraging each new child to speak. But each night would end disastrously.

The senior girls, so called not because of their age but because of the length of time spent in the dormitory, had listened to nights and nights of stories and greedily awaited this time of day. They were brilliant listeners and they prided themselves on their memories. They listened without inter-ruption, nodding at the right places or looking sympathetic, or laughing when required. But once a story was ended and was a few nights old we'd often hear it again. This time it would be told by a senior girl who had adopted it, but if questioned would swear on her life that it had actually happened to her. And this was where the trouble began. Though names and certain smaller incidents would have been changed, reworked in the quiet day to be ready for the night performance, its source could not be denied. Often the girl, the originator, who had told the story would hear it being claimed by a senior and react violently. Though her story may or may not have been true, there were surely elements of truth in it, and it often included the one sacred person, animal, object or incident that the child had treasured so completely, and now, hearing her own tale on another's lips, it was as if someone had stolen her life. Anna Tap explained that they had no possessions, no luggage, even the clothes they wore belonged to the orphanage. If a child arrived with her own clothes they would be removed, forcibly if necessary, and never seen again. Bullying had been reported, with stronger girls seizing such items of clothing and claiming by their possession an individuality that was not their own.

The stories that the new girls were tricked into telling were stolen and, like losing cherished photographs or letters, they felt that suddenly they had never belonged to a past, to a place, to people. Stories and memories were the only possessions left to them and they fought when they had been stolen, they violently struck out, bit, pulled hair. It often happened that two or more seniors stole the same story; for they grew bored of their own tales and changed them as often as three or four times a week. And when it happened that the same story was stolen by two seniors or three or four, a larger fight for ownership began, sometimes including the true author, sometimes with the true author looking on in tears.

With the beginning of the fights, the stories ceased for the night – the sounds grew ugly, crying now was often heard, beds being pushed about, other children yelling as the fights trod on them, heads being banged on bedheads. And then the wounded and the victor would slowly return to their beds and a quiet sobbing might be heard for a while and then silence. If someone, new girl or senior, were to say something then, even if in a whisper, a chorus of *shut up* would silence her. And the silence would continue until the next night when it all would begin again.

The dormitory was a museum of stories, original, stolen, fused. And the curators were the seniors who, rather than cataloguing the works, mixed them up, disposed of many, lost many.

Francis Orme remembered – 2.

The section of Miss Tap's history about children's possessions (or lack of them) reminded me of other children's objects. I remembered the attic rooms of Tearsham Park, and in the attic rooms furthest from the stairs, beyond the servants' quarters, I spent many hours discovering the objects of dead people. All the dead people's objects were kept out of the way there. Many of those dead people's objects were an embarrassment to the still-living people who dwelt down below. But some objects in the attic rooms were kept there because their dead owner was supposed to remain a secret. Hidden in a locked wooden trunk in one of the smaller rooms I found a child's possessions, among them a teddy bear without a mouth (lot 174).

Peter Bugg remembered – 2.

The prattle about dormitories, as Peter Bugg viewed it, about all-girls dormitories, reminded him of other dormitories, filled with boys, where he had turned the lights out at night and left the boys to their thoughts of girls. The names of some of those boys came sir-siring up into his head once more. And among those names was that of the boy who had died, that of the boy Peter Bugg was certain he had brought to death by his own mean ways. Tears rushed down his face as the boy, sitting on top of his bald head, slipped again under the lubrication of his excessive sweating into his eyes. Alexander Mead. He remembered so many boyhoods, so many school-days, so why could he not lift the image of this boy's face from his eyes. The boy stayed, smiled into Bugg's skull when he blinked.

This is a remembrance of his that he declined to share with Higg, Tap and Twenty. But he told me later on about the boys' dormitories . . .

... So that I, seeing girls and boys sleeping in beds, remembered a time when I was in possession of fifty-four porcelain dolls. The Time of Dolls boasts as its characters: myself, Master Francis Orme, then only recently after the Time of White Gloves, and fifty-four porcelain dolls. These dolls had belonged to my paternal grandmother and they were said to be extremely rare and valuable. Mother had not let me touch them. They lay in their various white cardboard boxes, lined with protective tissue paper, in those distant and out-of-bounds attic rooms of Tearsham Park. However, during the Time of Mother's Greatest Unhappiness, which coincided with the Time of Dolls, my mother kept herself locked in her bedroom and so was unable to see me up in the attic. I took the dolls from their boxes and, standing them all on their dainty feet, imagined myself married to every single one of them and saw myself living happily in the seclusion of the attic rooms of Tearsham Park. I saw myself, I remembered, strolling about nonchalantly under the pressures of marriage, and wherever I saw myself I was pursued by fifty-four diminutive porcelain wives. During the second stage of the Time of Dolls I undressed all the dolls and examined them very studiously. I became an expert in the anatomy of doll-kind. (At the waxworks I once tried to examine the wax flesh under the clothes of the wax people. The wax people did not have wax bodies, the wax people had bodies made of polystyrene and fibreglass – some of them, the ones with long dresses, even had wooden stumps for legs.) The third stage of the Time of Dolls, and sadly the last, found me returning all the still-unclothed dolls to their white boxes and numbering each of them. I found enough white cardboard around Tearsham Park to fashion for myself a somewhat larger white box. This I labelled fifty-five. I would lie down, also naked, save for my white gloves, in my box and meditate. The Time of Dolls ended abruptly: Mother, out of her room once more, though paler and thinner, discovered (naked) me with my fifty-four (naked) porcelain wives and divorced me from them immediately. The last time I saw my wives, I remembered, was during the auction that took place on the lawns around Tearsham Park. The dolls were clothed then and fetched an exceedingly high sum. (All but one, who managed to escape. Lot 192.)

Twenty remembered – 6.

Twenty, recovering progressively from her amnesia, thought of all the dogs of Tearsham Park Gardens. She told of how she had passed the time with them. She recounted unmentionable things. Unmentionable I say here because the appalled Peter Bugg refused to share them with me. She cried tears of remorse about all those dirty deeds. I wasn't always like that, was I? No. She remembered now, she remembered a flat with the number twenty on the door. She hadn't always been the Dog Woman of Tearsham Park Gardens. I've done such ugly things. She had done them for the love of Maximilian, whom she missed, she recalled, acutely.

Claire Higg remembered – 5.

Twenty's recollection of her, then quite recent, dog days reminded Claire Higg of those innumerable days of time equally ill-spent, though not in such unmentionable pursuits, that she had passed in front of her television set. I've lost so much time, she realized, aloud, tearing all the pictures of the deceased moustache man from her walls. What have I done?

She had been doing precisely nothing for over seven years and the sudden shock of it made her pull the television plug out of its socket and vow never, not for a single second, to watch her television again.

There was only one face for me, she remembered aloud, ripping the cut-outs of the moustache man into a thousand fragments. He was pale, she remembered. His photograph was on that wall. Look there, it was there! But it was there no longer.

Twenty remembered – 7.

And Twenty, seeing Claire Higg ripping up the magazine cut-outs of her moustache man, remembered another moustached man. This moustached man, she recalled with excitement and a slight laugh, did not have perfect teeth. This moustache man she remembered seeing outside the flat with the number twenty on it, and inside it too. He was, she exclaimed, her husband. But his marriage status and hair growth were temporarily all she could remember of him.

Then, exhausted as they all were, and momentarily out of memories, it was decided that another break should occur. They all left Claire Higg to her turned-off and unplugged television. Peter Bugg, after he had visited his own flat, knocked on the Orme family's door. It was then that he told me of all those remembrances that had been breathing upstairs in flat sixteen. He carried with him a photograph of a man, his father, which he said he could no longer share his rooms with. Though, he said, he could not bear to destroy it either. Could Francis, he asked, take care of it for him, just for a while. I could. He said, also, that he was being troubled by a certain matter which would not allow him to rest, and though he could not yet bring himself to share it with anyone, would Francis, if the time came, be willing to listen to it. I would.

Then Peter Bugg, troubled, crying and sweating on his way out, whispered a terrible thing:

Do you know where Chiron is?

And left without waiting for a response.

*A short voyage around the memory of the
teaching methods of Peter Bugg, as remembered
by Francis Orme.*

After the death of Emma it was decided, principally by
Mother, that I should be made to read and write. Father
spoke of his old tutor. Mother wrote to him and finding that
Bugg was then temporarily, as Bugg put it, out of work,
employed him. My parents had decided not to send me to
school, partly because of what I called my unwillingness
and they called my limited ability, but also partly because
Father had never been to school, so that it somehow made
sense that I shouldn't go either. I was taught exactly what my
father had been taught in his childhood. The years of civilization's progression between Father's schooling and mine
were ignored or else believed insignificant, and so for a long
while I was prepared for a world that no longer existed.

Peter Bugg, my new teacher, reeked of history; there
seemed to be nothing modern about him. His pale body
looked as if it had long since died and his clothes seemed to
have been tailored two or three generations earlier for people
that belonged in black and white photographs. Bugg was a
small man. He had a tiny, unmuscular body from the corners
of which came matchstick arms and legs. His neatly parted
hair was so black that it accentuated the pallor of his skin. He
had a huge head, which looked as though it belonged to
someone else. I believed that this was because he was always
exercising his head, but never his body.

I remember the first day I heard his raspy voice, we were in the large drawing room:

So this is the little scholar. Stand straight now. Chin up. We're to be chained together. Those hands of yours, those grubby fingers will be firing off essays before long. I shall call you *boy*. You shall call me *sir*. If you disagree I'll call my ruler and he'll call you cry baby bunting. Let's shake hands now. We shan't again till I've finished my work or it has finished you.

Father?

This is Mr Bugg, Francis. He was my professor, now he'll be yours. He was younger than me when he came to teach; I was his grown-up pupil, nearly ten years his senior. Term only began for me when Mr Bugg's school was on holiday. Mr Bugg is an intellectual. He's the author of a pamphlet entitled *The Benefits of Corporal Punishment in Education*.

A mere squib.

He has also read three thousand, six hundred and thirty-three different books.

Actually it's six thousand, eight hundred and sixty-nine, now. I've investigated into deeper oceans of cognisance since you last saw Chiron.

Chiron is Mr Bugg's ruler. There he is now.

Would you like to meet Chiron, boy?

Chiron makes his first appearance. Chiron was a long, thick piece of polished mahogany. I nodded in reply to Mr Bugg's question, believing that to be polite. It was polite. It was also foolish.

Put out your hand, flat, palm up.

I met Chiron. Chiron stung.

Next time it's the knuckles. That's Chiron.
Father!

Run along to lunch now, Francis. Lessons begin tomorrow. Enjoy your freedom.

Seven o'clock sharp.

The benefits of corporal punishment in education.

My father averted his eyes and let the education begin. He knew – how the memory must have stung his hands – he knew what I was in for. He had trembled through the nights of his early manhood trying to sharpen his brain. He tried to keep up, to stand equal with his teacher, but fell behind and Chiron was sent to catch him up. He'd struggled through a tempest of syllables and written words that blurred in his tear-filled eyes. He'd kissed his hands as they shook hours after, when the lessons had finished for the day, when he was free but his red, swollen knuckles wouldn't let him forget. He'd been called: Blockhead, Simpleton, Fathead, Mooncalf, Ignorance, Indolence. He'd crawled on the nursery floor, bit the table legs in his hysteria, he'd worked himself into black holes of distraction and distress. He'd bawled till he vomited, he couldn't sleep for fear that day would come again, he had pulled his hair out and groaned with terror when the clock doomed seven times. And yet here again was Peter Bugg, ready to pelt knowledge into his ignorant son.

I wrote my quaking A, B, Cs with Chiron hovering and swooping above and about me. I traced my Ands, Hows and Becauses on the school foolscap. I drew a margin every day in the corner of my page and slowly, with throbbing hands, wrote out my feeble pencil marks. Between breakfast and lunch I clawed through centuries of grammar on the axis of my blunt pencil tip. Between lunch and five o'clock I swam, sinking, rising and spluttering along the choppy surfaces of arithmetic conducted by the lightning shocks of a mahogany ruler called Chiron.

And every evening, appalled and cowering, I would be

pulled by the lobe of my left ear into the drawing room where my pedagogue would endlessly inform my mother that I was not worthy of his tutelage. I had to say, *Dear Mother, I am so sorry, I will try harder.* And sometimes the tutor, infuriated by my sloth, would send me out with twenty pieces of paper of which the first had inscribed at its head: *I am an idiot, weak and ungrateful x 1,000.* I'd run to the kitchen and passing pages to Cook and the other domestics we'd all work on a sheet of the lines. My handwriting unjoined and large was quick to copy. We made easy work of the punishment and drank hot chocolate or peppermint tea as we all sat, pencils in hand, around the large oak table. I hadn't come up with this idea. Father had. He'd done the same when he was a child. Sometimes he would join in the writing game; he'd agreed to becoming an idiot, weak and ungrateful.

One day we were all busy with our pencils in the kitchen when we heard a calm voice which made our hair stand erect with terror:

What's going on here?

It was Peter Bugg.

I was locked up in the nursery in order to write a novel which consisted of one sentence, endlessly repeated: *I am a deceitful, wicked and hideous child.* I had already had a long if rather one-sided conversation with a strip of mahogany.

I was however learning.

I could read and write.

I was progressing.

The fall of Peter Bugg.

About six months after Peter Bugg arrived, and shortly before Christmas, it was decided, principally by my mother, that I should be given a reward for my endeavours. Asked what I would like I replied immediately that I wanted see the museum of the wax people again. Bugg would accompany me, a taxi drove us past the frozen fields into the city.

Bugg called the taxi to a halt outside the city's largest toyshop, and though I protested he insisted we at least look in. Every child, I remember him saying, adores a toyshop, particularly at Christmas time. That day it was Bugg who played with the toys and I, strangely assuming the role of the adult, who watched over him as he picked up toy after toy with ecstatic giggles. *Look at this and look at this and look at this.* I remember seeing him transform, he seemed so happy now. All the bitterness had fallen from his face, I could feel him enjoying himself for the first time in years. He worked puppets, fired toy revolvers, pressed the buttons that released the torpedoes on little electronic games. He cuddled teddy bears, shot with bow and arrow, attempted to launch kites. He pulled me by my hand leading me from one object to another, grinning and shrieking in excitement. *Look at this and look at this and look at this.* I presumed my tutor was unwell, that he was experiencing some kind of fit, or that perhaps his extraordinary behaviour was an attempt at mimicking the obsessions of children and that he would very soon tell me – No, Francis, this you must never do. You must work hard, nothing but misery befalls those young adults who indulge in their childish ways when they should be growing up and studying hard. Those children become failures, their ways end in the prison.

But Bugg played on. Instead it was all *Look at this and look at this and look at this* with him. He was, truly, happy. We only left the toyshop after he was discouraged by a shop assistant from mounting a rocking horse:

Excuse me, sir, but I don't think that's designed to take people your size, do you?

In that moment he seemed to gain decades of life, lose all hope and love from his face. Peter Bugg began to cry, we hurriedly left the toyshop. He cried throughout our visit at the waxworks, in front of the wax figures. And each time I tried to stand by one of my wax friends and achieve some stillness, if only outer, I would be disturbed by his perpetual sobbing. How adult, how mature and brave he made the wax people seem. But I do not think my tutor looked at a single one of them. He sobbed and shuddered the entire visit. Finally, embarrassed and insulted by him in front of my wax friends, I suggested that we went home. He nodded sulkily, and let me lead him by his hand from the museum.

In the taxi on the way home Bugg dried his eyes and composed himself to appear unchanged in front of my parents. I began to wonder how I had felt so threatened by him before, this man who played with toys and wept like a child when challenged. And I began to understand that if I could control myself in the nursery, if I could pretend that the ruler didn't hurt me, then I might be able to defeat little man Peter Bugg.

Acquiring such discipline took me several months. I allowed my knuckles to be ripped and bloodied without attempting to protect them or even to attend to them afterwards. At first Bugg reacted to my seeming nonchalance by striking me harder or in different places – on the top of the head, on the back of the neck, across the ribs. But gradually he expressed his exasperation at my sluggishness by prolonged outbursts of vituperation, which were always fascinating to watch. He'd snort, his pale face would mutate into a phenomenal sepia, he'd grind his teeth between sentences, working himself up in a fit of expressiveness, and stamp his shoes to give weight to his words. And the words themselves would pour out in hatred, soaked with spittle and froth: all the fruits of his considerable vocabulary around the theme of stupidity, but even these were soon exhausted and he'd be forced to retreat to stamping his feet or whining in frustration. These tantrums were exceptionally watchable, even desired as welcome interruptions from Latin or Mathematics. He'd eventually steady himself by sitting with his back to me and muttering favourite chapters of the campaigns of Julius Caesar, or by setting himself some labyrinthine equation and deftly solving it. By degrees his incensed skin would take up its more accustomed white and the lesson would recommence.

My knuckles were healing.

Chiron grew grey with dust.

Muting mahogany.

Occasionally, and unexpectedly, he'd return to his old ways and thrash me again. Perhaps they were such a part of his teaching methods and so natural for him that he scarcely realized what he was about. This is being generous. I suspect he enjoyed delivering the punishment, I suspect he found the recipient's reactions profoundly satisfying. A satisfaction, perhaps, that was never equalled by anything else he did or saw. Perhaps it was his secret passion. Perhaps now I'm being less than generous.

It was on one of those odd days when Bugg returned to abrupt and momentary violence that Chiron was sentenced to eternal, long-awaited retirement.

I had, not unusually so, been charged with the indolence crime and Chiron, in an instant, shed his skin of dust and broke open the knuckles of my right hand in a single stroke. For once, because I had relaxed my self-discipline, I vocalized my pain. Bugg grinned.

Three o'clock the next morning, I tiptoed in the blackness towards a certain book-filled bedroom in which a certain book-filled gentleman was full of dreams of books. Peter Bugg with his black locks locked up in a hairnet was deeply dreaming, talking in his sleep with gentlemen and emperors of long, long ago. His door was opening but he did not know. His lids were closed with the weight of history. His library mind could not see that his library-cum-bedroom had been invaded, not by barbaric Goths, come to sweep away civilization, but by a single school-aged boy dressed in pyjamas, dressing gown and slippers, complete with an up-to-no-good look on his round face.

Peter Bugg had a bed companion, not imaginary, very real. The companion lay tucked up beside him. Neither male nor female the companion was nevertheless his virtual wife. If it had a voice it would have been crowing its master to arms. But it had none and did not call out when it was lifted from the bed and taken away from book-night and walked down to Tearsham Park cellar where it was thrown into a cold, damp tunnel and left there for ever. The same tunnel where my exhibition was, years later, to join it. The ruler became lot number fifty-two.

The criminal, then all smiles, returned to his nursery and sweet dreams of murdered rulers.

Adieu to Chiron, crawled over by insects who took him for a mere piece of wood, left alone down there for so many years, without books, without voices, without knuckles, with nothing to do. How did it feel to feel such loneliness?

All around Peter Bugg.

Of course he screamed, *Kidnapped!* Of course I was the only suspect. Of course the whole house was searched. But nobody found Chiron. And I insisted on my innocence. Everyone knew that I had taken the ruler, but they had no proof. I put on an exemplary display of sinlessness and even led the search myself. We went through all the servants' rooms, Father's library, Mother's drawing room. They upturned everything in the nursery. They scoured the garden, they sifted through the fields. Where could that ruler be?

They, we, looked everywhere. Nothing. Class was abandoned for two days, everyone was frisking everyone and everything. Mr Bugg sat in his bed with a hot-water bottle, silent in grief, trying to come to terms with his loss. But no one looked down a certain tunnel. That was out of bounds. A certain ghost of a certain fat and thin Cavalier lived there. The place: not to be disturbed. You're not to go there, Francis, do you hear?

On the third day, I was sent into Bugg's bedroom. I was to be taught while he lay struggling with his loss in bed. This was a gentler, kinder Peter Bugg. He spoke in a quiet voice:

Please, Francis, if you have Chiron return him. I swear I will never bring him into class again.

Sir, if I had him I'd gladly bring him to you. But I've no idea where he could have gone. I shall miss him too, he's taught me so much.

He was a present from my father. That's Father there.

Mr Bugg pointed to a photograph in a silver picture frame (the same photograph that Peter Bugg had given to me that night so many years later for temporary safe keeping). The occupant was a mean-looking man with dark hair and side-boards.

My father was a teacher like me. A phenomenal teacher, the best that ever there was. He'd read many thousands of books. He taught in a university. He was a real professor. When he died three hundred people came to his funeral. Never a greater man lived. So modest, so kind, so infinitely clever. Nobody lazed in his classes, everybody sat up straight, listened, was inspired, was in the presence of greatness. He published seven books. All masterpieces, all ground-breaking in their fields. Perhaps I'll show them to you one day, when you can understand them. Chiron was his ruler. Chiron is to be found in Greek mythology, he was a centaur but unlike the rest of his race who were loud and violent, Chiron was wise and kindly. He was a teacher, a famous teacher, he taught Jason and Achilles and Asclepius. My father underlined the dominant words in his works with that ruler. He never hit anyone with it. He had no need. He turned all his pupils into little genii. He left the ruler to me in his will, to bring me luck. That was all he left me. All the money and his books went to the university library. Do you know where Chiron is?

No, sir.

Some of the books you see here belonged to Father. I stole them. I cannot condone my behaviour but I felt it was important for me to collect some of his knowledge. I went to the library with a briefcase, I put the books in the case and walked out with them. Soon they began searching people's bags when they left. I changed my tactics: I put the books in dustbin bags and threw them from the library windows down on to the library bins below. I stole what should in a way have been my legacy, but it was illegal since Father had only given me his ruler. Do you know where Chiron is?

No, sir.

We spent the day not studying but talking. Bugg showed me many books, but never the ones written by his father. He spoke of Daedalus who lost his disobedient son in the Icarian sea; of King Minos who kept his stepson imprisoned in a labyrinth; of Oedipus who murdered his own father; of fathers and sons. He spoke often of his own father whose name was Peter Bugg. The other Peter Bugg, my tutor, was christened Ronald Peter Bugg but dropped the Ronald in preference to the Peter, in memoriam patris. At the end of each story or reminiscence he would always ask, gently, quietly – Do you know where Chiron is?

Clearing up his bedroom – we had made such a mess studying all his books and photographs – I noticed a large bottle of ink standing on the shelf next to his basin. As I went to put it on the desk, Peter Bugg stopped me. He instructed me to return it, that was where it belonged, he explained why:

It's a sad story, but I'll tell it to you. A confidence in exchange for a confidence. It's stupid really, but here it is. My father published his first book when he was twenty-six, when his hair was jet black and he was young and life and other works lay before him. I was determined to be like Father, to publish young. But when I was twenty-six I hadn't written anything. So I moved my goal, a more modest undertaking. I vowed to be published before my black hair turned grey. You see me here with black hair, but it greyed many years ago. It started greying when I was a mere thirty. It was as if my own hair was mocking me. One evening, in my boxroom at school, the fear that I would break my vow began to suffocate me. I sat in front of the mirror and tried to pull out each of my grey hairs. It was so difficult, such fiddly work! In frustration I took hold of a bottle of indelible black ink on my writing desk and dyed my hair with it. Since then I've done it regularly. I dye my hair with black ink, it gives me more time. One day I will write a book and then I will leave my hair to grey, sit out in the sun and breathe deeply. That's why the ink. So, Francis, dear child, now I've told you, and now you can tell me, please, where can I find Chiron?

Sir, I do not know. Please believe me.

Tomorrow I'll get up. Perhaps when I wake I'll find a length of mahogany beside me. Do you think so, boy?

I couldn't possibly say, sir.

That's it for today. Off you go now. I need to sleep. Seven o'clock as usual.

Seven o'clock, sir.

Perhaps I'll never write a book. What do you think, Francis? Perhaps I'll never.

Sir?

How could you know, you're just a boy. I was a boy once.

Can I go, sir?

Father confiscated my toys, kept me studying day and night. One day he picked me up, tapped my skull – What's in there, Ronnie? Is there anything in there at all?

Seven o'clock, sir.

But he wasn't listening. I left Peter Bugg sitting on the bony lap of that other Peter Bugg, the mythical father.

That night Peter Bugg sat up at his desk, watched only by the owls' eyes of so many books, which glared at him, showing him no pity. He wrote a page then threw it away, wrote another, discarded that and so his torment began. At seven the next morning he did not come to the classroom. I found him in his bedroom sleeping over his desk, small clouds of repudiated pages around his feet. I took the large bottle of ink and hid it in the nursery.

Some hours later:

Boy, have you taken my dyeing ink?

Yes, sir, I have.

Return it forthwith.

No, sir, I cannot do that, I've tipped it out.

NO!

I think it would be better, sir, if you let your hair find its proper colour, and if you turned up to lessons on time.

The sepia returned to Bugg's face.

You don't think I can do it, or is it that you're trying to stop me? Yes, that's it, isn't it? I won't be stopped. You'll see, I shall write . . . Oh, such a book! You'll see. You'll see.

He returned to his room. Four hours later Bugg with all his trunks of books was climbing into a taxi cab. He did not shake my hand on leaving as he had promised. His farewell was:

Do you have Chiron?

He closed the cab door and went out of Tearsham Park, out of Tearsham village to the city of his future.

In time he would stop dyeing his hair and shave it all off. I still remember the shock when I first saw that bald Bugg, like an ancient baby. He came back to us, when he had nowhere else to go. He was a different Bugg then, a broken, more nervous Bugg, a Bugg who had lost all authority. We placed him in one of the empty flats in Observatory Mansions. He had been evicted from his previous home after spending years there not writing the book that he had sworn to write. You'll see. You'll see. But there was nothing in the end to see. Was there, sir?

Memory pressure.

In the days that followed the memory pressure rose. Peter Bugg occasionally visited me, though less frequently, and these visits would always be ended by an enquiry into a certain lost ruler. He told me that Twenty had remembered the telephone number of her flat in that foreign country of hers. She had called the number but the owner of the flat had changed, was no longer her husband. Claire Higg had remembered that about the last time she saw the photograph of Alec Magnitt, she had been visited in increasing amounts by Francis Orme, and wondered if I might recall the where-abouts of her beloved's image.

But soon Peter Bugg stopped his evening visits. And I was left alone in the evenings after plinth work with just Mother and Father for company, which is much the same as being left alone. I felt myself being suffocated by those still regurgitating memories upstairs, so that when my day off arrived I decided that rather than spend the day sitting in the park, or sitting in flat six, or wandering up and down the line of exhibits in the tunnel, that I needed to get out, to visit some other, and less over-familiar part of the city. I also remembered, with frus-tration, that my fingernails had grown too long, and unless I had them cut soon I was sure to ruin a pair of white, cotton hands.

I pass my many colleagues.

Through the city I went, choosing to walk on this occasion and not take the bus. I passed en route to my destination my many colleagues, the street professionals of our city, who earned their money from their limited talents. They survived by presenting themselves to their public bursting with confident smiles and hiding, almost convincingly, the desperation that had bored holes through their spirits. They were dented and withered displays of man's eternal resilience.

I passed the man with the scales. I passed, a little further on, the nervous and irritable woman with a tic, called Mad Lizzy, who spent her day taking photographs. Mad Lizzy's photographs were all snapshots of people walking or running about the city. She was capturing, she once told me, the essence of city existence. She would later set up a stall to sell these photographs and scream at her potential customers that her photographs were great art. The fact that she sold so few of these photographs was to Mad Lizzy, by her curious logic, not only one of the great injustices of the world but also proof of their worth. I passed Pascal the blind accordionist; and Samuel the chain snapper (with his chains wrapped around his body); and I passed Moses the vociferous prophet (whose real name was Philip), with his fold-up cross folded out behind him and his three-coins-a-piece sermons lining the street before him; I passed Sad Eddy selling his red roses; I passed Claudia the tiny cellist (whose scratched and dented cello propped up a sign saying she had once played in the city's concert hall but had fallen on bad times, though *by* the concert hall would have been more accurate); I passed Herbert the syphilitic magician with his one-footed white dove (though it was really a common city pigeon which he had bleached); I passed Hamish the salamander, Hamish with his scorched lips and burn-scarred body, indications of his earlier amateur days at fire-eating; I passed Carlo, the oldest of the street professionals, who remained upright by the use of his one leg and his one twisted crutch that was made from a scaffolding pole, Carlo used to strap on and pull off his wooden leg for the public, but sadly someone had stolen this leg (lot 634). I nodded to them all. And finally I passed Constantin, called Spider Boy, the contortionist, and passing Constantin meant that I had reached my destination.

The wax museum.

The wax museum was a large, but otherwise quite ordinary, red-brick building which had been partly disguised by the addition of huge fibreglass pillars and caryatids, a simple knock on which would reveal their hollowness. That same waxworks museum which Constantin had for many years worked outside, a popular pitch which he had to fight for and won over tiny Claudia of the cello due to his extraordinary, though not entirely tasteful, talents.

It was in the waxworks that my only true friend worked with wax.

Meeting my only true friend.

The wax sculptors only took care over the heads that they sculpted, these would be painstakingly made to resemble so-called famous individuals. But the rest of the exhibit, the arms, legs, torso, being supposedly extremely similar on every human, would be cast from the bodies of the half-wax-half-human dummies. We dummies, having amongst our number both males and females, ageing from reasonably young to fairly old, were perfect for donating imprints of our bodies. In return it was a custom that the sculptor would in some way compensate the half-wax-half-human dummy for the time spent on the top floor of the waxworks, where all the exhibits were made. Sometimes this compensation took the form of money, sometimes of food, sometimes some little gift would be given, a piece of cheap jewellery or a cigarette lighter. But it was understood that the dummy must be tipped.

I was not aware of this tradition when I first began my employment at the waxworks. We half-wax-half-human dummies rarely communicated with each other, we were not paid to be sociable after all, we were paid to keep still. Only once during my employment at the waxworks was this law of unsociability profoundly broken. One male and one female dummy used to stare at each other across the entire length of the Grand Hall and occasionally wink, blow kisses or flutter their eyelashes. In time, of course, they were discovered and dismissed. Such was the penalty for excessive friendliness. And so, when I saw half-wax-half-human dummies walking up the stairs to the mysterious top floor of the waxworks and passing through a door labelled AUTHORIZED PERSONNEL ONLY, I had no way of learning why the dummy had been sent up there, nor what lay behind the door.

The wax sculptors were a noisy group who talked loudly in the staff cafeteria, without ever considering the sensibilities of the dummies. In truth, I am sure they thought of us as inferior creatures, as unskilled labour. They laughed, they ate noisily, scraping their cutlery against their plates. They made lunch breaks extremely unpleasant.

One lunch break I was particularly disturbed to discover that the sculptors were talking about me. At least, the words *new boy* and *gloves* kept being repeated and I had only just managed to convince myself that it was a coincidence, when one of the wax sculptors looked up from the midst of his colleagues and smiled at me. Deliberately. Unmistakably. I always sat at my own table, as far away from anyone else as I could manage; the sculptor could not therefore have been smiling at anyone other than me. He picked me out for his smile. He had chosen to give his smile to me and to no other.

The consequence of this sudden attack of friendliness was that I began to take my lunch breaks in the peace of the locker room, where I had no fears of being smiled at whatsoever.

I had been wearing my white gloves for a number of years before I was employed at the waxworks and had worked out by then the painful routine of cutting nails. Since cutting nails meant taking hands out of gloves, meant exposing naked hands, I detested the operation. It seemed to me vile, an affront to my glove wearing. But since unchecked nails could begin to cut through white cotton, I had to submit, whenever my nails progressed too far, to removing my gloves and, never actually looking at my hands, dismissing the offending growths.

It was on one of these unpleasant occasions, as I was bravely snipping my nails in the privacy of the locker room and, in a state of gross discomfort, moaning with despair and nausea, that I was distracted by a voice which asked the following question:

Would you like me to cut your nails for you?

It was the voice of the wax sculptor who had deliberately smiled at me. I hid my hands behind my back, called to the sculptor to please go away. But he wouldn't go away, instead he said:

I could cut them for you, if it would help. Come upstairs. I've some sharper scissors there.

I can't allow anyone to see my hands.

It won't take long, then they'll be covered again.

But it isn't allowed.

You're in a state. It will be far less painful if you let me do it.

But everyone will see.

No, not at all. We'll be very discreet.

And so, hopeful but nervous, with my hands once again hidden inside their gloves, I followed the man up the forbidden stairs to the top floor, beyond the AUTHORIZED PERSONNEL ONLY door.

We had entered one extremely long room divided into two. The first part contained numerous trestle tables on which were placed many unfinished heads and limbs of dummies yet to be. They looked as if they belonged to some extraordinary dissection academy, or an anatomy classroom, or a transplant factory, or as if the top floor of the wax museum held the remains of some sinister execution. Beyond the tables, in the second part of the room, were numerous cubicles where the sculptors worked quietly by themselves, sculpting clay that would then be covered in plaster to make a mould and then the mould would be filled with wax. The sculptor ushered me into his cubicle.

Sit down. Breathe deeply. Relax. It shouldn't take long.

Before he took off the gloves he kindly secured a blindfold over my eyes. He used his hands extraordinarily deftly and slipped the gloves off with ease. He managed the operation as gently as he could, but the nails had grown quite long and thick and they were not easy to cut. Each time he worked his way through one I would hear a loud snap and begin to feel slightly faint. But he managed, the nails were reduced and my gloves were replaced.

There you are. Nice short nails. Would you care for a cup of coffee, Francis?
I'm not sure.
I'm having one.
How do you know my name?
Everyone knows everyone's name here. You'll learn that once you've been here a bit longer. My name's William.

The coffee was thick and black. He drank it that way, he said, to keep him awake, often he would sculpt well into the night. I noticed he was working on the head of a young man, who was, I supposed, about the same age as me. William asked me if I recognized the young man. I shook my head. At that he looked a little disappointed, he showed me various photographs of the man and I saw, and commented, that the likeness of his clay head to the photographs was exceedingly accurate. But you still don't recognize him? The head and the photographs were apparently of a certain young, famous actor who had recently died and whose model was to be placed in the wax museum. As we talked that day, William discovered that I hardly knew who any of the wax figures represented. And so it was that I came to mention my home.

Where've you been, Francis?

Tearsham Park mainly and then, more recently, Observatory Mansions.

Where are they?

You've never heard of Observatory Mansions or Tearsham Park? Where've *you* been?

William had heard of neither place and I was forced to realize, for the first time, that in fact my home, the centre of my existence, was just another human dwelling. Tearsham Park, Observatory Mansions: unexceptional.

After I had finished my coffee I thanked William repeatedly. He said that it was nothing. He lied. It was indeed something. Something enormous. William agreed that in the future whenever my nails needed cutting he would be willing to oblige.

I left him to the head of that young famous actor who had been at the time of his death about the same age as I was when William first cut my nails.

A brief account of the founder of the waxworks museum.

Our Founder, for so we referred to her, had been dead many years. There was a wax dummy of her in the entrance hall. I had not known that it was her, I was informed of it by William, who told me her story. Our Founder was friends with some of the most famous people of her time. She was an artist, a sculptress. Our Founder had a famous friend who was very old and likely soon to die. She decided to preserve the memory of her friend. She made a cast of her face with plaster and filled the cast with beeswax. When the friend died Our Founder had a model of that friend to keep her company. In this manner Our Founder slowly began to make wax impressions of all her friends, and in due course her models became famous. To discourage her home, populated enough as it was (though by wax dummies), from being so continuously visited, she began to charge people money to see her strange possessions. To her surprise, she discovered that people were more than willing to pay the sum she asked to see the wax impressions of those famous friends of hers. So it was that Our Founder's home became an exhibition. Years later Our Founder, an old and wealthy woman, would often be seen walking around the waxworks of her friends. She had outlived them all, but she still kept the memories of their heights, faces, eye colour, hair colour, clothes and shoes clearly with her. She had also chosen the part of her friends' lives that she wished to remember; some she had sculpted in youth, others in old age. Shortly before she died she had a wax model made of herself, as she was then. This she placed amongst the wax impressions of her friends. She watched her wax self watching her wax friends, the memory of her friends and of her mourning of her friends perfectly preserved in wax. Then she had a heart attack and died. At the age of one hundred and two.

On human stupidity.

All of the wax subjects kept in the museum were of famous people throughout the ages. Their histories slowly became known to me through William's insistence. The wax sculptors had no freedom to choose their own subjects to sculpt. The subjects were decided by the Committee of Wax Museums which sat in the largest of all the wax museums throughout our country to be found in our capital city. The Committee decided who was famous and who was not; who would be sculpted and who would be ignored. They made and broke reputations, sometimes by commissioning sculptures of people no one had heard of, and sometimes by announcing the removal of a waxwork and plunging its subject into public ignominy.

What I had noticed though, and much to my disgust, was that the visitors to the museum became excited by wax replicas of people they recognized. It was a habit of theirs to have themselves photographed next to these insulted wax dummies. The visitors never understood that these wax dummies had an identity separate from their fleshy counterparts. The photographs taken of those visitors (insignificant humans) resting their filthy hands on the shoulders of some of my best wax acquaintances seemed to me entirely perverse. This preoccupation was a prime example of human stupidity. The visitors were trying to fool themselves that they had actually met these so-called famous people; as if by walking up to a wax duplicate of a so-called famous personality that personality would somehow rub off on them, that they would suddenly become a little famous themselves. They looked at the wax duplicates and made, oh, such profound observations:

I never realized she was so tall!
I'm taller than him, who'd have thought it!
To think I can stand so close to her!

The visitors were unable to see exactly what the waxworks museum was. They saw a hall of fame and they fooled themselves by taking photographs that, for an instant, they could be so close to fame even, they felt, touch it. No, that is not what the waxworks were about at all. The waxworks were an immensely eloquent dissertation on the wonderful ordinariness of mankind. We could forget about fame, what was important was that here we had people too: here we had noses, ears, eyes, etc. It was an exhibition that showed mankind in all its various ages, from babies to old crones, the fact that the subjects chosen happened to be celebrated was entirely irrelevant.

The whole point of the waxworks was to study in minute detail the human form, bring a magnifying glass, study the differences between human chins. But they did not see this at all. In the exhibition it was possible to do a thing that was impossible to do anywhere else: *get close to the human form, close enough even to touch.* With how many people in this world do individuals feel free enough to stop them mid-sentence and say – Excuse me, I'd like to examine your lips now, could you keep very still? I hope you don't mind. It shouldn't take more than twenty minutes. Just keep still and let me really stare at them. With how many people is that possible? Answer: very few. Even the most uninhibited person becomes coy when intensely stared at. Only in the waxworks, in that people museum, could the human being be really, truly examined.

The many hands of Francis Orme.

I was so impressed by William's kindness on the day of the first nail cutting that I visited him on various occasions when no nail cutting actually took place. William hinted about that famous young (dead) actor needing some hands to go with his head. The actor, William hinted, was the same age as Francis. Really? How fascinating? I think I'd better go now.

I did not visit William again until my nails had grown to a glove-perilous length. He refused to cut them unless I allowed him to make a mould of my hands. Was it a deal? No, never. I think I'd better go now.

It wasn't until I had almost begun to rip my gloves that I reluctantly returned to William and let him cast my hands so that he would cut my nails.

I did not see the wax casts of my hands when they were first ready. I insisted on that as one of the conditions of their being cast. They would be hidden from me at all times. This of course was possible when the hands were kept in William's cubicle but completely impossible when the dummy of the young actor arrived in the exhibition itself.

When I first saw those hands I was disgusted, but as time progressed I became less disturbed by them. I even, much later and shortly before my employment at the waxworks was terminated, touched them.

It was so extraordinary, watching all those other people that I had never met walking into the wax museum where my naked hands were on display. Of course, most people did not notice my hands, or if they did they gave them only the briefest of glances, but that did not matter, the fact that they were there, the fact that people did not point at them and double up with laughter, the fact that they were considered acceptable, even normal, made me feel strangely confident. But by then there were many impressions of my hands about the exhibition. My hands were not only used for male dummies, they also were to be found peeping through dress sleeves. My hands, said William, were virtually unmarked (there were some residues of Chiron's days to be found on them), they were proportionally slightly small to the rest of my body, as if by being out of sunlight so long, like a plant, they had ceased to grow, they were delicate, he said, they were perfect for women. For the male hands he often added hair, real human hair, for the women he added long nails. Actually William did not place either hairs or nails or eyes on to his models, these were separate jobs and were performed by different departments. I came, in time, to know all the other departments. The hair department was performed by a pair of twins, Laura and Linda; the nail department by a man named Julian; the eye department, by far the most fascinating of the three, by a woman named Ottila. Ottila had worked as a doll's-eye manufacturer before she had been employed at the waxworks and her eyes were so lifelike that I was surprised when they didn't blink.

On William and friendship.

William was my only true friend, and I grew ever closer to him during my employment at the waxworks. I was often to be found on the upper floor drinking his thick black coffee. I called him a friend though I have never actually publicly referred to him as such. Nor did I learn anything about how his life was spent beyond the waxworks. I never found out, for example, whether he was married or single, whether he had children, or even if he was happy in his work. Of course, I realized that he had used the excuse of cutting my nails so that he might cast my hands, that he had not cut them from any altruistic tendency, but that did not matter to me any more. In fact, it was because of this need for each other that I considered William a true friend. I could trust him, he had told me no lies about how much he liked me, he had not flattered and cajoled me into having my hands cast. And besides, he would never demand any personal favours from me, he would never cry on my shoulder. It was the business-like nature of our friendship that I cherished, I felt useful in his company. And even if William did often talk down to me, and even if he did chuckle at some of my observations, and even if he did enjoy telling stories about me to the other wax sculptors, he was, nevertheless, my only true friend. He was the man who cut my nails.

*An example of how even the truest friend can
prove irritating.*

When I met William that day, to escape from the pressure of
memories in Observatory Mansions, he simply pulled up the
familiar chair for me and took out his scissors. I placed on
the blindfold, he took off my gloves and cut my nails. When
the nails had been cut, when my gloves were safely returned
and I had taken off my blindfold, we sat, as was our custom,
drinking William's thick, black coffee.

I was somewhat overcome by a need to communicate and
told my only true friend of the terrible experience I was
undergoing in Observatory Mansions. I told him all there
was to tell about Miss Anna Tap, calling her at times Miss
Tap or the new resident or the orphan.

What does she look like?
Pasty, round face, glasses. Pointy nose.

As I described her William began to sculpt her face in
miniature out of clay, fiercely trying to capture her likeness.
We became excited trying to pin her features down, trying to
make my words guide William's hands around that upturned
nose, that round chin, that high forehead. I thought I had
remembered her quite well but the head we managed to
produce together had few similarities to Anna Tap's.

Francis, don't be angry with me, but there's something I'd
like to ask. You seem to be talking about this girl a lot.
Would you like her to be your special friend, Francis?
What do you mean?
Would you like to hold her perhaps? To kiss her?
I think I'd better go now.

I left William with my thick, black cup of coffee half
finished on his worktop.

Cigarette ends.

On my way back from William I came across Anna Tap leaving the church. I watched her walk through the graveyard, back towards Observatory Mansions. I followed her, always a few metres behind, and, careful for my gloves, retrieved all the cigarette ends that she dropped as she walked on. By the time I was safely in my bedroom, I had collected no less than four Lucky Strike cigarette ends and I laid them out on my desk and numbered them on their yellow filters. I had collected them to answer William's ridiculous questions; to find out whether I wanted to be closer to Anna Tap or not. I believed, of course, that I didn't, that I couldn't possibly, but I thought I needed to be sure. I considered the cigarette ends. Did I want to be closer to those cigarette ends that had been so close, that had even been kissed and bitten by Anna Tap? No, I considered, I did not.

I found the cigarette ends unattractive.

Lots 988 and 989.

We were by then far into the Time of Memories and had even started on the Time of the Four Objects. I was deeply concerned, as I have suggested, for my fellow occupants of Observatory Mansions, though they in their turn seemed not to be thinking of me at all.

In an attempt to end that Time of Memories, and longing for the time before Anna Tap arrived, feeling a little left out and disturbed by forming the collection of cigarette ends, I went to work that night.

Still were the inhabitants of Observatory Mansions, tossed only by their deep three-in-the-morning sleep. But someone was out of his place, leaving his bedroom all alone. This someone, named Francis Orme, tiptoed in the blackness to the outside night and leant the ladder against the window of flat eighteen. I climbed up to flat eighteen and entered its cigarette smelling confines. I tiptoed into the bedroom and found a woman, late twenties to mid-thirties, fast asleep, dreaming of orphanages and museums and the minuscule strands of textile fibres. Beside her bed was a spectacles case and in the spectacles case a pair of spectacles. Round frames. Steel. Containing thick lenses (lot 988).

Then I ventured up beyond the always-open door of flat twenty and found Twenty there snoring and barking in her sleep. Clasped in one of her paws was the dog collar with the name tag inscribed MAX. By sniffing around her head and hands – not a pleasant thing to do – in the fashion of a dog, I noted to my satisfaction, that Twenty let go of the dog collar to rest her hands on my shoulders and lick my face, whining happily. And when Twenty had licked enough, I took the collar (lot 989).

Through the eyes of Anna Tap.

After placing Twenty's former dog collar neatly within a transparent polythene bag and having catalogued the object, I turned my attention to the pair of spectacles. With one of the cigarette ends in my mouth and the pair of spectacles on my nose, I attempted to discover how it felt to be Anna Tap. I saw a blur. A thick blur. Blurred colours, blurred division between light and darkness. This, I thought, must be something similar to what she saw when she wasn't wearing her glasses. In this way I imitated Anna Tap, sucking her already smoked cigarettes and looking through her spectacles, for half an hour, just to be sure of my feelings for her. And I concluded that William had somehow been mistaken. I looked through them and smoked on for another ten minutes, just to be sure. Nothing.

Then I catalogued the spectacles, placed them inside a polythene bag, went upstairs to bed and fell into a happy sleep.

The next morning I was at work a little earlier than usual, and was out of the Mansions before any of the others had left their beds. I considered what a kind thing I had done for them all, for all that is except Anna Tap. Twenty had been happy as the Dog Woman of Tearsham Park Gardens, now she was reported to be sad, now she had no idea who she was. Claire Higg had been happily watching her television set until the presence of Anna Tap turned it off and reminded her of Alec Magnitt. Peter Bugg, too, had been tolerably content with his life until he had been reminded of his father, of his father's ruler and of school terms long since broken up. By removing the dog collar I had hoped to take away all evidence of Twenty's dead dog which had sparked off all her other memories, and so return Twenty to her former dog days. By returning Claire to her television and Bugg to his life filled with sweat and tears but not of worry, I had hoped to break up the Time of Memories in flat sixteen. By stealing Anna Tap's spectacles I had hoped to show her that she was still unwelcome in Observatory Mansions. If Twenty went back to the park, if Claire went back to her television, if Bugg stopped worrying, then Anna Tap would realize, only too clearly, that she was not needed here. She could sit in her bedroom, blind as a mole, and think about it. Then she could go elsewhere.

These were my happy thoughts as I stood, some time before the public arrived, on my plinth in the centre of the city. Waiting for a coin to drop.

Hand Armageddon.

On my way back from work I did not find Anna Tap coming out of the church, nor did I find her inside. She had been there though, or I presumed she had. Cigarette ends, Lucky Strikes with teeth marks, dotted the route back to Observatory Mansions. I gathered them but soon stopped: impaled on top of one of the spikes of Tearsham Park Gardens' fencing was a single white glove, my brand. My glove. I picked it up. Yes, mine! A little further on, lying this time on the dirty pavement, was another glove, not its pair. A left hand again. Further still, across the road, a pair of gloves were to be found nailed on to the Observatory Mansions sign. Spacious apartments of quality design:

OBSERVATORY MANSIONS
Spacious (Glove) *Apartments of Quality* (Glove) *Design*

My gloves, mine! Pierced in the palms, like Christ had been before me! My gloves. I pulled them down. My gloves ripped. My gloves dirty. On the ground floor a glove had been covered in dirt and was more black than white in colour – had the Porter used it as a duster? Up the stairs of Observatory Mansions, past the Porter's desk and all the way to the first floor were hands (some, I noted to my horror, had even been trodden on). The gloves on the stairs, looking like unhappy anaemic insects, seemed to be attempting to crawl their way back to their home. *My home!* Then I saw it: *the door of flat six! A new lock had been fitted!* The empty fingers of a white glove were peeping out from under the door, but flat six was locked from me. I screamed repeatedly. I sat on the stairs, gloves on hands, different gloves in my lap, trembling. Then with the help of that white, that cotton, I calmed myself enough to realize that the new lock was in fact the same new lock that I had purchased on behalf of Anna Tap and that I had the second key in my pocket. I let myself in. I wish I had not, for the sight before my eyes that cruel evening was not a thing that delicate Francises should ever be subjected to.

White gloves, a sea of white gloves, white gloves covered every bit of the floor of flat six of Observatory Mansions. I began to carefully pick the gloves up, petrified that I might step on one. I placed the gloves on surfaces higher than the floor, poor servants, poor skins. In Mother's bedroom the night light's rabbit was sheathed by a white glove. Mother's head lay on a pillow stuffed with white gloves, on Mother's chair sat a pair of Y-fronts filled with white gloves. In the bathroom there were white gloves taking a bath, there were discharged gloves in the lavatory bowl. Gloves had been tied on to the hot and cold taps of both the bath and the basin and were full of water; bloated hands, looking more like cows' dugs than sensitive touchers. In the kitchen part of the largest room of flat six there were cold gloves in the refrigerator, there were frozen gloves in the deep freeze, there were gloves boiling in water on the top of the cooker, there were burnt gloves inside the cooker. In the dining room section of the largest room of flat six, the dining table had been laid and on a plate in the centre of the table was an evil salad consisting only of white gloves sprinkled with olive oil, under the lid of a tureen there was white-glove soup, under the lid of a silver salver was a brace of white gloves with whole onions stuffed inside them.

In the sitting room section of the largest room of flat sat Father: Father with gloves on his ears and fingerless gloves six on his hands and with fingers, that formerly belonged to the white gloves on his hands, placed on the toes of his feet. In my bedroom there were three empty glove diary boxes. On my desk there was a single glove. The glove was positioned with a pen in such a way that it looked as if the glove had been writing. At the tip of the pen was a piece of paper. On the paper was written the following:

PLEASE RETURN:

1. A mahogany ruler, known as Chiron.
2. A passport photograph of Alec Magnitt, with declarations of love written on its reverse.
3. A dog collar, with a name tag inscribed MAX.
4. A pair of round, steel-rimmed glasses, containing powerful lenses.

THANK YOU.

We were deep within the Time of the Four Objects.

On late night visitors.

I had rescued my gloves, some were already back in the glove diary boxes, others were drying in the bathroom. I was busy at work sewing the fingers back on to the white gloves that my father had been wearing on his hands and toes, when the door to flat six was opened. The door was not knocked on, there was no *please can I come in.* It was unlocked and opened and people came into flat six without the word please being used once. And they didn't stop there, they came straight into my bedroom.

My room had never been so populated before. There stood Higg, Bugg, Twenty, and behind them the Porter holding the elbow of Anna Tap. How tiny Anna Tap's eyes looked without glasses. Higg, I noted to my disgust, was wearing some of my white cotton gloves on her person. She had put on a bra and had stuffed the bra with gloves, compensating by use of my white cotton friends for her tiny breasts. There were fingertips poking out from the cups of her bra. *My gloves were feeling Miss Higg's breasts.*

The Porter spoke first:

I have no cause for real complaint myself. I am here as Miss Tap's guide, she cannot see.

Get out.

They want various items which they believe you have borrowed, Francis Orme.

No. You've searched my home already and you haven't found them. Doesn't that make it obvious that I don't have them, that I am entirely innocent and therefore completely wronged?

You won't return the items then?

If I had them, I would not.

You don't have them?

Who moved my gloves? Why don't you ask that? It'll take me weeks to re-catalogue the glove diary. And even then it'll be incomplete. It's a far more serious crime. Who was it? Who?

Bugg giggled.

Higg giggled.

The Porter hissed (a giggle-like hiss).

Claire Higg began to moan something about milk bottles, Twenty began to bark, Peter Bugg to remember, aloud this time, his father, and Anna Tap to rub her, blind, eyes.

You will tell us, you will. Yes, you will.

It was the Porter who said those words, then he instructed Bugg, crying and sweating and smelling of a hundred smells, to hold me down in my chair, while he took one of my white gloved hands and, grasping it by the wrist, held it palm upwards. Claire Higg revealed a fountain pen, recognized as belonging to Peter Bugg, and holding the nib a millimetre from the perfect white cotton of my trapped hand, uttered the monosyllable:

Speak.

I would, in fact, have spoken freely, perhaps even betrayed my exhibition at that moment had it not been for Twenty, who by causing me terrible pain actually saved me. Twenty followed Higg's *speak* with a sharp doggish howl, which so shocked Miss Higg that her hand jogged, causing ink to spill on my white cotton hand.

What a loss! What a loss! Far superior to the loss of a thousand, thousand rulers or spectacles or passport photographs or dog collars. I felt more pain than any cut could give: there was ink on my gloves!

I showed Claire Higg and Peter Bugg, the Porter, Anna Tap and Twenty too.

Look what you've done. This is bad, this is bad! This is so, so bad!

I sat cross-legged on the floor with my hands resting, trembling on my knees. They were quivering as if they had been hideously burnt. I repeatedly closed my eyes and then opened them hoping, in vain, that in a magical second when I was not looking the ink would mysteriously vanish and my glove would return to its former beauty.

For some time I sat there, rocking slightly backwards and forwards, nodding my head a little, humming quietly, comforting myself, whilst they limply, the murderers, stood, without a cent of pride, profoundly ashamed of themselves around me.

I felt ill.

My heart shrieked inside me, each time I closed my eyes I

was sure I was going to faint. And my heart kept bashing against my ribcage, desperate to get out.

I feel sick. I can't calm down.

I tried listing the sacred paper entitled the Law of White Gloves, but I couldn't concentrate. I stood up. *I had to keep moving.* I walked around Twenty, around Claire Higg and Peter Bugg, around the Porter and Anna Tap. I couldn't keep still and all the while my heart thrashed inside me, begging to be free.

My heart wouldn't slow down.

I can't slow down. I can't slow my heart down. Why won't it slow down, why won't it slow down? What can I do to make it slow down? Am I going to die, is this what dying feels like?

Calm down, Francis Orme.

I CAN'T!

Anna Tap tried to calm me.

Sit down, Francis.

I have to keep moving.

No, you don't, sit down and you'll feel better. That's it. Take deep breaths.

I can't calm down!

Deep breaths.

My heart!

Count. Slowly.

123456789101112 . . .

Slower.

1, 2, 3, 4 . . . I can't!

Yes, you can.

What's happening to me?

It's nothing. It'll be gone soon. Sssh.

Help me!

Try lying down. Better?

I can't.

You can.

Better?

A little.

Deep breaths.

I feel faint.

No you don't, you feel sleepy. Close your eyes. Deep breaths.

I feel sleepy.

Close your eyes.

My heart!

Close your eyes, breathe slowly.

Eventually, I fell asleep.

When I woke up they had all gone.

Later that night (when I was wearing a new pair of gloves) I heard a knock at our door and smelt Bugg outside.

Francis, I know what you've done is very wrong. But I will forgive you my part of the wrong if you would just let me talk to you for a little while. Everyone's asleep and I must have someone to talk to. I can't stop thinking, I can't lose sight of the boy ... He's been smiling at me for a few days, but tonight he has begun to laugh. Francis, Alexander Mead's come back to haunt me. Let me in. I don't have a key to this lock. The Porter's got it and he's asleep. Let me in, don't make me be alone tonight.

I did not reply. Peter Bugg knocked a few more times, begged a little more (let him beg, that unforgiven Bugg) and then, weeping and smelling and sweating too, he went back to Alexander Mead.

The altarpiece of Tearsham Church.

The next day I was not visited. I spent the morning recovering a few more of my abused gloves. During the afternoon I heard the Porter and Anna Tap descend the stairs and listened to the following part of a conversation:

To the eye hospital?
No, to the church.

I ran down to my exhibition, all the way to the narrowest end of that tunnel and out again the other side. I pushed the stone cover of the false tomb away, wearing Father's old leather gloves over my white ones. I replaced the cover and stood up, a little out of breath, in Tearsham Church, in the private chapel of the Orme family, separated from the rest of the church by tall bars with spikes on their ends and by a lock, which only I and the priest had keys for.

The church had become increasingly neglected for some time. Few people visited it now, I myself had not visited it for some months. The priest had four other churches to look after and considered the parish that was once called Tearsham his most insignificant. Services had not been held there for several years and the church had begun its slow deterioration. Some of the stained-glass windows had been smashed and were boarded up, but pigeons still managed to get in, through the bell tower perhaps, and once in, defecating everywhere, they were unable to find their way out. They died in corners, their corpses encouraging rats. Rubbish from the city had found its way inside: sweet wrappers, rusting cans, yellowing newspapers. All the, once numerous, church paintings and tapestries from the various side chapels, together with the altar, candlesticks, chalice and even the church bells, had been removed long ago. Now all that was left behind were the dust-covered pews, the broken, ancient pump organ and the church's bulky and decayed, ugly altarpiece.

The altarpiece consisted of eight slightly larger-than-life-size wooden figures. One Madonna. One Child. Six saints. The Madonna sat on a throne with the Christ Child in her lap and three saints either side of her. These wooden people had been dressed like dolls, they were wearing clothes: real clothes that were now in a state of advanced disintegration, moth-eaten and faded, and which had in places fallen off the bodies and collected in strange ugly piles beneath them on the church's stone floor. The wooden arms, hands and faces of these heroes of old were once painted in flesh tints. Much of the paint, though, had begun to peel off, giving the impression that the martyrs were being martyred again, flayed alive in their various poses of beatitude. Many of the saints once had real human hair attached to their skulls, though much of it had been lost over time and the Virgin Mary looked among them particularly bald. The saints from right to left were as follows: Saint Catherine with a wheel, the instrument of her martyrdom; Saint Thomas Aquinas, clutching a book, the *Summa theologicae*; Saint Stephen Protomartyr, who had been stoned to death, holding large sharp stones; Saint Peter in the pope's triple crowned mitre, holding a pair of keys; Francis, that wooden Francis, not me, had his hands clasped together and looked towards the sky, probably hallucinating some sparrow or chaffinch. Saint Francis had no objects, he despised possessions. This malnourished man had great blisters in the centre of his hands and feet – his stigmata (whenever I visited the church, after my glove days had begun, I longed to place a pair of white gloves over Francis's scarred hands). And finally there was Saint Lucy who held a wooden plate on which were glued a pair of wooden eyes. Only Lucy among this group was in remotely good condition. She alone had a full head of hair running down her back; she alone had convincing, uncracked flesh; she alone was fully dressed and her clothes, extraordinarily, had retained their colours and even appeared clean and new. Anyone unfamiliar with the church, entering it for the first time, might initially assume that Lucy was a real person dressed in some bizarre costume. But when she didn't move they would become suspicious, they would walk up to her and then they would see her neighbours. Her rotten, disfigured neighbours, with such severe woodworm that it resembled leprosy and with all their faded and filthy clothes, would look like monochromatic ghosts.

The altarpiece was brought by my great-grandfather, a very different Francis Orme. He came across the wooden altarpiece (so runs the story in a volume of the *History of the Ormes*) when he was about his travels. With a considerable amount of difficulty, and an even more considerable amount of funds, he managed to purchase it on condition that it always be situated on Holy ground. My great-grandfather gave it to Tearsham Church. The Virgin, not bald then I presume, held, it is believed, an extraordinary resemblance to his dead wife. He used to sit, not, I imagine, thinking heavenly thoughts, in front of the wooden mother of God, confusing her with the mother of his son, yet another Francis Orme. One day my ancestor was found sitting naked on the Virgin Mother, and the Virgin Mother's son was found on the floor of Tearsham Church, having been forcibly removed: my ancestor was attempting to make love to the wooden Virgin. He ended his days in a cell in a hospital.

In time the Porter and Anna Tap arrived. Hidden behind the tomb of some dead Orme, I heard all.

Sacred Monologue.

What do you see?

Wooden people. Who's the one with the keys?

Saint Peter, the gatekeeper of Heaven.

Another porter?

The Holy porter. Describe to me the last saint on the left.

It is a young woman, Miss Tap.

It is Saint Lucy. What is she holding?

A plate.

What is on the plate?

A pair of eyes.

I come here for those eyes. I have been looking after Saint Lucy for several months now. When I first saw her she was like the others, she was so ill and frayed, her paint was peeling everywhere, there were cracks and stains all over her. I was supposed to conserve the clothes and hair of all of them. It was a commission from the city council, to preserve our churches and the objects inside them, but before I had a chance it was announced that this church would cease being used and the funds were withdrawn. It was too late for me, though, I had already started to become fascinated by Saint Lucy. I dreamt of her sad face at night; I believed she was calling me. I went to the library and looked up her history; I discovered all I could about her.

The disease in my eyes had already been troubling me for many years and I had been sent from optometrist to eye surgeon all around the city. They'd blown air in my eyes, squirted dye into them, injected them and even operated on them but my sight did not improve. My eyes, they predicted, would become hard, would become solid and cease to work. So it seemed to me that Saint Lucy had come to me for a reason. She is the patron saint of diseases of the eyes. She has two sets, one on the plate, one in her head, I thought she might lend me one. In her story an infidel fell in love with

Lucy's eyes, and begged her to marry him. Lucy refused and the man had her eyes pulled out, but miraculously another pair immediately grew in their place.

I decided that I must repair Saint Lucy, return her to her former state, and so for months, after work had finished for the day, I remained in the workshop treating her clothes, buying new material when necessary. Her hair was so frail that it had to be removed entirely. I placed a small advert in the paper: DO YOU HAVE LONG FAIR HAIR? Would you be willing to sell it? Please contact ... Many people responded, most of them inappropriate, but among them there was a girl with such long, beautiful, golden hair that I believed her almost the living Lucy, she was even wearing a small gold cross on a chain around her neck. I paid her well, she had her hair cut short. I collected it and sewed it, strand by strand, into Lucy's scalp. I paid a painting conserver from the museum to make her eyes and skin live again, and then a letter came informing me that Lucy was the property of the church and that I must return her within four days or appropriate action would be taken. I ignored the letter and five days later the police came to the museum and took her away. Who wanted her, I screamed at the police, who else cared for her but me? That wasn't the point, they said, it belonged to Tearsham Church. *It!* Her then, if it makes you feel better. And so I started coming here regularly, visiting her four or five times a week, praying to her always for my eyes. But soon that wasn't enough, I had to see her more often, so I moved my home. She looks so beautiful next to the others, doesn't she?

Look at them all in their straight line. They don't look at each other, they don't communicate. The art always used to be like that, but then it changed, later the saints were painted speaking with each other and with the Virgin and Child. They even called that type of altarpiece *sacra conversazione*, holy conversation. And those pictures often included the altarpiece's donor, its commissioner, kneeling down. So sometimes I think of these wooden saints talking to each other, not living in isolation, and then I think of myself as a kind of donor, with Lucy blessing me, and I am suddenly part of the altarpiece too. Saint Lucy's day is the thirteenth of December, a day which used to be celebrated as the winter solstice, the shortest day of the year, the longest night. The blindest date in the calendar. Each thirteenth of December since I met Lucy I've laid candles in front of her and begged for her to return my sight, each year, more and more, I feel the light by its heat rather than by seeing it. She hasn't helped me yet. But she will, she must. And it'll be this year, this thirteenth of December, that she saves my eyes, because if it isn't then it'll be too late, I'll be blind and my eyes will grow hard. Take me to her now, Porter, so I can touch her.

She stayed with Lucy for a little over an hour and then the Porter took her back to Observatory Mansions. I left the company of Virgin and Child with six saints and went back to my exhibition.

The borrower.

Leaving the tunnel locked behind me, a few hours later, I climbed the stairs to flat six where I found Anna Tap outside the door, waiting for me.

Francis? Francis, is that you?
Why don't you leave me alone?
I've been knocking and knocking.
No one answers the door but me and I've been out.
Francis, I want my glasses back.
Then you'd better find them.
I think I know where they are.
Well go and fetch them then.
Are they in the cellar, Francis? Is that where you've hidden

them? Is that why you were so keen to get me away from the cellar steps when I first met you? What else do you keep down there?

It's just the Porter's flat and the boiler room—

I could get the Porter to have a proper look.

I shouldn't do that—

I knew they were there!

—not if you want your glasses back.

Fetch them for me.

I can't do that.

Francis, we'll make a deal, you give me back my glasses now and when I see properly again you can keep them.

But what if you go blind?

I won't go blind.

But if you do, can I still keep them?

Please, Francis.

If you promise.

I can't see without them.

It's not usual. I have never lent an exhibit out from the exhibition before. I don't know whether such behaviour is permissible. Do you promise to return the spectacles once you're blind?

Yes. Anything.

Well, let's see. How long do you think it will be before you actually go blind?

I DON'T KNOW!

Roughly?

Months, but I won't.

Months, is it? A loan for an undisclosed number of months. Well, I would consider this a deal now . . . but there was that instance when you called me backward. I didn't like that.

I didn't mean it.

That's better. But is that enough?

I could call the Porter.

It's a deal. I'll give you the spectacles. You'll return them once you're blind, in a matter of months. There's no need to involve the Porter.

And what about the dog collar, Claire's photograph, Peter's ruler?

No, they can't have those. I've destroyed them.

I don't believe you.

I could also destroy your glasses.

No, Francis. I'm sorry.

I went to the exhibition and borrowed an exhibit. To be returned, it was understood, in an undisclosed number of months.

Back on ground level, in the entrance hall, I heard screams coming from the second floor. Claire Higg, the Porter, Twenty and Anna Tap were in flat ten (Peter Bugg was too).

The end of the Time of Memories, the departure of Peter Bugg, retired schoolmaster, retired personal tutor, etc.

Mr Peter Bugg, no longer sweating, no longer crying but still smelling of a hundred different smells, was at home. Mr Peter Bugg was wearing a school tie. Navy blue, with red stripes. He was wearing it the wrong way round. The knot was at the back of his neck. The tie was really wearing Peter Bugg. Peter Bugg, cold now and silent, possessing no thoughts for Alexander Mead or for his father or for his father's ruler, was in a vertical position some two feet from the ground. Suspended. He was not, however, flying.

Hung.

Strangled.

Dead.

The Porter cut him down and laid him on his bed. On his desk, where he had continued not finishing his book, were five envelopes addressed: the Porter of Observatory Mansions, the resident of flat twenty, Miss Anna Tap, Francis Orme (minor), Claire. These letters were the last writings of Peter Bugg, though even in their small quantity they exceeded the length of that other, never to be finished, opus.

We opened the envelopes.

To the Porter of Observatory Mansions.

My dear Porter,

I am sorry not to be referring to you in a more personal manner, but I discovered as I sat down to write this note that I never learnt your name. Forgive me.

I am exceedingly sorry for all the mess, personal effects, clothes, etc., that I have left for you to clear up. I fear it shall be you who performs this task. I enclose a banknote for your pains. Forgive me.

Yours sincerely,
    Peter Bugg

To the resident of flat twenty.

Dear friend,

Alas you have no name yet, but I have great confidence that you will remember it soon. I enclose a limited, but I think helpful, bilingual dictionary for you. I leave a list of phone numbers of police stations in your land. When you call these numbers I am sure that you will be aided in your pursuit. I have no doubt that you will soon be yourself again.

With my warmest regards and best wishes,
    Peter Bugg

(This letter was later translated by Anna Tap, word by word, using Peter Bugg's old dictionary.)

To Miss Anna Tap.

Dear Miss Tap,

I am afraid you will be very disappointed with me. Forgive?

I have to ask a favour of you. During my days in Observatory Mansions I have, over the last few years, committed myself to various little chores. These chores involve shopping (food mainly and occasionally some rather more unusual items) for Miss Higg and, this is the more taxing task, looking after Mr Francis Orme during the day, while his son is out. Would you mind? I apologize for this, but I have every confidence in your abilities.

Though I have known you for such a little time, you find me, yours ever,

Peter Bugg

To Francis Orme (minor).

My dear boy,

You must on no account blame yourself for not speaking to me last night. I would have gone some night or other. I have been haunted for many years by a certain memory which has, as I realized recently, caused me to sweat out of nervousness and to cry out of remorse. It is possible that you had not noticed this in your former tutor, or that you were good enough not to comment upon it. The boy's name was Alexander Mead. We were friends. He was my most intelligent pupil. But beyond that, when classes were over, we played draughts together, we were tiddlywinks partners and we rolled marbles. He was the truest friend I ever made in my life. He called me Peter out of class hours. We were so close. I wanted him to grow up. He wanted me to become a child. But somehow we managed to communicate so profoundly across the barrier of our years. One day in class he was so engrossed in the subject I was teaching that he called me Peter instead of sir. The class grew silent and waited for me to react. What could I do? I couldn't let it go. I had to do something and the class was baying for blood. Alexander looked so frightened, so feeble. I took out Chiron and beat him solidly for five minutes, on the knuckles, on his head, across his ribs. I had to, it was a matter of survival; a teacher can't be called by his Christian name by a pupil in front of a class. It is disrespectful. He had to be reprimanded. If I hadn't hit him, and hit him hard, and hit him repeatedly, then I would have become the victim. The class would see a germ of weakness inside me, and thus exposed I would lose my authority; the pupils would begin to disobey and ridicule me. I had to beat him and with each strike our friendship faded a little bit more. After five minutes of beating our friendship was dead. After class I tried to speak to him but his bedroom door was locked and he was silent behind it. The next morning when he didn't come to class I sent someone to find him. The door was still locked. It was forced open. The boy had hanged himself with a school tie. For weeks after his death I kept finding many school ties around my boxroom tied into nooses, hidden in large books, in cupboards, in drawers, in my bath and even, on one occasion, in my food. I did not ever see which of my other pupils were busying themselves with such an unpleasant task but I realized that it must have been several of them. It seemed obvious to me that they implicated me in the boy's death. I could not teach under such sorrow and quit the school, though I have to admit the headmaster was not sorry to see me go.

I am afraid to say that it was the remembrance of these ties that inspired my misuse of your glove collection yesterday.

I leave you, the only pupil that has stood by me, my book collection. You will find it somewhat depleted since our days of study at Tearsham Park; I had to sell many of them for a more bodily consumption. Among them are the various books written by my father. As regards my father's photograph, please be so good as to place it in my grave.

Concerning the tie, which may have been cut by the time you read this, knowing that you hold a great collectability for certain possessions which are precious to people, I leave it, once I am done with it, to your keeping. It was indeed a precious neck to me that first used it.

Please, if your father should ever shake himself from his illness, send him my heart-felt gratitude for the pension he so kindly granted me for so many years.

I have gone to Alexander Mead to apologize, but remain, in life as in death, your tutor,

Peter Bugg

PS. Do you know where Chiron is?

To Claire.

My dear Claire,

I do hope you will not mind my addressing you in such a familiar way, but you have been the closest I have ever come to a woman. I have to confess, and I hope this will not upset you too greatly (and try to forgive me if it does), that I have, for several years – I do not know exactly how long, these matters do not always, I believe, begin at definite moments – been in love with you. I did not for one moment believe that my feelings were reciprocated and so kept quiet on the matter. It was enough for me to be by you every day. I was deeply jealous of your former boyfriends, both real and fictional, and hope you will not mind the impertinence of my enclosing a small photograph of myself, in former happier days, when I had hair. If you do not wish to keep it, well and good.

If you do, however, you could do worse than place it in your sitting room, over that spot on the wall where Mr Magnitt was once to be found. I thought of this last night when we were returning up the stairs to your home and you mentioned how useful it would be if the lift was working. That comment reminded you, I am afraid, of Mr Magnitt's unfortunate end. If my photograph can in any way help you to make up for the loss of that other photograph which, I fear, you are never likely to see again, please do keep it.

    With my fondest love,
      Peter

So ended the Time of Memories.

IV

OBSERVATORY MANSIONS
AND TEARSHAM PARK

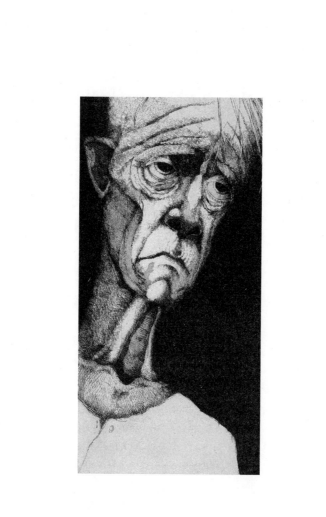

Peter Bugg remembered.

Twenty, Anna Tap and I were there as witnesses. Peter Bugg
was taken in a cheap box made of barely disguised chipboard
to the city crematorium. The chapel we were ushered into
had chairs laid out for forty or more, but we only needed
three. We felt so strange being the chief mourners that we sat
in the second row, as if we were somehow expecting other
people to arrive. The priest ran up the aisle chivvying the pall-
bearers along and looking nervously at his watch. He had a
skin disease, there were great yellow scaly infections on his
cheeks. When the coffin was positioned, I placed the photograph of Peter Bugg Senior on top of it, the priest gave me a
look of disapproval but did not take it away. With a photo-
copy of Peter Bugg's birth certificate in his hands he began to
say meaningless words about someone called Ronald Peter
Bugg, and I would have started giggling if it hadn't been so
sad. We sang one hymn, and during the third verse the man
who played on an electric keyboard – were we supposed to
think it was an organ? – turned the volume up slightly so that
we should all know that now was the time to look at Peter
Bugg for the last time. As soon as the hymn was finished we
were pushed out, through a different door to the one we came
in, other people with another coffin were using that door,
being rushed forwards by a different priest. We went home.

Claire Higg had decided to stay in flat sixteen. The journey
to the crematorium was too long, she said, for her. I do not
know whether she placed the photograph of Peter Bugg in

the position he had suggested. I was no longer allowed to enter her flat. Ever again, she said. And, indeed, I never saw it again. Miss Higg, contrary to her promise, returned the pet television's plug to its socket and continued her former entertainment, though, I gather, with less enthusiasm. When the power cuts came she was for a while taken out for her little walks, but on those occasions she was supported by two entirely different companions: Anna Tap and the Porter. The Porter, too, was absent from Peter Bugg's leave-taking, he had a skip placed beneath Bugg's window and threw all the former resident's possessions, those that were not left to anyone, out of the window into the skip. Those few, pathetically few, pages of Bugg's never-to-be-finished book among them. The residue of Bugg's life did not fill the skip. The half-full skip was taken away.

I considered how many skip loads each resident of Observatory Mansions would fill. My life would require many skip loads. Mother too would certainly require more than one skip. Claire Higg would require a single skip. Miss Tap would require one quarter of a skip. The Porter with his single box of unseen possessions and his uniforms, etc. would require an eighth of a skip. And Twenty, now even without her dog collar, would require no skip at all. For her a single dustbin bag would be sufficient. How much does the average person accumulate in his life?

We were seven again, as we had been before the new resident came to us.

The departure of Twenty.

Twenty called up the police officers in her country and after a week of silence her files were found. She was told that her name was not Twenty, was not Dog Woman, that her name was Anca. That she had married Stefan, and that Stefan and

Anca had no children. She had been twenty-six when she was lost, she was thirty-nine when she was found. But by the time she was found, by the time she had found herself, everyone had stopped looking for her. In her absence her father and mother had died, her father by suicide, her mother by failing health. This was told to her by her sister. She had not remembered having a sister. She asked her sister whether they had been happy together. The sister said, No they had not, they had hated each other; they had fallen for the same man and that man had married Anca not her sister.

Where is he now?
Don't you know?

No, Anca did not know, but she had remembered him, she remembered his moustache, she remembered him standing by the door of that other flat twenty. But he, she was told by her sister, had forgotten her.

He married again, Anca.
You?
No, he was never interested in me.
Didn't he wait for me, couldn't he have waited?
Anca, it wasn't a happy marriage.
Oh, I didn't know.
He hit you.
I didn't know.
You bought a dog to protect yourself, the biggest dog you could find, Max, you called him. I don't suppose you remember Max, a big softy. Such a huge dog in such a tiny flat. The dog didn't help you though. Then suddenly after what your neighbours said was a particularly gruesome fight, you disappeared. You and the dog. They suspected your husband of murder. Took him to court. But there was not enough proof to put him away for any longer than ten years.
Ten years!

He only served six of them, then he came out and married someone else. If I were you I'd keep yourself very quiet, I don't suppose Stefan would like to know he spent six years in hell for nothing. Everyone thought he'd killed you. Me too. By the end I think even he thought he'd done it, he just couldn't remember how.

I hit my head, I walked and walked.

Everyone was looking for you.

Can we two be friends?

I'm not sure, we used to hate each other so much.

You're my sister. I haven't got anyone else. Can we try?

If you like.

Thank you, thank you.

I've room in my flat. You can stay with me, but not for ever, you understand, just until you find a job.

Anca told Anna Tap these bits of her history very slowly, word by word, flicking through the dictionary that Peter Bugg had given her.

So, Anca, Twenty, Dog Woman, left us too. The Porter and I saw her to the bus, Anna Tap took her to the station. She laughed as she got on the bus, she laughed as she waved through the bus window at us. She laughed as the bus moved away, but there were tears in her eyes. Now we were six. We had, or rather Anna Tap had, a postcard from Anca, months later, written in our own language with many mistakes. Anca wrote that the moment she saw her sister she remembered that she hated her and they found it impossible to live together. She found a job at a canning factory, canning dog food, and now, with all her old possessions, she lived in her own flat. She had a pet cat, she wrote, named Anna. She also wrote that she had grown frightened of dogs and could not bear to be near them. Poor Anca, she still didn't really know who she was, but she was studying her old possessions to find out. She took up her old life without questioning its worth. Anna Tap said she didn't realize that she had other choices.

We never heard from her again.

The Porter cleared up Twenty's flat. It was damp from holes in the ceiling where the rain came through and it was also putrid; there were morsels of food rescued from bins decaying all over the floor, there were bones and dogs' hairs, dried blood, urine and shit. Poor Porter, he scrubbed it clean.

The Time of Silence.

Shortly after the Time of Memories had expired, taking Peter Bugg and Twenty with it, we entered the Time of Silence. Eventually even memories run out, even they have an end. No memory goes on for ever, to do so it would have to be connected with the present. And no one can remember the present. The present is the killer of memories. Father lived there, in the present, in that no-memory place. After so many memories had been related a feeling of dissatisfaction invaded us. We looked at each other, at those fellow residents who had told us their memories, and we thought – Is that all? Is that all that you are? Is that you? Ah, well if that's you, if that's all there is to you, then you're not so remarkable any more. I know your story now, there's nothing else for me to know and quite suddenly I don't know what to say to you. In truth, I find you a little dull, you shouldn't have told me everything, you should have kept something back to keep my interest alive. But now that I know everything about you I suddenly find myself unable to talk to you any more. I prefer to keep silent.

The Time of Silence, being a time of silence, had little to report about itself. Very little happened . . . except silence. No one spoke. We kept our silence to ourselves, fed it, slept with it, quietly breathed it in. Occasionally, though, it would happen that we passed one of our fellow residents, on the stairs perhaps or in the entrance hall, in the park or on the street. In these instances we would walk on silently, as if we had not seen the person, or, perhaps, we would nod at each other. But no words would come out. We could not speak, our tongues were anchored by a terrible paralysis. Our lips would open only for food or drink but at other times remained quite rigid.

I went to work as usual and achieved both inner and outer stillness. On my days off I visited the park. And on one of these visits to the park, the bathroom scalesman spoke to me, breaking for a few seconds the silence, before the pressure of that Time closed up his lips again. The girl, said the scalesman, and I presumed he meant Anna Tap, is getting thinner. That was all. I thought little of it.

Miss Tap continued to visit Saint Lucy, to pray to her in preparation for her day, and often on my return from work I would find her cigarette ends thrown casually along the pavements. These I continued to collect. The Porter was to be seen walking with Miss Tap, though in their afternoon perambulations they obeyed the Time of Silence. Indeed it seemed to me now that the Porter was spending a great deal of time with Anna Tap and though they barely spoke to each other there seemed a kind of warmth in their nods and smiles. The Porter seemed a happier porter then, he hissed and he tidied less.

Miss Tap took up Peter Bugg's chores: she shopped for Claire Higg and she changed my father. The Porter gave her a key to flat six – no doubt making another duplicate for himself first. I left a note for Miss Tap:

1. Do not enter my mother's room.
2. Do not enter Francis's bedroom.

On one of these visits of hers to flat six, she wandered into Mother's bedroom and when I returned from work I found a photograph of myself as a child holding in my hands a pair of pet mice. My hands on that photograph were white. I had painted them white. The mice lived and died before I wore gloves and after I began wearing gloves I sought out all the photographs ever taken of me and painted my photographed hands white. Under the picture, which Miss Tap had taken from my mother's room and placed on the dining-room table, was a note which said, simply:

Why?

That same day, when I returned the photograph to its rightful position, my mother extraordinarily broke the barrier of silence, broke out of her memory days for a fraction of time:

Francis?
Mother!
Francis, I don't want that girl in here. Keep her out.

Then she shut herself up again. I left a note in the same place where the why note had been left (that note I kept and stored). I wrote:

On no account enter my mother's room again.

And afterwards there were no other notes from Miss Tap when I returned home from work. Silence was back again. The only noises we heard, other than the movements of our solitary bodies, were those from the television set on the third floor. But this instrument of noise is designed to keep us silent.

Weeks passed. We watched our clocks. Unlike the Time of Memory, the Time of Silence kept perfect time, we always knew what the month was, what the hour was and usually the minute too. The Time of Silence lasted one month, three days and fourteen hours. It was broken suddenly one day from a most unpredictable corner. I was at work, silent and stationary on my plinth. A coin dropped in my box. I opened my eyes to find Anna Tap in front of me holding a sheet of paper on which was written:

Your father has begun to speak.

I left work early that day.

Father's first words.

Of course, I could not at first believe Miss Tap's note, but then, after much thinking, I considered it only too possible that it was now, rather than at any other time, that Father had begun to speak. He was tricked surely by the Time of Silence. Only during the Time of Silence could Father drop his guard enough, relax his brain sufficiently for it to be entered by a thought. The thought, presumably abandoned after the Time of Memories, must have somehow worked its way up one of father's nostrils and into the brain. Father was at peace during any time of silence and subsequently at his most vulnerable, A thought was in his brain, flying along all those corridors and its movements had opened his mouth.

Father did not, when I returned early from work, with Miss Tap, call me by my name. He did not look at me at all. Miss Tap had told me on our journey home, breaking that silence between us for ever, that all my father had said was – Plough. Over and over again. She imagined that he was referring to former agricultural days, when Observatory Mansions was called Tearsham Park. She was wrong. It was, however, a good sign. I sat in front of Father. He was smiling. He was speaking, or rather muttering. For the first few days all we heard from him were timid words, scarcely audible. They were words though, sure enough. Father was talking again. He whispered that first day:

Plough. The Plough the. Plough. The . . . the . . .
Hello, Father.

The Plough.
It's Francis.
Plough. Plough.
And there's also Orion, Father.
Orion, yes, Orion. How are you?
Well, Father.
How are you, Orion? Orion, the Plough . . .
The Pleiades.
The Pleiades!
Andromeda.
The Great Bear, Ursa Major!
Sagittarius.
Cassiopeia!
Perseus.
Sirius, Dog Star. Oh, goody, goody.

My Father was recalling the names of the stars or of constellations of stars. And in recalling them I fancied he saw himself back in his observatory. The Observatory Nights, or the Time of Father's Greatest Happiness, were spent by my father in total seclusion from the rest of humanity on a great contemplation of the universe. My father, many years before the observatory existed, had confused stillness with wisdom. He had not then learnt his incredible inner stillness that later I was to become so indebted to.

When Father was a child he was given a microscope for his birthday and so began his brave analysis of life.

Tiny Father and the microscope adventure.

The arrival of this gift coincided with Father's absence from outdoors. In those days he would be found in the nursery crouched on top of his toy, staring with one fascinated eye at a hair or the insides of a squashed ant, or at yeast, or water fleas. Father's world was minuscule then. And so were

Father's thoughts. Father's thoughts were so tiny that they were hardly thoughts at all, they were half thoughts or quarter thoughts. And all these fractions of thoughts were concerned only with reducing all that he saw around him to its tiniest element, to a single cell. Whenever he saw his father or mother, my grandfather or grandmother, he would wrinkle his brow and reduce his parents to the remembered dimensions and colours of a single blood cell, only then would my father relax. He stored in his mind a small visual dictionary of things tiny, things invisible to the unaided human eye. His mind would dissect everything until there was no further to go. There lurked Father, under the gaze of a mighty x 1000 lens. He lived there, that was the only place he could function. Father was turning dangerously into the tiniest molecule. He shied away from people, finding their vastness petrifying. If he happened to accidentally look out of a window he was terrorized by the expanse of the horizon. A mouse, he thought, was capable not of eating him, but breathing him in. A common housefly might step on him with one of its wiry feet and squash him quite to death. It was a perilous life for Father when Father confused an orbicular blood cell for a planet.

My father through his magnifying glass.

My grandparents at first believed Father's obsession with his microscope was due to a passion for science. For a while they even encouraged his long afternoons up in the nursery lost inside cells of mesophyll or epithelium. When it came to his next birthday he was given a chemistry set. My father never opened the chemistry set. He remained in the nursery, hunched in a corner quivering and mumbling. If moved, my father's whole body would shake, tears would spit from his eyes, his face would be frozen in an expression of unappeasable fear. Finally my grandfather came up with an idea that was one of the two moments of genius in his otherwise entirely prosperous and completely banal existence. A magnifying glass. Grandfather gave Father a magnifying glass. Father looked through the magnifying glass and immediately grew. Now Father was still small but large enough to abandon many of his fears. He was no longer a molecule, he was now about the size of a matchstick. Mice he still feared, and flies, too, but as long as there were no animals or insects around him he was perfectly calm and was even known to make occasional timid conversation. My grandfather, shortly before his death, had his second brilliant idea. One night, while Father was sleeping, he crept into the nursery and borrowed Father's magnifying glass. He replaced its round lens with a piece of ordinary glass and then returned it.

Then Father entered the next stage of his analysis of life. Father was now human size, six foot one to be exact. He was still known to approach objects and stare at them through his magnifying glass and I believe its circular frame helped him to concentrate.

Observatory Nights.

The Observatory Nights belonged to by far the greatest and most expensive of all Father's ventures to analyse life. They did not come about during one night in particular, they took many months of planning and when they finally arrived they were to change Father for ever (and later to give us a title for our new home – which was really our old home under a different name). Father had found a pair of field binoculars and, from the comfort of his library armchair (red, leather), he used to sit with them in front of his eyes and watch the world outside approach him – trees far away would suddenly rush their great trunks forwards. During that time Father used to imagine himself the size of trees. He would walk around Tearsham Park in great, sombre strides. One evening in his study, Father was so deep in his consideration of some copper beeches that he studied them through his binoculars until it grew dark. Father strained his eyes but the images of the trees had faded. He approached the window, still looking through his binoculars, when he caught in their eyes the night sky. He saw the moon, he saw stars. That was enough for Father, that's how it started. Father suddenly grew so large that he couldn't fit in the library, or in Tearsham Park, or in our country – Father was suddenly as big as the world. In an instant his phenomenal brain had transformed him into a planet. Father, condescending to bring himself momentarily down to our size, purchased a telescope. From that small, unremarkable telescope the idea of the observatory was born. Soon, at the expense of the Orme coffers, Father had the dome on the roof converted. The green copper cover was pulled off, a metal frame was carefully hoisted up, glass segments were added, one with a hinge so it could be opened and his newly acquired and extraordinarily powerful telescope could peek out.

My father in relation to the universe.

Father spent his days studying astronomical charts and playing with models of the planets. Getting to know his neighbours, he called it. He became friends with all the stars, called them by their names, would hop from planet to star all night long, breaking away only when the sun came out to ruin his enjoyment. Father knew the universe.

However, struggling though he was with himself, he was unable, that first night of his vocal return to us, to manage anything but the names of the stars. He tried, unsuccessfully, to get out of his chair but the chair was unwilling to release him. We hoisted him up, Miss Tap and I, and walked him carefully around the largest room in flat six. But soon we sat him down, exhausted. He closed his eyes and his thoughts immediately drifted up into the cosmos. As I watched Father's eyes close I realized what it was that had brought him back to us. His eyes usually so absent had suddenly focused on the magnified eyes of Anna Tap. Concave lenses brought Father to life. My father was ever the lover of a lens.

A *family reunion.*

In the night that followed Father's acknowledgement of his former companions, the stars, I slept badly. I was disturbed by Father's breathing, or what I at first interpreted as Father's breathing, but which I later realized was in fact Father calling out one word again and again. He was saying – Alice. Alice. Alice.

I left my bedroom to find Father sitting on an upright pine chair. He had somehow managed, unaided, to pull himself out of that red leather armchair which had held him mercilessly prisoner for so many years. Father was slowly shifting his new seat forward. Heading, with a snail's sincerity, towards the passageway. I stood and watched him, unnoticed. Even when I said – Father. Father, are you all right? he did not look up, all his concentration was spent on moving himself and the pine chair forward. And as he moved, in rhythm to his breaths, he called in his weak voice: Alice, Alice. Once in the passageway, Father slowly progressed towards my mother's room. Once he had eventually managed to open the door of Mother's room, he edged himself and his new chair towards Mother's bed. Alice, Alice. My mother was, I think, awake. I saw her eyes shifting beneath her eyelids. But she did not move. Alice, Alice. And she did not call to her husband – Francis, Francis. Francis Senior. My dear old father positioned his chair so that it touched the side of Mother's bed. In one unbroken, heroic gesture, Father managed to heave himself on to Mother's bed. He stretched himself out next to Mother, he did not touch her. He said – Alice, Alice – once more. Then he muttered, straining his head to look at her docile form:

Alice, Alice. We need another Francis Orme. Alice, Alice. I don't think this one will last. Alice, Alice, Orion, Cassiopeia.

Under Mother's eyelids tears had formed and they burst through the lids and wandered hurriedly down her flabby cheeks.

For a while, before returning to my own room and dreamless sleep, I sat on that upright pine chair by my mother's bed and watched Father close his eyes and breathe more calmly. Father's jaws moved from side to side.

In former times Father's placidly spent days would be counterbalanced at night by the ferocious grinding of his teeth. A terrible sound. We wondered what was happening in Father's brain to make his teeth gnash so excitedly. My mother hated that noise, it kept her awake in those nights when they used to sleep together. She would scream at Father ordering him to control his teeth. Father, awakened and back in his mild ways, would look devastated and through tear-filled eyes would assure her that he was incapable of such noises, that my mother should stop bullying him. So Mother bought a dictaphone and one night recorded Father's grinding teeth and played it back to him the next morning. Father looked shocked, he could not understand why his body, so polite and gentle all day through, would suddenly take up such menacing and unpleasant sounds during the night. He concluded that since his body spent the nights deceiving him it was not to be trusted. He waited patiently for his body's clandestine betrayals to grow braver, he waited for that time when his body would set out on a journey, perhaps only as far as the park, even after his mind had strictly forbidden it. One day my father's body did take my father to the park. Father used the only means he had left of defeating it. Father watched the people around him, Father heard noises, Father fell off the park bench. Father gave himself a stroke. Ever after the lower lid of his left eye drooped slightly, showing its pink inside, a memento of the battle between Father's body and Father's mind. But that was all before, a different time when Father had teeth instead of gums to grind.

When Father was sleeping and Mother's tears had dried, I considered that there was a term for what had passed that night: a family reunion.

Breakfasting Mother and Father.

There was more action that night, as I discovered when I awoke the next morning. I was in the kitchen preparing breakfast when I felt sure that I was being watched. Seated in that famous red leather armchair was an elderly figure. But it was not Father. Mother. My mother. Mother's eyes were open, Mother was looking directly at me.

Mother!
Good morning, Francis.
Mother!
Where's breakfast?
It's coming, it's coming.
Did you sleep well, Francis?
Yes, thank you.
I'm so glad.
And you, Mother, did you sleep well?
I did not sleep at all. There's a strange man in my bed.

We ate breakfast together at the dining table. We had not done this for many years. We did not speak as we ate. When Mother had finished watching me washing up (I was wearing those pink rubber gloves) she announced her intention of getting dressed, taking off her nightclothes and changing into day clothes, but she was not going to dress with a strange man looking at her. I went into Mother's room. Father was awake and mumbling to himself, lying on Mother's bed. I tried to move him, to pull him off the bed, encourage him to sit on the pine chair, but Father was too heavy and unhelpful. I needed some help. Mother would not help me, she refused to acknowledge Father. The Porter would not be allowed to help, not after the last time he looked after Father, when he dropped Father because of a drop of spittle. Claire Higg was too weak to help, was anyway not talking to me. Only one person remained. I knocked on Miss Tap's flat door, she followed me back down the stairs. Father's in Mother's bed, Mother wants to get dressed, I said. That was all.

We carried Father back out of Mother's bedroom and, as we were shuffling him forwards, Mother rushed into the lavatory and only came out again when Father was safely out of sight in the kitchen, then she darted into her own room and slammed the door.

When we aimed Father's bottom at that red leather armchair the old man began to panic again, shifting his weak body from side to side and whining in frustration. We propped him on an upright pine chair and fed him.

Mother in the mirror.

Mother saw herself in the mirror and said very calmly:

Look at that ugly old hag.

Mother washed herself, changed out of her nightclothes and put on a red dress. She brushed her hair. She put on a little make-up. Then Mother, looking in the mirror, said:

Good morning, Alice. Irresistible Alice.

Indeed, Mother was a fine-looking woman when she took the time to smooth out her ugliness.

Gradually our routines began.

Father, in those first days of his return to us, was able to move only with the greatest difficulty. Slowly though, with encouragement, Anna Tap and I taught Father to walk as parents teach babies. We stood, one behind Father and one in front, and softly dared him to take a few steps. Sometimes he fell, but we always caught him. What a heavy child Father was. But he progressed quickly and soon we were able to take him out of flat six and along the corridor. In time he learnt to climb the stairs, slowly, on all fours. Descending them, though, was more perilous. He grasped the banisters until his knuckles showed white and refused to let go. But slowly, with great patience, taking each step as an individual journey, we brought him back home.

Mother was making swifter progress. She was out of flat six on the first day she returned to us. A week later she managed, with supervision, a short walk in the park. Most of her days, though, were spent inside Observatory Mansions. She would walk from empty flat to empty flat; she hissed at the Porter and watched television with Claire Higg.

We found Father's false teeth in a drawer, dusted and washed them and said: Open wide. At night we would disguise the red leather armchair with sheets and pillows and place Father in its familiar comfort. He slept badly and was often heard calling to the stars.

We took turns to look after Mother and Father. Usually I took Mother and Anna took Father, but often we supervised one parent together. At first Mother did not like Anna Tap at all, she called her the photograph thief, and it was only after Anna had shown her many kindnesses that she began to consider her tolerable company. Mother would only ever refer to Father as *that strange man*, and when informed that that strange man was in fact her husband, she would invariably reply: Nonsense, my husband died of a stroke many years ago.

In the following weeks, time was divided into two. Mother and Father were imagining themselves in the same place but at different times. Father saw himself in Tearsham Park and could not understand why it had changed so much. Mother knew she was in Observatory Mansions, and not the Observatory Mansions in which she was happy; she was in the latest Observatory Mansions, the disintegrating Observatory Mansions, that the rest of us dwelt in, in real time. She understood that, she existed in the present, but she liked to wander into the past, and touching the walls of the various abandoned flats she would recall pictures that had once hung there. Mother was reminiscing, working her way backwards, remembering in reverse order, but Father was living the past. Father could not see that he had lost himself hopelessly in a time long dead. He believed he was in Tearsham Park and that Tearsham Park had become somehow alienated from him. He tried to redress this unfamiliarity by struggling to remember exactly where the rooms were that were temporarily avoiding him. Sadly, he found plasterboard walls in his way and would shriek – *The servants' hall is here, just the other side of this wall.* And we would have to shrug our shoulders and pat his hand and say: No, Father, you are mistaken. He was right, though. He was always right.

Together my Mother and Father heaved themselves back to life. And as they did so the building that was called Tearsham Park, that was called Observatory Mansions, began to fill with the people and objects of their yesterdays.

THE COMPLETE HISTORY OF
OBSERVATORY MANSIONS
AND
TEARSHAM PARK

as seen through the eyes of my mother and father
(retold with the assistance of Francis Orme and Anna Tap):

PART ONE.

Observatory Mansions.

My mother stood in the abandoned flat eight, in an empty bedroom. She wiped away cobwebs with her hands, blew all the dead flies into a corner and then sat in the centre of the bare, dusty floor. Here, where I'm sitting, she said, was the bachelor's bed. It was a large double bed, it made no noises. The bachelor lay here on this bed, every night and slept (said Mother, spreading her hands around the dust). Some nights while he lay here he did not sleep, some nights, and some days too, he had a companion. I am here, said my mother, to recall the last time I came into this flat. I stood here (she stood with only one foot inside the flat, the rest of her on the threadbare landing carpet). He did not let me in. I saw through the gap in the door that all his bags were packed and that his flat was cleared. He was going to leave the next morning, without saying goodbye.

There could have been a thousand things to say to him. But he didn't care for me any more and I couldn't make him care, the harder I tried, the more he pushed me away. As I stood on the landing, with only the smallest part of me in his flat, I thought: What's the point, what's the point of anything? And I just said a not very forceful *bastard* to him and left. I went to my bedroom in flat six, changed into my nightie, drew the curtains and got into bed. That's how it started.

Francis came to see me, he said: Mother, get up, it's not night-time. Listen Francis, I said, if I close my eyes I can be anywhere. I can imagine myself in any time I desire. I can always be in summer if I like. I can relive those rather better days that seem to have dried up for ever. Perhaps, if I want to see myself in flat eight with the bachelor, when I first met him, when we were happy, I can just close my eyes and be there. But perhaps it would be better if I had a little something of his to remember him by. Francis, I know you're a thief. You've been a thief since you could crawl, it's your nature, I've never complained, I've never reported you, even when I knew you were to blame, even when your victims were in tears and desperate. I could have, but I never did. So, now, Francis, I have a commission for you. You will be paid. Steal for me a pair of the bachelor's Y-fronts.

Francis Orme, aside to Anna Tap.

In time Mother and I drew out great plans. I helped to contain all Mother in one room. I stole back all the gifts that she had ever given. I piled objects into Mother's room. And she paid me for each object returned. When I had collected all Mother's memories I would sit in her room, holding hands with her, and we would laugh together. The Exhibition of Mother was one of the greatest achievements of my life; surpassed only by that other exhibition down in the cellar, in the tunnel that leads to the church. But how did Mother repay me for my genius? She shut herself up and loved only Mother's past and Mother's objects. Mother ghosted herself.

Tearsham Park.

My father complained that the smells were all wrong.

There was a damp smell all about Observatory Mansions and the musty, sweet scent of rats. It never used to be like that, he said, it always used to smell of wood polish, they were always polishing the oak floorboards. Or it would smell of the delicious odours from the kitchen. After his first attempts to rediscover the rooms of Tearsham Park had led only to off-white walls and ripped wallpaper, my father decided to begin again. He decided to start with his childhood and work his way forward, slowly, methodically. He was sure that this process of remembering would eventually reveal the entire and familiar Tearsham Park to him, that he had some-how forgotten something that might explain it to him, that the building was a complicated puzzle which he must unravel.

Observatory Mansions.

Mother said: Here I stand on the second floor facing flat twelve. To my right is flat thirteen, to my left is flat eleven. In flat twelve lives a mother. Either side of her live her two daughters. I open the door to flat twelve: here is the mother, she is called Elizabeth. I open the door to flat thirteen: here is the daughter called Christa. I open the door to flat eleven: here is the daughter called Eva. The sisters were twins, but never have I known such un-identical twins in my life before or since. Christa was tall and thin. Eva was short and fat. Elizabeth, their mother, was tall and fat, but she suffers from a terrible cancer that has made her progressively shorter and thinner. I close the door to flat twelve. Mother Elizabeth has died. I open the door to flat twelve, the mother is buried. Now in flat twelve are the two daughters, before so pleasant, but now screaming and clawing each other. They are dividing the complete possessions of their mother between them. The sisters used to be inseparable, they spent their days nursing their sick mother. I have never before or since seen such devotion in children. However, when the mother died and it came to the division of the mother's articles, never have I known before or since such harridan sisters. They are walking around the flat now. One holds a sheet of paper with little round red stickers on it. The other holds a sheet of paper with little round green stickers on it. They are walking around the flat placing the circular stickers on various items. They are arguing with each other, if one sees a red sticker on an object she demands that it be taken off so that it can be exchanged for a green sticker. And vice versa. Some objects have green or red stickers on them and directly underneath them, hidden from sight, are red or green stickers. Now they have both stopped before an object. This object is an eternity ring given to their mother by their long-dead father. It is a beautiful ring, its thick silver holds a precious diamond. Eva says the diamond is hers, Christa contradicts her. The diamond is covered by green and red stickers. They scream at each other, their screams are heard throughout the building, all the residents come out and stand in their doorways, trying to hear more. Both sisters say: This ring was given to my mother as a symbol of love, I loved Mother, I loved Father more than you, it is only right that I should have the ring. They curse each other. They slap each other. They accuse each other of never having loved their mother at all. They call each other selfish and materialistic. But they are unable to decide which sister should keep the ring. Finally, they resolve to break off their argument until the next morning. They lock the door to flat twelve. I close it. They return to their flats eleven and thirteen. I close these doors too. Behind them the sisters are sobbing alone. It is now night. Close your eyes. Open your eyes. It is now morning. I open the door to flat eleven. I open the door to flat thirteen. The two sisters bid each other a cold good morning. I open the door to flat twelve. The sisters enter flat twelve. The eternity ring has gone. It went in the night. Christa says to Eva, Give back my diamond. Eva says to Christa, Return my ring immediately. They accuse each other for many hours, they search each other's pockets and each other's rooms. They do not find the eternity ring. The police are called. The police do not find the eternity ring either. Three days later flats eleven, twelve and thirteen are empty. The objects of flat twelve have been divided among the sisters under the supervision of lawyers. The sisters leave Observatory Mansions with their own possessions and a half each of their dead mother's possessions. They never speak to each other again.

Tearsham Park.

Father standing in flat one said: This is the drawing room. It used to be, unless I'm much mistaken, about three times the size of this. It's so dirty! Where has all this rubbish, all these empty cans and newspapers come from? And someone has smashed the windows. There should be, just above me now, written into the stucco-decorated ceiling with its roses and leaves, a date: 1687. Here, said Father kicking a wall, should be a fireplace, a great marble surround with columns supporting the mantelpiece, its twin should be a few metres further down, the other side of the wall. There, that's in the way, that deceiving wall! There should be tapestries, it's all too, too small! With your imagination put a sofa here. On this absent sofa I sit with my mother. My father is sitting alone over there. He is reading the last volume of the *History of the Ormes*. He had written this volume. He is laughing. I am playing with a magnifying glass. Father closes the book. It is finished.

Francis, says my father, you are heir to a great and old family. Look after it when I am gone. Cherish it. Marry, get yourself a son, at least one. Never waste money. Extend

Ormeland. If you can't, keep it as it is. If you lose one inch of it you will be cursed by your ancestors.

My father takes me around the house showing me all our family's possessions. Look at them, he says, aren't they beautiful? Never lose one, Francis, he says.

Father takes Anna and me into the entrance hall and says: Here in the hall of Tearsham Park are many faces. Not bare and filthy wallpaper, and the floor should be black and white chequered marble, not threadbare carpet. Here are many faces painted in oil. Many proud profiles. Many old Ormes. One head on top of another, five heads high, climbing piggyback into the darkness. Many old dead Ormes. The dead that are frequently dusted, a chapel of history. All these faces arranged neatly in order of existence whisper *remember me*. All that spotless history. They look at me and there is no approval in their look.

Come here every day, says my father, as I have done. Look at these faces. If you *can* look at them then you are doing your duty, then these portraits will be your friends. If you *cannot* look at them then you are doing something wrong. Immediately right that wrong, Francis. If you buy land, and you will, you must go in and see the portraits. You will find them smiling at you. Never sell, Francis, extend, expand. That is the oldest Francis Orme up there at the top, Sir Francis Orme, who died in these grounds, in a tunnel that starts in the cellar. We are all his little children, he made us. In gratitude we borrow his name for our little lives and then pass it on. It is never ours to keep. Pass it on, Francis, keep it living. Read the *History of the Ormes* in the library, write your own. Do not let us down. Promise me you won't. Swear by these portraits and on your own father's life that you won't let us down. Promise, Francis, promise.

I promise.

Observatory Mansions.

Mother: This is flat sixteen. Its occupant is Claire Higg. Claire Higg is watching television. She has only recently taken up the habit of watching television and—

Mother suddenly stopped talking, she had heard Father moving about in the next door flat and rushed down a level.

Tearsham Park.

Father inside flat fifteen: This is Peter Bugg's room. This stern, jet-black-haired man is my tutor during his school's holidays. He used only to have one room but now, strangely, it has extended to four rooms. Three of these rooms are fictitious. Ignore them. On the walls are school photographs.

Observatory Mansions.

Mother: This, flat ten, belongs to Peter Bugg. This bald man who is always sweating and crying was tutor to my husband and to my son. He has only recently come to live here. His former home was repossessed. He keeps himself to himself and spends much of his time sitting at his desk writing. I do not know what it is that he is writing. There is a waste-paper basket by the window. It is filled with scrunched up pieces of paper. This wallpaper made of one huge photograph of a harbour with fishermen at work in strange looking boats has nothing to do with Peter Bugg. It was here before him. How ridiculous Mr Bugg's school photographs look here, hanging just above an ultramarine sea. This strange wallpaper was placed here by the old resident of flat ten, an old man, who had spent many years working abroad. This photograph wallpaper was the view he had from his house in that foreign land of his, which he missed so much. The old man, Mr Wilson, had had to return to this country, his job out there had finished. He hated it here and turned his flat into a museum of his old days spent abroad. Almost everything he placed inside it was from that foreign world. One day when he walked out, having not, I believe, left his flat for almost a week, he was so appalled by what he saw that he stood absolutely still, all his muscles tensed, and screamed and screamed and wouldn't stop screaming. The Porter called a doctor, the doctor called an ambulance. They took Mr Wilson away and they didn't bring him back.

Tearsham Park.

Father with tears in his eyes, back in flat one which he called the drawing room: Over there (he points to an empty, dirty corner) is my father. We think, my mother and I, that Father is sleeping. Mother goes to wake him, the gong for supper has gone, but Father will not wake up. Mother shouts at me. She tells me to go into supper alone. I never see Father again.

Shortly afterwards people will start demanding money from us, a great deal of money – taxes and duties that we have to pay entirely because Father has just died. They ask for so much money that Mother starts crying and we sell the two oil landscapes in the dining room, whenever we look at the gaps on the walls we are reminded of them. I see Mother at the desk in the smoking room, where Father kept his accounts. She says: In your grandfather's time this house had twenty-seven staff, there were butlers and under butlers, footmen, lady's maids and even lamp boys, but things have changed. That was a long time ago.

She sighs and tells me that we must further reduce the number of our staff. The house steward must go and one housemaid and the valet, too, and we can't afford even to keep the pantry boy on any longer or even the daily woman for that matter. There won't be enough people to keep the place tidy any more and there'll be no one to polish the floors.

Observatory Mansions.

Mother, back outside Claire Higg's flat (not rising to the third floor until she was certain that Father was away from the stairs and down on the ground floor): Claire has suffered a terrible loss. She sits alone, crying day and night. We have tried to take her out, we have offered her walks in the park and hot chocolate in cafés. She does not find our offers tempting. Every morning we come and knock on her door. She says she can't come out because she saw a dead sparrow from her window, lying at the side of the road. It's a bad sign, she says. On other mornings she says she can't go out because she heard a car horn which meant to her that a dangerous driver was roaming the streets and she might be knocked down. Sometimes she tells us that she can't come out because there is a storm about to break, though there is not a cloud in the sky. She stands at the window watching the traffic going around and around.

Tearsham Park.

Father in flat one, in his reduced drawing room: The room is filled with girls. Mother presides over them. They are taking tea. I am sitting over there, a little way away from them. Mother tries to get me to talk to the girls but I am frightened. I keep quiet. The girls come every day and talk happily to each other, they are old friends. They do not talk to me. Mother is trying to find me a wife. I tell her that I do not want a wife. She slaps me. When the girls come the next time I am made to sit with them. Halfway through tea I upset a cup and it spills on to the dress of one of the girls. The girl screams at me, she says the dress was new. She accuses me of upsetting the tea deliberately. She had a lovely face and a lovely smile. But the smile was only on her lips when she talked to the girls. When she screams at me, accusing me of deliberately ruining her dress, she does not wear her beautiful smile. The next time the girls come to tea, the girl with the smile is not with them. Slowly, there are less and less girls at Mother's tea parties. Then they are abandoned altogether. I am much relieved.

Observatory Mansions.

Mother still on the third floor, opened the sliding metal lift doors. She peered into the darkness. Mother: This is a prologue to what happened next, or before, before Miss Higg took herself away from the world. Look at that metal cord, that cord is one of the cords that used to gently pull the lift up or let it slowly come down. Look at the end of the cord. It is broken. There are rumours, that originated from Francis, that the lift cord was deliberately cut by the Porter. The police did think the cord looked a little too cleanly cut, if the cord had snapped from hard wear it would probably have been more serrated. But there was no proof.

Tearsham Park.

Father, still in his diminished drawing room, labelled one: I'm sitting here. No one else is in the room. The door is opened, a different door to this one which has the number one on it, and it wasn't such a cheap door, if you tapped it, it wasn't hollow like this one. I can see that other door, I can see that other door open, a girl walks into the drawing room. The door is closed, I hear a key in the lock. I am left locked in the drawing room with a girl. That girl is to be my future wife. She came from the city, not from such an old family as ours I am told later, but a good enough family all the same, according to my mother. She walks up to me and says hello. I look away. Now she comes closer and kisses me on the lips. I run to the door and beg my mother to open it. The girl follows me to the door and when I realize that my mother is not going to open it I turn around and the girl kisses me again. Her third kiss is longer than the other two. I stand frozen in absolute fear. I feel her tongue on my lips. Her tongue opens my mouth and wiggles about inside it. After a while she takes her tongue out and steps back from me. I realize that I have been holding my breath for a long time and feel dizzy. I breathe out. I must look upset because now the girl goes and sits in one of the chairs over there and starts crying. After a while I go and sit next to her. I pat her hand. She looks up at me. She smiles. I cannot disobey that smile. The girl smiles such a beautiful smile and says: Can I stay? I say: Yes, but not because I want her to stay. I say yes because it is impossible to contradict that smile. I hear a key turn in the lock. I hear my mother knock on the door. When I go to answer it my mother asks me, How are you, darling? I say, immediately without thinking, that I am in love. The words that have just come out of my mouth shock me. I think about them and I realize that in fact I *am* in love. I say it again: I am in love with ... Then I stop. I do not know her name. I ask her: What is your name? She says that her name is Alice. I turn to my mother. I say: Yes, I am in love with Alice.

Observatory Mansions.

My mother on the third floor, somewhere between flats sixteen and nineteen. Mother: There are milk bottles outside the doors of flats sixteen and nineteen. It is precisely seven thirty in the morning. The door to flat sixteen is opened. There stands Miss Claire Higg, dressed, suggestively enough, in her nightgown. Now the door to flat nineteen is opened.

Mr Alec Magnitt steps out, he is dressed tidily in an unfashionable grey suit with matching grey shoes. In one hand he holds a calculator. He picks up the milk bottle outside his door and, still keeping his door open, places the milk bottle in his fridge. Claire sees a little of his flat, that same fraction that she has always seen; she has never seen anything more. She sees a framed photograph of an old woman, possibly Alec Magnitt's mother. Mr Magnitt returns to the landing and locks his door. Claire Higg, still posted outside the door of flat sixteen, smiles lovingly at him. He smiles nervously back. Alec Magnitt walks towards Claire Higg and places something in her hands. He opens the lift shutters and walks into the lift. He closes the lift shutters behind him. Claire Higg returns to her flat and closes the door behind her. She looks in her hands. She finds a passport photograph there of Alec Magnitt, on its reverse are written words full of love. Alec Magnitt, inside the lift, presses the button that says G on it, for the ground floor. Outside the lift a terrific noise is heard, the sound of something swiftly descending from a great height. Suddenly there is an enormous bang. Dust rises and spews out of the lift shaft on the first and second floors. Miss Higg opens her door again. She is no longer smiling. She rushes to the lift entrance on the third floor and pulls back its metal shutters. She looks down the lift shaft. She sees the broken metal cord dangling beneath her. Claire Higg screams.

Tearsham Park.

My father gradually ascended the stairs, my mother hearing his approach rushed up to the fourth floor. My father stopped outside flat sixteen. He heard voices coming from inside the flat. Father: This door for some unknown reason labelled sixteen, has nothing to do with the number sixteen. This door is the door to my bedroom. (Father bangs on the door.) I will not be locked out of my own bedroom. (Claire Higg curses inside. Father kicks the door. We beg him to stop, we beg him to imagine his old bedroom. He complains a little more and then, touching the door, he closes his eyes and smiles.) On the other side of this door I am lying on my four-poster bed, under the covers. I am alone. It is midnight. During the day that has just passed I have been married to Alice who I have fallen in love with; a small service in Tearsham Church. Alice is sleeping in Tearsham Park for the first time tonight. Her bedroom is two floors below. As I gaze at my ceiling I am disturbed by a knocking sound, a hand tapping on wood. Who is it? I ask. It is Alice, says Alice. The door is opened, without my permission, and Alice walks into my bedroom and closes the door behind her. She is wearing only her nightclothes. Now, hardly any time later, she is wearing nothing. Alice, completely naked, steps forwards and pulls the sheets and blankets away. Then she replaces the sheets and blankets with her naked self. She pulls down my pyjama bottoms and sits on me. She moves up and down. As she moves up and down I am overcome by a feeling of considerable pleasure. Shortly after this Alice looks down at me and asks – *Already?* I do not know what she is talking about and ignore her comment. Alice returns to her room. She will come back again on the next few nights and the procedure will be the same. I begin to look forward to these nights. Soon she stops saying *Already?* and stays with me for longer.

Observatory Mansions.

My mother, on the fourth floor, walked into the empty flat twenty-three. Mother: This, the smallest flat in the building, was once the home of Lord Aloysius Pearson. Lord Pearson lived alone. He was once the owner of a castle which was so large and so full of treasures that in the month of August he opened it to the public and, for a fee, toured his visitors around. The castle was, however, in a bad state of disrepair, and to make things worse, a cedar tree had collapsed on its roof during a thunder storm causing considerable damage. Lord Pearson could not afford to personally finance the restoration of his home. He had just one option: to hand it over with all its treasures to a trust. This trust would repair the castle and keep it open to the public all the year round. The trust stated:

a. That it would not be possible for Lord Pearson to remain in the castle.
b. That it would not be possible for Lord Pearson to show visitors around the castle. (See note below)
Note: The trust has a team of specialists in history and architecture, <u>professionally</u> trained to entertain the public.

Lord Pearson left his castle assured that it would be repaired and that it would keep for ever all his family's treasures. He came to the city and bought, with the majority of what money he had left, flat twenty-three of Observatory Mansions. This building, he said, had such a feel for history, and besides, he said, the flat (formerly servants' rooms) was so reasonably priced. Here he lived and here he died. Before he died he would often invite the other residents into his flat and show them around it as if it were a stately home. He would say – This is the drawing room where Lord Pearson sat and watched television. This is the bathroom and in this plastic bath Lord Pearson washed himself with lemon-smelling soap. This is the kitchen and at this table Lord Pearson sat and sipped his consommé soups. And so on. Lord Pearson died by taking an overdose of sleeping tablets. His money had run out. He had no idea how he could possibly earn any more. On his body which was smartly dressed in a tweed suit was a note that said:

This is Lord Pearson.
A stately relic dating back to the beginning of
the century.
Please bury in the family vaults.

Tearsham Park.

Father stood in abandoned flat twelve. Father: This is my mother's room. My mother is lying in her bed. All around the room are her collection of porcelain dolls, staring at me. It is day. My mother no longer gets out of her bed any more. My mother tells me to remember to keep the Orme family alive. She tells me to study the *History of the Ormes* so that I may be able to pass it on to my children. Then she starts crying. She tells me that she is being persecuted by my wife. She tells me that my wife is deliberately changing the positions of all the objects in Tearsham Park. Mother tells me that Alice has been moving objets about to undermine her authority. Mother complains that when she can't find these missing objects Alice points to the objects which have been deliberately repositioned and tells her that as far as she was aware they had always been kept there. Mother tells me that this has happened so often that the servants have begun laughing behind her back. When she asked for the where-abouts of a missing object last time, Alice asked her, in front of servants, if she was feeling well and wondered if she wouldn't be better off in bed.

Mother says to me, Sit with me, Francis, my darling boy. I say, I can't, I told Alice that I would go for a walk with her. The next day my mother tells me that Alice has turned all the servants against her. I tell Mother that she is being cruel to Alice and that I will bring Alice up to the bedroom later, so that Mother can apologize to her. Mother orders me out and tells me never to come back. During the night she dies in her sleep. We bury her. I move all her porcelain dolls to the attic storerooms. My wife said: I can't stand those dolls glaring at me. Take them away, Francis, before I smash them.

Observatory Mansions.

Mother, inside flat nineteen: It is the evening before the lift fails. Alec Magnitt is sitting at his desk pressing the buttons of his calculator. He hears a voice outside on the landing. He approaches his front door and puts his ear to the keyhole. He hears the Porter talking to Claire Higg, knocking on her flat door.

> Can I come in?
> No.
> Please will you come for a walk with me?
> No, I don't want to.
> I want to kiss you. I love you.
> Leave me alone.
> Open up, I want to kiss you.
> Go away!

The Porter leaves the door of flat sixteen and kicks the landing skirting board leaving a dent which you see here. Then he walks away cursing. I know all this because I was in flat sixteen with Claire Higg. We heard Alec Magnitt walk out of his flat and up to the door of flat sixteen. Inside the flat Claire looked excited. Then we heard the footsteps walk away and the door of flat nineteen close. Claire looked disappointed. That night Alec Magnitt wrote, on the back of a passport photograph of himself, a confession of love.

Tearsham Park.

My father stood in Mother's bedroom in flat six. Father: Finally! Yes, this is right, this is my wife's room! The same walls decorated with the same red flock paper. Perhaps it's a little more cluttered than before, but it *is* her room. Look there, I recognize that night lamp, it belonged to Francis.

Add a cot now. Put it here, by the night light. In that cot sleeps a baby. The baby is male. He is called Francis. All the first-born sons of the Orme family are named Francis. He is very small and very white. This is our baby. This is the baby that Alice and I made together.

The portraits are smiling.

Observatory Mansions.

Mother: I am in the entrance hall. It is evening. Alec Magnitt is coming back home from work. He gets into the lift and is carried to the third floor. Now Claire Higg comes into the entrance hall. She has been following Alec Magnitt. She walks up the stairs to the third floor. Here comes a third person. It is the Porter. The Porter has been following Claire Higg following Alec Magnitt. His face is red. He is jealous. He descends the stairs to his basement flat. Here comes the fourth and final person. It is I, Alice Orme. I have been following the Porter following Claire Higg following Alec Magnitt. I realize the Porter has grown attached to my friend Miss Higg. There is something dangerous about him. He never showed interest in her until he discovered that Alec Magnitt loved her. Perhaps he is one of those people who can only love people who are already loved. Perhaps only then does he feel a person is worth loving. Perhaps he needs to see a person being loved in order to imagine what love is like. Then, when he sees it, he wants to steal it.

Claire follows Alec, the Porter follows Claire, I follow the Porter. It is not an unusual occurrence. It happens a few times each week. The only person completely unaware of it is Alec Magnitt.

It is strange that after Magnitt's death, the Porter no longer pays any attention to Claire. He immediately loses interest, as if without Alec being there he can no longer see what it was that made Claire lovable.

Tearsham Park.

Father, in flat fourteen: I know that this room is the nursery, even if someone has taken the nursery tables and chairs away to fool me. And there used to be tiles the colour of bluebottle flies on the floor and halfway up the walls. In this bit of wall here, I'm sure it was here, I scratched my name. Look! Plaster! They've covered it up, but I was here! This *is* the nursery! I sat just there with my microscope. But that was long ago, now, years later, I see our child sleeping in the nursery bed. The doctor has just left, one of many doctors who we have called for these last months. Our child is five years old. He is not well. He is diseased. His head has begun to swell and he is very pale. He complains of headaches. He is sleeping now and as I look down at his pale, thin body I begin to cry. The head on that body is too large. It is out of proportion. The cheeks are very swollen. The flesh of his face looks so tight that I imagine it to be on the point of ripping.

Observatory Mansions.

Mother, in flat eight, where her bachelor lived: I am in the bedroom. I am not alone. I am smiling.

Tearsham Park.

Father, in flat fourteen: My son's illness has progressed. While his head has expanded his body has become thinner. I notice he smiles a great deal. He is smiling now. Wrinkles have developed around his eyes. My son is holding one arm of his teddy bear. He has ripped off the mouth, the smile from the teddy bear's face. My son does not want to smile. I think it is the disease affecting his face that has stretched his skin into a smile. My son has very fine, fair hair. It is parted. It is so fine that you can almost see his skull through it. I am looking at my son and I am thinking that my five-year-old son looks like an old man.

Observatory Mansions.

Mother, still in flat eight: I am in the bedroom. I am not alone. I am smiling.

Tearsham Park.

Father, in Mother's bedroom, in flat six: My wife is in bed. She spends most of her days in bed now. She has not been in to see our son for a long time. I am wearing my pyjamas. It is night. I get into bed with my wife. I say to her: Alice, I've been sitting with the portraits. Alice, we need another Francis Orme. I don't think this one will last.

Observatory Mansions.

Mother, up in flat eight: I am in the bedroom. I am not alone. I am smiling. I am in love with a bachelor. I have never been so happy.

Tearsham Park.

Father, in Mother's bedroom in flat six: In the cot that should stand here sleeps our second child. He is another boy. He is called Thomas. Alice looks after him very carefully and cups her hands around his head every hour to check if it is swelling. She is sighing with relief. My other son, who is usually kept in the nursery by his ailment, cannot stop smiling now. His eyes, though, I notice show no happiness. He has seen the baby. He studies the child carefully, as he looks at the baby's face he strokes his own cheeks. My wife will not allow our eldest son to touch the baby. She pushes him away when he comes near. There he is now with his back to us, walking up the stairs that lead to the nursery. He is six years old but looks sixty.

There are two doctors around my son's bed. My son is wailing and holding his head. I ask the doctors: Can't you do something? He's hurting. Now I scream: Do something! The doctors say nothing else can be done. They have given the boy morphine. My son is feverishly scratching his head. *DO SOMETHING!*

Observatory Mansions.

Mother in flat twelve: I have just given the two sisters a present. I gave Eva and Christa a record player. This is the last present I will ever give. Today I have learnt that the only unoccupied flat, flat eight, has been bought by a very hand-some bachelor. The bachelor, whose name is Dominic, smiled at me when he came to look around the flat. There was something in that smile. He asked me my name and if I was married. I said my name is Alice and I am a widow. The sisters unwrap the record player and put on a record. They have already said: Thank you very much, Alice, you are very kind. All these presents you have given us! We listen to a famous love song, and as we do I think of the bachelor.

Tearsham Park.

My father walked out of flat fourteen, his feet remembering differently carpeted stairs. His hands were stretched out as if he were carrying an object. In that moment I could almost see Father when he was younger, almost see his hair darker and fuller, his spine straight.

Father: This is Francis Orme eldest son of Francis Orme. I wish he weighed more. I feel as if I am carrying nothing. He looks like a little old man. He stopped breathing. His big head doesn't work any more. This is my son. This was my son. My son is dead and I feel sick.

Mosquito bites and lip cream.

Just because my parents had chosen to run around Observatory Mansions and wade forwards and backwards through their histories was not reason enough to drop our own lives. I continued, with the few hours of the day that I could leave my parents to the care of Miss Tap, to stand atop my plinth in the city's centre or to wander down the alleyway of my exhibition. And Miss Tap was relieved by me as often as she required it, so that she might visit the wooden altarpiece of Tearsham Church and pray to Saint Lucy to save her fading sight. Once, when I returned from my plinth I found Anna Tap alone sitting at the kitchen table in flat six (Father was down in flat four in what used to be part of the old library; my mother was taking a nap in her bedroom). Anna, I am not mistaken in this, was wearing a pair of white gloves and when I walked in she quickly hid her hands. I only saw them for a second but she was nevertheless wearing white cotton gloves. Gloves not taken out of my glove diary boxes, gloves still unaccounted for after the terrible Gloves Armageddon Experience.

We had entered the summer months now and summer is a time that I loathe. The heat makes my hands sweat, but far worse than that, summer is the time of the year most frequented by mosquitoes.

I was terrorized by mosquitoes; they rushed into flat six during the day and lined themselves up on the ceiling of my bedroom, during the night they swooped down and bit me.

The mosquitoes bit me on the legs, on the arms and on the face. Mosquito bites are dangerous things. The little bits of my skin that swelled up into small red mounds itched. And when I itch in this way I want to scratch myself desperately. I want nothing more in the world than to scratch. But I cannot scratch. Scratching is the enemy of gloves. Bothered and broken mosquito bites after scratching leave a stain on the tips of cotton fingers. I cannot scratch with my hands. So, during summer months, I wandered miserably around the world of Observatory Mansions rubbing my arms against window ledges or my legs against the sides of doors. And I was altogether miserable. When I stood on my plinth and closed my eyes I could sometimes achieve outer stillness but never the inner stillness that the job required, for all I could think about was the itching of a thousand mosquito bites.

That summer was different, though, from all those other mosquito-bitten summers. That summer I was as usual bitten in many places, but I did not scratch. I itched a little but never for very long. Anna Tap bought a miraculous spray that stopped my itching mania; I sprayed myself and the spray felt very cool and soothing.

Later that same summer, Anna came up to me in flat six and told me that my bottom lip was swollen. I knew this very well, I was entirely aware of every feature, handsome and not so handsome, on my thirty-seven-year-old body. Anna held in her hand a small tube of cream. I bought this for you, she said. It is for your lip, it will stop the swelling. I held the tube of lip cream in my white hands. For a few moments I considered it and then said: I can't accept this. I mustn't get cream, whether it's white or transparent, on my fingers.

Anna took back the tube of lip cream.

Anna placed some lip cream on one of her, ungloved, fingers.

Anna's finger touched my lower lip. She put cream on that

lower lip. Anna's finger rubbed that cream all over my lower lip until I felt a little faint and had to sit down.

That night I lay on my bed thinking that *Anna Tap's finger had actually touched my lower lip.* As she touched it, I recalled this thoroughly, her face was extremely close to mine. I could smell her breath, which smelt of cigarettes, and see very clearly the freckle that lived on the middle of the end of her nose. I saw also, at very close range, the lips of Anna Tap.

Every day for two weeks Anna applied the cream to my lip. And every day she applied the cream I was able to study her face very closely. Sometimes when I looked at her face I looked into her eyes, and once she looked into my eyes at the same time. Not for long. I felt faint again. At the end of the two weeks my lower lip was no longer swollen and Anna ceased applying lip cream to it.

I remember this with regret.

I suppose it was at around this time that I began to reconsider my thoughts on Anna. I had at first thought that there was nothing pretty about her at all. I realized that this was not true. I found her nose pretty and her lips not unattractive, and her smile encouraging. Even her eyes, perhaps because they were so fragile, held a certain unconfident beauty. And she had the most moving shoulder blades I have ever seen, when she was reading, crouched over a table, they looked as if they belonged to a small bird.

One night in the street.

One night when Mother was sleeping and Father was up in the broken observatory with Anna, I went out into the street. I whispered her name into the night. Anna, Anna, I said. To the streets, to the park, to the houses. I heard the sound of her name on my lips. I heard her noise lift out of me quietly and sound so small and precise in the summer night air.

Anna.

Anna.

Anna.

Tell me about gloves, Anna.

Tell me about gloves, Anna.

This was a good way of passing time. Even if I asked her to tell me about gloves ten times in one day, she would smile and begin again:

Hands are measured by the glove tailor: the width across the knuckles; the span from outstretched thumb to outstretched little finger; the length from the centre of the wrist to the tip of the longest finger; the thickness of the hand. The shapes of the hands are traced on a sheet of paper. Two pieces of material are needed to form a glove. The first, the largest piece, is of the hand, minus the thumb. It has seven fingers. Picture it as if the skin of a hand had been removed and laid out flat so that the little finger is twice the width of the other fingers because, unlike the others, its nail side and palm side are still connected. This piece is folded in half at the little finger, making the shape of a hand and then it is sewn together. There is a hole in the glove at this stage where the naked thumb would peek out if it were worn. The second piece is a small length of material, itself to be folded in half and sewn together, in the shape of the thumb, which is of course inserted into the hole in the glove. Now you have the complete glove. In addition, two lines or more of raised fabric which tuck in some of the excess material and stop the glove sagging are often added, these are called darts.

But the more Anna told me about gloves, the more I realized that what I enjoyed in these descriptions was not the content of her sentences, which were loaded with the profession's dry language, but the fact that she was speaking to me.

I realized that something must be done to end this infatuation.
I began to fear for the exhibition.

A commission for William.

I went to see William, my nails were quite long but they didn't really need cutting. I had them cut anyway. When we were drinking the thick black coffee, William said: I'm glad you've come back. I was sure you would in the end.

I told him that I had come to give him a commission. A bust. In wax. As soon as possible, please. Tell me how much, I'll bring you the money all in one lump or in weekly fees. We can draw up a contract if you wish it. I'll pay you extra for speediness, but I shan't penalize you if it arrives late. I have money, don't be worried about that.

I'm very busy at the moment.
Find time for Francis.
Francis, have you any idea how much it costs to make a wax head?
I have money.

I placed all my saved money on to William's work table, coins from my plinth, notes from when I helped Mother to collect herself up into one room. William counted it.

It's not enough.
It must be. You haven't counted it properly.

William saw my disappointment and, sighing, he asked:

Who's the subject?
A woman, late twenties to mid-thirties.
I'll need photographs.
I'll get them for you.
Is this person living?

The subject of the commission's life, whether past or present, has no bearing on your work.

If she's alive I could do the portrait from life. Francis, it's not the girl we talked about, is it?

Consider the subject dead.

Why do you want it, Francis?

That is no concern of yours.

The photographs will have to be detailed. Every angle of the face. Close ups.

Certainly. One other thing: you will of course employ Laura and Linda to give her hair and Ottila to give her eyes.

Unless you want her bald and blind.

Now, as far as Ottila is concerned she must not, on any account, copy the eyes she sees in the photographs. Of course, she will discover the colour of the subject's eyes from these photographs but that is all the information she is required to take from them. The subject's eyes are damaged. They are bloodshot and yellow, the irises are cloudy. These details are to be ignored by Ottila. She is to give the head perfect eyes. Is that understood? I'll bring you the photographs in a few days and then you can set about your work. Let's nod on it. Good. Goodbye, William, I thank you for your time.

I'll do what I can, Francis, but you'll have to get me more money.

Everything I earn from now on.

A commission for Mad Lizzy.

I was in a very business-like mood that day and went straight on to my second commission: photographs of Anna Tap. I found Mad Lizzy dashing and twitching around the crowds of the city, busy recording life. I stopped her and invited her for a coffee in a particular café where I am known, on occasion, to waste my hard-earned money. This café has nothing very extraordinary about it. Its coffee, however, is excellent but that is not reason enough to visit it. I visit it because of its single waiter, George, a young man in his twenties, skinny and nervous and eager to please. The reason I like George is because of his lie. He lies only on one subject. And as he came up to take the order from Mad Lizzy and myself, he lied, predictably enough:

Francis, how wonderful it is to see your lovely white hands again. I'm glad you've come today, now we have a chance to say goodbye to each other. I am leaving for the capital tomorrow. I shall have a new life. One coffee and a bowl of chips, instantly.

Whenever I visit this café I always, by some bizarre coincidence, arrive the day before George is to set off for the capital city. I do not think that George will ever get there. But I don't suppose George thinks that: every morning he gets up, smiles at his lean face in the mirror and says – Tomorrow, you naughty boy, you'll be out of here.

Why are you buying me chips, Francis Orme?
I have a commission for you.
I'm too busy.
There's money involved.
I can't spare the time. I'll miss something important. All for nothing.

We were sitting outside, Lizzy pecked at her chips and suddenly dropped one, pulled up her camera and shot off seven photographs. Three tourists had walked by, that was all. Lizzy's body bobbed and jerked. From her mouth:

Got 'em! Yes. Hee hee. Now I'll remember that for ever. I'll develop it tonight and put it in the book of photographs for this street. What a shot, what a shot!

And she patted herself on her bony thigh in congratulation.

This commission, Mad Lizzy . . .

Stuff it.

It's outside.

Where? Where? City outside? Or outside city outside?

City outside. Tearsham Park Gardens.

Who? Who? City person? Or outside city person?

A city dweller.

Money? Give it. Give it to Lizzy, please. Thank you. Good.

I gave Mad Lizzy half her fee and described to her Anna Tap and that she must take photographs of her face from every angle and be as inconspicuous as her twitching would allow her. Eleven o'clock, I said, in Tearsham Park. You'll know her, I said, because I'll be standing near her.

Got it. Got it. Off I go. Go. Bye-bye, blackbird.

And off went Mad Lizzy, busy in her body's peculiar eccentricities. Mad Lizzy was always rushing but she seemed never to get anywhere of any significance. Her days were spent trying to capture city life. But she was unable ever to pin the city down, it kept changing, the most extraordinary things kept happening and she couldn't be everywhere at the same time, she missed so much. She would need many people's lives to finish her work. But the worst of it was that Mad Lizzy was photographing the city in order to feel somehow a part of it, and the more she photographed the more distanced she felt. She was frequently seen dashing around the city streets trying to tire the city out, but she was only exhausting herself.

At eleven o'clock the next day, while we were walking with Mother in Tearsham Park, Anna was distracted by the clicks of a camera and the twitches of a photographer. I excused Lizzy, explaining that she was, in fact, quite demented, and Anna seemed content with that. I received the photographs three days later. They had a certain charm about them and described Anna's face satisfactorily from every angle and a good deal of Tearsham Park Gardens besides. I gave the photographs to William and he began his work.

Observatory Mansions and Tearsham Park.

It is now time to return to my father and mother. Mother had worked her way back to her gift-giving days. Father had positioned himself in flat four, where the old library used to be. All along we had been keenly aware that, as Mother rushed backwards through her Observatory Mansions experience and Father stumbled forwards through Tearsham Park time, there would come a moment when their two journeys would meet. It was not yet time for that to happen, but we knew that it must.

THE COMPLETE HISTORY OF
OBSERVATORY MANSIONS
AND
TEARSHAM PARK
as seen through the eyes of my mother and father
(retold with the assistance of Francis Orme and Anna Tap):
PART TWO.

Mother's gift-giving days.

At this stage of the history of Observatory Mansions Mother
was to be found wandering hurriedly around the empty and
few still-occupied flats of Observatory Mansions. Mother, the
gift giver, became obsessed with presents during the first
years of Observatory Mansions. Every new resident was given
a gift from Mother, and those residents who reacted to those
gifts and showed Mother some affection would sometimes
receive visits and gifts as often as twice a week. With each
gift, Mother explained, she gained an entrance into a flat. She
gave a book on ballerinas to the fat girl who went to ballet
classes, who lived with her meagre father and meagre mother
in flat one. She gave a yucca plant to the young couple who
lived in flat two. She gave a pouch of pipe tobacco to the
unsociable stamp collector who lived in flat three. She gave
a mirror to the three ugly brothers who lived in flat four.
She gave a radio to the lonely old woman who lived in flat
five. She gave nothing to flat six, she lived there. She gave a

protractor to the old man, whose back was bent so badly that everyone called him Mr Right Angle, who lived in flat seven. She gave nothing to flat eight, it would remain unoccupied until the bachelor arrived and she would give him herself. She gave the young, newly wed couple who lived in flat nine a pamphlet about how to write a will. She gave a ticket to the zoo to Mr Wilson, a man who loved anything from a certain strange land, who had left his home abroad to live in flat ten. She gave a set of four teacups to fat Eva who lived in flat eleven. She gave a set of four sherry glasses to old Elizabeth who was dying in flat twelve. She gave a set of four tumblers to Christa in flat thirteen. (Always four of each, so that she might be invited to drink with the mother and her two daughters.) She gave a book of common prayer to the defrocked vicar who lived in flat fourteen. She gave a bottle of vodka to the young and single man who lived in flat fifteen, he played the piano in a bar in the centre of the city. I think Mother found him attractive, until, that is, he started bringing a different woman friend home with him almost every week. She gave a book called the *Good Sex Guide* to Miss Claire Higg who lived in flat sixteen. In flat seventeen she gave a picture frame to the woman who had just lost her little daughter in a car accident just outside Observatory Mansions. Mother knocked on the door of flat eighteen and gave the retired army officer and his wife a plastic toy tank. Mother knocked on the door of flat nineteen but the shy resident, called Alec Magnitt (never to be seen without a calculator), did not come to his door, she left an abacus outside it. For flats twenty and twenty-one she gave, in that order, a canister of deodorant and a book called *Decorating with Style*. The resident of flat twenty-two was a portrait painter and she gave him a book on how to paint portraits. She gave Lord Pearson, of flat twenty-three, a book on modern architecture and she gave the resident of flat twenty-four, the furthest flat from the stairs, a report on how many people burned to death in houses without adequate fire escapes. Not all of the gifts contained my mother's unsubtle humour and not all of the residents understood that humour. She would return to flat six and say after she'd seen the insides of another flat – I'm living, I'm living!

Mostly the residents ignored Mother after her first visit, but some let her inside again. In this manner Mother made her friends. She was happy. She enjoyed giving, it occupied her days.

Tearsham Park.

Father is in unoccupied flat four. Father: Here, where I am standing there should be a red leather sofa. Over there should be one of two red leather armchairs. The other armchair should be just here by the shelves where the *History of the Ormes* are kept. This chair, I know for a fact, has been maliciously moved to my wife's dressing room.

Imagine that chair back here and place me, with the help of your thoughts, in it. I am reading. I am studying the *History of the Ormes*. Years have passed since the death of my eldest son. We have almost succeeded in forgetting him. The few possessions that he had accumulated in his short life, including his birth and death certificates, have been packed away inside a box. The box is in a locked trunk, out of sight in one of the attic rooms. All the photographs we ever took of him have been destroyed. All but one, that is. I kept one, I hide it from my wife inside a volume of the *History of the Ormes*, I use it as a bookmark. A little boy with a swollen face holding a mouthless teddy bear.

We have remembered to call our second son Francis now and not Thomas. Francis, Thomas but not Thomas, has not been told about his deceased brother. He is a slow child, who would never have learnt to talk were it not for the efforts of a woman from the village. And, more recently, his tutor Peter Bugg left the house, refusing to return.

Since the tutor left, Francis spends most of his days sitting on the bench by the war memorial in the centre of Tearsham Village. Francis sits on that bench staring into the school playground, watching children his own age. Two weeks ago, to stop this display of public loneliness, I bought him two mice. Pets to be his friends. My son named them Peter and Emma. I took a photograph of him holding the mice. He seemed very happy. All went well for a few days but then my son returned to his habit of observing the children in the playground. I asked him if he was no longer happy with his mice. He told me he was. Extremely happy, he said and went back to the bench by the war memorial. Whilst he was away I went in to the nursery, I could not at first find the mice anywhere. Their cage door was open and the cage was empty. I presumed that he had accidentally let the little creatures escape, but then I found them hidden away under papers in the nursery desk. They had been nailed to two neatly sawn blocks of wood. Underneath each unfortunate creature was written in ink, in extremely neat handwriting on a piece of white card, the names of the deceased. *Peter. Emma.*

Observatory Mansions.

Mother: Today my son has been missing all afternoon and some of the evening. The Porter told me that he had gone out many hours ago. I am standing in our flat, which is flat six, just by the dining table. My son has returned, he is sitting at the dining table. He says to us, to me and to the man who used to be his father who is sitting pathetically in his chair in the corner, that he has some wonderful news. My son tells us that he has found a job. I am pleased for him; I did not ever think that my child was employable. He is smiling an unusually large smile. I ask him what the job is. He tells me that he is going to work in a museum in the city centre, a waxwork hall of fame. He is to be employed to stand still and pretend to be made of wax. My son has surely been taken on to be laughed at: some hideous little employer thinks Francis will attract comments, be a talking point because of his white gloves. My son will be displayed surely as a curiosity, a freak. He sees that I am disappointed. He looks to the man who used to be my husband. Francis says that his father is smiling. I reply that that is of no consequence, the man often smiles and it means precisely nothing. I say to Francis that I will not allow him to take up this degrading employment. To my surprise he says, Yes, Mother, if that is what you wish. We do not talk of it for the rest of the day. The next morning Francis will go out early and begin his work at the wax house. When I see him in the evening I reprimand him and he says – Try and stop me.

I do not. I keep his employment secret from all the other residents. I am ashamed of it and of my son. Now I spend the days completely alone in flat six. I decide I need to make some friends. I decide to buy many gifts.

Tearsham Park.

Father, in flat four: A volume of the Orme history has been stolen. The volume that I was reading. The volume with the photograph inside it. It was stolen in the night. I ask the servants about it. They shake their heads in ignorance. I ask Francis. Francis says he does not know. I begin searching all over the house.

Observatory Mansions.

My mother, in the entrance hall: I am greeting the residents of Observatory Mansions. They come with luggage, with vans full of luggage. They are making new homes for themselves so close to mine. I am very happy. I shake hands with every one of them. I say, Welcome. Welcome to Observatory

Mansions. Francis is standing behind me. He looks very serious, he spends more time regarding the new residents' possessions than the new residents themselves. He does not shake hands with them.

Tearsham Park.

Father, in flat twenty-four: These are the attic rooms, for some reason they have been tidied. They were always as dusty as this but before they were crammed with objects. I have come here to look, unsuccessfully, for the missing book with the photograph inside it. I have found instead that something else is missing. This is what I see: this empty corner. There was a wooden box here, in it were kept various objects that no longer have a use in Tearsham Park. Among the objects was a teddy bear without a mouth.

Observatory Mansions.

In the largest room of flat six, my mother speaks: Today my husband was sitting in the park when he had a stroke. The doctor says he might recover, he can stay here or he can be put in a hospital. We must decide. My husband does not speak, he looks vaguely ahead. There is no expression on his face. Oh, why didn't he die?

I say yes to the doctor, take him away, put him in a hospital, get him out of my sight. Francis says no, absolutely not. Francis says: I shall look after Father. I say: Suit yourself, but don't expect me to help.

I consider my husband dead and myself a widow. I wear black. Sometimes I catch myself crying – I don't feel any sorrow, why should I be crying? I dry my eyes and scold myself.

Tearsham Park.

Father, in my mother's bedroom in flat six: The priest has been to visit us. Something dreadful has happened, something unspeakable; something unmentionable has been stolen. Not the toys, not the last volume of Orme history, not the photograph or the teddy bear, something else. Francis denies all knowledge but I know that he is guilty. We have searched the house and we have searched the grounds. We have not found what we are looking for. I have horsewhipped the child. He asks me: Don't you love me, Father? I tell him later, when I am a little calmed: I shall always love you, but never, I fear, shall I like you again.

What have I done to create such a monster of a child? How could he do such a thing? What made him steal such a thing? I try not to think about it. I daren't look at the child for fear I shall start thrashing him again. I daren't look at him, he disgusts me.

When we told my wife of Francis's crime she vomited. We took her up to her bed. But now she never leaves her room. She has stopped speaking altogether. She lies in her bed and does not move.

A short conversation between Anna Tap and myself.

Usually on our adventures with my parents, Anna Tap and I would freely be taken along by them, never questioning their stories and rarely discussing them afterwards. In truth, this was mainly because I stopped Anna whenever she started to talk, but on this one occasion, so shocked by my father's performance, at seeing him in tears, she continued to question me, even after I had begged her to be quiet.

What was stolen, Francis?
I don't know.

What did you steal?

Can you steal what no one wants?

Why were your mother and father so upset? What happened?

They are very nervous people, my parents.

Francis, what did you do?

I seem to have forgotten.

Francis.

I think I'd better go now, Mother's calling.

Observatory Mansions.

Mother, walking around the landings and in and out of flats: Tomorrow the painters will have finished their work. Look at the skirting boards, look at the window sills. Look at the new ceilings. Come with me into flat two, it used to be the drawing room, so much wasted space. Look up there: the ceiling's so smooth and white. There used to be hideous roses and leaves up there sculpted in plaster, they've all gone now. Isn't that better? Clean and white, ready and new, waiting for life.

Tearsham Park.

Father, in Mother's bedroom in flat six: The puppy arrived today. The puppy was my idea, she was bought on my initiative for my wife's recovery. The doctor thought her a good idea. I can see, in the near future, my wife walking her, feeding her, cuddling her. I see a new life for my wife inspired by the jolly waggling of a canine's tail.

As an idea it was one of my best. I hoped it would work. I hoped my wife would soon quit her bed and return to life. And so I have called the dog Hope. A collar was bought, the collar had *Hope* inscribed on to it. Hope wore *Hope* round her little neck and went into my wife's chamber and licked my wife's hand. But my wife did not stir, did not look down at the creature, ignored its yapping.

I have shut Hope in with her.

Observatory Mansions.

Mother, up and down Observatory Mansions stairs: The builders promise me that their work will be finished in two days' time. All the flats have doors and electricity and gas. It's so exciting! Tomorrow, the locksmiths are coming. They'll put locks on every flat door, ours as well. It's really happening! People are going to come here. Really. Really.

Tearsham Park.

The dog has become savage with unfulfilment. It has grown wild, it no longer trusts humans. Left, shut in, not alone but at the same time in complete solitude, it has become terrified. It has defecated all over the bedroom, clawed at the door, chewed the edges of my wife's sheets, ceased barking and even refused food. At the sight of an alert human it will either baulk with fear or approach and bite.

Today the creature was found gnawing at my wife's hands.

I have put the dog out, it will never return to my wife's bedroom.

Observatory Mansions.

Mother, up and down the landings: The electricians are everywhere planting wires of life. The plumbers are putting in radiators and connecting taps. Look, here's the lift shaft! And there's the lift! I just press this button and listen: it's alive!

The history of the dog Hope.

Father, back in his library, flat four: For a long time the dog was forgotten. But one day Hope returned to us, thin with the wild, matted hair of a tramp. She no longer bit, she no longer ran away, she sniffed and padded off uninterested. She seemed to be searching for something, but could not remember what. Everything she came across was rejected. She refused all the food we put out for her. She was trying to remember something, the effort of this search was killing her.

I thought at first that she was looking for my wife but later, after her death, I believed it was an abstract happiness that eluded her. She was in pursuit of a life that she had meant to have, the life of a dog loved by a family, walked, fed, protected and enjoyed. Hope was now an ugly dog, not in looks but in another way. An internal ugliness. Francis combed her, washed her, cut her thick, taut hairs but there always remained the unattractive and unmistakable pressure of desperate and all-embracing loneliness. We did not and could not love the dog Hope, the very idea of it sickened us.

After months of longing she finally gave up her search. She tried to die. She lay in remote parts of the park, slept, like my wife, and tried never to wake up. But somehow she would be found by Francis and force-fed in time and would grimly, listlessly continue her being. Until one day she began the last terrible stage of her appalling suffering.

Hope the dog scratched herself to death. It began with her collar. Hope's collar hung loose around her neck. She chewed it. The collar made of stiff leather had serrated edges which cut into her hair. The cuts, the worst being just behind her ears, were detected and the collar was taken off to allow the wounds to heal. But Hope could not stop her scratching once it had begun. With each new scrape from the sharp nails of her forepaws her injuries grew until the poor creature had no hair either side of her face, just vulnerably pink flesh. Her

hind legs duplicated the actions of the front legs and introduced many new glistening lesions across her ribs. Soon the
entire being, dog Hope, was involved solely in the business
of self-destruction in which every hedge, every coarse brick,
every corrugated tree bark was called upon for help. It seems
this unhappiness was infectious since somewhere during
Hope's inexhaustible preoccupation with self-laceration my
son Francis began to itch. For a short while this imitation,
performed in private, went unnoticed until he handed in for
washing a grubby white shirt which had a large brown dried
bloodstain around its collar. The doctor was informed and
Francis's neck was bandaged. But his scab was inspected every
night and we discovered that the bandage had been removed
during the course of the day and the wound irritated. Francis
began to itch in other places too, but his bath times were
observed by our house maid, and the decline in the child's
skin was reported. Francis was taken to the doctor, the dog
Hope was taken to a vet. The doctor prescribed plenty of air
and a white cream to be rubbed on the infections thrice daily,
the vet prescribed for Hope no bandages, since air was a great
healer, and a white cream to be rubbed on her wounds three
times a day. Every night Francis would come downstairs in
his pyjamas to bid me good-night. Francis would be made to
strip so that his recovery could be inspected. But he was not
getting any better. He particularly attacked any mole, birth-
mark or natural blemish on his skin, as if he were attempting
to remove his own identity. The dog continued to scrape
herself apart, Francis copied her with energetic reverence.

The vet prescribed antibiotics: a bottle of white pills which
were to be pushed into a piece of cheese and deviously fed
to the unsuspecting Hope. The doctor prescribed steroids
for Francis. The steroids made Francis sleepy, he spent the
majority of days in bed, but after pulling back the bedcovers,
the sheets were discovered to be speckled with blood.
Hope was given a lampshade collar that stretched from her

shoulders like a funnel. The collar frightened and panicked her but did not stop her scratching. The doctor gave Francis a pair of white cotton gloves. For a while, Francis, he said, everything you touch will be monitored, everything you touch will leave a trace on those gloves, so that we will know what you have been up to. He was instructed to wear them all day and all night, that they were to remain white, that if there was even a hint of blood on them, no matter what the excuse, he would be beaten. To prevent him from simply taking these gloves off, irritating his sores and then replacing them, two lengths of string were tied around his gloved wrists so tightly and with such an array of complicated knots that he could not possibly undo them. Together the dog, with her preposterous collar, and Francis, with his immaculate gloves, walked pathetically, in complete frustration, around the garden, always on the same route stipulated by me that circled the house but was not so wide as to stretch up to the numerous outhouses and stable buildings where the unfortunate duo could perambulate unseen. But once these hours were ended by the sounding of a handbell, Francis dismissed himself from Hope and ventured to the upper landings of the house where he could, in all privacy, scrape himself against the back of a chair, the corner of a bookcase or with the aid of a stiff hairbrush.

On the day of his thirteenth birthday all scratching ceased entirely. Just as Francis was leaning on tiptoes over his birthday cake to blow out the candles the servants' bell rang. Standing in the pantry corridor was a farmhand holding a newspaper parcel in which lay the wretched and bloody dog Hope. She had somehow wandered into one of the chicken runs to scratch herself against the wire fencing and the chickens, excited by the sight and smell of blood, had pecked her quite to death.

Francis, complete with a cortège consisting of maids, cook, the housekeeper and myself, buried her by the kitchen garden.

Francis took the old, chewed collar and the new lampshade collar and kept them in the nursery. Without his inspiration he stopped his itching. The string was cut off and he was invited to remove his gloves. He refused. He said that the white gloves had taught him too much about life for that. He said Hope's death had been ugly and messy, he said the gloves had taught him to keep his distance from suffering. And also, he believed the gloves made him look smart. He found the clean white cotton comforting. He said he liked to monitor everything he touched, it would make him more cautious in the future.

In this way my son began his habit of wearing gloves. I found the following article in the nursery:

The Law of White Gloves.

1. White cotton gloves are your own skin, so treat them as you would your own. If they get torn it is as if you have been cut open.

2. The moment a glove, or a pair of gloves, are dirtied then it is as if they were a pair of hands that have been scarred for life. They can never be clean again.

3. The washing of gloves is not permissible.

4. The utmost care must be made never to dirty the gloves. However, we are quite prepared to accept that accidents do happen, but ... (see 5)

5. The loss of a pair of gloves is a profound misdeed. When gloves are lost (loss = dirtied or scratched) the pain undergone in the loss is felt the same as if the careless wearer had chopped off his own hands (which is, in fact, exactly what he has done).

6. Dead gloves should then be put quietly to rest as a good, loyal friend who has excelled in service and has now earned his peace. It is forbidden to walk around with dirty gloves.

7. Dead gloves cannot function. The hands underneath them will never be able to pick up, touch or move at all. They are dead.

8. Dead gloves should immediately be changed for live, new ones.

9. When changing gloves it is not permissible to look at your own naked, former hands in their ugly state. Only when they are wearing, proudly, their new white skin is looking again permissible.

10. It is forbidden to let any person see your naked hands.

Observatory Mansions.

Mother, in the entrance hall: This used to have old oil portraits of dead Orme people all over it. Now look: a blue and white wallpapered wall. The chequered marble floor has been pulled up and sold, they've put in new floorboards and they're going to place blue carpet over them. Newness is everywhere!

Tearsham Park.

Father, in Mother's bedroom in flat six: Without fail, I told my wife my daily news as she sat absent from us, in her bed. Eyes closed. Lying still.

Today, though, I'm sitting by her bed and I tell her that I've had to sell some Orme land. Nothing else could be done. There are increasingly less farmhands. All the young are being encouraged to work in the city, where they are paid higher wages, they say there's nothing in the country for them any more. They resent their parents and their old ways, they want to see more than fields and early mornings. The estate needs money, I don't know how it could have got so bad. There's so much repair work to be done, and our machinery is terribly out of date. And there are rumours I heard from one farmhand that it is all my fault, that I am incapable of running a farm. I do not know how it happened, but it has; somehow we are in debt.

I can't bear to look at the portraits. The people who bought the land promised me that they would not build on it. But they did not sign on that issue. They said, We'll call it a gentleman's agreement. I feel ashamed. I sit by my wife holding her hand and say – Alice, my darling, I've had to sell some land.

When I finish speaking I see my wife's eyes flick open as if my sentence were the key to her lock.

I never go into the hall any more, I cannot bear to look at the portraits. I always leave by one of the side doors, through the kitchen or the pantry.

Observatory Mansions.

Mother, in the ruined observatory: My husband has been sheltering from the builders in here. He complains about the perpetual noise of the workmen. He yells down at them to turn off their radios and they laugh at him and raise the volume. He whispers: I have known the feel and the scent of grass. He looks over the parapet muttering: Oak, sycamore, ash, beech.

Tearsham Park.

Father, in flat one, formerly one part of the drawing room: My wife spends her time reading books about foreign climates. Sell all the land, she tells me, sell everything, Francis, and we can start again. She says: I can't live here! Everything is suffocating me! You. Our son. Everything looks so old! It's making me old. Look at me, I'm wrinkling already! Sell everything before it turns me into an old hag. Send me on holiday. Divorce me. Murder me!

My wife finds my son, naked, playing with my mother's porcelain dolls. She confiscates the dolls. Days later she talks to him, she orders him to take off his gloves. My son runs away and will not speak to her again for many months. When my son asks me to buy him new gloves, I look at him sadly and nod. I am a weak man. I send the housemaid into the city with him to buy them. I will do anything to get the boy away from me.

Today Francis has found a till receipt on the driveway. It is a warning from the city. It says: I am coming.

Observatory Mansions.

Mother, in the entrance hall: Today our porter arrived. He has settled into his basement flat and wears his uniform proudly. There are no residents here yet, save me, my husband and my son, but already he is prepared for his work. He holds a great bunch of keys. What is your name? I ask him. He says: Porter. Call me Porter.

Tearsham Park.

Father, looking through the window of flat three: Today our servants left. I watched them leave from this window. They walked away and did not look back. They blame me. I know they blame me. They would not even say goodbye.

My wife dismissed them all. She has had lawyers around and lawyers' doctors too. She says I'm incapable of looking after anything. She says she should be allowed to take charge. The lawyers interviewed me. I started crying. The lawyers watched as my wife pulled me into the hall of Tearsham Park where the portraits are hung. I ran from the place. The lawyers called in their doctors. The doctors asked me such stupid questions that I refused to answer them and started crying. The doctors tugged me into the hall. I started screaming. The doctors went away. The lawyers went away. My wife has taken charge of my bank books.

Observatory Mansions.

Mother, restless in the entrance hall: The builders say their work will take them another six months. When I tell them about my bedroom, they say that they've been given orders not to change that room, that it's to stay the same. The room remains a bedroom on their plans, they say, best to leave it as it is. But I want it changed, I scream! It has to be different. No, it's not changing they say, it's staying the same, exactly the same. Even this hideous crimson wallpaper is going to stay.

Mother and her wallpaper dance.

Here my mother began clawing at the wallpaper, making fresh wounds next to those old scars where she had ripped the wallpaper for exactly the same reason years ago. As before, only a little yielded and it cut into the skin beneath her nails. Then she spat at the walls and kicked them, but finally she slumped to the floor. I knew she would do this, I had seen it before, it surprised me then. But I was ready the second time, and when Mother had stopped moving I gave her a handkerchief, which I had taken out of my drawer for her exclusive use, and went in search of Father.

Tearsham Park.

Father, in flat four: I have grown into the habit of looking out of the window with a pair of field binoculars before my

235

eyes. I am watching the trees: Oak, sycamore, ash, beech, poplar, fir, yew, lime.

Upstairs, from a window in the attic, I can see the city. It is closer now. Tearsham, just beyond the parkland, is more of a town than a village.

Observatory Mansions.

Mother rushed out of Observatory Mansions and returned with a plastic shopping bag full of boxes of teabags and jars of coffee. All afternoon Mother made mugs of tea and coffee for her imagined workmen and ran around the abandoned flats depositing them in front of plasterboard walls, by bricked-up fireplaces, in the basement by the new boiler, by the lift shaft. She took away all the mugs from our flat and all of Claire Higg's too. She kept the kettle boiling all day. At night we fetched the mugs and emptied the cold, undrunk teas and coffees down the sink.

Mother, just before she went to sleep: They've put a door next to my old dressing room and labelled it six. But they still haven't changed my bedroom, though I do keep reminding them.

Tearsham Park.

Father, looking out from a window of flat four: Oak, sycamore, ash, beech . . . the rest have gone.

Observatory Mansions.

Mother, in the entrance hall: I dance to the builders' music from their radios, sometimes they dance with me. They smoke roll-up cigarettes. They have stored sheets and sheets of plasterboard and chipboard in the cellar. They say that they will divide up the rooms of Tearsham Park with them. They say ideally the divisions should be made with brick, but their orders were to use board, they say boards don't last that long, they can be dislodged fairly easily, but they're much cheaper.

They've pulled out my old round enamel bath and halved the room. Half will be a much smaller bathroom, the other half will be a small bedroom. They're making my dressing room into a kitchen and sitting room. It's all so new. They've only to change my bedroom now.

Tearsham Park.

Father, through a window of flat four: Oak.

Observatory Mansions.

Mother, in the entrance hall: My husband says he can hear the house screaming. I tell him that it's the workmen sawing and drilling but he won't believe me. They have begun knocking the outhouses and stable blocks down. How easily they fall, it's as if that's all they've ever been longing to do.

Tearsham Park.

Father, in the observatory: I am happy here. I have been allowed to spend much money and I am happy. My wife says that if we keep spending money, something ultimately will happen to us. I try not to think of it. Not up here, not here in the observatory. Not while I'm with my telescope. At night I watch the stars and the planets, in the day I sleep or consult my astrological charts. In this way I can keep sane. In this way I only look upwards. I dare not look down. Beneath me they are building on old Ormeland. Beneath me they are pouring asphalt on to the grass.

Observatory Mansions.

Mother, in the entrance hall: Here are the architectural surveyors. Proud and stout! I have arranged that we will stay in the house, the new house – how wonderful that sounds. We will live in that part that smells least of the Orme history, by which I mean, of course, that part which I have been living in, my apartment. A smaller bedroom will be made for little Francis. My husband asks me where he is to sleep. When I tell him that, of course, he will sleep with me, he looks horrified and even starts to cry.

Tearsham Park.

Father, in his observatory: Today when I came up here, I saw that they had taken my telescope away.

Father, descending the stairs: The rooms of Tearsham Park are bare. There are only two beds left in the house. All else is gone. They've gutted my house. All my family's collections are out on the single strip of grassland left.

Father, sitting on a bench in Tearsham Park Gardens: All around are my family's objects. I look about me. There is my telescope! There are oil paintings too: *the portraits of my ancestors!* They are crying! There is porcelain and pottery. There are mahogany chests and rosewood tables. There are books by the metre: the complete chronicles (lacking but one volume) of the Orme family. There are mirrors and tapestries. There are my mother's dolls and my father's shotguns. The marquetry tables and the dressers, the kitchen pots and saucepans, garden furniture, the sundial. Even my clothes are here. *There are my pyjamas!*

Everything here has a little tag tied on to it. They each say lot and then a number. Over there stands a man behind a desk. He has a wooden hammer. He calls out numbers. People nod at him. There are people everywhere. People and objects. The people are buying the objects.

I see my field binoculars on a table with the number 386 by it, I pick them up. When nobody is looking I slip them into my coat. Surely I cannot be arrested for stealing my own binoculars.

I sit in one of the red leather armchairs that have been pulled from the library. I rip its tag off. I cover the chair's arms with my coat and jacket, so that no one can see it, so that no one will buy it.

It can't all be true, I think, surely it's not true. The man with the hammer keeps calling out, selling history. Sometimes I listen, sometimes I hum to myself so I won't hear.

Lot 1945   An exceedingly grand pair of twenty-two-inch bronze vases.

Lot 1956   A family portrait in oils of a Cavalier, impeccably framed.

Lot 2432   A mahogany kneehole leather-top writing table with nine drawers and extra slope.

Lot 2978   A handsome set of ivory chessmen in a carved ebony box and two chessboards.

Lot 3671   A blue and white breakfast service, one hundred and four pieces.

Lot 4648   A patent steam bath with gas apparatus.

Lot 6043   Two paraffin lamps, an earthenware foot warmer, pair of lamp scissors and brushes.

Lot 6743   A very valuable astronomical clock by Pratt.

Lot 7021   A fine telescope fashioned by H. Muncie, six foot with five inch diameter.

Lot 7347   1. Lalandes's catalogue of stars and total solar eclipses.
2. Philps's Practical astronomy.

Lot 7986   A fine morocco-bound edition of *The World of Comets* by Guillemin.

Finally, they reach the last item:

Lot 8029   Eight cacti and one camellia.

The people begin to leave. Oh, what a long time they take about leaving, finally only hurried by the disappearing sun. I am suddenly aware of my wife leaning over me, she says: We were out of money, Francis, we have had to sell everything, the banks demanded it. We have just enough money for a few rooms somewhere. We shan't be going so very far. I've sorted everything out. We will start afresh, Francis, we will begin again.

But I don't want to begin again.

Everything is sold except for the red leather armchair I am sitting in and the field binoculars that I have hidden in my coat. Someone has bought my pyjamas. *What am I going to wear tonight?*

I am left alone sitting on my armchair in what remains of the parkland. The people have left their rubbish on the grass. My son comes up to me and says: Mother is dancing naked around the house.

Observatory Mansions.

Mother, standing outside Observatory Mansions: I am holding the hand of my husband. This is a very sacred moment. Before us, raised from the ground on two metal posts, is a large marble sign, at the moment covered by a sheet. I look at my husband. My husband does not understand. I triumphantly pull the sheet away and I see . . .

Tearsham Park becomes Observatory Mansions.

Father, walking out of the entrance hall: My wife is very excited, she is dragging me outside our empty house. Before us, raised from the ground on two metal posts, is some sort of sign that has been inexplicably planted outside the main door. My wife is looking at me. I do not understand. My wife pulls away the sheet covering it and I see ...

OBSERVATORY MANSIONS
Spacious Apartments of Quality Design

My mother and father.

Standing before the polluted exterior of Observatory Mansions my old parents stared, together for once, at the name of our home badly chiselled on fake marble, chipped and very dirty. After they had looked at the sign, they looked at each other. Finally they spoke, raising their voices above the circling traffic:

You!
You?
Francis?
Alice?
Is that really you, Francis?
Alice? Alice!
I thought you were dead.
I lost sight of you.
My wife!
My husband!
Where have you been?
Observatory Mansions, flat six. First floor.
I didn't know where to look for you.
And you, where have you been?
Inside Tearsham Park, of course.
No, Francis, that building doesn't exist any more.
Where's it gone, Alice?
It's dead, Francis.

There was a long pause.

Is it really dead?
Quite dead, Francis.
I was born there, you know.
We must move on.

Another long pause. Father was trying to understand, trying to link up facts in his head.

Someone's taken the telescope from the observatory.
Don't worry, no one's touched the stars.
I am glad.

There was another long pause, though my mother's last sentence cheered my father a little he still looked worried. He was mumbling to himself. At last he spoke again.

Alice?
Yes, Francis.
Alice? Alice! *ALICE!*
Sssh, Francis, what's the matter?
Alice. Alice, if I haven't been in Tearsham Park where have I been?
I seem to remember now that you were in the room next door to me. You were so quiet, I thought you were dead.

Yet another pause. My father looked for a long time at the shape of the exterior of Observatory Mansions. In puzzlement he read the graffiti – *And even you can find love* and, later on, *Enjoy the taste* – but when he stared at the columns of the entrance portico his face changed, and when he next spoke he seemed to hint at some knowledge which had before evaded him:

I have been very ill, haven't I?
You're well now, Francis.
I feel a little cold.
Then let's step in, Francis.
Is it cold, Alice?

No, Francis, it's summer. It's hot in the summer.
Oh good, it's just I can't feel the temperature any more.

My mother slowly, carefully, gently took my father back up the stairs of Observatory Mansions, pausing every second or third step, into flat six. She took him into the largest room and sat him down in a capacious red leather armchair.

Have a little sleep, Francis. You'll feel better.
Just a little nap, Alice. It's been rather a tiring journey.

Father closed his eyes.

V

SAINT LUCY'S DAY

Demolition experts.

One autumn day the demolition experts returned to us. My mother saw them through the park fencing, they were making notes in their files. When Mother came back from her walk (after having eaten her supper, visited her friend Claire Higg, watched some television with Claire Higg, returned to her own flat, dressed in her night attire) she said, with a yawn: I saw the demolition experts back again. Anna Tap, who was in flat six with us, asked who they were. We answered that we didn't really know, that they never really seemed to do anything except make notes in their files every half year or so. They were quite peaceful people, these demolition experts, we had decided. But Anna Tap said:

Has it never occurred to you to ask them what they are doing here?

No. It had not.

Father remembered – 1.

We buried Father in the Orme chapel of Tearsham Church. The priest came and unlocked the chapel gate. Some days before, I had seen Mother up earlier than was usual for her and well dressed, walking out of Observatory Mansions clutching some silver: candlesticks, cutlery and a salver. These were from Tearsham Park, I remembered them from when I was a child. How was it that they hadn't been sold in the auction? Where had they been kept all these years? I went into Mother's bedroom, her bed was stripped and her mattress had been ripped open – Mother had used that most well known of hiding places to keep the silver away from me: she had lain on top of it for such a long time, in a place she knew I wouldn't consider looking. With the money from the silver, with all that was left of Tearsham Park, Mother bought a much more beautiful box for Father than the one they had put Peter Bugg in.

When we entered the Orme chapel I was frightened that the priest might have the wrong tomb lid lifted, that the tunnel passageway would suddenly be revealed, that my exhibition would be discovered. But the priest selected the right tomb for Father, which was also where his parents and grandparents were kept. There were other stone boxes of course, with all the other dead Ormes inside them, all containing quality goods.

Mother, Anna Tap and I were present. No one, save the priest, spoke. Mother was wearing black again. Claire Higg had decided to stay at home, the journey to the church was too long for her, she said, I really am too busy. She was forgiven, she had never met Father, to her he was a preposterous fiction.

As they pulled off the lid from the great, lead-lined stone bin to dispose of dead Father, I understood that God collects us all. As they lowered Father into the darkness, I realized that there is absolutely no other option, we have to die with God, we are all offered up to him in the end. Whether good or bad, whether hell or heaven bound, or just left there to rot, our heavy, lifeless bodies are pushed under the sign of the cross. It's just another type of skip. God, refuse collector.

Father remembered – 2.

For weeks after Father died I kept seeing him from behind, walking along the city streets. But when I approached him – shouting, *Father! Father!* – it was not Father who turned around but some unfamiliar old man.

I talked of Father. I talked of nothing else. My father and the stars. My father between blood cells. My father as tall as trees. My mother at the same time spoke nothing of Father, she talked only of the days of the week and of shifts in the weather, she watched television with Claire Higg; she busied her days with non-father-thinking devices.

I took the red leather armchair from the largest room in flat six. I heaved it down the stairs. I dragged it outside on to the concrete enclosure. I bought a can of petrol, poured it over the chair and set light to it. The chair moaned and crackled and flattened itself out until no one could sit in it ever again.

Father remembered – 3.

For some time Father's false teeth remained submerged in a glass of water on the kitchen table in flat six. We sometimes caught each other looking at those teeth, Anna Tap, Mother and I. When we ate we found it hard not to look at them, smiling at us in their glass of water. They robbed us of our appetites.

In the end, at night whilst everyone else slept, I took them away (lot 994).

Father remembered – 4.

Without Father there, the world was suddenly unconfident; it could not understand what to do without Father's inner strength to guide it. The world became brittle. After Father died we moved with caution, we felt it inconceivable that life would be allowed to carry on as if nothing had happened, we expected phenomena of nature – eclipses, hurricanes, earthquakes. We felt cheated when they didn't come. We wanted the world to mark Father's death with catastrophe. We were sure that something would match the sorrow of our bleeding hearts: the sun was bound to come tumbling down today or tomorrow. But nothing happened.

Soon we realized what it was that Father's death meant to us: it meant that death was possible. Once we had realized that we started shivering and we walked stooped over with short strides. Only *Father's* death had taught us this, had taught us such profound sadness and anger and fear. All the deaths that had gone before, even way back to the first dead man, were only try-outs, dry runs for Father's death. They seemed somehow effortless. Who cried for those dead people, after all?

But Mother's indifference to Father's death soon helped me to realize that no one was suffering as much as I was, and that when I thought *we* I really meant *I*.

Father remembered – 5.

I visited the observatory at night. With Father there we had been able to conjure the glass back on the dome; we had looked through his field binoculars and imagined ourselves seated behind his giant telescope. But without him the observatory faded: the metal dome-shaped frame was rusty again, pigeons' shit lay everywhere, there was a dead pigeon by the entrance.

Up in the observatory with Anna Tap, I pointed out the stars and planets. Though Anna no longer had any duties to perform for my parents she would often come and smoke in flat six and we would go for short walks together. I think we were becoming friends. I talked to her all about Father business.

One night she started to cry. Poor Anna had no Father, none that she knew of. But that was not why she was crying. Francis, she said, can you see me? Do you notice me at all? I could see her, I said, she was sitting with me, up in the observatory, looking at the stars. She said that that was not what she was talking about. My thoughts, I told her, were all Father full at the moment. She knew that, she said, because all I had talked about for weeks now was Father. Wouldn't it be better if I made room for someone else, if I let someone else in. Perhaps there was someone who wanted to get in, Francis, she said. Consider who that might be, she said, and left.

Father remembered – 6.

When I returned that night to flat six I heard noises coming from my mother's bedroom. The gnashing of teeth. My father's teeth. I opened the door, excited, wondering if perhaps I might find Father inside Mother's room, perhaps he hadn't died after all. Mother was asleep. On her bedside table, next to the night lamp was a dictaphone playing the sounds of Father's teeth.

This became a habit of Mother's. When she got into bed she turned on the dictaphone, only with the sound of Father's teeth would she be able to sleep.

Anna Days.

Then came a brief and happy time called Anna Days. In Anna Days, all shining with autumn sun, I spent my time with Anna. I did not talk about Father. Anna said that I could, just not all the time. I thought it safer not to, at all. Anna seemed, I thought, very happy. She laughed at some of the things that I said (but only when I wasn't trying too hard to make her laugh). Sometimes she would close her eyes and say – I can feel the sun on my face.

That was Anna when she was with me that autumn. So, why, when I went alone to the park, did the bathroom scalesman always say:

The girl is getting thinner.

I was Anna's friend. We did not speak of friendship in definite terms, but surely that was unnecessary. We walked into the centre of the city sometimes. On these walks she said: So much of the city is kept from us. We only know those parts where we live or have friends or go to work. We know our routes, our little paths, our certain streets, but that is all we know. I haven't been here before. If I hadn't come on these walks with you, I would never have seen this or this or that. I would never have known it existed. It's not part of my life. I don't know anyone who lives or works here. But at least I have seen it, Francis.

I visited the church with her and watched her stroke the eyes and face of Saint Lucy. She told me that when the pain begins in her eyes, when her eyes start to harden, then surely Saint Lucy's eyes would become soft. All this time we spent together, so why, whenever I went alone to the park did the bathroom scalesman always say:

The girl is getting thinner.

She had long stopped going for walks with the Porter, considering my company preferable. And the Porter, I noticed, had begun to tidy more fiercely, and he would hiss at me whenever I came near.

Anna would ask me to tell her everything about myself and when I refused she would look away. She would ask me what I kept in the cellar. I would not tell her, but she kept asking all the same, she would not let the subject drop. One day, furious with her repeated questions, I told her: Love,

Anna, love is kept in the cellar, nine hundred and ninety-five objects of love all nicely wrapped up. Let me see them, Francis. No. No, I can't do that.

She asked me to take my gloves off. No, never, I can't do that.

Soon she stopped coming for walks but would still sit with us in the largest room of flat six. By then we did not talk, there was suddenly little left for us to say. I looked at my gloves or at the floor but she looked at me all the time. And whenever I went to the park on my own the bathroom scalesman always said:

The girl is getting thinner.

I knew what was happening to her but couldn't see how to stop it: she was becoming sad like the rest of us.

One afternoon while we sat together in flat six, Anna asked me:

Will you hold my hand, Francis?

But I didn't hold hands, it was understood. Then she said:

Would you like to kiss me, Francis?

I had not been expecting that. And my heart bumped-bumped out of joy. So why was it, why, after I heard a question that made me jump inside, that made a little movement in my inner inner, why was it, why, when I so loved that question, why was it that I replied:

I think I'd better go now.

Autumn leads to winter.

The winter months were approaching. I was known to love wintertime. People wore gloves in wintertime. Not white cotton gloves for sure. In wintertime the children wore bright colourful gloves with faces sewn on to each finger or they wore mittens. In wintertime the men and women put on woollen gloves: black, red, green, blue and pink. Or leather gloves with soft wool or silk on the insides. Yes, I loved this wintertime glove mania; it made me feel closer to humanity.

The love dress of Anna Tap.

The days became less like Anna days and more like Francis days until they were entirely Francis days and made up of those various well-known time-passers which have already been indicated. True, Anna did often visit us in flat six but she had grown timid in my company and often did not look at me when she spoke. Once she left a note, slipped under the door of my bedroom, which I was unable to comprehend, it said:

If not now, then when?

She would come and sit with us bringing with her one of her blue dresses, a needle and some black cotton. At first I thought she was mending some holes but gradually I began to understand that Anna was stitching words into the dress.

The first word she wrote on it was Peter. The second word she wrote was loved. The third word she wrote was Claire. Anna was straining the light out of her eyes.

As weeks passed she wrote other sentences with black cotton on her dress:

> Claire loved Alec.
> Alec loved Claire.
> The Porter loved Claire.
> Mrs Orme loved a bachelor.
> Mr Orme loved Mrs Orme.

This is my love dress, Francis, she told me. I am writing out sentences of love, so that I shall never forget them. So that if I go blind I will be able to read the words by touch, even when I wear them.

On Francis and lovers – 1.

It is well known that lovers hold hands. It is well known that I wear gloves. It is well known that I never touch anything that could be dirty (human flesh being but one example). I could not then hold hands with my lover. Therefore I have no lover.

Inside a cardboard box.

One day a large cardboard box was delivered to Observatory Mansions by a courier. The box said: *Property of Francis Orme*. The Porter brought it up to flat six. Within minutes everybody in Observatory Mansions knew of its existence. Mother saw the Porter delivering it, she immediately rushed to tell Claire Higg and Anna Tap. But I took the box to my bedroom and closed the door behind me, away from everyone else. Claire, her thoughts clouded by the television she watched, thought it might be money inside the box or perhaps even a severed head, but was too busy to leave her flat to find out. Mother and Anna knocked on my bedroom door. Let us in, Francis, what's in the box? Go away, Anna. Go away, Mother. Leave me alone.

Inside the box were many chips of polystyrene for protection and, as my gloved hands felt cautiously for more, I discovered hair, and even a face, and a neck, and a pair of shoulders. A bust made of wax. And when I looked at the face for the first time its accuracy made me frightened. I stared at her, she didn't frown or look away.

There was a postcard in the box, a photograph of the wax model of Our Founder, on its reverse was written:

> Francis,
> Enclosed, the head of your choosing.
> I do not advise kissing wax,
> flesh is much softer.
> William

It was such a good likeness. Save one thing. The eyes. The eyes were ordinary, healthy, beautiful green eyes. William had perfected Anna.

I heard Anna, the real Anna, outside my room, talking to Mother in the kitchen, otherwise I would have been sure that I had her head in with me. It was difficult at first to believe that she could have two such similar heads and that one of them was entirely mine. I touched it. I touched the eyes, I felt the hair, I kissed the lips. I learnt the face. Here was Anna, I could touch her as I wanted to touch her. I could stroke her hair. Anna would never have let me touch her like that, and even if she did I might run the risk of dirtying my gloves. Now I could touch her and be sure that my gloves would remain unharmed.

The bust never complained, I pretended it quite liked my attentions. I fooled myself that it was really Anna I touched, that my cotton fingers were really feeling her skin. But what was it that the wax head really meant? That I need never feel lonely again.

I told Mother and Anna that the delivery was a new glove box. They seemed to believe me, though they could not understand why I spent so much more time in my bedroom than before.

I found it hard to leave that head alone.

Even for a moment.

To save the exhibition.

But I was unable to stop thinking of the real Anna. The wax bust only increased my thoughts of her. Whenever I was out of my room I would be with the genuine Anna Tap, and I would look at her lips or her ears or her hair and I would yearn to touch them, I would long to be back in my room with the wax bust.

Francis, I said to myself, you must think quickly for the exhibition is suffering. Francis, I said to myself, with use of that bust you must think of Anna as a child's toy or as a new object. And saving yourself all the pain of human contact, and having the object of love (the wax bust) without the irritating messiness of love (Anna Tap), love the object, ignore the person. Busy yourself with it for as long as it takes, soon you will become bored. Then you'll no longer want it near you. And it slowly began to work: I began to convince myself that I was tiring of both the wax and the flesh Anna Tap.

One night.

One night Anna came in to us a little tearful and a little more needful of company than usual. She stood by the dining table waiting for Mother or me to ask her to sit down with us and offer her a coffee. Neither of us did. Mother had fallen asleep and I let Anna hover there, passing her weight from one foot to the other, looking more and more desperate. Until finally she spoke:

I have been staring at the bottle marked dihydrocodeine tartrate. Today I felt some new pain in my eyes, when I held the bottle of pills I felt safer. I shouldn't, I know. I should trust in Lucy. But when I put the bottle down I felt the pain coming back. It's only Lucy testing me, it's only Lucy wanting me to trust her, isn't it?

Isn't it time you left Observatory Mansions?

Francis?

Hasn't it gone on long enough? Don't you feel we've grown tired of you now?

I'm waiting for Saint Lucy's day.

Why? Nothing will happen.

It will, you'll see.

I don't think so. You're going blind, you'll be blind soon. Then what?

I shan't go blind.

Don't expect us to look after you. Oh no, we won't have it. Perhaps you'd better leave here now, get into a home or something where you can be properly looked after.

I shan't go blind.

I'm only thinking of you. You *should* leave. As soon as possible. I could call a taxi now. I could do that for you.

You can pick up a leaf and point it to the sun. Then you see everything about that leaf, everything that's going on inside, all the veins within, nothing is hidden. Anna looked a little like that after I had spoken to her that night. Her face showed such an anxious expression that I thought I could read by it everything that went on in her brain and in her body: I could see how ill she was, how easy to lift up or to throw away.

258

On Francis and lovers – 2.

Soon Anna stopped talking when she came to visit us and just sat with her love dress, she was stitching a new sentence on to the dress, on the place where her bottom would be when she wore it, on the backside of her dress:

Francis loves no one.

12th December.

On the twelfth of December, a date so close to Christmas that many people's thoughts are only full of the forthcoming holiday, a strange incident occurred. The day began with Anna entering flat six to say: Tomorrow, Francis, is Saint Lucy's day. Tomorrow, I'll be able to see properly again, Francis, you'll see.

In the evening Anna discovered her wax head. I was out. I was licking my lower lip down in the tunnel in the cellar. Anna was with my mother but Mother had fallen asleep. Anna walked around flat six and let herself into my bedroom. She found the wax bust. She went back into the kitchen and fetched a knife. She scarred the face of the wax head. She smashed the eyes, then she went to her flat and locked the door.

She would not let me see her, she would not even talk to me behind her door. So I decided that the next day, the anticipated December the thirteenth, I would steal the wooden eyes of Saint Lucy and place them inside the wax head.

Saint Lucy's day.

It was obvious from looking out of the window on Saint Lucy's morning that it was a day in which nothing wonderful would happen. The winter weather made it feel heavy. It was perhaps a day for going immediately back to bed and falling asleep again and not waking up until December the fourteenth. But for those who had to get up and venture out, it was another unpleasant winter day, cold and pessimistic.

I was reminded of my plan the moment I woke and saw from my bed the vandalized wax head, with scars worked into its wax flesh, with raw holes for eyes, where I was sure sight had once been. As soon as I was dressed I walked, neither quickly nor slowly, to Tearsham Church – I was convinced of the fairness of my plan, and the fairness gave me an even, confident pace for my journey. If people had seen me on that particular morning as I moved from Observatory Mansions to Tearsham Church, I feel convinced that they would have thought of me as some kind of official, someone whose every move was backed by laws and declarations, such was my business-like gait. If people had seen me they would be sure to have stepped out of my way, certain that the path I took was far more mine than theirs and that they were trespassing. However, I cannot recall anyone on my route to the church and though it is conceivable that I did pass people, or that people even moved out of my way, they made no impression on me; my mind was too focused on the wooden eyes of Saint Lucy.

When I stepped into the church I saw immediately that the dust had recently been disturbed. But I quickly convinced myself that it was I who had moved the dust by opening the church door. Besides, I couldn't see anyone in the church. But once, as I stepped towards the wooden altarpiece, I thought I heard a faint hissing.

The saints themselves stood, reassuringly enough, just as they had always stood, and I was encouraged and calmed by their dignified poses. It was an uncomplicated task that I had to perform: I must simply remove the wooden eyes from Saint Lucy's plate and then be gone. I would disturb the church no longer than was necessary. But it must be remembered that I had a right to be there, I had a right to those eyes. My eyes, the glass eyes inside the wax head, had been destroyed – it was only fair that the wooden ones should become mine. In compensation. Surely the church could understand that.

Saint Lucy stood in her usual position beside her fellow saints and martyrs, the Virgin and her Child. Her right hand, as was to be expected, held a wooden plate. The plate, contrary to all expectations, was empty. There were two small scars where objects had once been glued, but there was no pair of wooden eyes.

Of course the great injustice of this should have made me scream. It perhaps should have convinced me to drag the wooden woman from the church by her golden hair and take her apart, shatter her against a wall. But scarcely had I opened my mouth to launch my frustration when I noticed, lying on one of the pews, the body of a young woman wrapped up in a blue dress and a black coat. Gently breathing Anna Tap. With her hands clenched tight at her side, surely holding my eye treasure, one eye to each hand. I quietly moved along the pew until I was beside her. I crouched down until my head was at the level of her hands. Her hands were dirty, smudged with dust. I put my father's leather gloves over my white cotton skin, blankets of protection, and began to unpeel Anna's right hand. She held on tight, I pulled at her fingers harder. She opened her eyes, ugly, sore eyes, spheres that shone with pain, with eyelids torn and ruddy from scratching. She had been attempting to remove her pain by scraping at it. How much did it hurt, Anna Tap? Did you cry? Did you scream?

As I worked, stooped over her, busy about my compensation business, she continued to stare at me, but I could not at first be sure if those terrible eyes were seeing anything at all. Then she quietly spoke.

Why won't the wooden eyes become soft, Francis?

I continued my work at her fingers.

If my eyes are going hard then why won't the wooden ones becomes soft?
I shan't be here long.
They should be soft.
Just give them to me and I'll be gone.
I can't stop the hurting.
Take a pill.
I've taken one.
Then you'll feel better soon.
I've been sick.
Then take another pill.
I didn't know it would hurt so much. It made me sick.
Take another pill.
They're in my pocket.

I reached into her coat pocket, found a pill. I asked her to open up a hand so I could put the pill there, but she sat up and opened her mouth instead. I dropped it in, the pill fell from my hand into her mouth, there was no connection between my hand and her lips. She swallowed. And winced.

The wooden eyes are mine, Anna.
They don't work.

You broke my eyes, I must have these.

They don't work, Francis. They're of no use.

Please give them to me.

Then Anna smiled, an unkind smile created to make me feel stupid and awkward. But which only made me feel angry and would even have made me rush from the church were it not for the fact that she still held on to my wooden eyes.

Why did you have a wax head made of me, Francis?

The eyes, please.

Didn't you know you can touch the real thing?

Eyes, please.

I would have let you.

Eyes, now!

Do you feel embarrassed that I found out? Poor little boy.

I think I'd better go now.

Then Anna stopped laughing and began to cry. She rubbed at her eyes with her fists, almost thumping them, and when she had calmed a little she announced, so simply and without any suggestion of doubt:

I'm going blind.

And then she said it again:

I'm going blind.

And sighed.

And suddenly the wooden eyes weren't important any more, and I suddenly realized that what I must do while I still had the chance was to take Anna down into the tunnel and show her the exhibition. She must see it all, she must see all of it, before she went blind, from the very beginning up until the very last object, *The Object*. I had never intended to show the exhibition to anyone, but in that instant I believed that I must, that it was the most important thing I would ever do. (Perhaps this was because I felt pity for Anna, suffering from her eye disease. I do not rule that out. I am not incapable of pity, and pity is perhaps not incapable of, temporarily, commanding me. That is possible. However, at the time I felt that something very different was moving me to open up my exhibition, if only for a limited period, to a limited public.)

She agreed to come with me. At first she smiled and said – Not now. But then she stopped herself and said that of course, if I was willing she would come now, and that perhaps now was the right time after all. Keep your eyes closed, you must keep them closed or I won't show you anything. You must see it all in the correct order, as it is supposed to be seen. If you open your eyes before it is time then we'll have to come back up immediately. I pulled Anna's coat up over her head. What can you see, I asked. And she said – Nothing, I can't see a thing. Good, I said, let me guide you.

Still wearing my leather gloves, I pulled her forward by the wrist, calling out instructions. I unlocked the Orme chapel gate. I pushed aside the tomb lid, and we moved slowly down into the exhibition. Be careful to step slowly, I said, you're not going to be sick again, are you? She said that she couldn't see anything. That's all right, I said, you will when we're at the beginning, keep to the right. When we arrived at the other entrance, in the cellar of Observatory Mansions, I lit a candle.

This is my exhibition, I said, I have never shown it to any-one before. Open up your eyes now. Please look. I gave her the exhibition book, instructing her to read my words on every object. I wanted her to see it all, even the final object, even that. She placed the wooden eyes inside her coat pocket. She took out her glasses, polished them against her dress, and began.

Lot 1: a till receipt.
Being the property (briefly) of either: 1 – a bus conductor; 2 – an inventor's assistant; 3 – a pregnant housewife; 4 – a policeman; 5 – an air hostess; 6 – a rat catcher; 7 – a street

cleaner; 8 – a trumpeter; 9 – a kindergarten teacher; 10 – a cloakroom attendant; 11 – a pigeon fancier; 12 – a head librarian; 13 – a jukebox maker; 14 – a boy who committed matricide.

(All of the above have been most thoroughly considered.)

Anna read and looked on, she had reached:

Lot 49: a love letter.
A badly written epistle from a house maid to a valet, originally slipped under the valet's door but rescued before the valet knew either it or the house maid's love for him existed.

Anna stopped, crouched down again:

Lot 110: a tontine salver (silver).
Previous property of the Orme family, to signify a bet made between a long-since deceased Francis Orme and his friends. The bet being who should live the longest. Francis Orme did. Prized possession of my grandfather being proof of his family longevity. Prized possession of my father, because his father loved it so.

Anna rubbed her eyes and cleaned her glasses, she continued.

Lot 163: a Morocco-bound book
(a volume of Orme History).
Taken from Father to remind him that some Ormes are still alive.

Anna said she wanted a break, but I begged her to read on. She smiled. She even said: Thank you for showing me this, Francis. Keep going, I said, you have to reach the end.

Lot 238: a ballet shoe
Belonging to the fat little daughter (and hopeful ballerina to be) of the slim parents of flat one.

Anna cleaned her glasses again. Keep going, I said, don't stop.

Lot 301: a pair of walking sticks.
Belonging to the man in George's café who couldn't go anywhere without them and had to get George to make a call on the café telephone and then to wait for two hours to be collected by his also decrepit wife (who arrived by use of a Zimmer frame and with two spare sticks hooked over it).

Anna said her eyes were burning. She suggested that we stop for a while but I said that I'd rather she kept going. I gave her another pill.

Lot 353: a pair of pearl earrings.
Previous property of the man known as Mr Right Angle of flat seven, being proof of the life of his mother.

Anna said to me: Francis, stop being a blur, come into the light. I said: I am in the light. She said: I can't see you properly, what's happening? I said: Do you want to go upstairs? She said: Not till I've finished.

Lot 380: a television's remote control.
Claire Higg, flat sixteen, when she wasn't looking, when she went to make me a cup of tea.

Anna told me that she needed to rest, she couldn't concentrate any more. We walked on to the end of the tunnel. We climbed up the steps.

We are in the church again, I said. We walked out of the church. Anna held on to my back.

We sat on a bench in Tearsham Park Gardens. Anna said: Is it really day? Is it really light? I said: The sky is an unhappy shade of blue. She said: I can't see. She said: I can't see anything at all.

We agreed that Anna was blind.

Anna held my arm. We went inside.

266

VI

LITTLE PEOPLE

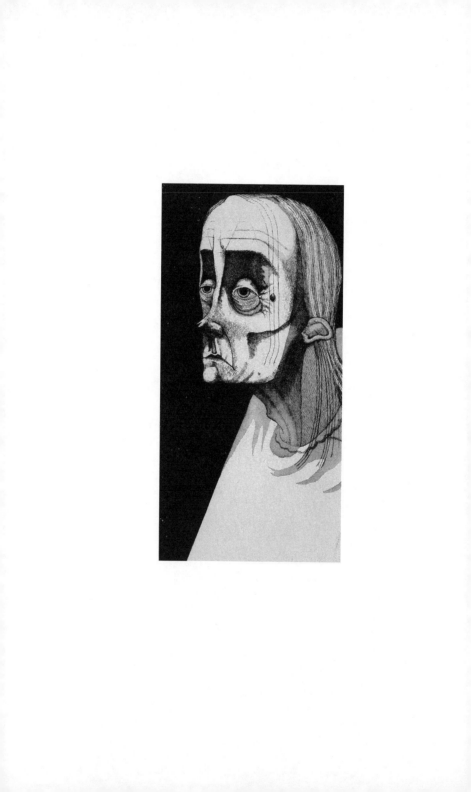

The philosophy of Mark Daniel Cooper.

For days they would not let me be with Anna. Claire Higg and Mother looked after her, they dressed her, spoon fed her, brushed her hair, bathed her, read her good-night stories; two old women playing dolls with a blind girl. They preferred it if the blind girl didn't speak, if the blind girl only smiled. But sometimes the blind girl screamed and wouldn't stop screaming.

Someone had stolen my wax bust of Anna. It had been taken from my room during Saint Lucy's day. I presumed that it was Mother, who, disapproving, disposed of it. If it was her, she never mentioned it and I was too frightened of her reproaches to ask for its return. Without the bust I was forgetting Anna's face again, or remembering it wrongly.

Sometimes at night I would go for walks around the city, crossing the streets that surrounded Observatory Mansions, thinking of Anna, trying to remember her, smelling her in every smoker that walked by.

On one of these nights, perhaps a little later than usual, I was walking somewhere between Tearsham Park Gardens and Tearsham Church when I became aware that someone else was with me, standing very close, hissing. I turned around, expecting to see the Porter.

A young man with a pock-marked face wearing a dirty tracksuit was spraying the city walls with paint from a canister. The words bursting out at high pressure seemed

269

almost to be hissing or whispering their way on to the walls. The following words:

For the softest skin.
The whitest teeth, the freshest breath.
And even you can find love.
Turn back the clocks, say goodbye to your wrinkles.
Because you're worth it.

Finally, I had found the man who had been making his marks around the city, spraying the walls at night, passing on his messages, so they could be read by everyone in the morning.

I so longed for company but it took him some time to feel relaxed with me. He spoke with a terrible stutter. He was called, as far as I could understand him, Mark Daniel Cooper and he would often spend his nights with his spray cans. The work on Observatory Mansions' walls too, he admitted, was his own. He explained that he found it so difficult to speak to people that people preferred to leave him alone. To remedy this he at first wrote in notebooks all his feelings. But often, he told me – more with the help of gestures than words – he was so angry that his letters became angry too, and angry letters, he said, he gestured, are huge in size and he filled his notebooks too quickly. But nobody read his notebooks, once he had shut them, they just lay there, useless. One day he saw some graffiti sprayed on the walls of a school playground and he suddenly knew what he had to do. He felt so happy scrawling his innermost thoughts on the city, that all his pain and frustration had dwindled almost to nothing. He was more confident afterwards and soon he ran out of things to say but he could not give up graffitiing the city walls, it was all that made him feel alive. In time he began to write out sentences from advertisements everywhere. They were so confident, those adverts, he told me. Nothing in the world was so confident. He said the Coca-Cola signs in the city, which had been there for as long as he could remember, made us worth something. If the Coca-Cola company felt happy to be here, then it had faith in us, and that therefore we should have faith in ourselves. If the Coca-Cola signs were taken away then we would be worthless. With them here we truly belonged to the world.

Copying the confident words from adverts down, he felt their confidence glow within him. He told me this smiling and laughing between his broken words and wrote:

Enjoy the taste.

He let me borrow one of his cans so that I could write this word on to bricks:

Anna.

But no, he said, he gestured, I had made the word far too small and he sprayed a whole street with large bold Annas. Anna Street, we called it.

When he decided it was time for him to leave, he sprayed his goodbye on the wall, nervously smiled at me but without looking into my eyes and rushed off into the early morning before it became too light.

Observing Anna.

In time, of course, they became careless. Their love for their blind doll began to wane. Mother had a key to Anna's flat, which occasionally she left, inadvertently, by the playing dictaphone at night, so sometimes, when everyone was asleep, I'd leave flat six and climb the stairs to Anna's flat clutching mother's key. I'd walk into Anna's bedroom and watch her sleep, just look at her for a long while. I'd discover new lighter freckles that I hadn't seen before. I'd want to touch, but I never did. Anna's closed eyes (what was happening beneath those lids?), Anna's nose, Anna's little ears. I'd imagine her whole body concealed beneath the sheets. Anna's hidden legs and arms, Anna's hidden stomach, Anna's hidden breasts. But I'd creep away again before she woke.

During the days when I was not allowed to see her, when I was not even allowed to wait outside her flat door, I had to find other preoccupations. I occasionally returned to my plinth, but I was incapable of concentrating. I spent hours with my exhibition, looking at those objects that Anna had looked at, talking to that most precious of all objects, *The Object*, at the end of the exhibition, an object which Anna never reached, which she would never see now.

A visit to Mr Behrens' glove shop.

Many people, when they are feeling a little low and need some cheering up, are often known to buy. Some buy clothes, some buy food. In those times, to console myself, I bought gloves, white cotton gloves from Mr Behrens' glove shop. Mr Behrens was a tiny man who also wore gloves, though his were made of leather and were black. He wore his gloves to hide his hands which had been badly burnt in a war he preferred never to talk about. Mr Behrens' glove shop catered for all types of glove wearers, he sold gloves every colour of the spectrum, he sold gloves made of wool, of leather, of rubber, cotton, fox skin, calfskin, kidskin, moleskin, wire. I was prized above all his other customers. I had been coming to him for many years and always bought several pairs of gloves whenever I came. Most of his customers, Mr Behrens said, make their gloves last for years, sometimes decades even. But among my customers, he said, are you, Francis, loyal and almost regular in your visits and always requiring, in bulk, the same traditional white cotton gloves, boxed and wrapped in tissue paper.

On that day, some months, it was estimated, before my required time of purchasing, I left Mr Behrens and his glove shop with ten new pairs, ten new membranes neatly stacked, waiting peacefully for the day when I would call them to life; when the fingers would operate and timidly learn the world.

The Christmas present.

Soon Anna felt more confident and was allowed to go on accompanied walks. Sometimes she went with Mother, sometimes she was allowed to go with me. She never went with Miss Higg. Claire Higg did not appreciate outdoor places. Anna's eyes had begun to completely cloud over, now there was no proof in them that they had ever seen. The irises, the pupils, were all a milky white – they were hard now too. When she was still, she was like a waxwork that someone had forgotten to paint eyes on. She kept touching her white eyes, pushing them, scratching them. I asked her if she remembered what most things looked like. Yes, she said, by memory and by touch. Anna said to me:

Please let me touch your hands, then I'll be happy.

It was Christmas time, at Christmas time people are known to wrap objects in paper. Anna Tap wanted to touch my hands and, since it was Christmas time, that would be my present to her. I would gift-wrap my hands.

Dressed in my costume (the costume I wore when I was employed in the waxworks), in buckled shoes, in tights, in a white shirt with frilly cuffs, in a long gabardine and on top of my head a long curled wig, I entered the wax museum through the side door with the combination lock that we half-wax-half-human dummies had always used. Still were the inhabitants, as silent as wax. Did they dream? Did thoughts move inside their wax interiors? Was a person seen through the glass eyes of the wax dummies, moving about them? Some of these wax men and women moved themselves, in daylight hours, when the exhibition was open, when electricity warmed their bodies and let them shift in their ugly and jerky movements. But they did not move that Christmas Eve when I walked amongst them again.

I stopped in front of a certain wax model of a film star, young, deceased. My white gloved hands touched his youthful wax hands.

I heard the security guard walking about upstairs, doing his rounds. Silently, I twisted the hands off the film star, the wax hands rotated slowly, slowly. There was something appalling in the way those wax hands went round and round: why wasn't the wax mouth of the wax head screaming?

Then I held two wax hands, my hands, but made of wax.

The security guard came down the stairs. I stood still by men in suits, women in ball gowns, fat kings and fat queens in their regal togs. I was kept company by the famous and the infamous and I was altogether welcomed among them.

The light from the torch entered the room and the security guard came after it. He walked around us. He shone his torch in our faces. He stopped in front of each of us. He was trying to catch us out, but none of us moved, or rather only one of us moved, but it was not me. Further away, at the other end of the exhibition hall, stood, in wax company, a model of a man, about six foot high with brown hair, thin, wearing a pinstripe suit. The eyes of this exhibit moved. They moved in one continuous action from staring straight ahead to staring at me. I knew this exhibit. His name was Ivan. He was not a wax dummy, he was a flesh dummy. He had been working as a flesh dummy before I came to the wax museum but was dismissed from employment on the same day as me.

That night I saw him again, silent and still, save for the single movement of his eyes. The security guard did not notice those eyes move, he saw nothing unusual in the frozen figures before him, he did not notice that one wax figure had lost his hands, or that another had taken them. As he waved his torch about us his expression did not change. Then he put his torch down and started to take off his clothes.

Now I only achieved outer stillness, the inner, I confess, had quite gone. The security guard, quite naked, walked up to a certain wax figure and hugged her. He felt her body and kissed her lips, he brushed his hands through her hair. He sighed and he moaned. He stroked the polystyrene breasts and felt under the dress, way up the fibreglass legs. This was a model of a certain celebrated beauty, a singer. He rubbed his body all over her wax, fibreglass and polystyrene skin.

After he had masturbated, he cried. He dressed himself, walked up to the wax figure he had abused, kissed her on the forehead and murmured sincere apologies:

I love you. I'm sorry. I hope I didn't startle you. I love you and I am not worthy of your love.

He picked up his torch, shone its beam around us, particularly at his beloved, and then quietly descended the stairs.

When he was no longer heard I left my outer stillness and, still carrying wax hands, walked over to Ivan. I stopped just in front of him, smiled and whispered:

Happy Christmas.

Don't tell anyone, Francis. Please. I don't do any wrong. I just come here to be with them. I don't touch them or hurt them. Don't tell anyone, please.

I promise. Are you here every day?

Every other day.

How do you eat?

I always bring sandwiches and a drink with me. I creep in at night, like you did, through our old entrance while the guard does his rounds. Then I stay with them all day and some of the night before returning home. I sleep for a day and then come back. I am happy here, I'm not doing any harm.

Will you come out with me now or have you just arrived?

Just arrived, just before you. I couldn't leave them alone over Christmas.

Poor Ivan.

Francis, why have you stolen those hands?

They're a Christmas present.

If you don't put them back, I'll be forced to report you.

And they'll ask you how you know. How did you witness the theft? And when you explain they'll look at you strangely and call doctors and lock you away ... They'll find new hands, Ivan. He'll look the same.

But I'll know.

Happy Christmas.

Francis, don't go.

I must, the security guard could return.

I'm frightened. It's because of the young man without hands. People should have hands, he doesn't look like a person without them, he just looks like a model. He makes the others look like models. Please put the hands back.

Happy Christmas.

Then take the whole figure.

I only want the hands.

I'm frightened. Look, my hands are shaking, my hands want me to cut them off and give them to the young man.

Ivan, he's made of wax.

You're betraying us.

Why don't you come out now?

Stay here with us. It'll be like before.

I've got to go home. I must deliver these.

I think one day someone will come in here, one of the officials, and remove me from the exhibition. They'll lift me up and drag me away. They'll put me in a cold room and lock the door. I'll stand still even then. I shan't move. And maybe days or maybe weeks later they'll come into that room and pull off my arms or legs and give them to somebody else, to some other model. Then they'll burn the rest of me. And what's certain is that when I am burning, my flesh will drip from me, like wax.

I think you should leave the exhibition, it'll be fine without you. Come outside.

You're jealous.

No, Ivan.

Ivan resumed his stationary pose and would not talk again.

Christmas morning.

On Christmas morning I went to flat eighteen. Anna Tap sat across the table from me.

Anna, you can touch my hands.

Wax hands at the ends of my jumper sleeves, my own gloved hands up my jumper holding wax wrists. She touched both my elbows and slowly crept her fingers down my forearms. She touched my hands.

They're so cold.

She felt them.

They're so hard.

She took hold of the fingers and gently pulled them towards her. The wax hands came free. She felt the weight of them. They banged on the table. Anna screamed.

They are my hands, they are my fingers and knuckles. Wax casts made by my friend William.

Another commission?

Not for me, for the wax museum. They were for a wax model. They're yours now. My hands, from me to you. Happy Christmas.

And what did Anna give me for Christmas? A pair of spectacles. Spectacles that were mine already. Spectacles that belonged to the exhibition, that were on loan. So was it a happy Christmas? Not really, no.

A shadow called Tap.

Anna Tap, blind, mid-twenties to early thirties, in a blue dress, in black shoes, needed, she said, to be by me always. She said she felt uneasy if I wasn't near. She didn't want to be left alone. When she was left in the largest room of flat six she would sneak away in search of me. She followed me down to the cellar and found the door to the tunnel and knocked on that door and wouldn't stop knocking until I had let her in:

I'm busy now. Go back upstairs.

I won't disturb you. I'll just sit here. I won't make a sound, you won't know I'm here.

I would resume my work.

I do like your exhibition, Francis. Or almost. I don't think I quite understand it. You said that it was an exhibition of love. But I didn't see that, I just saw abandoned and stolen objects. Perhaps you should tell me about the other exhibits I didn't get to see. Perhaps you should read me your catalogue.

No, never.

When I went into the city to stand on my plinth, she would insist on accompanying me. She would stand near to the plinth and smile whenever a coin was thrown into my box.

I could never be alone.

She was still losing weight, as the bathroom scalesman was eager to inform me whenever Anna and I went to the park. I sometimes tried to leave her with the chalk artist. I walked towards the broken fountain, sat Anna down on the nearest bench to the chalk drawings and told her I'd come and get her soon. She called after me, she looked frightened. She took Saint Lucy's eyes from her pockets and passed them nervously from hand to hand. But despite my irritation at the almost perpetual presence of Anna Tap, I found that I could never leave her alone for very long. I felt guilty when I walked away, I saw her pathetic expressions and heard her rubbing the wooden eyes together. I often felt guilty enough to return to her and say – Yes, all right, you can come. But the moment I said that the irritation would reappear. So I sat her down somewhere else and promised to return. So she called out to me. So I felt guilty and sad. So I let her come. So I felt disgusted by her.

I was a solitary person. I was happiest with just myself for company. But now I could no longer talk to the most precious object in my exhibition because she was there; I could no longer achieve inner stillness because she was there; I could no longer think because she was always there. Silences would be interrupted by – Francis, what are you doing?

She said to me once, when we were in the tunnel: I am filling your days with love, Francis. You'll get used to it. Be patient.

I would ask her – Are you still alive behind those white eyes, Anna. They make you look dead. I'm still alive, Francis, she'd say, come closer.

She was always smoking. It dirtied everything. I was sure that if I spent too much time with her that my gloves would become tobacco stained.

I stole her toothbrush. I threw it away (it wasn't worthy of the exhibition). I complained that her breath smelt, asked her to keep her distance. I climbed up to her flat whilst she was with my mother and moved her possessions about. I placed bricks outside the entrance door, I saw her fall over and cut herself. I would take her for a walk in the city and leave her there and hear her scream out my name and follow her as she desperately asked people for help. I would follow her all the way home, and even watch her standing on the curb, panic-stricken, listening to the traffic rushing around Observatory Mansions and see her waiting there for an hour, begging every passer-by to take her across.

She would bear all the little abuses I subjected her to with patience and pretend I was just tired, that I didn't mean what I said. She would always forgive me: I forgive you, Francis. But I thought it would be more interesting if she didn't forgive me, if she shouted at me and insulted me and left me in peace. My days were filled with the fug of Anna Tap and I struggled for clean air.

She gave me gifts: she gave me her spectacles case, she gave me her love dress (which I had every intention of stealing anyway, lot 995).

I know this is hard for you, Francis. I know it will take time. But do not worry, I am patient.

Of eyes and sticks.

I walked Anna to the eye hospital. They gave her a white metal stick with a rubber end. People taught Anna how to use the stick and kept her away from me for hours while she tapped the ground and was given instructions on how to know the streets by beating them. And strangely, when Anna was away at her lessons, I wanted her back, I was bored without her. When she had finished at the eye hospital for the day I would be there waiting for her. With each lesson she was regaining her confidence.

The eye hospital had ordered some glass eyes for her and expected them to arrive in a number of weeks. But she wanted to wear wooden eyes in her skull and screamed and kicked when the eye people refused her. Unhygienic. Unsavoury. Unmentionable.

Tap walks alone.

After she had been a few weeks with the eye people, Anna was happy walking alone. She would not allow me to guide her, she did not cling on to my arm or try to grip my hands as she had before. She stood erect and alone, and if when following her I came a little too close I was struck by the stick. Anna Tap was confident again. She stopped giving me presents.

Anna Tap no longer visited me in the tunnel, even when invited. She spent a lot of time with her stick tutors, girls of a similar age to her. Plotting.

An outing.

One mid-January day was, and is, my birthday. On that particular birthday I was given as presents:

1. From the Porter: a hiss.
2. From Claire Higg: nothing.
3. From my mother: a pair of red cotton gloves.
4. From Anna Tap: an outing.

This outing of Anna's was a surprise outing, one she said that she had been busying herself with for several weeks, in fact ever since a certain person, who was wearing white gloves, announced (dropping this unconnected information casually between sentences) that his birthday was approaching. The outing began with a bus journey. I sat in the front seat next to Anna Tap. I noticed, slightly frightened, that the bus was not heading in the usual direction towards the city but away from it, in a direction I was unaccustomed to taking, we were moving towards the countryside. Ever since Tearsham Park changed its name I had somehow forgotten that the countryside still existed. After half an hour we had arrived. The bus moved off without us.

What do you smell, Francis?
Decay, rotting.
Is it a pleasant smell?
No.
Look up, Francis. Are there any birds?
Pigeons and seagulls.
What is in front of you?
A metal wall stretching out for miles.
Is there an entrance?
There's a metal door.
Open it, we will walk inside.

A man ran up to us dressed in a filthy boiler suit, wearing boots and thick rubber gloves, a helmet and with a paper mask over his mouth and nose. Anna took a piece of paper from her pocket, the man read it and left us alone, instructing us first, for safety's sake, to remain on the perimeter.

What do you see, Francis?
I don't know ... there're things everywhere, old mattresses, old bicycles, smashed televisions, ruined cars, carpets, suitcases, papers, magazines, bags, curtains, books, bones, cardboard boxes, rotting food, rubble ...
Are you crying?
No.
Good, then keep going.
There're broken chairs, floorboards, window frames, twisted and smashed shop's mannequins, clothes, till receipts, beams, lamps, cans, record players ... all smashed ...
Stop crying and go on.

I'm not crying.

Keep going.

There are tables with three legs, there are plates and clocks. There are cups, smashed glass, bottles, paintings, posters, tyres, cartons, wires, shoes, spectacles, wigs, wardrobes, drawers, doors . . .

Don't stop.

Please can I stop?

Go on.

I think I'd better go now.

KEEP GOING!

There are pens, suitcases, briefcases, filing cabinets, sheets, blankets, buckets, saws, iron poles, plaster, a caryatid missing its head, tiles, coats, rocks, mirrors, a doll's leg.

On! ON!

There are bed frames, dresses, plastic jewellery, telephones, photographs, a blackboard, a tricycle, a doghouse, a chimney, a snooker table . . . a walking frame . . . I want to stop.

Besides the objects, what else do you see?

People walking about it all – It's so high in places, it's like mountains!

What are the people doing?

Collecting?

No, they're scavenging.

What is this, Anna?

It's all the rubbish from the city.

No, it's not rubbish, not all of it.

Describe the smell.

I can't.

It's decay, it's rotting, it's the smell of everything that we throw away, heaped together. It's the smell of everything we don't want any more.

It's so sad.

It's the smell of dying objects, Francis.

Objects don't die.

Here, Francis, are kept out of sight all the dead objects, all the rejected objects of dead people and living people. The things we don't care about any more. Our things will be sent here one day.

Not my things. Why are we here?

I thought you might find it entertaining. It's a little like your exhibition, don't you think? Less ordered of course.

NO.

There are similarities.

My exhibition is full of love. I feel sick.

Then be sick.

Look at it. It's so, so sad.

I can't look. I can't see.

I want to go home.

Touch it, Francis. It's so dirty! Touch it. Touch it and then look at your gloves.

Stop it. Please, please stop it.

This is the shit the city laid.

There's a rat over there! I feel sick.

Look at the rat, Francis, look at it. Is it wearing white gloves?

In the bus on the way back she told me she had shown me the mountains for my own good. She asked me to take off my gloves again. I didn't say anything. I moved away from her, we sat at different ends of the bus.

That was my birthday outing.

Afterwards, if Anna came into flat six, I left it. If I went to the tunnel I would always lock the door after me.

The demolition experts came back again. They talked to the Porter. I ignored them all: Anna, Mother, Claire Higg, the Porter, the demolition experts.

That white.

That cotton.

That exhibition.
That favoured object.
That's all.
That's all there was for me.

Porter.

The Porter brushed on, dusted on, mopped on, moped on. He would sometimes be seen scrubbing a small patch of carpet with a wire brush, and would only leave his work after the carpet had been scrubbed completely away and the floorboards were visible underneath. But he continued to empty our bins and he continued to hiss and we continued to avoid him.

Higg.

I shopped for Miss Higg now. Mother brought the food up to her. She thought Miss Higg was deteriorating, she said:

Claire has let herself go. She watches the television all day and all night. She no longer sleeps in her bed. After the programmes have finished for the night and the channels only transmit a single, high-pitched, continuous screech, Claire watches the blank screen and hums along with the screech all night.

Miss Higg complained that early one morning, when she was dozing, someone crept into her flat and turned off the television. She said that someone had stolen her hairbrush. Everyone looked at me. But I hadn't stolen the hairbrush. What would I want with Claire Higg's hairbrush?

Mother.

Mother spent as little time as possible within her bedroom and had me cover all her objects with sheets. She got up early, before the rest of us, and dressed always in smart clothes now but would never go out, not even to the park.

Tap.

Anna Tap was ignored by me until the night when she was visited by a man wearing white gloves.

The man in white gloves.

Late at night, when everyone was asleep, someone was out of his place, walking up the stairs to the third floor. He stopped outside the flat numbered eighteen, he turned the door handle with a white-cotton-gloved hand. The door was locked. He took out a key. He unlocked the door to flat eighteen and stepped inside.

Fast asleep in her bedroom lay the gently rising and falling body of Anna Tap. She was asleep, she did not know that someone had entered her flat and was even slowly approaching her bedroom, was even slowly approaching her bed.

The visitor knelt down when he reached the bed. He stayed there for a little while looking at the closed face of Anna Tap. He brought his white gloved hands up to her face and gently, gently touched her dark hair. He stroked it for a while, gently-gently so he wouldn't wake her. He grew brave. He touched her skin. He brushed her cheeks with his fingers. A finger traced the outline of her nose. He felt the closed lips. He touched the eyelids. But when he touched the eyelids, the damaged globes underneath them began to move. They opened and the broken eyes looked out and saw nothing.

Who's there? Someone's there. Is it you, Francis?

The visitor touched the face of Anna Tap once more. Anna's hands grasped his.

Francis. Francis.

The gloved hands of the visitor held the cheeks of Anna's face. They squeezed.

Not so hard, Francis. Be gentle.

The gloved hands stroked her hair.

That's right.

And then pulled it.

No, Francis, gently.

The gloved hands gently touched her lips.

That's right, Francis.

The gloved hands pushed a gloved finger inside Anna's mouth. And then two fingers and then three and even four. Anna Tap pushed them away, choking.

Francis, please!

The visitor kissed the forehead of Anna Tap and the cheeks and the lips. Hard. Hard kisses.

Gently, Francis, you must be gentle.

The visitor's lips gently kissed those of Anna. And Anna kissed back. Anna felt the visitor's face. She learnt it with her hands. She felt the visitor's lips and then she stopped. The visitor's lower lip was not swollen. The visitor didn't even have Francis's smell.

Who is it?

The visitor held Anna's face.

Who's there?

The visitor kissed Anna.

Stop it. Please.

The visitor kissed Anna.

I'll scream. Please, please go.

The visitor kissed Anna.

Anna screamed.

The visitor hissed, gently, quietly. A hiss which did not mean - Go away - a hiss which meant - It's me, I'm here. Haven't you longed for me? Well, here I am.

Anna screamed. The visitor placed one gloved hand over Anna's mouth, with the other he pulled back the blankets.

Anna's screams had awoken the house, and I, with Mother not far behind and pushing me on, knocked on the door of flat eighteen. As I opened the door I saw the Porter. He was wearing white gloves, stolen, no doubt, from the Gloves Armageddon Experience. The freckles of imperfection seemed to quiver on his face. He was shaking. He pushed roughly past me and shoved my mother out of the way before hissing and descending to the cellar depths. The screaming continued and did not stop even after my mother had pushed back Anna's nightdress and was hugging her and shushing her and even crying herself.

He tried to . . . He tried to . . . He tried to . . .

Anna comes to stay.

Anna came to stay that night and never slept in flat eighteen again. She lay, instead, in my bedroom. During the first night of her visit she did not sleep at all. Mother held her hand, I would have offered her one of mine but it was never asked for. Mother told me to go away.

I did not sleep. When daylight came I opened my bedroom door and saw Mother asleep on a chair and Anna asleep in my bed, still holding hands.

I walked out into the park, feeling impotent. I kicked some trees and hurt my feet, which only made me feel more useless. Returning from the park I saw the Porter within the circular wall of Observatory Mansions. He had made himself a fire. He had burnt his broom and his dustpan and brush. The dustpan and the brush handle were made of plastic, they were dripping in the heat. When a drop of liquid plastic fell it made a hissing sound very similar to the Porter's hiss, the noise of anger.

The Porter did not look at me as I returned home, he was staring grimly into the flames, crying.

One of the brass buttons on his uniform jacket was missing.

The little people.

We did not think of calling the police about what had happened to Anna. If we had, we would probably not have been heard on the telephone, or we would have quickly returned the receiver the moment someone from beyond Observatory Mansions spoke to us. We moved rarely and announced our moves before we made them:

I'm just going to the loo now. I'll only be gone a little while. I'll come straight back.

I'll just turn on the kettle and make us a little tea.

I'm just going to have a little lie down.

Anna smoked nervously, she dared not sit without a cigarette in her hands. My mother watched Anna always and would order me away when she started crying. Only I left Observatory Mansions now. I bought the food and the cigarettes. Once, I tried to steal something from a shop, to prove to myself that I was still that infamous Francis Orme, serial thief. A loaf of brown bread. I was caught, the shop-keeper laughed at me. He said it was the clumsiest act of theft he had ever seen. He didn't report me. I paid for the bread.

We were little then, tiny mice people, sniffing for danger.

Claire Higg comes to stay.

A night or so after Anna was visited by the Porter, my mother decided that we must all live together in flat six. She brought Claire Higg to our home and then went upstairs again to fetch the television set. Claire Higg was only partly Claire Higg by then, she had lost the rest of her somewhere, somehow misplaced it. She seemed to have only half a face and half a body and her eyes only focused when she watched the television screen. She was nervous when anyone spoke and started scratching herself whenever Anna cried. Sometimes Anna would become violent, she smashed some glasses and threw books down from the shelves, she spat on the floor. And during these fits, Claire Higg scratched herself or chewed the ends of her hair and looked completely exposed, as if she was the only human left in the world, sitting in an arid land on an upright pine chair, chewing her hair, scratching, waiting for the something indescribable that we were all waiting for to come to her and say: Boo!

It was Mother who calmed Anna down and if I came to help her she would push me away – Don't touch, Francis. Go away. Go and sleep.

Anna continued to sleep in my bed, Miss Higg slept with my mother in her double bed, I slept in the largest room of flat six, on a bed made of cushions and folded eiderdowns.

The whole world had shrunk to the size of flat six, Observatory Mansions. If I talked I was told not to disturb the television. If I offered to help with the cooking I was told to either go away or go to sleep or both. If I sat somewhere I was told to move. If I stood somewhere I was pushed on. When the others spoke they did not speak to me, or even look at me.

I was allowed to put the dustbin bags outside the door. But they were not taken away any more. They were mounting up.

Pyloric stenosis.

Then pyloric stenosis hit us. It wasn't just that there were fifteen or more dustbins outside the door of flat six, or just that those dustbins had begun to stink. It wasn't just that one morning when I went down to do the shopping I noticed that all the windows on the ground floor had been smashed. It wasn't just that the carpets remained unswept. And it wasn't just that the whole house smelt of rotting food. It was something else. It was the feeling of defeat. We gave up all pretence of not noticing that our home and our lives had decayed and sat moaning on various upright pine chairs, waiting for the real pain to begin.

No one had seen the Porter for many days. I was the last person to see him, on my way back from shopping. As I fumbled with the keys to flat six, the Porter came out of unoccupied flat eight, where I think he had been waiting for me. He tore the bags of shopping away and threw them down the stairs. He started kicking me. He pulled my hair. He punched me in the stomach and left me trying to breathe on the floor. That was the last time we had seen the Porter. That was the last time any of us had left flat six.

Under the terrible inertia of pyloric stenosis we tried to move no more than was necessary, movement was painful to us now, painful to us and to our home – too quick a movement might bring us down, might collapse floor on to floor. If our home was to die, and we realized it must, then, definitely, we should die with it. We could not imagine a life without Observatory Mansions.

One afternoon we looked out of the window of the largest room of flat six and saw that the Porter was still with us. He was talking to the demolition experts. On the afternoons that followed we often saw him talking to the demolition experts, but we could not hear him. The demolition experts nodded at him, they made him sign some papers, they shook his hand.

While we, watching from above, said nothing. And one day a van actually drove into Observatory Mansions' circular yard and stayed there for several hours. And on that day we heard a small explosion from a long way beneath us and felt the whole building briefly shudder. But afterwards the van drove away and we were left without an explanation.

We sat in a circle and remembered to breathe. We all knew that our end would soon be here to fetch us. We had some tins of food left which we divided equally among us. We did not need to conserve the food, we had enough; we would need no more food very soon. We stopped watching television, those creatures that appeared on the screen, though having forms vaguely reminiscent of ours, were otherwise alien to us. Besides, we only wanted quiet now, we were listening, waiting for something to happen.

The time was coming soon. We put out no more rubbish, we kept it with us for company in the largest room of flat six, where we all slept. Now that Anna had run out of cigarettes, she worked her way through full ashtrays smoking the remains of abandoned cigarettes. When the ends held no more tobacco, she would sit with an unlit butt in her mouth quietly sucking.

We heard the Porter hammering just outside our door. We thought: soon, the day is coming soon.

And then it did.

VII

DEMOLITION

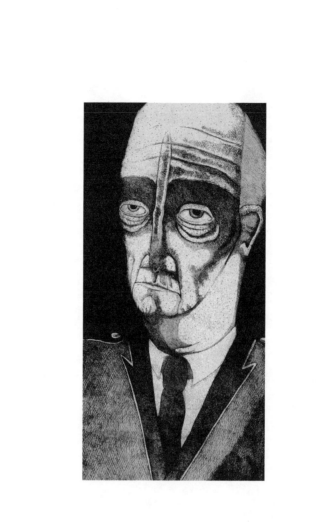

The day came.

On the morning of the day that we had been waiting so long for, we woke up to a strange silence, everything seemed wonderfully peaceful. We sat in our circle, as always, and waited. We had been waiting for an hour and a half when Anna had one of her violent fits. It began with her spitting a cigarette butt from her mouth. Then she stood up and we watched her as she kicked over her chair and threw all the unwashed plates from the sink on to the floor.

I can't keep still any more. Why should you? Get up! I want a cigarette. I want some noise, some noise and a cigarette. I can't stay in here any more. I won't be patient! Leave me alone. DON'T TOUCH ME! I'm alive! I don't want to be dead. Don't just sit there. Please, move. Show me you're human. Francis, move. Speak. ONE OF YOU! I can't do this alone. Why do you just sit there? I won't accept it. It's not over. Why do you say it's over when it's not? It doesn't have to be. I'm going out. I'm going out and I'll face the Porter alone if I have to. Will nobody help me? Nobody? Alice? Claire? Francis? *Come on, Francis!* Why are you so frightened? I'll just open the door, let the air in and then you'll feel better. Then you'll come, won't you? Then you'll come, Francis.

Don't touch the door.

Sit down.

Don't talk.

Keep still.

I'll just open the door a little.
Come away from the door.
I'll just open the little door a little.
You mustn't touch the door.
You must keep still.
You must return to your chair.
Let go of the handle!
Come away.
Don't turn it!
You mustn't turn it!
Leave it alone! Please!
Come and sit down. There's a good girl.
Come and sit with Claire.
Come and sit with Alice.
You can hold Francis's hand if you like.
She's turning the handle!
Oh my God!
Let it go, let go!
She's turning it, turning it!
The handle's come off! The door's locked, it won't open.
Someone's locked the door! There's something in the lock,
someone's sealed it up! *Someone's locked us in!* Help!
Sit down!
Help!
Keep still!
Help!
Come away from the door. Someone might hear you!
HELP!
SIT HER DOWN!
Go to your chair!
Please, please help.
To your chair!
Sssh, now. Sssh. We're nearly there.
Just be patient.
It'll all be over soon.

That's it, just sit still.

Can you open the window for me? I need a little air.

Is that permissible?

Only a fraction.

There you are, now just wait quietly.

Can I stand closer to the window?

Is that permissible?

If she promises not to talk.

Do you promise?

I'll be quiet. I just need the air.

But the moment Anna Tap was positioned by the window she pushed it wide open, leant out and screamed – *Help! Somebody help! We're locked in here! Help us!*

After she had called out she seemed to relax. She sat back down on her chair, she smiled a little and we all sat around her and listened to our excited breaths. We smelt the fresh, cool air. By simply opening the window and calling out for help, Anna had destroyed the peace inside us and we were becoming angry, we were growing finally. Anna's scream had given us a little hope, her voice had sounded so loud, we had not realized that among us there was someone who could achieve such loudness. We had been quiet for so long and now, suddenly, we could not bear the quiet any longer. Claire Higg began to hum the note the television played when all the programmes had ended, Mother began singing, I began quoting the Law of White Gloves, Anna began laughing. Soon we were all shouting, all leaning out of the window, shouting and singing and whistling and giggling.

But we became quiet and frightened again when we heard a distant knocking.

Our saviours.

Our saviours, there were several of them, were on the other side of the door. But they sounded so far away, as if they were in another building. They asked, shouting hard, if there was anyone there, we shouted back: Yes, we're all here, Alice and Claire and Anna and Francis Orme.

Our saviours told us to move away from the door, they were going to break it down. Move away now. Move away.

They smashed the door down, it moaned and cracked and finally yielded. Then we saw what had happened: someone had shoved putty into the keyhole and nailed plasterboard over our door, and even wallpapered over the plasterboard so that it looked as if flat six didn't exist at all, that it was simply a wall. Our saviours must only have been able to find our door because the wallpaper over it was conspicuously cleaner than anywhere else. The Porter, the Porter had blocked us in.

We saw our saviours. They were four men. Identically dressed in white boiler suits. They wore plastic helmets which each had a sticker above the visor: Demolition Experts. They looked at us, puzzled. We looked at them, puzzled.

Will you come downstairs?
Why? Mother asked.
I think you'd better.
Then we'll come.

They took us down the stairs, out through the entrance hall. Tapes marked with DANGER KEEP AWAY and signs saying DEMOLITION IN PROGRESS were all around Observatory Mansions. Iron barricades had been lined up along the surrounding streets, wooden boards had been hammered over the windows of the neighbouring houses. There was no traffic at all.

People stood behind the barricades, crowds of people forming a circle around the island of Observatory Mansions:

the city had come out to watch. When the other people saw us they cheered. We were embarrassed: so much noise, all for us. The crowds even pushed and shoved so that they could get a look at us. People with television cameras and microphones ran across the empty road. They asked us questions. We did not answer the questions, we were so shocked by the cheering that we had temporarily forgotten how to speak, but we smiled for the cameras. A man in a brown suit with a clipboard came towards us. We recognized him immediately as one of the senior demolition experts who we had seen talking to the Porter. He told us that our home had been thoroughly searched, that no one had been found. Where had we been hiding? We said we hadn't been hiding, but that the Porter had wanted us hidden. He said that we couldn't possibly go back into Observatory Mansions, we could never go back in there again. He couldn't change the schedule, the police had been called in, the traffic had been stopped, diverted about the city – Do you know how much organizing that takes? he asked us. Everything must continue according to the schedule. We were sure to be compensated, he said, even though his company was not to blame. But the schedule must not be altered, not at all.

Where was the Porter? Nobody knew. He had been seen earlier that morning, he was even helping plant wires in the cellar, he wouldn't leave the workers alone. Mother asked:

What are you going to do?
We'll remove the vertical supports, madam. Gravity should do the rest.
I don't understand.
We'll destroy the basement columns, madam, then, of course, the structure's weight will tear itself apart. It's a fairly simple procedure and shouldn't take long. Go and join the crowd now, stand behind the barrier like everyone else.

But I couldn't just leave it like that. How could I leave it like that? I knew that something must be done.

Quickly, before it was too late.

I moved through the crowds, pushing my way from Tearsham Park Gardens towards Tearsham Church and as I left I heard someone who sounded like Anna Tap calling, *Francis? Francis? FRANCIS!*

Incidents in the cellar.

How could I just leave the exhibition, with the weight of all the Ormes threatening to fall upon it, just leave it, like an unwanted child, to such an ending? I could not. Nor would I be able to live with myself afterwards, the failed guardian of all that love. Nor could I be sure that I would remain Francis Orme after every significant moment of my life recorded there had been destroyed. And what would my life mean once its only purpose had been removed? It would mean nothing, it would be a dull nothing.

I unlocked the Orme chapel, removed the lid of the false tomb, climbed down into the tunnel, sliding the lid back behind me. Striking matches to light my way, firing off wild, dancing shadows, I progressed along the narrow passageway – I saw the city retreating through history as I rushed along, I saw myself growing younger, all my mistakes, all my victories. I ran past Anna still with working eyes, past the death of Father, past Peter Bugg's tie, past the beginning of Observatory Mansions, past the end of Tearsham Park – losing years of life in my strides – past my schooling, past Emma, until finally, out of breath, I reached lot 1, a till receipt. There would be time, if I was quick, there *must* still be time to collect it all. All time was there, in that tunnel, neatly documented, could I not leave behind a year – leave behind those objects that indicated a year's existence – trade them in for a few kind minutes to help me move my magnificent collection?

As I crouched by the love-worn till receipt, I heard a male voice from within the cellar, someone was still inside. He was calling out – *Anna, Anna!* I dropped the receipt. Anna was in the cellar? She must leave. She must have heard: they've decided to remove Observatory Mansions today. She must get out. I tried to open the tunnel door, but it was locked from the other side. I was shut in, kept in by my own padlock. I called to her, kicking the tunnel door – *Anna! Anna!*

And my calls to her were met with the echoing calls of that other voice in the cellar, just the other side of my tunnel door.

Anna! Anna! the voice called.

Anna! Anna! came my reply.

I banged on the tunnel door, smashing my elbows and shoulders against it. *Anna! Anna!* came the call again. I began ramming the tunnel door with my shoulder, again and again, fiercer and fiercer, until the wood of the door, rotten with woodworm, broke free.

I was in the grey cellar of Observatory Mansions, there were wires all along the ground. There were holes bored into the pillars and in those holes the wires ended, or began, with a harmless-looking cylinder of grey putty. There was even a pile of rubble where a practice demolition had removed a pillar. The sound of its collapse had been vaguely heard by us the day before, up in our prison in flat six. *Anna! Anna!* – came the wailing again. These corridors had known butlers come to collect wine, had known laundry maids come to stoke the boiler, had known pantry boys come to pick up firewood. And in my confusion I thought I saw them all again, as busy and as panicked as I was, hurtling along; our different shoes beating out the times of different years on the same cold brick floor – each of the servants shocked into life by some scent of danger, or as if those holes in the pillars had opened up time and let the past come bleeding out. I imagined, at that moment, upstairs in the drawing room lamp boys must be struggling to light lamps, housekeepers must be rushing about looking for dust, ladies' maids must be running baths, praying for the water to move faster. And also I imagined my ancestors running from room to room or sitting up in beds around the house, ringing the bells, trying to understand what it was that had suddenly made them feel so unsure. And with them also, caught in the upheaval of the moment, dodging between servants and masters, would be all the pale faces, with grey-blue circles under their eyes and with frightened, anxious looks, of the shadows of the old residents of Observatory Mansions: the piano player disturbed in his practice; the dying mother with her two grown-up daughters, each come to their neighbouring doors with the same frightened instinct; the bachelor suddenly disturbed in his afternoon's lovemaking, not by a noise but by a feeling; the young mother hearing the car shrieking just beyond the wall of Observatory Mansions as it thuds into her little daughter; Alec Magnitt stepping into the lift. They were all suddenly awake, wondering, what has called us, what has called us? And – What's going to happen, what's going to happen?

I reached the place where the calls originated, I stood in front of the three-roomed cage of undiluted tidiness. The Porter was in his flat, dressed in his now dirty porter's uniform, still with a brass button missing. He was sitting on his padlocked metal trunk by his bed – the trunk that was presumed to contain all his personal effects and memories. Anna Tap was lying in his bed, lying still, not panicking, nor even showing any awareness that I had just entered the room. She lay under the bedcovers, with only her neck and head visible. The Porter was brushing her hair, with Claire Higg's hairbrush, and calling out the single word Anna. She looked so ill, her face had somehow shrunk, the skin was dull and lifeless. Why was she keeping so still?

Anna, get up!

The Porter took hold of Anna's hair, scrunched it up in his fist, and making one prolonged wail of effort he pulled it, heaving Anna from the bed. And Anna's head came off. He held it up to me! What had he done? Anna! I screamed and as I screamed the Porter began to laugh, shrieking with pleasure. And then I saw that Anna had no eyes at all, that there were huge scars across her face and that her body was cut off so neatly just beneath the shoulders. Her body had been made of pillows. The Porter was holding up the wax bust of Anna Tap.

The Porter hissed and very quietly spoke:

Who let you out, Francis Orme?
They're blowing the place up.
You're not supposed to come down here . . .
We have to leave.
But we'll make an exception, won't we, Anna?
There's no time left.
Anna wants you to sit down. Do come in and sit down.
You must leave now, there's no time.
There's always time for friends. Come in, Francis, do. You know Anna already, don't you?
You can't stay.
I've mislaid a button. Have you seen it?
You've got to get out.
Shall I close the door, so we won't be disturbed?
I'm going. I've told you, now I'm going.

The Porter hissed.

Get inside! Close the door.
Get out of here!

I rushed back towards the tunnel. My footsteps were soon joined by another set of footsteps, rushed steps, hammering in my ears. And a voice, calling out – Where's my button? Has anyone seen my button?

And as I moved, I thought to myself: I think you can go faster, don't you, Francis? And even a little more fast, if you please, Francis. Can you manage that? I'll certainly try. Yes, this is quicker, but I think that's the limit. No, that won't do. You'll have to go a bit quicker still. How about this? And some more, please. This? More, please. I'll try, but it can't be guaranteed. Any better? Yes, but more, Francis, more. Still more? I'll try, of course, but—

And then I stopped completely, just a metre away from the broken tunnel door. The Porter was with me, he had hold of my hair and banged my head against the wall.

A blast from the other end of the cellar made him let go. The blast had a wind all of its own which rushed through the cellar and made the Porter's cheeks wobble. And then in a moment the dust settled and I saw my white cotton hands, dead, dirty, ugly.

Look what you've done! You did this. You did it.

The Porter spat in my face and said:

Goodbye, Francis.

And smiled.

Another blast, louder, much louder. And this time the wind came with plaster and pieces of brick, all over the spot where the Porter and I sat in the cellar of that building called Observatory Mansions and above us came the sound of the whole world creaking and beginning to give way.

A moment outside of time.

The Porter didn't move. I didn't really see him, not all of him, or even most of him. Just a part of him. His right hand. Dusty. Freckled. Peeping out of rubble.

I looked around the cellar, one half of it was filled with dust and rubble, the other half still retained its columns and vaulted ceiling, pretending that nothing had happened. I stood up and brushed myself down with my forearms, taking care over my appearance, keeping calm, trying not to worry. I had heard that people behaved in this manner when faced with approaching peril, they take solace in the most banal activities; I had once been told of a man who knew he was shortly to die, who began insisting that he have reading glasses, since he was afraid of ruining his eyes. Similarly, I brushed all the dust from me and then, with slow deliberate steps, calmly, to hide my mounting fear, I moved inside the tunnel. I began to collect my exhibition, to bring it back out with me, scooping each exhibit up by a corner of its polythene bag, not willing to lose a single exhibit but leaving the cardboard slips with the lot numbers behind. I could re-catalogue later. But this was so difficult, I could no longer use my hands, and was forced to scoop up the exhibition with my wrists. I kept dropping precious objects. Shall I go back for that? What was it? Lot 9, an empty vinegar bottle. Oh yes, I remember that, lot 9's good. You'd better pick that up. Oh, and something else has gone. What is it? Lot 6, a pencil stub. Leave lot 6 here? Never. Pick it up. But now lot 18's gone. The empty small brown cardboard box? Pick it up immediately. Stop fumbling, Francis. Now's not the time for fumbling. And with each dropped object the panic began to return.

I had hardly begun to retrieve the exhibition when the third and largest blast went off and threw me to the tunnel floor.

Incidents inside a tunnel.

When I opened my eyes again I could see nothing. The light from the cellar, that had barely lit the tunnel before, was gone. Something pressed down on my legs, stopping me moving. Some of the old wooden beams that supported the tunnel's ceiling and walls had collapsed, bringing part of the tunnel down with it, covering my legs. As I moved my head up slightly it touched a beam: the way ahead was blocked too. I was wedged in, in both directions. I did not dare to feel about with my hands, I tried not to think about them at all. What state had they been reduced to now? How dirty could they be, dead gloves, dead hands, paralysed with filth?

I gradually became aware of the rest of my body. I was lying on top of my exhibition. My chin was resting on a tobacco tin. There were objects piled in front of me, I could feel their polythene bags against my cheeks: the beginnings of my exhibition, lying where I had dropped them in my fall.

I knew that I should probably try to get up, that that would be the best thing, heave my legs away from all that rubble, try to carry on along the tunnel, try to find the church. That's what I should have done, but I was frightened to move my legs in case they hurt, I didn't want to feel any pain. There was dust in my lungs and the taste of blood in my mouth and my head felt thick and alien. Run, Francis, run, I thought, that's what you ought to do, but instead I just closed my eyes and drifted into a sleep.

When I woke, I woke because of the pain in my legs. I tried to move the rubble; I tried to roll over, but was unable to. I felt my hands throbbing, insulted, I pressed them to my mouth, kissed them. That beautiful white was ruined for ever, one of my fingers had burst out of the cotton.

I took some deep breaths and tried only to concentrate on my feet and ankles and legs, tried to remember how they were connected to me, what they felt like, how they moved.

And the moment I pictured them, I felt their pain drilling through my body. I tried to roll a little, to feel my legs moving. But the more I shifted, the more it hurt. But I wriggled on with tiny, controlled movements, and slowly I began to creep forwards, eventually, advancing inch by inch, the rubble was left behind and I sat as best I could, crouched beneath the wooden beam, hugging my wounded knees.

It would be good to light a match, I thought. It would be good to see something, no matter how bleak it was, something to take away this thick blackness, if only for a moment. I was scared of the dark, like a child. How, I wondered, did Anna feel, trapped in perpetual night. But though there were still matches in my pocket I would be unable to strike one without the use of my hands. But I tried, I shifted the box out of my trouser pocket using an elbow, and even clamped it still on the floor between my feet, but I could not open it. Then I tried holding the matchbox between my wrists and sliding it open with my tongue. But I had hold of the box the wrong way round, and as I stuck my tongue out and pushed the cardboard drawer away from me, all the matchsticks fell to the floor. Howling in frustration, I ground the matchsticks up under my shoes, cursing them. I was alone in the dark. I had lost my one chance of light, tipped it out on the floor of the tunnel.

Then I began to frighten myself, muttering, if you don't get out you will die. If I stayed here, I thought, I would become one with the famous fat and thin Cavalier. My ghost might wander up and down and spook anyone who came to look for me; and those intruders would never return to the light again, even if they screamed out at eighty decibels, for no one would come searching in the tunnel for them because that is where the phantom of the white gloves lives with the fat and thin Cavalier, and no one wants to disturb those two. But I could not move the rubble in front of me, that was impossible, the Law of White Gloves forbade it:

Rule 7. Dead gloves cannot function. The hands underneath them will never be able to pick up, touch or move at all. They are dead.

I would scream for help. How convenient it would be for me if people came to save me. They would do all the work of shifting the rubble, while I just sat here kissing my fingers, ordering the people to hurry up. Yes, that's what would happen. I needed only open my mouth and with one brave effort, call out. What remained of the tunnel walls would surely echo and duplicate the sound until someone heard it, then everyone would immediately start moving rubble and set about the business of rescuing me. I felt considerably better. But when I opened my mouth to scream, I could not make any noise. My throat was too dry, all I was able to hear was a thin whispering sound, which faded as soon as it was uttered.

I was like a Pharaoh buried amongst his life's objects. But I was unable yet to let go of life. I began to aim my elbows at the rubble in front of me, scraping away in ugly, desperate gestures, trying to dislodge it. But it did not move. I thumped the rubble with my wrists. But it did not move. I kicked at the rubble. And it did not move.

Perhaps if I used my hands . . . but that was not permissible. Rule seven was firm about that. I would just sit here then, cramped against the jagged tunnel wall, and try to sleep the end out, try to keep quiet, try to achieve a little of that inner stillness which I had so enjoyed and loved when extinction wasn't threatened. But, in my state of fear, I was unable to achieve inner stillness, so I attempted a prolonged session of outer stillness to calm me down. But I was incapable even of that. I fidgeted, my bleeding legs kept shaking, my hands throbbed, my brain pictured the words of the seventh rule of the Law of White Gloves and began to reduce the print size until it couldn't be read any more, until it was out of sight.

No! I could not break the law! If I broke the law what would that lead to? The end, surely. I might become one of those other people, I might take up talking, I might even stop collecting and leave that most welcome of plinths in the centre of the city empty, I might take a movement job, and in that movement job my superior would be bound to say: Take off those gloves, Francis, and sit down, there's a good man. And I might even become a good man and take off those gloves and what then? No, I was a glove wearer, it was understood. Glove people are a magical people, wearing gloves, monitoring everything you touched, was like floating above the world, watching everybody in it, watching all the suffering, always observing it, but never touching it. It was best not to think about breaking the Law of White Gloves, it was better just to die quietly down here in the miserable darkness.

But it was very hard not to think, there was really very little else to do. I tried to remember the names of the stars, but I needed my father's help for that. And one thought, no matter how hard I tried to extinguish it, kept repeating itself within me, and the power of that thought was so great that it opened my mouth and made me whisper:

Rule 11. It has recently been decided that in one certain extraordinary circumstance dead hands may continue to function. When a gloved individual is suffocating and bleeding down in a dark tunnel and surrounded north and south by rubble, it has been agreed, by popular demand, that hands with dirty or ripped white cotton and even hands lacking white cotton altogether may move and be put to work.

My fingers began to shift rubble. Piece by piece, cutting that most vulnerable part of me open, progress was rewarded with more rubble and more cuts. My poor hands were being ruined for ever. They stung, they ached, but on they worked. And slowly I began to build the rubble up behind me and to move, shifting loads, slowly, slowly along the tunnel, until after three or four breaks and curses that the rubble would never thin out, I was able to push backwards an obstructing beam and climb, scraping against the tunnel ceiling, forwards on top of the rubble. And then, finally, dusty and bloody, I felt myself descending and I was able to crawl along the floor itself.

A while later I felt the tunnel steps and slid open the tomb lid, the light burned my eyes. The first thing I saw were my betrayed hands, ugly and ashamed. My nails bled, tiny strips of jagged skin hung from ungloved fingers, the gloved fingers all had red tips. Sitting with my legs dangling, half in the church, half in the tunnel, panting and crying, I looked back into the dark. In the distance, just touched by the light, I could see a sad still life. Untidy, uncared for, lay a few, too few, objects from my exhibition, smashed and broken.

I could just see the rounded top of my last exhibit, lot 996, that most precious of all the objects. The object for which the exhibition was made. The ever-moving exhibit, destined always to be placed in the furthest spot, always to appear the most recent possession. I slipped back down, into the semi-darkness.

In the tunnel the lives and loves of so many people were represented. Father was there and Twenty and Claire Higg and poor Peter Bugg and Emma, too, and even Anna Tap. But most of all, there was a person of such importance stored down there that his love was proclaimed by me as being above all those other thousands of people exhibited: lot 996, a skeleton.

I picked up this exhibit, held in its three transparent bags. I felt its polythene skin. For a moment in the half-light I thought he was alive. I thought I saw flesh grow on his skull, his eyes push out into his sockets and a large ever-smiling mouth. I thought I saw his breath caught in the polythene bag, but then the life faded again, only the head continued to smile, a skull's smile. The rounded top of his skull was well polished, it glistened, I had looked after it so, such a wonderful roundness. I kissed it. I studied the bag that held the precious object's hands. I brought the bags up into the church, and laid them out on the church's cold stone floor. I spilled out one bag, positioned the bones, there were carpals and metacarpals and phalanges too; delicate family. What tiny hands, they were. They had touched, they had collected, they had been put together palm against palm to pray, they held things, other hands among them. Brother hands to my hands. Brother skull to my skull. Brother Francis to his younger brother Thomas. My elder brother. Brother object above all other objects, the object for whom I would come to be loved always but never liked.

I slid away the cover – which only a few months ago had been removed for Father – so that only half of it was open and then I began to tip the contents of my brother on top of Father's coffin. Up-turning the polythene bags, I began to spill my brother's bones, back from where I had taken them. One, at least one object would be returned, I could do that much. I could at least give Father some company. I could remind him that he once had two sons, no matter how hard, for the portraits' sake, he tried to believe that I was his eldest son. Home the bones went, each splinter, each chipped fragment of the little brother who was my senior. Back to his stone bed, stick by stick. Finally the skull, but first one final polish.

Francis, Francis?

Someone was calling.

Francis? Francis?
I'm here, Anna.
You missed it. How could you miss it? It's fallen down, Francis. Your mother said like a once mighty elephant, its

knees buckling before it fell, groaning. They said it was a magnificent thing to have seen. You should have stayed. I called out for you. There were some huge explosions. You should've heard them.

I did.

The people cheered when it fell. They took photographs and cheered. There're still lots of them there, they've gone among the rubble, they're playing over what's left of our home. It took me so long to get away. The chalk artist brought me here.

The Porter's dead.

No one's seen him.

He's quite dead. The exhibition's gone.

Yes, I suppose it must have. I'm sorry, Francis.

He was squashed, and they squashed the exhibition too.

Where are we going to sleep tonight?

All that work, all gone.

They'll probably find us somewhere. Surely they will.

Anna, five steps away, seemed to want to come closer. She felt her way forward, made brave by the events of the afternoon. She put out her hands, searching for me through the air, striking her hands upon the chapel bars until she found the open entrance gate and then, stepping forward, her fingers rested on the object that I was holding. Her hands moved about, they felt the skull, the teeth, her fingers slipped through the eyeholes.

Francis!

It's all right.

What is it?

It's from the exhibition. I'm putting it back.

What is it?

Neither of us spoke. Then, after Anna's breath had calmed, she whispered:

It's a skull.

I'm putting it back.

You stole it.

But I'm putting it back.

You stole a skull.

He's going back. I'm putting him back now.

Whose was it, Francis?

It's the object Father was so upset about. They wanted him forgotten. But I remembered him. It's my brother.

Put him back.

Back in his box.

In went the skull. I closed the lid. Lights out. I locked up the chapel. Anna was sitting on one of the front pews, if she had eyes she would have been looking at Saint Lucy. I sat beside her.

Anna, I've run out of gloves.

When she began to take off my ripped gloves, I did not stop her. Nor did I complain or pull away when she placed my hands to her face. Skin on skin. Skin on skin.

VIII

CITY HEIGHTS

Porter.

The Porter, whose real name we never knew, died in the demolition of Observatory Mansions which he had helped to bring about. Among the rubble of our former home it was said that certain scavenging children found a metal trunk, identical in description to the one that was seen in the basement flat where the Porter lived, in which it was supposed all that remained of his private life was kept, all proof of his existence before he began his work in Observatory Mansions. The trunk was badly dented in the explosion and its aftermath, one of its padlocks had been ripped off – but one still remained. The children, it has been related to me, smashed open the surviving padlock and when they lifted the lid off the trunk to look inside they found nothing. The trunk was empty. This is conjecture. A rumour. It may or may not be believed.

Claire Higg.

Claire Higg is dead now too. She died a little before the Porter, on the same day. During the build up to the destruction of our former home, television cameras were filming the crowd, which was large, which stood and shrieked, waiting for action. One of these television cameras was pointed in the direction of Miss Higg. The television crew had positioned monitors which displayed the various pictures being filmed by the surrounding cameras. These monitors were very near to Miss Higg, and Miss Higg was happily watching them, feeling by their presence quite relaxed in the outdoors. Miss Higg, watching one particular monitor, suddenly saw on its screen a figure of a woman, watching a television monitor, who she knew she had once known, but couldn't quite place. She looked at that old woman on the television monitor, that old woman had greasy hair, was bony and pale and certainly dirty. Who could it be? Concentrating intensely, she scratched her forehead. As Claire Higg scratched her forehead she noticed that the old woman on the television monitor scratched her forehead too. That disgusting old woman, who looked like she'd been kept in a shoebox for decades, even seemed to be wearing the same nightdress as her, she noticed as she looked at herself and then back at the monitor. She noticed too that the old woman had, coincidentally, exactly the same dirt patches on that identical nightdress. Then Claire Higg, former resident of flat sixteen, once loved by Mr Alec Magnitt (deceased), once perhaps loved by the Porter (soon to be deceased), realized in fact that she was that unpleasant-looking old woman. In the instant that Claire Higg saw who she was, in the instant that she saw what she had become, she immediately leapt into one of those moments of high consciousness and, filled with mounting horror, disgust and breathlessness, decided to have a heart attack on the spot. She died, of course. But she may have been comforted to know that the last moments of her life made very watchable television. This is not conjecture. This is to be believed.

Mother.

My mother is still alive but I no longer live with her. Mother lives in a large white building on the other side of the city. This building is one of several, specifically organized to look after old people. When the crowd began to disperse after the demolition, Mother was forced along with it. And the crowd, moving far quicker than her old body could easily endure, spat her out, pushed her aside and rammed her against a wall. Mother collapsed. When the last people were drifting away someone found her and called for help. She was carried away on a stretcher, into an ambulance, and disappeared into the city. It took us a week to find her again. We telephoned all the hospitals but none had admitted her, had never even heard of her. Finally, someone suggested we call the large nursing home. The ambulance drivers had taken her there immediately, to the tiny hospital adjacent to it, where so many old people have been seen to, which nobody thinks of as being a hospital but only a sanatorium within the nursing home grounds. Mother had broken her hip. They gave her a new one but told her that she would never be able to walk without sticks or a frame ever again.

The nursing home has a staff of eighteen nurses and three doctors, but is otherwise filled with old people. The old people are packed tightly together, and there they talk about old things and other old people and old objects that can't be bought in the shops any more and old food which everyone has forgotten the recipes to. Mother is furious at the old people, she screams at the nurses and asks them why she is being housed with drooling idiots who constantly wet themselves and don't know who they are any more. She says she is not like the other old people; she is still aware. The nurses smile at Mother and give her some pills. Mother hides the pills. She has begun a great collection, which she keeps in a little plastic bag immersed in one of the nursing home's lavatory tanks. I am very proud of her, there is no doubting that we are related.

The nurses do not allow her to play the tape of my father's teeth and she complains that she gets no sleep. Mother has her hair brushed every day.

Anna Tap.

Anna Tap has chosen to look after me. After Observatory Mansions collapsed she said I became quite helpless. We spent our days on long walks around the city. For a long time these walks took us to the place where Observatory Mansions used to be. The rubble had been taken away, skip by skip, and on those walks we would often go into Tearsham Park Gardens. The bathroom scalesman was still there and he said, each time we met him, that Anna was putting on weight. Indeed, she became quite fat. Her stomach showed through her dress. Soon she had to buy new dresses made of a stretchy material, large enough to keep her and her growing belly inside. For a while she even gave up cigarettes. Now, though, she has become thin again, not dangerously thin as she was before, but as thin as she was when she first came to Observatory Mansions.

Certain changes have been made to her eyes. The glass ones arrived at the eye hospital but not before another pair had been made and Anna wears those eyes and never the hospital ones. The eyes she wears are partly constructed of glass and partly of wood. Ottila, the eye maker at the waxworks, assembled them. It was William who organized this for us.

So, in the end, Anna did get to wear Saint Lucy's eyes, the surface of which has been carefully glued on to glass balls and fit Anna's skull wonderfully well. And she looks beautiful with them. They make her happy too. (Sometimes when Anna keeps still with her eyelids open, showing her wooden eyes, I think that Anna has become an object. But then she talks, and I am reminded that she is the real Anna Tap, made of flesh.)

City Heights.

Anna and I live together in a building just opposite Tearsham Park Gardens. We have been living here for a few weeks now. It is a modern building but it suits us well enough. Our new home is built on exactly the same spot as Observatory Mansions, as Tearsham Park, it is called City Heights and it has twenty floors, all of which are identical.

They have built a tunnel out from City Heights stretching towards Tearsham Park Gardens, a concrete subway so that all the new residents can walk beneath the traffic of the roundabout and have no fear of it. This tunnel has yellow strip lighting which makes it feel claustrophobic and hostile. There is some graffiti there too, the work, I believe, of Mark Daniel Cooper.

But even though Observatory Mansions has gone and City Heights has taken its place, it is possible, if you're really quiet, to hear the old building. Sometimes I can hear Miss Higg's television set or Twenty barking, and occasionally I think I can smell the one hundred smells of Peter Bugg. If you're really still, so still that your heart almost stops, you can just pick up Tearsham Park sound, you can just hear the dog Hope scratching or my father talking to the stars or even Emma telling a story. And perhaps, if you're as proficient at outer and inner stillness as I am, you might hear, might, and then only barely, the troubled breathing of my brother, of that other Francis Orme.

Francis Orme.

I wore white gloves. I lived with my mother and father. I had a swollen lower lip. I no longer wear white gloves. I live with Miss Anna Tap. My lips are not swollen.

I no longer work on the plinth in the centre of the city. I was offered employment by the company who own City

Heights. I accepted their offer. They have given me a wonderful blue uniform with golden epaulettes and they have given Anna and me a wonderful two-bedroom flat in the basement. Anna says I make a fine porter. I know everyone who lives in the building.

Anna and I spend most of our time together around a new object. This new object has absolutely no understanding of either inner or outer stillness and keeps moving all the time and makes loud, loud noises that keep us awake at night. The new object is alive. It is a female new object and we have called her Frances.

When I first saw our baby daughter I cried because she had such tiny hands. Now they are larger. Now they grip and won't let go.

I have been painting our new home white. Sometimes I dip my entire hands into the pot of paint. On those occasions I walk to the mirror and look at myself with white hands, and then I feel sad.

APPENDIX

FRANCIS ORME'S
EXHIBITION OF LOVE

(Lot Numbers 1–996)

1. A till receipt.
2. A used envelope (white).
3. A used envelope (blue).
4. A white plastic bag.
5. An empty wine bottle.
6. A pencil stub.
7. An empty can of plum tomatoes.
8. A red plastic bag.
9. An empty vinegar bottle.
10. An empty can of pineapple chunks.
11. An empty cardboard box (white).
12. A rusted and bent nail.
13. A brown paper bag.
14. A quantity of pencil shavings.
15. A goose's feathers.
16. A light bulb (blown).
17. An old mop head.
18. An empty cardboard box (brown).
19. A number of fish bones.
20. An out-of-date calendar.
21. A collection of toenail clippings.
22. A quantity of various dogs' faeces in a glass jar (sealed).
23. A cotton handkerchief (unclean).
24. A sealed jar containing used bathwater.
25. A collection of ash from a fireplace.
26. A bent hairclip.

27. A quantity of potato peelings.

28. A newspaper.

29. A snapped metal coathanger.

30. An apple core.

31. A china teacup missing its handle.

32. A used disposable razor.

33. A fuse (blown).

34. A cork (from a wine bottle).

35. A cigar butt.

36. A bent staple.

37. A sock with three holes.

38. A teddy bear (small).

39. A tin soldier (infantry).

40. A clockwork robot.

41. A stuffed fox.

42. A plastic frog.

43. A collection of shattered glass.

44. A tin of tobacco.

45. A wad of black cigarette papers.

46. A miniature ivory elephant.

47. A marriage casket (tortoiseshell and metal marquetry).

48. A dinner gong (copper and tin).

49. A love letter.

50. The eighth volume of an encyclopedia.

51. A pair of brass doorknobs.

52. A mahogany ruler.

53. A large bottle of black writing ink.

54. A hairnet.

55. A pair of wooden doorknobs.

56. A soup ladle.

57. Four curtain pulls.

58. A photograph of a shooting party.

59. A photograph of a hunt.

60. An oriental wooden cockerel.

61. A globe (terrestrial).

62. A leg from an old ice chest.

63. A piano stool.

64. A book on the science of physiognomy.

65. A gold signet ring.

66. Various parts from four scarecrows.

67. A punch bowl (silver and tortoiseshell).

68. A two-handed sword (steel).

69. A pine draining board.

70. A riding crop.

71. An ivory shoehorn.

72. A family tree (on parchment paper).

73. A carving knife.

74. A pair of nail scissors (silver).

75. A miniature steam engine.

76. A corner of a tapestry (wool and silk).

77. A pestle.

78. A photograph of a woman with a number of porcelain dolls.

79. A clothes brush.

80. A brown leather shoe (gentleman's, right foot).

81. A black leather shoe (gentleman's, right foot).

82. A pepper pot.

83. A porcelain swan.

84. A gilded beechwood candlestick.

85. A brown trilby.

86. A soup tureen (porcelain).

87. A wooden croquet ball (red).

88. Two crystals of glass from a chandelier.

89. Twelve cash books.

90. A silver-gilt ewer.

91. A marble bust of a bald gentleman.

92. A chair leg (pine).

93. The bit from a bridle.

94. A snuffbox (ivory).

95. A book entitled *The Eucharist* (black goatskin binding).

96. A tiara (gold, silver, emeralds).
97. An ash pan.
98. An illustrated book of moths and butterflies.
99. A salmon fly-fishing rod.
100. A pair of silver and diamond earrings.
101. A book of maps of modern cities of the world.
102. A small sculpture of a classical figure (boxwood).
103. A straw doll.
104. A wheel-lock musket.
105. A large terracotta flowerpot.
106. A stained-glass window of a family crest.
107. A silver letter knife.
108. Two eggs made of malachite.
109. A charcoal drawing of a large house.
110. A tontine salver (silver).
111. A parasol.
112. Three silver napkin rings.
113. A newspaper rod.
114. An apron.
115. A copper kettle lid.
116. A gate latch.
117. A screw from a microscope.
118. A toboggan.
119. Two china teacups.
120. A wooden lavatory seat.
121. A bottle-corking machine.
122. A watering can.
123. A pair of cricket bails.
124. An illuminated manuscript.
125. A cushion with an embroidered cover.
126. A pin box.
127. A cooking thermometer.
128. A book containing botanical drawings.
129. A pair of prints, of fighting cocks.
130. A book of anatomical drawings.

131. A metal bolt.
132. A gardening glove.
133. A watercolour of a beautiful woman, two centuries dead.
134. An hourglass.
135. A bottle of old port wine (unopened).
136. A silver-gilt and glass salt cellar.
137. A weathervane.
138. A quantity of bookplates (with heraldic design).
139. A fountain pump.
140. A pair of dice (ivory).
141. Two wooden pieces taken from a game of backgammon.
142. A castle from a chess set (ivory).
143. A castle from a chess set (wood).
144. A stick for cleaning shotguns.
145. A pair of oven gloves.
146. Seven drying-up cloths.
147. The winding key to a grandfather clock.
148. The winding key to a grandfather clock.
149. The winding key to a grandmother clock.
150. The winding key to a carriage clock.
151. The winding key to a table clock.
152. A magnifying glass.
153. An amount of turmeric.
154. An amount of garlic salt.
155. Two bay leaves.
156. A cut-glass decanter containing malt whisky.
157. A silver sugar bowl.
158. A naval cutlass.
159. A pair of bellows.
160. A fire poker.
161. A porcelain vase.
162. A psalter.
163. A morocco-bound book (a volume of Orme history).
164. A photograph of a boy with a teddy bear (black and white).

165. A wading stick.

166. A silver-gilt and glass pepper pot.

167. A wrought-iron fireguard.

168. A coal scuttle.

169. Twelve book dust-wrappers.

170. An iron mantrap.

171. A fish kettle.

172. A black leather riding boot.

173. A glass-crystal fruit bowl.

174. A teddy bear without a mouth.

175. A wooden spinning top.

176. A wooden yo-yo.

177. A cricket bat.

178. A puppet (of a boy with a long nose).

179. A tricycle.

180. A birth certificate.

181. A death certificate.

182. The remains of a mouse nailed to a board (labelled).

183. The remains of a mouse nailed to a board (labelled).

184. A light switch.

185. A shooting stick.

186. A chewed dog collar with name tag (inscribed).

187. A lampshade dog collar.

188. Eight hinges from a dressing screen.

189. A bedside light.

190. A letter of resignation.

191. A bell pull.

192. A naked porcelain doll.

193. One half of a pair of curtains.

194. A number of tapers.

195. A farewell letter.

196. A letter of apology.

197. A letter from a master to his housekeeper.

198. A housekeeper's keys.

199. A servant's livery.

200. Two ice trays.
201. A set of children's building blocks.
202. Six dismissal letters.
203. A hookah pipe.
204. A clockwork toy train.
205. A tub of floor wax.
206. Seven screws taken from a boiler.
207. A dustpan and brush.
208. Four postcards from foreign cities.
209. The key to the servants' hall.
210. An antique box camera.
211. A tin of silver polish.
212. A shoe grate.
213. A tear-stained confession (ink on paper).
214. A letter to notify termination of contract.
215. A monocle.
216. A tennis racket bracket.
217. A lavatory handle.
218. A mummified cat.
219. An oriental rug.
220. A dog bowl.
221. A globe (celestial).
222. A quantity of green baize (from a door).
223. A bottle of aspirin tablets.
224. A list of items to be auctioned (booklet).
225. An auctioneer's hammer.
226. A cheque made out to an auctioneering company.
227. Two rolls of wallpaper.
228. A drum of household electricity wire.
229. A hacksaw.
230. An electric drill.
231. Two boiler suits.
232. A carefully cut length of skirting board.
233. An industrial floor polisher.
234. The insides of a telephone.

235. A tool box.
236. A fuse box.
237. Thirteen paintbrushes.
238. A ballet shoe.
239. A new resident's first set of keys.
240. Seven invitations to a house-warming party.
241. An unused doormat.
242. A length of bandage.
243. A number of photographs of the sun's chromosphere.
244. A travel book.
245. A metronome.
246. A will.
247. A cashmere scarf.
248. A medal (silver, ribbon).
249. A map of Western Europe.
250. A map of Eastern Europe.
251. A photograph of a wedding.
252. A tennis racket.
253. A wooden clog.
254. A bugle.
255. An X-ray of a pair of lungs.
256. A plastic male doll.
257. A dried globe fish.
258. A paraffin lamp.
259. A trumpet.
260. A pair of spectacles.
261. A pebble.
262. A Ventolin inhaler.
263. A leather boxing glove.
264. A dog collar (for a priest).
265. A quantity of communion wafers.
266. A book of fairy tales.
267. Four lace bonnets.
268. A military sword.
269. A can-opener.

270. A book of instructions (for a child's model kit).
271. A piece of cardboard with writing on it (belonging to a tramp).
272. A passport.
273. A number of guitar strings.
274. A discus.
275. A death mask.
276. A hand-drawn map.
277. A shopping basket.
278. An umbrella.
279. A pair of aeroplane tickets (non-returnable).
280. A cross-cut saw.
281. A pencil drawing of a hunchback.
282. A woollen mitten.
283. A crucifix.
284. A gold sports medal.
285. A reel of barbed wire.
286. A tap-dancing shoe.
287. A leather punch bag.
288. A dog whistle.
289. A calfskin gauntlet.
290. A record player.
291. A lawnmower blade.
292. A death threat (letters cut from a newspaper glued on to white paper).
293. A length of stair carpet.
294. The transcripts from a trial.
295. A tin of dried tea leaves.
296. A tax rebate (cheque).
297. A collection of scissors (twenty-six pairs).
298. A pair of moleskin trousers.
299. A list of records from a jukebox.
300. A bottle of massage oil.
301. A pair of walking sticks.
302. A nail brush.

303. A blue shirt.
304. An appointment book.
305. A quantity of keys on a keyring.
306. A road sign.
307. A zoetrope.
308. A quantity of dried chillies.
309. A bird's nest.
310. A shopping list.
311. A puppet on a stick.
312. A child's potty (enamelware).
313. A Bible (leather bound).
314. The top of a human thumb (wrapped in cotton wool).
315. A tin foot bowl.
316. A school photograph.
317. A guidebook to a public abattoir.
318. A component from a washing machine.
319. A book of philosophy.
320. A glassblower's iron pipe.
321. A child's story book.
322. A dog-leg chisel.
323. A black leather belt.
324. An address book.
325. The peddle from a sewing machine.
326. A microphone.
327. A silver teaspoon.
328. A dried starfish.
329. A book on dieting.
330. A quill pen.
331. A Noah's ark (containing twenty wooden animals and two wooden people).
332. A plastic doll that wets itself.
333. An oboe reed.
334. A urine sample (inside a test tube).
335. The lid of a baptismal font.
336. A rudder.

337. A child's drum.

338. An electric toaster.

339. A gym slip.

340. A Petit's tourniquet.

341. A wineglass with a lipstick mark on its rim.

342. A betting slip.

343. A bottle of liquid paper.

344. A Jew's harp.

345. A blow pipe.

346. A plastic toy tank.

347. A political manifesto.

348. A bull's-eye (from a dartboard).

349. A knuckle duster.

350. A poster of a screen idol.

351. A tin of straw-hat varnish.

352. A telegram.

353. A pair of pearl earrings

354. A paper flag on a wooden stick.

355. A metal detector.

356. A dinosaur model kit.

357. A code book.

358. A library book.

359. A library card.

360. A piece of shrapnel.

361. A pair of pyjama bottoms (unclean).

362. A length of tartan material.

363. A number of exhibition catalogues.

364. A flag.

365. A tooth mug.

366. A tube of spot cream.

367. A kazoo.

368. A medical dictionary.

369. The tusk of a narwhal.

370. A battery-operated torch (rubber casing).

371. A handwritten map of the whereabouts of a grave (paper).

372. A pair of boots, one with raised heel and metal supports.
373. A cardboard theatre.
374. A book of illustrated stories.
375. A quantity of sand stored in a glass receptacle.
376. A pair of earphones.
377. A fob watch.
378. A soldier's bayonet.
379. A blood-stained tea cosy.
380. A television's remote control.
381. A saline drip.
382. A cheap piece of jewellery (engraved).
383. A roller skate.
384. A top hat.
385. A smoke alarm.
386. A corduroy jacket.
387. A brass doorknocker.
388. A fingerless shooting glove.
389. A medical bracelet.
390. A darning egg.
391. A boomerang (karenya wood).
392. A beer mat (with a telephone number written on it).
393. A radiator tap.
394. A job contract (to work at a waxworks exhibition).
395. A list of rules and conditions in the workplace.
396. A city map.
397. A hat pin.
398. A fragment of a wax ear.
399. A wooden hoop.
400. An ink pad.
401. A rubber stamp.
402. A blue sock.
403. A paintbox.
404. A nurse's uniform.
405. A dunce's cap.
406. A harmonica.

407. A miniature statue of Buddha.
408. A Saint Christopher medallion.
409. A pair of candy-striped braces.
410. An ostrich feather.
411. A soldier's helmet.
412. A bottle of arsenic.
413. An artist's preliminary sketches.
414. A circular saw blade.
415. A sculptor's spatula.
416. A silver propelling pencil.
417. Moulds from a wax head.
418. A quantity of fair hair.
419. A wax foot.
420. A glass eyeball.
421. A silk headscarf.
422. A machine for counting notes of money.
423. A quantity of brown hair.
424. A postcard of the founder of a wax museum.
425. A kaleidoscope.
426. A black and white photograph (a family portrait).
427. A pair of black leather gloves.
428. A packet of cigarettes (unopened).
429. A metal cog.
430. A hot-water bottle.
431. An architect's plan.
432. A number of matchstick boxes (all empty).
433. A quantity of ginger hair.
434. A wilted rose.
435. A sports trophy.
436. A silver bracelet.
437. A bow and arrow.
438. A wax pear.
439. A pair of tortoiseshell spectacles.
440. A child's raincoat.
441. A dog's lead.

442. A piano key.
443. A pair of swimming goggles.
444. A chorister's gown.
445. A wind-resistant cigarette lighter.
446. A set square.
447. A protractor.
448. A compass.
449. A blunt pencil.
450. A schoolboy's homework.
451. A silver tiepin (engraved).
452. A rifle's telescopic lens.
453. A quantity of red ribbon.
454. An epaulette.
455. A black cotton waistcoat.
456. A pair of leather slippers.
457. A wheel from a hospital bed.
458. A bar of soap (lemon smelling).
459. Four tins of consommé soup.
460. A hearing trumpet.
461. An anglepoise lamp.
462. A ball, chain and ankle cuff.
463. A plastercast of a person's teeth.
464. Milkshake powder in a plastic container.
465. A chocolate sculpted penis.
466. A tortoise.
467. A bottle of oil of cloves.
468. A dwarf's dress.
469. A club membership card.
470. A reflex hammer.
471. A list of numbers to open a combination lock.
472. A police file.
473. A number of children's paintings.
474. A photograph of a first communion.
475. A No Smoking sign.
476. A hip flask (full of brandy).

477. A lottery ticket.

478. A photograph of an old woman.

479. A human rib (believed to have belonged to a saint).

480. A snooker cue.

481. A meat pie.

482. A personal stereo.

483. Silk underwear.

484. Two floorboards.

485. A record.

486. A number of hair curlers.

487. A brass cigarette lighter.

488. A number of moth balls.

489. A stamp album.

490. A briefcase.

491. A receptacle for the remains of a dead person (plastic).

492. The remains of a dead person (ash).

493. A screwdriver (plastic handle).

494. A red satin bra.

495. A magnet.

496. A contact lens.

497. A fencing foil.

498. A pair of sunglasses.

499. A child's first pair of shoes.

500. A fur hat with ear flaps.

501. A dentist's grinder.

502. A mortarboard.

503. A pair of leather jackboots.

504. A bone drill.

505. A letter from a mother to her son.

506. Four peacock feathers.

507. A book of criminal statistics.

508. A book of fingerprints.

509. A wheelchair (collapsed).

510. A blue and green bobble hat.

511. A sextant.

512. A photograph of a six-year-old's birthday party.
513. A number of chocolate eggs.
514. A wind chime.
515. An employee-of-the-month badge.
516. A washing line.
517. A piece of primitive pottery.
518. An unwashed shawl.
519. A camera obscura.
520. A collection of cat ornaments (china, porcelain, plastic, rubber, glass).
521. The leg from a small clockwork ballerina.
522. A boy's collection of stolen bras (twelve pieces).
523. A matchstick model of a single-span bridge.
524. Two pig's hearts in a pine box.
525. A pair of stonewashed jeans.
526. A children's encyclopedia.
527. A large cactus.
528. An electric fan heater.
529. A silver cigarette case.
530. A hearing aid.
531. A photograph of a woman water-skiing.
532. Several teeth of a tiger.
533. A jar of mustard.
534. A bottle of pills (labelled).
535. A signed lithograph.
536. A clown's make-up box.
537. A typewriter ribbon.
538. A pair of sunglasses.
539. A cine camera.
540. Cine film (exposed).
541. Reels of cine film (developed).
542. A polo-neck jumper.
543. A quantity of postcards.
544. A can of air freshener.
545. A steel and plastic fountain pen.

546. A phial of supposed virgin's blood.

547. A music stand.

548. A stilt.

549. A terracotta ashtray.

550. A threadbare doormat.

551. A nun's wimple.

552. A map of a foreign country.

553. An opium pipe.

554. A dry-cleaning collection ticket.

555. A dental brace.

556. A spark plug.

557. A nappy pin.

558. A china inkwell.

559. A book of children's folk tales.

560. A handbag (with numerous contents).

561. One half of a ten-year correspondence (479 letters).

562. A piece of a jigsaw puzzle.

563. A scapular (cloth).

564. A university degree certificate.

565. An air pump.

566. A photograph of a teenage girl.

567. A number of sparklers.

568. A marriage licence.

569. A quantity of sheet music.

570. A hardback novel.

571. A photograph of a political rally.

572. A collection of chewing-gum wrappers.

573. A manhole cover.

574. A schoolboy's lines (thirty sheets of paper, completed).

575. A dissertation on castrati (handwritten).

576. A coarse blanket.

577. A wooden idol.

578. The seat of a wicker chair.

579. A collection of hotel stationery.

580. A quilted bedspread.

581. An ounce of hashish.
582. A number of spent gun cartridges.
583. A prayer wheel.
584. A pager.
585. A suitcase full of bananas.
586. A schoolgirl's diary.
587. A doll's house.
588. An ankle band.
589. A collection of pinned moths.
590. The complete handwritten love poems of an amateur poet.
591. A circus poster.
592. A blindfold.
593. A sheath of cooking recipes.
594. A boatswain's call.
595. A photograph of an old man and a young girl.
596. A collection of menus.
597. A sewing kit.
598. A bottle opener.
599. A hymn book.
600. A pearl necklace.
601. A box of medical gloves.
602. A letter from a solicitor.
603. A dictionary of an extinct language.
604. A small painting of the Virgin Mary.
605. A shooting target (used).
606. A doctor's night bell.
607. A television.
608. A seat from a swing.
609. A wooden rod from a banister.
610. A collection of cartoon magazines.
611. Part of a motor from inside a mechanized waxwork.
612. A plastic, yellow toothbrush.
613. A photograph of a man speaking to a large crowd.
614. A traffic policeman's whistle.

615. An edition of twelve etchings.

616. A paper bag containing sherbet lemons.

617. A martyr's palm (plaster).

618. A tin of caviar (opened).

619. A For Sale sign.

620. A pickled human cerebellum.

621. Twelve bottles of home-brewed beer.

622. A sun hat.

623. An auditor's report.

624. An eyepatch.

625. A language learning course (four cassettes, one book).

626. A back scratcher.

627. A cinema poster.

628. A letter terminating work.

629. An exhibition catalogue of a wax museum.

630. A final pay cheque.

631. A purple ribbon.

632. A gabardine.

633. A pair of black buckled shoes.

634. A false leg.

635. A chipped urinal bowl.

636. A brass cockleshell.

637. A portable gas cooker.

638. A coral necklace.

639. Seventeen detective novels.

640. A milk bottle (unopened).

641. A pair of a celebrated magician's white gloves.

642. A group photograph of a school reunion.

643. A radio.

644. A notebook (containing weights of human beings).

645. A number of (developed) slides.

646. A slide projector.

647. A registered letter (unopened).

648. A pack of cards (pricked).

649. A book on dry cholera.

650. The name of a dead soldier from a war memorial.
651. A starting pistol.
652. A wedding dress (satin).
653. A bicycle pump.
654. A bottle of glue.
655. A snorkel.
656. A play script.
657. An architect's plan for housing poor families.
658. A compact mirror.
659. A pair of chequered trousers.
660. A cat flap.
661. A stuffed salmon (in a glass case).
662. A doily (cotton).
663. A milk bottle (unopened).
664. A sex discovery manual.
665. A box of assorted fireworks.
666. A lock of black hair.
667. Lipstick (vermilion).
668. A number of grooved lead and nickel bullets.
669. A dinner jacket and trousers.
670. A violin.
671. A shower head.
672. A chest wig.
673. A silver picture frame (empty).
674. A cravat (silk).
675. A business card.
676. A pair of ankle-length leather boots.
677. A photograph of a spotty male adolescent.
678. An oil painting of a blue Persian cat.
679. A milk bottle (unopened).
680. A scabbing hammer.
681. A woman's vibrator.
682. A bird table.
683. A clock's pendulum.
684. An astrology chart.

685. A pair of tailor's shears.
686. A group of photographs of voluntary patients of a mental asylum.
687. An ivory roulette ball.
688. A ventriloquist's dummy.
689. A tide chart.
690. A man-made pair of wings.
691. A colostomy bag (empty).
692. A penny whistle.
693. A bottle of shampoo.
694. A tin of biscuits.
695. The top of a lectern (ash).
696. A white linen suit (three pieces).
697. An eternity ring (diamond, silver).
698. A paper and wood fan.
699. A gobstopper.
700. A skull cap.
701. A lint-removing device.
702. A coathanger.
703. A self-portrait.
704. A leather bookmark.
705. A cotton nightdress (white).
706. An anchor.
707. An oven door.
708. Skin moisturizing cream.
709. A packet of cigarette rolling papers.
710. A candle.
711. Four cans of lager beer.
712. A penknife with sixteen different blades.
713. The remains of a tulip.
714. An aviator's compass.
715. A drawer's handle (brass).
716. A wallet full of money.
717. A pair of jogging bottoms.
718. A pair of cinema tickets.

719. A Pyrex coffee pot.
720. A canister of petrol.
721. Certificates of shares.
722. A tape-measure.
723. A bull's nosering.
724. A worker's overalls.
725. A milk bottle (unopened).
726. A blackboard rubber.
727. A length of cane.
728. A schoolroom stool.
729. A camera lens.
730. A dog's bone.
731. A pair of child's gloves with faces knitted on to the fingertips.
732. A fire extinguisher.
733. A suitcase.
734. A hairdryer.
735. A guidebook to a foreign city.
736. A canvas bag.
737. A broken calculator.
738. A nail file.
739. A ballcock.
740. A first-aid box.
741. A hinge from a door.
742. A starched collar.
743. A leather sports bag.
744. A sheath of paintbrushes.
745. A metal trunk.
746. A pair of false eyelashes.
747. A brown leather satchel.
748. A Father Christmas costume.
749. An elephant's hoof umbrella stand.
750. A tin of fluorescent paint.
751. A uniform from a vanquished army.
752. A kneeling cushion from a church.

753. A suitcase with wheels.
754. A dumb-bell.
755. A canister of hair-styling foam.
756. A used condom.
757. A mosquito net.
758. A corkscrew.
759. A pair of starched shorts.
760. A jar of porridge oats.
761. A photograph of a man with no nose.
762. A bottle of scent.
763. A souvenir plaster statue of an ancient church.
764. A book on genocide.
765. A dried sea horse.
766. A thank-you letter.
767. The rod from a sundial.
768. A coffee grinder.
769. A tube of tooth glue.
770. A passport photograph (inscribed on reverse).
771. A bottle of suntan lotion.
772. A straw hat.
773. A false moustache.
774. A nutcracker.
775. An Instamatic camera.
776. A flat cap.
777. A thermometer.
778. A silk dressing gown.
779. A bill from a lawyer.
780. A book of autographs.
781. A bottle of vodka.
782. A chocolate bunny.
783. The results of a pregnancy test.
784. A chequebook.
785. A cheque-guarantee card.
786. A cut-throat razor.
787. A railway platform ticket.

788. An engagement ring.

789. A packet of ground coffee (vacuum sealed).

790. A blade from a kitchen blender.

791. A wedding ring (gold).

792. A length of hosepipe.

793. An unopened box of chocolates.

794. A military cap.

795. A gallstone (in a glass jar).

796. A photograph of a ship.

797. A cork from a champagne bottle.

798. An Alice band.

799. A car's number plate.

800. A red dress.

801. A photograph of teenage males marching.

802. A vacuum cleaner.

803. A brass button.

804. A man's wristwatch.

805. A set of six wineglasses.

806. A bronze bust of a famous politician.

807. A photograph of an amateur theatre production.

808. A bottle of cough mixture.

809. A doctor's handwritten journal (seven volumes).

810. A pair of shoes, formerly belonging to a giant.

811. An eyewitness report of an alien sighting.

812. A stamp (franked).

813. A plaster angel.

814. A stethoscope.

815. A pair of white gloves, from a military band's trombone player.

816. A photograph of a bulldog.

817. A plastic bottle of washing-up liquid.

818. A barometer.

819. A tattoo design.

820. A conductor's baton.

821. A gas mask.

822. A Valentine's day card.
823. A silk underskirt.
824. A box of soft-centred chocolates (unopened).
825. A football.
826. A change of address card.
827. A set of liar dice.
828. A digital watch.
829. A list of people.
830. A pair of theatre tickets.
831. A toupee.
832. A baby's dummy.
833. A jeroboam of very old wine.
834. A number of photographs of naked children.
835. A wallet full of foreign currencies.
836. A black tie.
837. A bicycle saddle.
838. A gimlet.
839. A quantity of fruit-machine tokens.
840. A verruca sock.
841. An answer-machine tape.
842. A bottle of bubble bath.
843. A bride's bouquet.
844. The skeleton of a fruit bat.
845. A christening gown.
846. A bottle of essence of vanilla.
847. A dead goldfish in a plastic bag of moulding water.
848. A grey overcoat.
849. A bottle of formaldehyde.
850. A name plate.
851. A plastic comb.
852. A kite.
853. A pair of taxidermist's blunt-tipped scissors.
854. A woman's swimming costume.
855. An invalid's hand bell.
856. A polka-dot bow tie.

857. A prison uniform.
858. A rosette.
859. A knife used by a celebrated murderer.
860. A fossil of an ancient centipede.
861. A rabbit hutch (empty).
862. A snowstorm within a plastic dome (souvenir).
863. A spirit level.
864. A number of newspaper cuttings.
865. A turban.
866. A strait-jacket.
867. A number of plant seeds in a packet.
868. An oar.
869. A plastic dustbin.
870. A future chemist's first periodic table.
871. A conker on a length of string.
872. A history book.
873. A plastic toy astronaut.
874. A hospital patient's chart.
875. A driving licence.
876. A handkerchief (initialled).
877. A bottle of vitamin tablets.
878. A number of mouse traps.
879. A satellite television disc.
880. A plastic water pistol.
881. A laptop computer.
882. Four pieces of lead guttering.
883. A dried locust.
884. The left speaker from a hi-fi unit.
885. A builder's helmet (plastic).
886. A car's aerial.
887. A red beret.
888. A cymbal.
889. A bath plug.
890. A skeleton key.
891. A china teapot.

892. A number of Christmas cards.
893. A photograph of a naked woman and a horse.
894. Seventeen volumes of photograph albums from one family.
895. A child's molar.
896. An architect's pen.
897. The pin from a door lock.
898. A theatre programme (autographed).
899. A syringe.
900. The centrifugal governor from a lift.
901. The space bar from a computer keyboard.
902. A pair of handcuffs.
903. A cheque.
904. A doorbell.
905. An alchemist's chart.
906. A chalk sculpture of an owl's head.
907. An ancient and inaccurate map of the world.
908. A number of naval sea charts.
909. A recording of a concert pianist.
910. Three theatrical masks.
911. A photograph of a city immediately after it was bombed.
912. An obituary (cut from a newspaper).
913. A rosary.
914. A conch shell.
915. A stop watch.
916. The provenance of an oil painting (ink on paper).
917. A photograph of a dead man.
918. A pocket electronic game.
919. A bottle of methylated spirit.
920. A miniature wooden yacht.
921. A radio interview (on tape).
922. A requiem mass (sheet music).
923. A street sign.
924. A swan's egg.
925. A fur collar.

926. A box of coloured chalks.
927. A postcard of a Renaissance painting.
928. A rabbit's foot.
929. A pair of inflatable armbands.
930. A quilted jacket.
931. A remote-control toy car.
932. A schoolgirl's end of term school report.
933. A blow-up female dummy.
934. A telephone doll.
935. A hospital appointment card.
936. A transvestite's wig.
937. A writer's notebook.
938. A quantity of confetti.
939. A tummy-button ring.
940. An ancient coin.
941. A monograph on an artist.
942. A pack of tarot cards.
943. A baseball cap.
944. A train timetable.
945. A phonecard.
946. A videotape.
947. A revolver.
948. The keys to a hotel bedroom.
949. An etcher's needle.
950. A collection of pornographic magazines.
951. A monk's habit.
952. A photograph of a man in uniform.
953. A plastic mouse from a computer.
954. A sculpture of a pair of hands clasped (marble).
955. A bank statement.
956. A car's cigarette lighter.
957. A photograph believed to be of a ghost.
958. An accordion.
959. An old man's collection of photographs of his life's female conquests.

960. A number of unused balloons.
961. A reel-to-reel tape recorder.
962. A missing person poster.
963. A toy hand grenade.
964. A mobile telephone.
965. A dictionary of architecture.
966. A collection of dead flies (in a large matchbox).
967. A thermograph.
968. Two identical black and yellow dresses (formerly belonging to twins).
969. A page from a manuscript.
970. A face mask to hide burnt flesh.
971. A Breathalyser.
972. A scented love letter.
973. A photograph of a nudist group's annual reunion.
974. A visitors' book (leather bound).
975. A number of paperback romances.
976. Seventeen computer disks.
977. A photograph of two naked women.
978. A white silk negligee.
979. A wooden horse on wheels, with a lead.
980. A tuning fork.
981. A dried newt.
982. A birthday cake.
983. A number of fly-papers.
984. A pill-box (containing numerous pills).
985. A christening gown.
986. A toy Concorde aeroplane.
987. A sable stole.
988. A pair of steel-framed spectacles.
989. A dog collar with name tag (inscribed).
990. A schoolboy's tie.
991. A handwritten note.
992. A canister of mosquito repellent.
993. A tube of lip cream.

994. A set of false teeth.
995. A blue dress (inscribed).
996. *The Object.*

About the Author

Born in 1970, Edward Carey has written several adaptations for the stage, including Patrick Suskind's *The Pigeon* and Robert Coover's *Pinocchio in Venice*. His own plays include *Sulking Thomas* and *Captain of the Birds*. He is also a freelance illustrator. This is his first book.